17

(

To

Issue: 07

NECESSARY EVIL

NECESSARY EVIL

Shaun Hutson

timewarner
books

A *Time Warner* Book

First published in Great Britain in 2004
by Time Warner Books

A CIP catalogue record for this book
is available from the British Library.

ISBN 0 316 72593 5

Typeset by Palimpsest Book Production Limited,
Polmont, Stirlingshire
Printed and bound in Great Britain by
Clays Ltd, St Ives plc

Time Warner Books
An imprint of
Time Warner Book Group UK
Brettenham House
Lancaster Place
London WC2E 7EN

www.twbg.co.uk

For my wife and daughter.
Simple as that.

Acknowledgements

Well, what can I say . . . this one was a marathon and I hope you all enjoy it. As usual, certain things, people and places featured in and during the writing of it, so here they are . . .

Many thanks to my publishers and everyone concerned with them, particularly Barbara Daniel, Andy Edwards, Carol Donnelly (no honestly, and not one mention of football, Carol . . .), Kirsteen Brace, Sarah Shrubb, Sheena-Margot Gibson and everyone concerned at Time Warner.

Special thanks to my sales team, as ever a true 'Wild Bunch'.

I owe a huge thank you (well, several of them really) to my agent, Brie Burkeman. Seldom have I received kicks up the arse so frequently and so accurately delivered. She's ferocious, she's demanding (she's always bloody right too which can be irritating . . .) and she makes jam. 'Nuff said.

Thanks also to my accountant, Peter Nichols and everyone at Chancery.

To James Whale, Melinda (Frisbee, of course) and Ash.

Many thanks to all at Sanctuary Music, particularly Val James and, of course, Maiden themselves.

Thanks also to my good friend and penalty-taker *extra-*

ordinaire, Martin 'Gooner' Phillips for, among other things, organising another match. I've still got the scars from that one . . .

Thanks to Ian Austin.

To Claire at Centurion. To Ted and Molly. To Hailey, emerged from the primordial swamp at long last. Welcome back H. To Zena, Terri, Becki and Rachel, Nicky, Adele Hartley, Sandi at Waterstone's in Birmingham.

Thank you to Graeme Sayer and Callum Hughes for their continued work on the website www.shaun-hutson.com and to all of you who've visited, commented and contributed, many thanks.

A special thank you to Jason Figgis and October Eleven Pictures.

Thanks also to Eric Cooke at Demolition Records.

Many thanks to Alison and all at The London Dungeon for allowing me such a memorable Hallowe'en (sorry to the lady whose foot I stood on when the body dropped through the trap . . . It's a long story, trust me . . .)

A word, as usual, for two men, both sadly deceased but who, for the genius of their work, will always live on in my memory. Sam Peckinpah and Bill Hicks.

As I seem to spend most of my waking hours watching films, I'd like to say a very special thank you to all the management and staff at Cineworld in Milton Keynes. Particularly Mark, Richard, Ti, Debbie, Terri, Theresa (the 'pert' one . . .), Tasha, Paula, Kojo, Paul and everyone there I might have forgotten. You all make my cinema going a bit more . . . er . . . colourful . . . I'm still not sure about that bloody coffee machine though. All the best from Cappuccino man . . .

Another thing I spend a lot of time doing of course is watching Liverpool Football Club. So, to the mighty Reds, a huge thanks. Especially to everyone in the Commercial Department, Sue, Joanne, Debbi and Kirsty. Those in the

Bob Paisley suite, especially Steve 'a quarter of sportsman's' Lucas (and his adventures inside a lift with a camera . . .) and Paul 'fair as ever' Garner. Thanks also to Aaron 'look it's Stonehenge' Reynolds. A pat on the back to the men in Red, a kick in the nuts for SKY . . .

I'd like to say a special thank you to all the staff at Northampton Hospital who looked after my mum last year.

And, while I'm on the subject of my mum and dad, special love and thanks to them both as always.

To say thank you to my wife, Belinda, would be too inadequate a word. I've said this before but I'll say it again, how she puts up with me sometimes I have no idea. What she does amazes me, her strength astounds me and, quite simply, without her, I wouldn't be here now.

To the other girl in my life, what can I say? We're still arguing over Barbie outfits but now she's borrowing my CDs too . . . A pound on Harry Kewell every home game, a trip to the pictures every time the Reds haven't got a match, drives to grounds where the game's called off (sometimes . . .). But I can still beat her at Jenga . . . This one, like all the others, is for my wonderful daughter.

The last thank you always goes to you lot. My readers. Some have been there from the beginning, some have just joined the ride. Whoever you are, thanks.

Let's go.

Shaun Hutson

'. . .We were born of risen apes, not fallen angels, and the apes were armed killers besides . . .'

Robert Ardrey

Al Hajof, Eastern Iraq, 1990

If they could reach the village they might stay alive.

All three men knew that.

As they ran over the burning sand they kept their wide eyes fixed on the minaret rising from the cluster of red stone buildings in the distance. In the heat haze it was like a beacon, beckoning them to what they prayed would be safety.

The sand dunes and the village swam before them, behind a curtain of shimmering heat. A product both of the blistering sun at its zenith in a cloudless sky, and also of their dehydration.

They'd been running for hours. Now they sought reserves of energy they thought they didn't have. But fear was a great motivator. Somehow they forced themselves on, across sand that was, by turns, as hard as concrete or as soft and shifting as mounds of dust.

Sweat soaked their clothes. One of the men had discarded his tunic. The raw weals on his back open to the glare of the sun. When he fell, particles of sand stuck to the wounds and the congealed blood. But he hauled himself on, sucking in great lungfuls of burning air. It was like inhaling the fumes from a blast furnace.

1

All of the men were weak with thirst and exhaustion. The second of them occasionally slowed his pace as the pain in his right leg became too intense. But, despite his suffering, he drove himself on. Towards the village that promised shelter, even if it was only for precious minutes. They would be minutes out of the savage sunlight and a respite from the heat that felt as if it was boiling the blood in their veins. And there might be water there. The thought spurred all three of them on.

They crested one of the sand dunes, the first of the men stumbling. He hit the hot sand and rolled to the bottom, coughing and spluttering. He spat the dried particles from his mouth. One part of his mind told him to lie down on the sand and wait for death. Wait for the sun to burn him, to suck up what little moisture remained in his body. It would all be over then. All the suffering. All the pain.

But the other part of him wanted to live. To continue running. To survive. To escape.

The other two hurried down behind him, trying to dig their feet into the slope to slow their headlong progress. Neither waited to help the first man to his feet. There wasn't time. They couldn't afford to think about anyone but themselves.

The fallen man clawed his way across the sand for a few yards, the palms of his hands burning on the surface. Then, with a gasp of despair, he hauled himself to his knees. Fighting for breath he managed to stand, swaying uncertainly for a second. Then he began to move again. Somehow he forced his legs to carry him on across the scorched terrain.

The village couldn't be more than half a mile away now. Ahead of him, the other two continued on their stumbling way, never once looking back at him.

He stopped for a second. Every breath drawn into his lungs was like inhaling fire. He wiped sweat from his stinging eyes and blinked to try and clear his vision. Half a mile.

Move.

Something grabbed his ankles. Something that moved beneath the sand. It gripped him with incredible strength and now, despite his breathlessness, he found the power to scream.

The other two men turned and looked back at him. Saw him rooted to one spot, his arms flailing, his eyes staring madly down at his feet.

He looked to them imploringly for interminable seconds then, as they watched, he was dragged down into the sand. With one dizzying movement, he disappeared beneath the shifting particles like a drowning man beneath the waves.

A huge gout of blood fountained up from the place where he'd disappeared, rising like a crimson geyser before spattering the desert all around.

Every muscle screaming, their hearts and lungs on the point of bursting, the other two men ran on.

1

London, the Present Day

The public bar of the King George in Islington was busy. Like most pubs it offered the delights of big screen satellite football, a jukebox and food. But, in the manner of more traditional establishments, it also boasted pool, bar billiards and, on a weekly basis, live music.

The pub was usually full on those nights, particularly at the weekends when singers and bands whose styles ran from jazz to rock would air their talents before mostly discerning listeners. Genuinely talented musicians could perform for a reasonable fee, while simultaneously lamenting the fact that the business they had chosen to make a living in cared little for creativity any longer, but chose instead the manufactured nonentities that polluted the nation's radios and TVs.

As Matthew Franklin drained what was left in his pint glass and pushed the empty receptacle in the direction of a passing barmaid, the same thought occurred to him. He nodded and smiled at the barmaid who refilled his glass and took his money. Franklin's eyes never left the band who were performing that night. Particularly their singer.

Amy Holden was twenty-eight, two years younger than

Franklin. A petite, thin-faced young woman dressed in a white shirt worn over a dark blue T-shirt and leather trousers that hugged her shapely thighs and backside gratefully.

Franklin took another sip of his lager and ran appraising eyes over her, from the tip of her high-heeled boots to the top of her light brown, shoulder-length hair.

There was power in her voice that belied her small frame. She and the three musicians backing her (a drummer, guitarist and bass player) had already run through several covers. The one of the Stones' 'Gimme Shelter' had sent an already appreciative audience into raptures. But Franklin had been glad to note that the two songs Amy had penned herself had been greeted with equal enthusiasm. After the second one (a ballad called 'At the End of Time'), she had looked across at him and smiled.

The gesture had sent a shiver down his spine. She had written it for him. She'd told him one night as they lay in bed. She'd first read the lyrics to him then sung them softly as she'd gazed down at him.

Now he watched and listened with the same combination of awe and pride that he felt whenever he watched her perform.

They'd been together for the last five years. They had met in a pub similar to this and a hundred other smoky establishments all across the capital. He'd watched her sing that first time and been struck by her looks as much as her talent. He'd offered to buy her a drink and she'd refused but, the next night, she'd accepted during a break in the set. They'd talked and found there was a very strong attraction between them. She'd moved in with him three months later. Franklin smiled at the recollection.

Amy didn't earn a fortune pursuing her dream but it was a help. The rent on their flat in Clerkenwell wasn't cheap and any extra money was greatly appreciated.

He heard two men close by murmuring something under

their breath, one of them pointing at Amy. Both smiled lewdly and one licked his lips.

Have a good look, dickhead. That's as close as you'll get.

Franklin was used to that kind of reaction. In fact, he'd have been disappointed if Amy *hadn't* elicited it. Nevertheless, it didn't prevent him from shooting the two men a look of contempt.

Pricks.

He was about to down what was left in his glass when he felt the vibration from the mobile in the pocket of his leather jacket. He pulled the Nokia free and checked the caller's number.

It was the call he'd been expecting.

Franklin got to his feet and moved quickly through the other drinkers, away from the band and Amy.

Only when he reached the pavement beyond the main doors of the pub did he answer the phone.

'Yeah, I'm on my way,' he said tersely. 'I'll be there in fifteen minutes.'

Al Hajof, Eastern Iraq, 1990

Death was close.

Now the two remaining men knew that for sure. It was very close.

Urged on by the fate of their companion, they found extra strength. Drew on reserves of energy that could only have been found by what they had witnessed.

They ran past several rusty corrugated iron huts on the outskirts of Al Hajof, glancing over their shoulders every few seconds.

The dusty dirt road that led into the village snaked past a small petrol station and a market, then opened out into a large square. Straight ahead of them was the mosque, the minaret now towering almost mockingly over them. To their right was a bombed-out school. To their left were the foundations and metal supports of a building that had been started but never finished.

Al Hajof was deserted.

There was no one to be seen although both men still wondered if there were eyes upon them – watching from some vantage point that they could not detect.

The rusty shell of an estate car stood to one side of the square, all four wheels missing, the bodywork decaying like

7

a rotting corpse. Paint was peeling off the chassis like leprous skin. One of the doors was slightly open and it swung in the hot breeze that whipped across the square. The hinges groaned, and every now and then a particularly strong gust would slam the door back against the frame of the abandoned car, making the whole thing vibrate. Surveying all of this were countless posters and murals of Saddam Hussein. Saddam as a soldier. Saddam as a teacher. The lifeless painted eyes stared blindly at them from every direction.

The second man dropped to his knees momentarily, looking back fearfully along the dusty road.

When they came, that was the route they would take.

He tried to say something to his companion but his mouth was so dry with thirst and terror that he could utter only a low croak.

The third man was dashing backwards and forwards madly as if searching for something.

Some shelter from the sun?

Somewhere to hide?

They both knew *that* was impossible.

The second man saw a stone well and scrambled towards it, praying that it was not dry. The red sand dust on the structure made it look as if it was constructed from lumps of congealed blood.

He looked over the rim and found himself gazing down into blackness. His heart sank but then he grabbed a stone and dropped it into the well. There was a second's delay, then a loud plop as it hit water. Gasping, but still ever vigilant, he reached for the battered wooden bucket that hung over the well and began to lower it into the darkness.

The other man joined him, watching as the bucket was hauled up once more. It was full of rancid water but neither man seemed to care. They pushed their hands into the dark fluid, supping some, ignoring the foul taste. The rest they splashed on their cracked and burning skin.

The water made the third man retch but he persevered, gulping down more from his cupped hands. He was more concerned with slaking his raging thirst than with the vile state of the fluid he was drinking.

He used both hands to splash his face and torso, then moved away from the well towards one of the nearest buildings. His companion remained crouched over the hole, intermittently coughing loudly and gulping down the rancid water. He was gripping the rim of the well with one bloodied hand, as if unable to straighten up.

The other man reached the building he sought and stepped inside.

Even under cover it was stiflingly hot. Flies buzzed in the heavy air and there was a stench of rotting food. He moved through into the back of the building where there were several wooden tables. On two of them lay the carcasses of animals and the man realised he was standing in what had once been a butcher's shop. Recently abandoned too by the look of it. There were two metal rails running across the low ceiling, each one bearing five or six meat hooks. The tip of one was still dull with congealed blood.

He could only guess at how long the carcasses had been there. Each one was covered in a seething blanket of black flies. He looked around the room, scanning it for anything he might use as a weapon.

There was a long knife lying on top of a metal worktop and he snatched it up, wielding it before him.

Perhaps now he would have a chance. He had something to fight back with.

A slight smile creased his face.

It vanished instantly as he felt incredibly powerful hands grab his shoulders.

He shrieked as he was dragged backwards, lifted off his feet like a puppet.

The movement happened so quickly he hardly realised. Only as he was spun round did it register. Then he was rushed towards the nearest meat hook. His screams grew in intensity as he was raised higher, moved closer to the point.

Then he was slammed downwards.

The point of the meat hook pierced his throat and tore the flesh as he was jammed on to the metal, the hook ripping effortlessly through his bottom jaw then upwards into his skull. Blood burst from the wounds as he was forced even further on to the hook, until the tip finally cracked the top of his skull and protruded an inch through the bone. His body twitched madly as it hung there and blood splattered noisily onto the ground around him.

His assailant was already gone, moving out into the square, towards the well.

The other man was nowhere to be seen.

2

London, The Present Day

'It's on for tomorrow night.'

Jeff Adamson perched on the edge of the desk and regarded the four faces that gazed at him with expressions ranging from determination to relief.

Matt Franklin took a drag on his cigarette and then ran a hand through his hair.

The room he and his companions occupied was above the gym that Adamson owned. It was a small place in Gray's Inn Road. Jeff had bought it five years ago with the profits from one of their most successful jobs. All four of the other men had been with him then and on a number of subsequent outings.

Adamson sipped at a glass of mineral water and looked around at his companions.

He trusted them all. Trusted their abilities. Trusted their friendship and their loyalty. They were important qualities for men who worked in the kind of field he had chosen. He'd learned the value of trust in the army. Three years in the Royal Greenjackets. It had been one of *their* arsenals that he and his companions had robbed shortly after he'd left the service. Proceeds from the sale of the weapons had financed the purchase of the gym.

Adamson looked at each in turn.

Steven Cutler was the best driver he had ever worked with. Cutler was thirty-one. A tall, good-looking man who looked immaculately groomed whatever he happened to be doing. Even now he was inspecting his fingernails, removing a piece of dirt from beneath one.

Next to him, sipping from a can of Carlsberg, sat George Nicholson. He was a year younger and dressed in jeans and a leather jacket. Nicholson illegally imported cigarettes and booze and sold them. He had recently branched out into another commodity that could be easily brought into the country.

For two thousand pounds each (although Nicholson *was* prepared to accept Euros too), refugees, illegal immigrants or any other pieces of human flotsam and jetsam that could afford it, would be transported into England by lorry drivers only too willing to risk their livelihoods, not to mention possible prison sentences, for what Nicholson paid them.

Joe Maguire was a different proposition. He was Liverpool born. Huyton specifically. Huyton was a Liverpool suburb that allowed all its denizens the same generic nickname – Two Dogs. 'Two Dogs fightin', Huyton.' At thirty-six, he was the oldest of the five men in the room.

Maguire was a heavy-set man with several tattoos on his exposed forearms. His hands were like ham hocks. He was a regular visitor to Adamson's gym and it showed in the girth of his chest and his general build.

He frowned and shot a derisory glance at Franklin as the younger man puffed on his cigarette.

'Those fucking things are no good for you, you know,' Maguire told him.

Franklin slowly turned the pack over in his hand. 'May cause harm to unborn babies,' he read. 'Fuck it. I've found my brand. Just don't get the ones that say lung cancer.'

'Soft twat,' Maguire snorted.

The other men in the room chuckled.

'Are we sorted?' Adamson wanted to know, attempting to maintain some semblance of order among his colleagues. 'You all know what you're doing? Where you're meant to be? Who with and when?'

'We've been over this before, Jeff,' Nicholson said wearily.

'Yeah, and we'll go over it again, George. I don't want any fuck-ups.' He looked at Cutler. 'Steve?'

'The cars are fine,' Cutler assured him. 'Matt and I only nicked them yesterday.'

More laughter.

Franklin grinned back at him.

'What about explosives?' Adamson wanted to know. 'If we have to blow our way in—'

Franklin cut him short. 'I've got fifteen pounds of Semtex,' he said. 'I could put them in orbit if I used it all.'

'I don't want them in orbit, Matt. I just want to be able to walk in if it comes to that.'

'Matt just wants to make sure he won't have to kill anyone, don't you, sunshine?' Maguire smiled, ruffling Franklin's hair.

'Fuck off, you scouse bastard,' Franklin chuckled, pulling away. 'I never *have* and I don't intend to start *now*. I can do the job without that. That's how *true* professionals work, Dogs.'

'A round of applause for Matty-boy,' Maguire continued.

'How much will they be carrying?' Nicholson enquired, his harsher tone cutting through the temporary burst of laughter.

'Anywhere between a quarter and half a million,' Adamson told him.

'How can you be sure?' Maguire insisted.

'It's a big army base. At least a thousand squaddies, plus the civilian staff who work there. That's a lot of wages, Dogs.'

Maguire nodded.

'What are you going to buy with your share, Dogs?' Franklin asked.

'A fucking fan, to keep your fag smoke away from me,' the older man retorted.

The other men laughed.

Adamson walked to a cupboard that ran the length of one office wall. He unlocked it using a small key and pulled out two large black holdalls, his muscles bulging under the weight of them. He put them both down on the desktop and unzipped the bags.

As the others watched, he began to lift out the first of the guns.

Al Hajof, Eastern Iraq, 1990

He heard the screams. From somewhere behind him the second man heard shrieks of first terror and then agony. He knew only too well what had happened. Knew now that he was the last.

Using the back of his hand he wiped sweat and water from his eyes, blinking away moisture as he tried to focus. His head jerked from side to side as he scanned the wind- and sand-blasted buildings all around him. He scrambled to his feet, then fell, lay sprawled in the hot sand then hauled himself upright again, his breath already rasping in his lungs as he began to run once more.

The muscles in his legs were throbbing. His chest was tight as his heart pounded with such ferocity he feared it would burst through his ribs.

His head spun. Should he run on? Into the desert beyond Al Hajof? What would he find there? There would be no more shelter for miles. Nowhere he could hide.

He thought about running into one of the buildings. If only there was refuge to be found. Perhaps he could remain hidden until they passed by.

Perhaps . . .

He hurtled towards the nearest house, his lips moving soundlessly, mouthing silent prayers.

He actually had one foot over the threshold when his head was grabbed in a vice-like grip.

The only sound he could utter was a high-pitched, strangled moan as he was lifted off his feet, the pressure growing on his skull. He slapped at the hands that held him, trying to prise them loose, but it was futile. And all the time, the pressure increased. He was lifted up towards the flat roof of the building from where his attacker had struck. Higher and higher he rose, legs kicking madly. It felt as if someone had filled his head with air. Air that was now expanding. His eyes bulged in their sockets. The world turned red as several blood vessels burst and spilled crimson across his retinas. He flailed at the hands with even less strength now as he heard the first bones crack.

Blood was running down his chin now, spilling onto his chest.

The grip tightened inexorably. The pressure became too much. As if propelled from inside his skull, one of his eyeballs finally burst free of the socket like a glutinous ping-pong ball. It hung on the tendril of the optic nerve for a moment then dropped to the sand beneath his shaking body.

Seconds later, his head collapsed. His body, now topped by a mangled flux of pulverised bone and macerated brain matter, dropped to the ground and lay still.

On the outskirts of Al Hajof the first of the vehicles arrived.

Three Scania lorries painted in the colours of the Iraqi army were followed by two dust-shrouded Mercedes and a jeep. The entire convoy came to a halt in the main square, engines idling.

From the three trucks, uniformed men jumped down onto the sand as NCOs barked orders. They drew themselves to attention as the doors of the Mercedes were held open and the occupants of the leading car clambered out into the blistering midday sun.

Saddam Hussein, medals glinting on the breast of his uniform, looked impassively around at the images of himself that stared back from the walls all around the square. The Iraqi leader, flanked on both sides by men of his Republican Guard, stood impatiently in the sun as a second man emerged from the car.

Unlike his superior, he was not dressed in combat gear, but in a simple charcoal-grey suit. He was a tall man with narrow eyes and thick eyebrows that knitted together over the bridge of his nose to give him the appearance of wearing a perpetual frown. He signalled to an officer who had emerged from the second of the Mercedes and the commissioned man nodded and hurried off in the direction of the body they could both see lying on the far side of the square.

'I think we can consider the test a success, your Highness,' said the tall man. 'Less than one hour from beginning to end.'

'I want to see them,' said Saddam.

Doctor Kalid Sharafi nodded.

'They are coming, your Highness,' the doctor told him. 'And I believe they have a gift for you.' He motioned to a point behind his leader.

Saddam turned, the breath catching momentarily in his throat.

Sharafi nodded, a smile on his thin lips.

Saddam swallowed hard and nodded almost imperceptibly as the gift was dropped at his feet.

The three severed heads, torn bodily from the corpses of the men who had fled across the desert, lay at the Iraqi leader's feet in a spreading pool of blood.

'Pity the infidels, your Highness,' Sharafi smiled. 'And all those who oppose you.' He gestured before him.

Saddam looked at those who had dropped the heads and, despite the blistering heat, he felt a cold chill run along his spine.

3

London, the Present Day

The pub was closed by the time Franklin got back.

He knocked on the door and nodded a greeting to the landlord who let him in then locked up behind him once more. Inside, tables were being wiped down and glasses washed. The smell of stale cigarettes and booze was strong in the air.

Franklin looked at his watch then in the direction of the bar. Amy was perched on a bar stool, a gin and tonic held in one hand. She looked at Franklin and raised an eyebrow as he approached.

'Sorry I'm late,' he told her, kissing her lightly on one cheek.

'An *hour* late,' she reminded him, sipping her drink.

'I said sorry. We had a lot to talk about.'

'I bet you did.'

He sat down on the stool next to her and rested one hand on her right knee.

'Don't get comfortable,' she said, her voice full of mock rebuke. 'I want to go home.'

She drained what was left in her glass, fastened her coat and slid down from the stool. She called a farewell to the landlord and she and Franklin headed for the main doors.

As they stepped out onto the pavement, Amy shivered and pulled her coat more tightly around her. Franklin hurried to open the passenger's side door of the Toyota, holding it open for Amy as she climbed in, then he walked round to the driver's side, slid behind the wheel and started the engine.

The car moved smoothly away from the kerb and into the sparse traffic.

'Good gig?' he asked.

'They seemed to enjoy it,' she told him.

'And what about you?'

'I always enjoy it, Matt.' She touched his thigh without looking at him. 'What about *your* business?'

'Everything's set for tomorrow night. There's no reason why things shouldn't run smoothly. We've been planning it for more than two months.' He swung the car right.

Amy took her hand from his thigh and gazed out of the side window.

'Something wrong, babe?' he asked.

'Why should there be?' she answered, a slight edge to her voice. 'I mean, you all know what you're doing, don't you?'

'Amy, what's the matter? Everything'll be fine. It's a straightforward job.'

Her only answer was a long sigh.

'Trust me,' he continued.

'I do,' she said, turning to look at him. 'I also love you. That's *why* I worry.'

'The job's been planned to the last detail. Just like every one that we do. It's been like that since you've known me. If anything looks dodgy we pull out.'

She nodded.

'Stop worrying,' he urged. 'None of us want to take any risks. We've all got too much to lose. Jeff and Two Dogs are both married. George has got his little girl to think about. Steve's got Sue and I've got you. You think any of us want to piss that away?' He looked at her and smiled. 'We're good at what we do, Amy. We *don't* make mistakes. Our jobs are planned. We don't run into fucking corner shops waving replicas.' He tapped his forehead. 'Have I got "Born to lose" tattooed on there? No.'

Amy laughed.

He guided the car down two or three more narrow streets, flicking the wipers on when the first drops of rain spattered the windscreen.

Amy pushed a cassette into the machine and music filled the car.

'. . . *When the lights turn green and your body screams, melt-down time, 'til we're blind . . . Burning rubber, oh, body heat . . .*'

'That'll be you one day,' Franklin said, nodding towards the cassette. '*Your* album playing. *You* singing.'

'You really believe that, don't you, Matt?' she smiled.

'I *know* it,' he told her, defiantly.

'. . . *Burning rubber, cover me . . .*'

Another ten minutes and they were home.

4

There were two basement flats beneath the large edifice called Cavendish House. Franklin and Amy occupied one of them. The other had been empty for more than a year.

People came and went. Most stayed in it for a month or so, but no one seemed willing to settle there permanently. An Irish guy had been the last tenant. He'd lived there for over six months, then suddenly one morning, they'd discovered that he and all his belongings had gone. So, too, had everything in the flat that wasn't nailed down and, Franklin thought, a few things that *had* been nailed down.

So they enjoyed a certain amount of privacy in the basement that the other residents who lived in the flats stretching up to the twelfth floor did not have.

They were on nodding terms with half a dozen of the other residents, but nothing more. London, like all cities, allowed people to live in both close proximity and anonymity simultaneously. That suited Franklin.

As he pushed the key into the lock and stepped back to allow Amy inside he felt the warmth pour out to meet them. The rain that had threatened during the drive home had given way, instead, to a biting wind. The warmth inside the flat was welcoming.

There was one bedroom to the left as they entered, a bathroom straight ahead and, to the right, a living room. In one corner of that area there was a sink, cooker and a worktop. The large windows opened out onto a tiny courtyard and Franklin noticed, as he drew the curtains, that there were several empty beer cans scattered across the cracked flagstones. They'd more than likely been dropped out of the window of one of the flats higher up in the block.

Untidy bastards.

He shrugged off his jacket and put the television on while Amy busied herself making tea.

Franklin flicked channels, found nothing worth watching and switched the set off again. He lit up a cigarette for himself then did the same for Amy and propped it in the nearby ashtray.

Amy set down two mugs of tea and sat on the sofa beside him, pulling off her boots and then drawing her feet up beneath her.

They sat in the silence and warmth, his arm around her shoulder, the noises of a night-time city seemingly miles away above them. A siren sounded somewhere in the distance.

'We should go to bed,' he said, blowing out a stream of cigarette smoke.

She sipped at her tea and nodded.

The clock on top of the TV showed 12.49 a.m.

'Matt,' she said quietly, her head resting on his chest, 'what if I don't make it?'

'What do you mean?'

'I mean, what if singing in pubs is as good as it gets? It wouldn't be *so* bad, would it?'

He lifted her head slightly and looked into her eyes.

'Where's *this* coming from?' he wanted to know. 'How long have you been thinking like this?'

22

'I might not be *able* to carry on singing forever.'

'Why? What's going to stop you?'

'I might not be able to find a babysitter.'

'Well, then . . .' he began, then her words seemed to hit him like a sledgehammer.

Amy was smiling.

'Babysitter?' he whispered.

'I'm pregnant,' she told him, her grin widening.

His eyes seemed to bulge.

'Pregnant,' he repeated. He shook his head, grinning like a maniac.

'I did a test yesterday.'

'Why didn't you tell me straight away?' he wanted to know.

'I wanted to be sure. I did another one this afternoon. They were both positive.'

'How far gone are you?'

'Only a couple of weeks.'

'Jesus,' he chuckled. 'I don't believe it.'

'I can do another one if you want me to.'

He held her tightly to him.

'Amy,' he murmured. He could think of nothing else to say but her name and he said it two or three more times, his eyes closed.

'I haven't told anyone else,' she informed him. 'We should keep it quiet until I've had the first scan. Just to be on the safe side. If anything goes wrong . . .' She shrugged.

'OK,' he beamed. 'If you think that's best.'

He stroked her hair gently.

'Don't you think you should stop singing *now*?' he wanted to know. 'I mean, there is so much fag smoke in those pubs. It's not good for the baby, is it?'

'We both smoke. The baby'll be fine. I'll keep singing as long as I can.'

'A baby,' he murmured. 'I don't fucking believe it. I'm going to be a dad!'

The sound of the siren outside grew louder but, as Franklin and Amy embraced, it didn't seem to matter any more. Nothing did.

Bassarra Military Base, Eight Miles North of Baghdad, 1990

The two Republican Guards positioned on either side of the door saluted stiffly as Doctor Kalid Sharafi passed between them.

He nodded curtly and continued through the door along a short corridor towards a single lift.

There was a panel of numbers beside the door and he jabbed the required digits, waiting as the lift car rose to his floor. The doors slid open and he stepped in, keying in another six-digit number to reactivate the lift. It began to descend slowly.

Sharafi glanced at the notes he held as the lift continued its journey into the subterranean depths. When it finally reached the bottom of the deep shaft, the doors slid open once more and he stepped out into a brightly lit cylindrical corridor. The floors were polished and gleaming in the light of the fluorescent tubes that flickered on both the ceiling and walls.

Sharafi, his mind seemingly focused on something else, began his journey along the corridor. It curved round in a gentle arc before finally straightening out once more, widening slightly at the far end.

He passed metal doors on both sides of him, each one equipped with a keypad. Sharafi knew what was going on behind each of those doors but it was the room at the far end of the corridor to which he walked with such urgency and purpose.

There were no soldiers on this lower level. He would not tolerate their presence here. They could bring in germs that would affect the work being carried out. Besides, he reasoned, there was no need for them here.

He reached the door and jabbed in another six-digit code. A small metal flap about six inches square slid open to reveal a round glass panel. A thin beam of red light was moving vertically back and forth across the white background.

Sharafi leaned forward and pressed his right eye to the panel.

'Retinal scan confirmed,' said a metallic voice from a microphone next to the keypad. 'Proceed with fingerprint identification.'

Sharafi pressed the tips of his long fingers onto a different panel and watched as another beam of red light moved back and forth.

'Fingerprint identification confirmed,' the metallic voice said.

Sharafi pulled the laminate that was hanging around his neck from inside his jacket and inserted it into a slot beside the door, swiping it like a credit card. There was a loud hydraulic hiss and the double doors opened. He stepped through.

The room beyond was dimly lit. It was difficult to see more than five feet in any direction. On the far wall there were half a dozen computers, each screen bearing images. Men were working at each of them, tapping away at the keys and occasionally speaking animatedly to each other. As Sharafi entered they all stood up and bowed in his direction.

He nodded a greeting and ushered them back to work with a wave of his hand. Then he turned towards the wall on his right.

One single pane of glass ran the entire length of the wall. It was thirty feet long and beyond it lay another room. It was vast, stretching back two or three hundred feet from the glass partition.

This room was filled with men lying motionless on gurneys, naked but for a small cloth that covered their genitals. Each one had a drip connected to his left arm. There were electrodes attached to each man's chest that led to a cardiogram. Sharafi watched the heart rhythms of the nearest man moving evenly across the small screen on top of the heart monitor. Other machinery also measured blood pressure, respiration and oxygen levels in their blood.

Sharafi moved away from the glass partition and reached for some notes that were lying on the desk that faced it.

One of the men working at a computer on the other side of the room approached him, handed him more paperwork then retreated quietly to his terminal.

Sharafi scanned all the information without speaking. Occasionally he would run his middle finger along one of his thick eyebrows but, other than that, he remained still. Only his gaze moved back and forth, over the printouts that he had been given.

'Are there any problems?' he asked finally.

One of the men turned away from his computer screen and looked at Sharafi.

'There is one, Doctor,' he said. 'The same one we encountered at the beginning of this project.'

'His Highness will not want to hear that,' Sharafi said dismissively. 'It is a problem that can be dealt with.'

The other man opened his mouth to speak but Sharafi raised a hand to silence him.

27

'If you disagree,' snapped Sharafi, 'perhaps *you* would like to be the one to tell his Highness.'

The other man shook his head almost imperceptibly.

Sharafi glanced once more through the long glass partition then, accompanied by another of his companions, he made his way towards a thick metal door at the far end of the room. Both of them were again confronted by retinal scans and fingerprint identification and once those had been accepted, they passed into the huge room that housed the immobile men.

There were a number of other white-coated orderlies moving among the gurneys, one occasionally stopping to adjust the angle of a drip or double-check the curve on a cardiogram. As Sharafi passed, each of them bowed reverentially.

'They bring their blasphemies to our land and expect us to be subservient,' Sharafi said as he walked. 'They dictate to us and demand our obedience. They threaten us and assume we will kneel.' He stopped at one of the naked figures and looked down at it, his fingers gliding along the plastic tube that led from the drip to the needle inserted in the man's arm. 'They will not triumph. They will not impose their will upon us. They will see the sands run red.'

He touched the arm of the man on the trolley.

The eyes snapped open and fixed him in an unblinking stare. Sharafi smiled down at the figure.

5

Matt Franklin worked the slide on the SPAS automatic shotgun, chambering a round.

The sound seemed to be amplified within the confines of the car, but despite that, Steven Cutler didn't even look at his companion. He tapped gently on the steering wheel, his eyes fixed firmly on the road and the traffic that sped along it.

The car was parked on a slight rise overlooking a section of dual carriageway that cut across open country between St Albans and Watford. The lights of houses could be glimpsed in the distance, but the area where the car stood was dark, hidden from the eyes of passing drivers by the trees and bushes that surrounded it. A narrow, rutted dirt track led down to the road.

Franklin laid the SPAS at his feet then reached inside his jacket and pulled out the Smith & Wesson .459 automatic that nestled in the shoulder holster he wore. He worked the slide on that too then flicked on the safety and replaced it. Reaching into his jacket pocket he touched the two spare fifteen-round magazines he had placed there.

Just in case.

Cutler had already checked his own weapons. The Steyr

GB automatic was in a shoulder holster. The Ithaca shotgun lay beneath a blanket on the back seat.

Franklin ran a hand through his hair and glanced first at his watch then at the dashboard clock.

'Why's Jeff got it in for the army?' Cutler asked, his eyes never leaving the road.

'He hasn't, as far as I know,' Franklin said, warming his hands near the heater of the Ford. 'What makes you ask that?'

'First job we ever did together was nicking guns from an army base, now we're about to knock over one of their payrolls.'

'He was *in* the army. He knows how they work. It's as simple as that. I don't think he's got an axe to grind. Look, Steve, he set this job up, that's all I'm bothered about.'

'Why did he leave? He's always banging on about how great life was when he was in.'

'He *had* to leave, didn't he? They accused him of negligence.'

Cutler glanced at his companion.

'He never told me that,' he murmured.

'Probably because you never asked him,' Franklin observed. 'When he was doing a tour in Northern Ireland, one of the geezers in his unit was killed by a sniper. They said Jeff hadn't checked the area thoroughly enough before his men arrived, or something like that.'

'So he *has* got it in for them then?'

Franklin merely shrugged.

'Who cares?' he said, reaching towards the glove compartment.

'What are you looking for?' Cutler wanted to know.

'I was going to put some music on.'

'Fuck that. Leave it.'

Franklin inspected the array of cassettes and chuckled to himself.

30

'It's a good job your taste in clothes is better than your taste in music, Steve,' he grinned. 'Dire Straits for Christ's sake.'

'What's wrong with Dire Straits?'

'And Genesis? When was the last time you bought an album?'

'Put them back. Just because I don't like the same kind of shit that you do.'

Franklin grinned and replaced the cassettes.

'How's Amy getting on with her singing?' Cutler wanted to know.

'She's getting on fine.'

Don't say anything about the baby. Amy asked you not to mention it.

'Sue's talking about leaving her job,' Cutler mused.

'She's still working in that club in the West End, isn't she?'

'Yeah, but you know bar work, Matt. And I don't like the sound of some of the bastards who go in there. Flashing their fucking money around. They think they can buy Sue as well. It'd be better if she found something else.'

'Is that what *you* think or is that what *she's* said?'

'*I* want her to leave. I want us to settle down. She doesn't need the fucking job.'

'It gives her a bit of independence.'

'She doesn't need independence. And I bring in enough money for both of us.'

'So what do you want her to do?'

'Marry me.'

'Then ask her again.'

'And risk getting blown out again?' Cutler shook his head. 'Fuck that. If she'd wanted to marry me she'd have said yes the first time that I asked her.'

'Maybe not. Why did she say she wouldn't marry you?'

'She said the time wasn't right.'

31

'There you go then. Ask her again. That was a year ago. She might have changed her mind by now.'

Cutler tapped gently on the wheel with one index finger.

'I just want us to be like you and Amy. You're settled,' he observed.

'We're not married.'

'I know that, but . . .' He allowed the sentence to trail off.

'Ask Sue again, Steve,' Franklin persisted.

'Haven't you two thought of getting married?' Cutler wanted to know.

'We've talked about it. Maybe . . .'

Now there's a baby on the way?

'Maybe what?' Cutler urged.

Shut it. Keep it to yourself.

'We'll see,' Franklin said.

The two-way radio on the parcel shelf crackled and he picked it up.

'Yeah,' he said into the mouthpiece.

The voice at the other end belonged to Jeff Adamson.

'They're on their way,' he said. 'They should be passing you in about ten minutes.'

'Got it,' said Franklin. He looked at Cutler and nodded. 'Party time.'

6

The Securicor van slowed down slightly and the driver edged it in behind an Astra.

There was no hurry.

They had plenty of time.

If anything, they were *ahead* of schedule.

The driver checked his wing mirror and saw that the road behind was practically empty. A motorbike shot past in the outside lane doing eighty or more and the van driver merely shook his head as he watched the Kawasaki hurtle out of sight into the darkness ahead.

The sodium glare of the van lights illuminated the dual carriageway and reflected back off the wet tarmac. It had rained for about twenty minutes a little over an hour ago. Just long enough to soak the road and persuade the driver that a steadier pace was safer. He glanced disdainfully into his wing mirror as another car hurtled up behind them, then shot past him like a bullet.

Up ahead, there were fewer lights and the road began to turn more sharply around bends. On the passenger side, thick bushes and a narrow grass verge were all that separated the road from the open fields beyond. The landscape sloped upwards in a number of places and the driver noticed that there were lights burning inside a house atop one of the ridges that flanked the road.

His passenger seemed unconcerned by what was happening around him and contented himself with gazing straight out of the windscreen, his face impassive. Large spots of rain began to hit the glass, thudding loudly against it.

The driver flicked on the windscreen wipers as the shower got heavier. One squeaked annoyingly every time it swept across the glass.

The Securicor van drove on through the ever increasing downpour.

'Just what we bloody need,' muttered Cutler as the rain began to spatter the Cosworth.

Franklin ignored him and fiddled with the controls of the radio transmitter perched on the dashboard. As he twisted the frequency dial the car was filled with crackles of static, hisses of interference and, every now and then, a disembodied voice.

'You got them yet?' Cutler wanted to know.

'If they're not transmitting, I can't pick them up,' Franklin told him. 'I can tune to the frequency they use but, like I said, if they're not saying anything then . . .' He shrugged and allowed the sentence to trail off.

The two-way crackled and Cutler snatched it up.

'Go ahead, Jeff,' he said into the mouthpiece.

'Less than five minutes from you,' Adamson told him, his voice disappearing momentarily under a crackle of static.

'Where are you?' Cutler asked.

'About two hundred yards behind them. I'm moving up in a minute.'

'What about George and Two Dogs? Are *they* in position?'

'Everything's set,' Adamson answered.

The two-way went dead.

34

Rain was now beating hard on the Ford, battering a tattoo on the roof and windscreen.

'Will this rain fuck the signal up?' Cutler wanted to know.

Franklin shook his head.

'Not enough for it to make a difference,' he said, eyes still fixed on the transmitter and the green lights that danced on it.

There was a particularly loud blast of interference then Franklin smiled.

'Got them,' he grinned. 'I've found their frequency. All we've got to do now is listen.'

'Perhaps they've got nothing to say,' Cutler mused, his eyes never leaving the road ahead.

'They will have in a minute,' Franklin murmured.

Jeff Adamson pressed his foot down on the accelerator of the Audi, the headlights cutting through the rainy darkness. One short burst of speed and he was within sight of the Securicor van. It was still moving along at a steady sixty, about fifty yards ahead of him. He eased off the accelerator a little and allowed the vehicle to drop back slightly.

A hundred yards.

There wasn't a great deal of traffic heading down the opposite carriageway. Occasionally headlights would cause him to squint, but for the most part, he kept his gaze on the Securicor van moving steadily along in front of him.

He moved up to within seventy yards, the needle on the speedo arcing.

Without taking his eyes off the van he reached onto the passenger seat and, with one gloved hand, gently touched the frame of the Heckler & Koch MP5K sub-machine gun.

Joe Maguire looked anxiously at his watch then out through the rain-drenched windscreen.

He was about to reach for the two-way when George Nicholson stopped him.

'What are you doing?' Maguire wanted to know.

'What are *you* doing?' Nicholson countered.

'I want to know where the fuck they are.'

'They'll be here. If anything had gone wrong we'd have heard.'

Maguire held his companion's gaze for a moment then put the two-way back down. Instead he picked up the twelve-gauge Ithaca 'Deerslayer' in front of him and began pushing cartridges into the magazine.

'Are you set?' he asked.

Without looking at him, Nicholson patted his jacket. In a shoulder holster beneath his left arm the SIG-Sauer P220 9mm automatic was loaded and ready.

'Do you think this is all right?' Maguire asked quietly.

'What?'

'This job.'

'Jeff's never let us down before.'

'I know he hasn't. It just seems too easy. A Securicor van with no escort?'

Nicholson merely shrugged. 'How many of them are escorted, Joe?' he mused.

'But this one's carrying army money,' the Liverpudlian insisted. 'You'd have thought they'd at least have sent someone with it.'

'Like who? The marines?' He chuckled.

'Very funny,' Maguire snapped.

'You worry too much, Dogs.'

'You can *never* worry too much,' Maguire told him.

'If it goes tits up we just walk away. It wouldn't be the first time. No mess. No fuss.'

Maguire shrugged.

'Jeff knows what he's doing,' Nicholson insisted, flicking the wipers of the Saab on. They cleared the rain momentarily giving them a clear view of the road. 'He's been planning this job for months, you know he has.'

Maguire nodded, seemingly placated by his companion's assurances.

He worked the slide of the Ithaca, his eyes fixed on the road.

'Come on then, you bastards,' he grinned.

'That's them.'

Franklin pointed and nudged Cutler but he had already seen the Securicor van as it swept past below them.

He turned the key in the ignition. The engine wouldn't start.

'Come on,' Cutler hissed and tried again. This time it burst into life and he guided the Cosworth down the muddy track and onto the dual carriageway, immediately moving into the outside lane.

Franklin reached for the two-way and pressed the Call button.

'We've got them, Jeff,' he said. 'Where are *you*?'

'Have a look out your back window,' Adamson told them.

Franklin turned and saw the headlights of the Audi cutting a swathe through the darkness about fifty yards to the rear in the inside lane.

'Just hold your position for five minutes,' Adamson instructed. 'Then get in front of them.'

'Got it,' Franklin answered, glancing at the Securicor van.

Cutler saw more headlights in his rear-view mirror as a car sped up close to his rear. 'What's this prick playing at?' he murmured.

The driver behind flashed his lights, anxious to get past.

'Fucking wait,' Cutler said, momentarily dazzled by the halogen glare. 'It's no wonder accidents happen, is it? Look at this cunt.' He pointed over his shoulder. 'Right up my arse in weather like this!' He shook his head irritably.

The car behind flashed its lights once more.

Cutler accelerated slightly then pulled in behind the Securicor van, allowing the car behind him to overtake.

As it did, Cutler glared through the rain and darkness in the direction of the other driver who shot past doing well over eighty.

'Dickhead,' Cutler rasped in the direction of the other car.

He manoeuvred the Ford back into the outside lane, sitting about thirty yards to the rear of the Securicor van.

Franklin twisted the dial on the radio transmitter, listening for any sounds coming from inside the target vehicle.

There was only static. The men inside were still silent.

So far, so good.

Another car cruised up behind the Ford then dropped back slightly. Once more Cutler eased the vehicle into the other lane, allowing the driver to pass, then moved back to his previous position. He looked in the rear-view mirror to see that Adamson had accelerated slightly and was now much closer to the Securicor van. The two pursuing cars were now less than thirty yards from their prey.

Headlights from cars coming along the opposite carriageway flashed into the Ford but neither Franklin nor Cutler paid them any attention. Cutler was too busy holding the car at a steady speed while Franklin continued to turn the dial on the transmitter.

'They're speeding up,' Cutler observed, watching as the Securicor van suddenly increased its pace.

He eased down on the accelerator to ensure the van didn't get too far away.

Beside them, Adamson did the same.

'Do you think they've sussed us?' Cutler murmured, never taking his eyes from the target.

Franklin shook his head.

'Still nothing on here,' he said, indicating the transmitter.

'Fuck this!' muttered Cutler.

He hit the gas and drew up alongside the larger vehicle before cruising effortlessly past it and moving slowly into the inside lane about fifty yards ahead. The needle on the speedo touched seventy-five.

Like a small convoy, the Ford, the van and the Audi all moved steadily along the carriageway through the driving rain.

'If they *have* clocked us we'll know soon enough,' Franklin said, glancing over his shoulder at the van.

Nothing came from the transmitter. The men in the cab of the Securicor van were still silent.

Jeff Adamson stepped on the brakes of the Audi and brought it quickly to a halt.

Leaving the engine running, he swung himself out of the car. As he did, he glanced back down the carriageway and saw nothing but darkness.

Just as planned.

Moving hurriedly, he ran to the boot of the car and pulled out several orange and white plastic bollards. These he spread across the full width of the carriageway then he returned to the Audi and pulled out a large triangular sign and the metal stand that would support it. Adamson placed the sign in front of the bollards and regarded it carefully.

ROAD CLOSED

Rain spattered on it and dripped from the sign.

Adamson ran back to his car and got in, stepping hard on the accelerator.

7

'He's speeding up.'

Cutler glanced in the rear-view mirror of the Ford and saw the lights of the Securicor van looming larger. He winced slightly as the light from the powerful beams filled his vision. Then he glanced down at his speedometer. The needle was still swaying around the seventy-five mark.

The Securicor van indicated and moved into the outside lane. It increased its speed and drew up alongside the Ford, driving parallel for a moment before moving ahead, still in the outside lane.

'Masks,' said Franklin and both men hurriedly pulled on the woollen sheaths that revealed just their eyes and mouths.

'Stay with them.' The voice belonged to Adamson and came from the two-way.

Franklin snatched it up. 'I don't know if they've figured out what's happening,' he said, his eyes never leaving the van in front. 'They haven't said anything.'

'Have they switched frequencies and you just can't hear them?' Adamson wanted to know, his voice harsh over the two-way.

'No,' Franklin told him. 'They're not saying a word.'

'Fucking hell,' murmured Cutler, forced to push the Ford

to eighty to keep within thirty yards of the speeding Securicor van. 'They know. They must do.'

Behind him, the Audi also accelerated, Adamson anxious not to lose touch with the target vehicle.

'Get in front of them and stay there,' he ordered through the two-way.

Cutler pressed down more urgently on the accelerator and the Ford moved smoothly up the inside of the van, overtaking it. As the two vehicles drew level, Cutler glanced in the direction of the van's cab and saw the passenger staring out at him through the darkness and rain. For fleeting seconds their eyes met, then the passenger turned away from Cutler's masked visage.

Franklin again adjusted the dial on the radio transmitter slightly, wincing as a burst of static erupted from the set. 'Still nothing,' he said.

The Securicor van suddenly swung back into the inside lane.

'What the fuck is he doing?' Cutler hissed, blinking rapidly as the powerful headlights momentarily dazzled him.

'It can't be more than a mile to the next slip road,' Franklin mused, glancing over his shoulder into the blazing headlights of the van. Even as he spoke, he saw the first countdown marker loom out of the rainy darkness.

The Securicor van lurched wildly into the outside lane again, tyres screeching on the wet tarmac. The driver seemed to be trying for more speed, anxious to be away from the Ford and the Audi which was moving up rapidly.

Cutler turned the wheel slightly and sent the Ford into the right lane ahead of the van. As he did so, the Audi sped up alongside the van, preventing it from moving back inside.

All three vehicles were now doing well over ninety, oblivious to the treacherous road conditions.

The slip road came into view and Franklin saw the Saab

41

come hurtling onto the carriageway from his left. It shot across into the outside lane then moved back more steadily into the inside about seventy yards ahead of the three speeding vehicles.

There was a burst of static from the radio transmitter then a muffled voice.

'. . . *behind us* . . .' More static. '. . . *two cars* . . .'

'They know they're being followed,' Franklin said.

The Securicor van suddenly swung back into the inside lane, almost slamming into the Audi.

Adamson hit the brakes, the car skidding slightly on the wet road but he kept control and forced it on, squinting through the rain-spattered windscreen.

Up ahead, Nicholson allowed the Saab to drop back slightly, blocking the inside lane. It was practically level with the Ford, the two vehicles forming an impassable barrier to the security truck.

Another hiss of static from the transmitter.

More muffled words.

'. . . *past them* . . . *go faster* . . .'

'They know we're on them, Jeff,' Franklin said quickly into the two-way.

'Keep them boxed in,' Adamson said, bringing the Audi closer. 'Once they radio for help we're going to have about ten minutes. That'll be the response time. A police car can't reach them any quicker where they are now.'

'Let's hope not,' Cutler said, guiding the Ford along the wet tarmac a few yards behind the Saab. The other vehicle was still speeding along in the inside lane.

The Securicor van suddenly accelerated. Cutting across lanes, it slammed into the back of the Saab which lurched violently.

'What the fuck is he doing?' Cutler hissed, watching as the armoured vehicle rammed the Saab, sparks flying into the air as the collision came.

Nicholson regained control of the car and sped away a dozen or so yards, pieces of the back bumper spilling across the carriageway like metallic confetti.

'Mad bastard,' Cutler said, frowning at the Securicor van.

Franklin leaned closer to the receiver.

He heard two voices now.

'. . . *hit them again . . . inside lane . . .*'

'. . . *overtake . . .*'

Franklin reached down by his feet and lifted the SPAS onto his lap. He fixed his eyes on the armoured vehicle and rested one index finger against the trigger of the shotgun.

8

'Why aren't they calling for help?'

Franklin watched as the armoured vehicle again accelerated and slammed into the back of the Saab, shattering one of its back lights.

'They know what's going on by now,' Franklin murmured, gripping the SPAS more tightly.

No sound came from the radio transmitter. The two men inside the cab of the Securicor van had fallen silent once more.

Franklin snatched up the two-way and spoke quickly into it.

'Jeff, they know what's happening,' he blurted.

'I can see that,' Adamson replied, his voice hissing from the two-way. 'Have they called for support?'

'No,' Franklin told him. 'Nothing. Not a word.'

There was no answer from Adamson.

'Jeff,' Franklin persisted as the Cosworth drew alongside the armoured vehicle.

'I heard you,' Adamson said finally.

'Why haven't they sent out a signal?' Franklin wanted to know.

The armoured vehicle suddenly swung madly towards

the Cosworth, trying to catch it broadside. Cutler pressed his foot down on the accelerator, roaring away from the van. It clipped his rear bumper and the Ford shook violently but Cutler gripped the steering wheel tightly and held it under control. He glanced into the rear-view mirror but saw only the blazing white headlights of the van.

'Take them now,' Adamson's voice seemed to grow in volume inside the Ford.

He gave the same instruction to Nicholson and Maguire.

As the two-way went dead, Franklin saw the Audi accelerate and swing out into the outside lane, gaining then drawing level with the Securicor van. He saw the passenger's side window of the car slowly roll down.

There was a burst of brilliant white light as Adamson's finger tightened on the trigger of the MP5K.

In the blink of an eye, half of the thirty-round magazine drilled into the side of the Securicor van, blasting holes in the metal. Some of the 9mm slugs screamed off the armoured chassis, sending pieces of steel flying. Empty shell cases spun out onto the road.

The Securicor van veered violently to one side, its nearside wheels gouging a path across the verge beside the road. The driver struggled with the vehicle but managed to keep it under control even when a second blast from the sub-machine gun raked over it. One bullet blew off part of a wing mirror. Another stove in part of the driver's side window.

'Still no signal,' Franklin said, his eyes fixed on the armoured van. 'Why aren't they calling for help?'

'Be grateful they're not,' Cutler murmured, bringing the Cosworth level with the van. 'Hit the bastards.'

Franklin lowered the passenger's side window. Wind rushed into the car, sweeping through his hair, driving rain into his face. He swung the SPAS up to his shoulder, prepared himself for the recoil, then kneeling on the seat he opened fire. When he squeezed the trigger, the weapon slammed back against his shoulder as it spat out its lethal load.

From such close range, the shot barely spread. It hit the armoured vehicle in one mass and punched a hole in the side of the van. Franklin, teeth gritted, worked the slide and sent another round into the target. The second discharge powered into the cab. It obliterated what remained of the wing mirror and blasted out a portion of the windscreen.

'Get in front of them,' Franklin roared, forced to shout to make himself heard above the wind and the deafening roar of the shotgun. He fired again as Cutler swung the Cosworth across the path of the van.

The shot punched a hole in the radiator grille. The next hit the windscreen. The glass spiderwebbed and Franklin saw the driver frantically punch out a portion of it so he could still see where he was going.

Again Franklin worked the slide and fired. The SPAS roared and slammed back against his shoulder. Franklin shouted furiously, his face demonically lit by the brilliant white light of the muzzle flash.

Another shot hit the radiator and blasted it in. Pieces of twisted metal rattled across the carriageway and steam rose from the buckled front of the vehicle.

He fired again, this time aiming for the tyres.

The front offside tyre exploded and Franklin's eyes blazed triumphantly as he saw the Securicor van begin to skid. The driver was losing control.

Up ahead the Saab began to slow down.

From behind, the Audi accelerated and Adamson raked the stricken vehicle with another burst of automatic fire, also aiming low for the tyres. Another was hit and punctured.

The armoured vehicle suddenly jack-knifed, its rear end spinning round, almost colliding with the Ford.

Cutler pressed down on the accelerator and guided the

car away from the van that was now listing dangerously to one side.

The armoured vehicle suddenly seemed to be moving in slow motion as first it pivoted then began to topple. Unable to grip the tarmac with two shredded tyres and moving too fast to stop, the Securicor van swayed towards the driver's side. Its weight, so useful as a battering ram against the cars that had surrounded it, now doomed it as it fell sideways. The van slammed down onto the carriage-way and skidded, sparks flying out as it skewed across the wet tarmac.

Franklin watched impassively as it continued to skid across the ground, finally coming to a halt close to the crash barrier.

Smoke was rising from the stricken vehicle and, even through the rain, Franklin could smell the stink of burning rubber and the pungent odour of petrol.

'Move it,' roared Adamson through the two-way. 'We've got about five minutes.'

Up ahead, the Saab screeched to a halt then reversed at breakneck speed until it was less than ten yards from the motionless hulk of the Securicor van.

Cutler swung the Ford to a stop near it and stepped out just as Adamson also joined them, the engine of the Audi still running.

In the pelting rain, the men surveyed the wreckage. Glass, pieces of metal and lumps of rubber were strewn across the road in all directions. Slicks of oil were also smeared over the surface. More worryingly, there was petrol spilling across the carriageway, seeping from the van's ruptured tank like blood from a fresh carcass.

'If I try to blow it open the whole fucking lot'll go up,' Franklin said, rain already soaking through the wool that covered his head.

Adamson was standing motionless studying the battered

armoured vehicle, the sub-machine gun still gripped in his fist. 'See if the guys in the cab are still alive,' he snapped.

'There's usually one in the back too,' called Maguire as he hurried over towards the cab and hauled himself up onto the door.

He looked down into the cab and saw that both men were still alive although the driver was bleeding heavily from several cuts on his face and neck.

Maguire pulled the door open and thrust an arm in, hauling the passenger up into the rain.

The second man was also badly cut around the face and his left arm dangled uselessly at his side. Maguire wondered if it had been broken in the crash.

'Get out,' he rasped, pushing the barrel of the Ithaca into the man's face. 'Come on.' He pulled the man free then motioned to Nicholson to help him.

Holding the SIG 9mm in one hand, Nicholson helped the stunned guard down. The man immediately dropped to his hands and knees and vomited violently.

'Where are the others?' Adamson wanted to know, standing over the guard.

The man merely moaned something unintelligible.

'Are there more men *inside* the van?' Adamson persisted, dropping to his haunches and shoving the barrel of the MP5K against the guard's cheek.

Franklin held the SPAS at his hip, the barrel pointed at the guard.

'He's concussed, Jeff,' Nicholson offered. 'He doesn't know what fucking day it is.'

'He knows if he's got mates in the back,' Adamson hissed, resting his finger on the trigger of the sub-machine gun. He leaned closer to the guard. 'If they're in there, tell them to open the doors.' He dragged the dazed man to his feet and half-walked, half-carried him towards the rear doors of the van.

Franklin saw a car approaching on the other side of the carriageway. It sped past and he was sure he could see the driver peering at the tableau behind him.

'Come on, let's move it,' he shouted anxiously.

'Get the fucking doors open,' Adamson hissed to the guard.

The guard merely swayed uncertainly, his eyes bulging. He was staring past Adamson like a blind man.

'We'll have to blow it,' Cutler insisted.

'Not with all this petrol,' Franklin said, wiping rain from his face. 'It's too risky.'

'The bastard must know the combination,' Maguire offered, jabbing a finger at the small panel on the rear door. He grabbed the guard by the throat and pinned him against the van. 'What is it?' he barked at the dazed man.

The guard merely shook his head slowly.

Maguire stepped back and raised the Ithaca to his shoulder, the barrel aimed at the guard's face. 'I'll count to three,' the Liverpudlian hissed.

The guard merely gazed at him blankly.

'One,' Maguire began.

'He's concussed, for fuck's sake,' Nicholson repeated, sharply.

'I heard you the first time,' said Maguire before returning his attention to the guard. 'Two,' he continued, his finger now pressing a little harder on the trigger. 'This fucking shotgun's got a three-pound pull on it and I've got about two pounds on it right now. What's the combination, you prick?'

The guard opened his mouth but all that came forth was a ribbon of blood that dribbled over his lips and ran down his chin.

'Three,' Maguire snarled. He squeezed the trigger.

The eruption missed the guard's head by inches and tore into the armour-plated doors of the van with a deafening clang.

Maguire swung the butt and caught the man across the temple. The guard dropped like a stone and the Liverpudlian raised the shotgun once more, this time bringing it to bear on the keypad attached to the door. He fired twice.

The panel was obliterated by the close range impact.

Adamson stepped across and dug a hand into the hole that had been blasted by the shotgun. The metal was still hot but he ignored that and pulled. The doors moved slightly.

He lowered the MP5K and pointed it in the direction of the rear of the van. 'Just in case,' he whispered, his words barely audible in the driving rain.

'Very subtle, Dogs,' said Cutler, his ears still ringing from the thunderous blasts of the shotgun.

'What the hell would you have done?' Maguire snarled. 'How else were we going to get the fucking doors open?'

'Shut it,' Adamson said. 'Let's get this lot loaded quick.'

All five men moved closer to the overturned van, all eager to see the contents. All desperate to get their hands on the money inside. They would have to move fast to transfer their haul into the boots of their waiting cars.

Franklin, Nicholson and Cutler pulled torches from their jackets and shone the beams on the doors.

Adamson nodded and Maguire stepped away.

One of the doors fell open. The Liverpudlian pulled hard on the other and it flapped wide.

Three torch beams swung on the inside of the van.

'Oh my God,' murmured Nicholson, his stomach contracting.

'What the fuck is *this*?' gasped Cutler, his voice barely more than a hoarse whisper.

Franklin, staring wide-eyed into the rear of the over-turned armoured vehicle, could not even find the breath to speak.

9

'Jeff,' Cutler whispered, rain blurring his vision. 'What's going on?'

Adamson had no answer. Like his companions he was transfixed by what he saw in the back of the van. He took a step closer.

Franklin also moved forward, not really *wanting* to see, but driven by a mixture of curiosity and fear.

He held the SPAS tight to his hip, the hand that held the torch shaking slightly as he played its beam over the contents of the armoured vehicle. It took a moment or two for it to register that what he was staring at were human bodies. Or at least they *had* been.

Franklin wiped rain from his eyes, recoiling suddenly from the foul stench emanating from the back of the van. 'Shit,' he rasped, turning his head slightly, trying to breathe through his mouth so as not to inhale the vile odour.

Maguire stood beside him, the Ithaca lowered, his gaze travelling everywhere the torch beam went.

'There must be fifteen of them in there,' he said quietly.

'Looks like more,' Adamson murmured.

'It smells like they've been in there for a while too,' Franklin said through gritted teeth.

'Where are the heads?' Nicholson added.

'Jesus,' Cutler breathed. 'What the fuck is going on?' He looked at Adamson.

The ex-soldier could only shake his head almost imperceptibly.

'Jeff, I'm talking to you,' Cutler persisted.

'I don't *know* what's happening,' Adamson told him.

Franklin, still trying to breathe through his mouth, continued shining the torch over the van's grisly cargo. Adamson was right. There were more than fifteen bodies in there – a lot more.

The corpses had been packed tightly. When the van had overturned, they had spilled across the inside of the vehicle so that they now formed one huge, bloodied and putrescent pyramid. Every one bore the same signs of mutilation – every one was headless, the skull having been severed roughly level with the shoulders.

As Franklin looked he noticed that it wasn't just the heads that were missing. On every single body, both hands had been hacked off just above the wrist. The same was true of the feet. All had been severed at the ankle. Pieces of jagged bone still showed through the mass of congealed blood and rotting flesh at the hewn joints.

'This wasn't in your fucking plan, was it, Jeff?' Cutler said, looking at Adamson with recrimination in his eyes.

'The driver might know what's going on,' Nicholson suggested.

'He's unconscious,' Maguire said.

'Yeah, and so is the other guard,' rasped Cutler, turning his attention to Maguire. 'Because *you* laid him out.'

'Fucking right,' the Liverpudlian snapped.

'They wouldn't have known what they were carrying,' Adamson said. 'They were civilians.'

'What the hell does it matter who knew?' Maguire snarled. 'The job's fucked. That's all that counts now.'

'Who are they?' Franklin mused aloud, still staring at the bodies.

'Who cares?' Nicholson said, tearing off his woollen mask and jamming it into his pocket. 'Let's get out of here before the law arrive.'

Adamson nodded, also removing his mask.

He could see headlights coming down the opposite carriageway. At any second he expected to hear the wail of a siren.

What he *did* hear was a sound he knew well.

It was the high-pitched scream of a bullet as it cut through the darkness.

10

For interminable seconds everything seemed to freeze. Even the rain appeared to stop falling, each droplet suspended in mid air. Then, the film was running again.

George Nicholson opened his mouth as if to shout something.

A warning?

His features froze in that position as most of the back of his head was blasted away in a reeking flux of blood, brain and pulverised bone. His body remained upright for a moment then pitched forwards onto the wet tarmac, blood pouring out from around what was left of his head.

The other men looked at the body then at each other, spinning madly, looking for the direction of the shot.

Franklin thought it had come from behind them.

Who had fired it?

His heart thudded hard in his chest as he swung the SPAS up, eyes bulging in their sockets as he tried to see through the darkness.

There was another high-pitched whizzing sound as a second bullet tore through the air just inches from Franklin. It came from another direction, although in the wet conditions, it was practically impossible to pinpoint the source.

What the fuck was happening here?

Franklin looked down at Nicholson's body, the pistol still gripped in his hand, the fingers having spasmed around the metal. The hole in the back of his skull was large enough to fit two fists into.

Another shot.

It caught Maguire in the face, powered through his right eye and erupted from the back of his head. Before his body could topple over, another shot hit him in the chest. It shattered his ribs and tore on through his lung, puncturing the fleshy sac before bursting out of his back carrying gobbets of pinkish-purple matter and slivers of flesh and clothing. He dropped to his knees, the Ithaca skittering away from his dead fingers.

Franklin turned and ran towards the Cosworth, aware that Cutler was also hurtling across the carriageway to the vehicle.

It suddenly didn't matter who was firing the shots or where they were coming from. All that mattered was reaching the car.

To remain out in that cold, rain-soaked night meant death.

Simple as that.

Cutler tore open the driver's side door and scrambled behind the wheel, twisting the key in the ignition. A bullet screamed off the bonnet, tearing a channel in the metal fully half an inch deep.

'Come on,' Cutler roared, pushing open the rear door.

Franklin ran, the breath searing in his throat. Behind him he heard another of those insidious high-pitched sounds then a louder, more strident crack.

It was breaking bone. A bullet had hit Adamson in the shoulder and pulverised his collarbone. He dropped the MP5K and clutched at the wound, blood pouring through his fingers. He staggered and tried to run towards the Ford, but another bullet hit him in the small of the back. The impact spun him round and he crashed heavily to the ground.

Franklin turned and saw his companion lying there, his head raised slightly, one arm stretched out before him, the fingers of his hand flexing imploringly. He sucked in another hacking breath, momentarily frozen between the waiting car and the stricken Adamson.

'Leave him,' bellowed Cutler, revving the engine.

Franklin shook his head.

'Do you *want* to die?' Cutler shouted after him as Franklin ran towards Adamson and caught his outstretched hand, dragging him to his feet.

Adamson was muttering something under his breath as Franklin dragged him towards the Cosworth, the sounds punctuated by groans of pain.

Another bullet tore into the road, inches from them, blasting lumps of bitumen into the air.

Franklin finally reached the Ford. He pushed Adamson across the back seats then climbed in behind him, slamming the door in the process.

'Go, go,' he shouted and the Ford shot forward as if fired from a catapult. More bullets struck the ground around it. Another sang off the roof.

Cutler, hunched low over the wheel, guided the vehicle up the road at breakneck speed, flooring the accelerator until the needle on the speedo hit one hundred and stayed there.

There was a slip road two hundred yards ahead. It led up onto a more brightly lit road.

Franklin kept low in the back, the SPAS gripped in one hand, his eyes moving back and forth between the bloodied body of Adamson and the rain-spattered windows.

There was an explosion of glass as one of the rear windows was blasted in. Franklin hissed in pain as a piece

56

of the crystal shrapnel caught him in the face, carved effort-lessly through the wool of his mask and opened a cut on his cheek just below his left eye.

Cutler pressed down harder on the gas pedal, trying to coax more speed from the car. The engine roared protest-ingly but the vehicle sped on. Away from the scene of death and destruction.

Away from so many bodies.

Away . . .

Another bullet obliterated the driver's side window and caught Cutler's right hand.

He shouted in pain as it ripped away most of his little finger, the digit flying into the air then falling uselessly onto the floor of the car at his feet. Blood spouted from the wound and pain travelled the length of his arm but he held onto the wheel, teeth gritted against the agony.

There was less than fifty yards to the slip road now.

Franklin tore off his mask and, blood streaming down his cheek, pressed the wool to the savage wound in Adamson's shoulder.

The older man was moving his lips but no sound was coming forth and there was a dribble of dark blood running from one corner of his mouth. Every now and then he made a gurgling sound in his throat.

Thirty yards to the slip road.

Cutler held the wheel as tightly as he could, his eyes screwed up because of the pain and the driving rain.

Twenty yards.

Headlights from other vehicles on the opposite carriageway cut through the darkness like lasers but he seemed not to notice them.

Ten yards.

Franklin remained bent low in the back of the car, not daring to raise his head for fear it would be blown off.

The Cosworth took the slip road doing a hundred, sped

up it as if it was some kind of launch ramp then slowed as Cutler slammed on the brakes. Steam and spray fountained up from the tyres as they struggled to grip the slippery surface. There was nothing else on the road as they careened onto it.

Sodium lights bathed the car and its stricken passengers as Cutler guided the Ford on as best he could, the pain in his right hand growing more intense by the minute.

'Anyone following us?' he demanded, checking his wing mirror.

Franklin finally raised his head long enough to look out of the back window. He gripped the SPAS in both hands.

What are you going to do if there is someone following?

He could see nothing that looked like a pursuit vehicle.

'No,' he said breathlessly.

Just because you can't see it, doesn't mean it's not there.

'I think we're clear,' he gasped.

He prayed to God he was right.

11

A train rumbled past, the sound amplified within the high-ceilinged garage. The fluorescents flickered and buzzed like angry blow flies. Panes of glass so dusty they were opaque rattled in their wooden frames. The air smelled of petrol, oil, sweat and the coppery odour of blood.

The lock-up was less than a hundred yards from Harrow & Wealdstone station, the direct line into Euston. It was one of a row of twelve identical garages, only two of the others were in use. The rest were boarded shut or sealed by rusted chains and padlocks.

Franklin had no idea how many trains had passed through the station since he and his companions had arrived just over an hour ago. Numbers, like time, seemed to have lost all meaning. His head was spinning. His mind struggling to comprehend what had taken place that night. Now, with midnight approaching, he paced slowly back and forth inside the garage. Occasionally he would lean against the tarpaulin that covered the other car in the lock-up. Beneath the dusty material sat a dark blue Peugeot 405.

'What are we just sitting here for?' he wanted to know.

'What else are we going to do?' Cutler demanded. 'What

do you *want* to do, Matt? Where the fuck are we going to go?'

Cutler took a long drag on his cigarette. His right hand was crudely and heavily bandaged, blood still soaking through the gauze at the place where his little finger used to be. The appendage was beginning to look like a crimson boxing glove. Franklin had applied the dressing before putting a large plaster on his own cut cheek.

He'd been relieved to find that his wound wasn't too deep. It had bled a lot, but the cut itself hadn't been as bad as he'd first feared.

Propped up in the back of the Ford, Adamson drifted in and out of consciousness. Every now and then his glazed eyes would clear and he would experience a moment of lucidity, but with it came a fresh onslaught of pain and he would slip back into his semi-conscious state.

Franklin glanced at his companion and noted how pale his skin looked. His complexion was waxy, covered by a thin sheen of perspiration. His lips were blue at the corners and there was blood trickling from one nostril.

'If we don't get him to a hospital he's not going to last the night,' Franklin said.

'We can't take him to a hospital,' Cutler said flatly. 'What are we going to tell them? He's got two bullet wounds, for Christ's sake.'

'We could drop him off and—'

Cutler interrupted angrily, 'The fucking robbery will be all over the news by now. Every copper in the south of England will be looking for us. If we drop Jeff off at a hospital they'll find us.'

'Robbery?' Franklin said, sucking in a deep breath. 'What fucking robbery? There *was* no robbery, Steve, remember? There was no *money* in that fucking van, was there?'

'You know what I mean,' Cutler said, lowering his voice

60

at the recollection. 'The guard and the driver could talk. They could identify our voices. They're—'

'They're probably dead too,' Franklin said, cutting him short. 'Maybe whoever killed George and Two Dogs killed *them* as well.'

'I doubt it.'

'What are you saying?'

'That it was *us* they were after.'

'*They?*' rasped Franklin. 'Who the hell are *they? Who* was after us?'

'How the fuck should I know, but the whole thing stinks. Somebody knew what we were pulling.'

'Who?'

'I told you, I don't know.'

'Say what you're thinking, Steve.'

'We were set up. No money in the van. Somebody waiting for us. Somebody who knew where the job was going to take place. It was a fucking set-up.'

'That's bullshit.'

'Is it? Then *you* explain what happened.' He pointed an accusatory finger at his companion. 'You saw what was inside that fucking van. Explain *that!*' Cutler winced and looked down at his damaged hand. The two painkillers he'd swallowed an hour ago had done little to ease his discomfort. It felt as if his right hand and lower arm were ablaze.

'I can't explain it. Just like I can't explain why someone started shooting at us. Even if it *was* a set-up, who stood to gain from it?'

'We won't know that until we know who grassed us up.'

'If it was a set-up then it was done by someone close to us. We were the only ones who knew about the job.'

'Obviously not.'

'Who knew, other than the five of us, what the job was and where it was going to happen?'

'People talk.'

61

'You're saying that one of us let the others walk into a trap knowing we'd be killed?'

Cutler didn't answer.

'What did any of us have to gain from that?' Franklin demanded.

Cutler merely shook his head.

'Come on, Steve, you're the one with all the questions,' Franklin snapped. 'All the opinions. Who do *you* think set us up? And why?'

Both men turned as they heard the loud pump-action of a shotgun.

Adamson, leaning unsteadily against the side of the Ford, had the barrel of the SPAS aimed at them, his finger hovering on the trigger.

12

'Yeah, Steve, tell us who arranged the set-up.' Adamson coughed, as if the words he'd spoken had been too much of an effort. He winced in pain, flecks of bloodied sputum spraying from his mouth, but he remained upright, the shotgun pointed at his two companions.

'How do we know it wasn't you?' he continued, his voice weakening. 'After all, you wanted to leave me behind back there on the road – didn't you?'

'All I was bothered about was getting away,' Cutler said defensively.

'Saving your own fucking neck, you mean,' Adamson rasped.

'All right, I panicked,' Cutler said angrily. He held up his bloodied fist. 'I was shot too, you know. This isn't a fucking flesh wound.'

Adamson shook his head.

'Put the gun down, Jeff,' Franklin said quietly.

'Why should I? According to Steve, *one* of us is a fucking grass. How do I know I can trust *either* of you?' He coughed again, his hands tightening on the SPAS, his body shuddering.

'Take it easy,' Franklin offered.

He took a step towards Adamson but the older man raised the SPAS barrel slightly and shook his head.

'I'll take it easy when we get this shit sorted out once and for all,' he said, his watery gaze moving back and forth between the two men.

With infinite slowness, Cutler slid one hand inside his jacket, his fingertips brushing the butt of the Steyr automatic.

'Don't even think about it, Steve,' Adamson coughed. 'I'll cut you in half before you pull it.'

'Both of you just shut the fuck up will you?' hissed Franklin. 'This isn't doing *anybody* any good. We should be trying to figure out what happened, not pointing guns at each other.'

'Perhaps it's time you picked a side, Matt,' Adamson said. 'Or perhaps you did when you pulled me off that road. Perhaps I don't have to worry about *you*.' He glanced at Franklin. '*Do* I have to worry?' He wiped blood from his mouth with the back of one hand.

'This is bullshit,' Franklin snapped.

'Tell *him* that,' Cutler said, pointing in Adamson's direction. 'He's the one pointing the fucking gun at us. Why are you doing that, Jeff? Things go wrong back there? Want to finish it properly now?'

Adamson managed a smile.

'Listen to yourself,' he said. 'Look at me, you stupid cunt.' His voice had suddenly taken on an edge. 'If *I'd* set us up would *I* be the one in this state?' He tried to swallow but his throat was dry, lubricated only by the blood that occasionally rose in it when he coughed.

Cutler held his companion's gaze for what seemed like an eternity then finally shook his head almost imperceptibly.

'Thanks for that,' Adamson chided, lowering the SPAS slightly.

'You've got to admit, Jeff, it looks like someone was waiting for us,' Cutler said.

'Someone *was*. What we've got to figure out is *who*?' Adamson sat down heavily on the bonnet of the Ford. 'I planned that job down to the last detail. I knew every route that van could take from the base to where it was heading. How much it'd be carrying. Everything.'

'Except what was in the back of it?' Cutler offered. 'Why the fuck would there be bodies in there?'

Adamson could only shake his head.

'That's not what matters,' he said, closing his eyes momentarily as a wave of pain swept over him. 'All we should be bothered about is who was waiting for us. Whoever they were they were well organised.'

'Could it have been the law?' Franklin asked.

'They'd have arrested us, not tried to kill us,' Adamson replied.

'And no signal went out from the van,' Franklin reminded them. 'They never called for help or assistance.'

'Probably because they knew what they were carrying wasn't worth taking,' coughed Adamson.

'Could it have been another firm?' Cutler mused.

'Like who?' Adamson wanted to know. 'Who else do we know with that kind of organisation? How many other firms have we ever crossed? None that'd want us all dead. None that *I* know of.'

A heavy silence descended which was broken finally by Franklin.

'So now what?' he asked.

'We wait until morning,' Adamson said quietly. 'Get some sleep. Then we use *that* to get out of here.' He pointed at the tarpaulin-covered Peugeot.

'You need medical help, Jeff,' Franklin insisted.

'Can't take that chance. Not yet. Steve was right.' He looked at Cutler. 'Leave it until morning.'

'You might not be alive in the morning,' snapped Franklin.

'Leave it,' Adamson insisted, walking unsteadily to the rear of the Cosworth. He lay down across the back seats, the SPAS on the floor beside him.

Cutler took a last drag on his cigarette and ground it out beneath his foot.

'Sleep,' he murmured. 'Who the fuck can sleep after what's just happened?'

Franklin ran a hand through his hair. He headed towards the rear of the lock-up, towards a partition made up of wide hanging lengths of plastic.

'I'm going for a piss,' he said wearily.

Cutler watched him disappear through the plastic curtain.

Franklin headed for the tiny lavatory at the back of the building, needing to empty his swollen bladder.

But, away from the prying eyes of his companions, there was something else he had to do.

Something more urgent.

13

There were more than twelve emergency vehicles parked on either side of the carriageway, their blue lights turning silently in the rainy night. Ambulances, fire engines and police cars were parked at various angles on the road that had now been closed both ways. Unmarked official vehicles were also stationed among the throng. It was from one of these that Detective Inspector Vincent Crane had stepped when he'd first arrived at the scene. He'd retreated to the shelter of the vehicle twice since arriving, once to take a message from his superior, the second time to finish a cigarette and momentarily dry off.

Now he stood on the carriageway, hands buried deep in the pockets of his coat, surveying the tableau before him, his forehead even more deeply lined than usual as he frowned. Crane had been in the police force for more than twenty years. Enough time to give anyone a few extra wrinkles. He guessed some of his colleagues might be sporting even more after what they'd seen tonight.

Crane walked slowly back and forth, stopping occasionally to hunker down near one of the bullet holes in the tarmac, or to more closely inspect some of the bloodstains not yet washed away by the rain. He had a cigarette between his lips but it wasn't lit. Only when he drew nearer the overturned Securicor van did he finally pull out the Zippo from his pocket and light the Marlboro.

'I thought you were giving up.'

The voice came from behind him, but Crane didn't need to turn around to know that it came from his second in command.

Detective Sergeant Derek Kingston was four years younger than Crane. He was a tall, powerfully built man, with a burn scar on his left cheek that made it look as though he was constantly blushing on one side of his face. He ran a hand through his wet hair and stood alongside his superior.

Crane blew out a stream of smoke, watching as yet another of the bodies from inside the van was removed to a waiting ambulance.

'How many's that?' Crane wanted to know.

'Fourteen so far,' Kingston told him.

'Forensics keeping busy?'

'They've dusted what they can. Inside and out *and* the two cars.' The DS nodded in the direction of the Saab and the Audi stationary further along the carriageway.

'Any info on the bodies yet?'

'Too early, guv. It'll be another couple of hours at least, I reckon.'

'What about the two we found on the road?'

'We should have something pretty soon. At least as far as ID goes.'

Crane nodded and took another draw on his cigarette.

'Do you reckon they shot the driver and the guard?' he wanted to know.

'They were both shot in the head from close range. There are powder burns around the wounds – execution style. Maybe they put up a struggle. Who knows?'

68

'Thanks, Del,' Crane murmured, stepping away from his companion.

Kingston watched his superior but let him go. He didn't want to interrupt whatever thoughts were tumbling through the older man's mind. Besides, he had enough of his own to contend with.

14

As Franklin emerged from the toilet, he slipped the mobile phone into the pocket of his jacket.

'Private call?' asked Cutler, appearing before him from behind a pile of cardboard boxes.

The two men held each other's gaze for a moment, the silence finally broken by Cutler.

'Who were you calling, Matt?' he wanted to know.

'I was trying to ring Amy,' Franklin said. 'Tell her what happened.'

'You don't usually do that after a job,' Cutler intoned.

'Our jobs don't usually end up like this one, do they?' He began to wash his hands in the small sink nearby.

'Why make the call out here?' Cutler persisted. 'Why not make it back there?' He hooked a thumb over his shoulder. 'Or did you have stuff to say that you didn't want us to hear?'

'What the fuck are you talking about, Steve?'

'I just want to be sure about who you were calling.'

'Don't start that shit again. I told you, I was trying to call Amy.'

'But you couldn't?'

'There was no answer from her mobile. Or from the flat.'

'Let *me* try.' He held out his left hand. 'If I hit redial then she might pick up.'

'I told you, she's not answering.'

'Let me try,' Cutler said more forcefully. He took a step towards his companion.

Franklin's expression darkened somewhat.

'Leave it, Steve,' he said impassively.

'Why? What have you got to hide? Or maybe it wasn't *Amy* that you were trying to call.'

Franklin finished washing his hands and flicked some water at Cutler.

'Fuck you,' he said dismissively, reaching for the towel that hung on a hook next to the sink.

'I want to see the phone, Matt,' said Cutler through clenched teeth.

'And what if I say no?'

'Show me the fucking phone.'

Franklin dug into his pocket and dragged out the mobile, ramming it towards Cutler's right hand. 'Go on,' he snarled. 'Take it, you paranoid bastard.' He pushed it hard against his companion's injured hand, forcing him back against the wall.

Cutler reacted with a combination of anger and pain. 'I've got good reason to be paranoid,' he said. 'Perhaps you should be too.'

'Take it.'

Cutler tried to hold the phone, blood from his bandage smearing the casing.

Franklin slipped his own right hand inside his jacket and pulled the .459 automatic from its shoulder holster.

'Press redial,' he snapped, raising the Smith & Wesson to within inches of Cutler's forehead. 'Do it.' His voice was low but full of menace.

Cutler hesitated.

Franklin thumbed back the hammer on the pistol.

71

'You want to play fucking games,' he hissed. 'I can play them too. You want to know who I was calling? Then press the fucking button.'

Cutler hesitated a moment then jabbed redial and waited, his eyes flicking between the phone and the barrel of the automatic, yawning close to his face.

A number flashed on the display.

'Amy's number,' Franklin said, holding the gun steady. He heard a click then her voice, distant and reedy through the phone.

'Satisfied?' demanded Franklin, snatching the phone back. 'Amy, it's me, babe,' he said into the mouthpiece. 'I'll call you back in a minute.' He pressed the Call End button. Very gently, he eased the hammer forward then flicked on the safety catch before sliding the .459 back into its holster.

'I'm sorry,' Cutler said quietly. 'It's just that, with what's happened, I—'

'I'm sorry too,' Franklin told him. 'Sorry you couldn't trust me. Why don't you go and check on Jeff? And before you do, you should ring Sue. Let her know what's happened.'

Cutler nodded and wandered back through the plastic partition.

Franklin pressed redial and waited.

15

'Are you OK?'

Amy Holden sat up on the bed, her slender legs tucked beneath her, the duvet wrapped around her shoulders.

'Has something happened, Matt?' she wanted to know. 'There was something on the news about an accident. A robbery.'

He ignored her question and wanted to know why she hadn't answered the phone when it had first rung.

'I was watching a film on TV, I must have dozed off,' she said. 'Tell me what's happening.'

She listened as he explained briefly what had occurred that night.

'Are you hurt?' she wanted to know.

He told her about Maguire and Nicholson's deaths. About Adamson having been shot.

The chill in the flat suddenly seemed to deepen.

'If you're hurt, *please* tell me,' she implored.

He mentioned the cut on his cheek but assured her it was nothing to worry about.

'What do you want me to do?'

Franklin told her that she had to leave the flat.

'Why?'

He said that until they knew what had happened, nowhere was safe.

'I could go to Sue's—'

He cut her short. That wasn't a good idea. If there *was* someone after them then spending the night at the home of Cutler's fiancée didn't make much sense. *She* might be a target too.

'I'll check into a hotel,' she said. 'I'll ring you back when I get there.'

He instructed her to use a land line, a public phone, when the time came.

'If Sue's in danger then I should call her too,' Amy suggested.

Franklin said that was a good idea, but that he'd told Cutler to contact his fiancée and explain what was happening.

'I'll get a cab round to her place to pick her up,' Amy said. 'We can go together.'

He asked how she was feeling. Asked about the baby.

The baby.

'I'll be fine,' she assured him. 'We *both* will.'

He told her to take care.

Told her that he loved her.

'I love you too, Matt,' she whispered. 'Please be careful.'

There was a moment's silence on the other end of the line, then he spoke the words she'd been expecting. She needed to protect herself.

Just in case.

'I know,' she said.

He told her to go immediately. To pack what she needed and leave.

'I love you,' she said, then hung up.

For what seemed like an eternity, Amy sat on the bed, as if the conversation she'd just had was part of a bad dream from which she might wake at any instant. But she knew that was not to be. She swallowed hard and swung herself off the bed.

She moved quickly around the small bedroom, pulling a black overnight bag from the top of the wardrobe. Into it she stuffed some tops, underwear, jeans, leggings and some footwear. That done, she hurried into the bathroom and grabbed a toothbrush and some other necessities. These she pushed into the toiletry bag she recovered from a cabinet on the wall behind her. That too went into the overnight bag.

Amy dressed quickly. She pulled on jeans, stepped into a pair of ankle boots and fastened a fleece over a T-shirt before slipping her arms into a long leather coat which she fastened by tying the belt at the waist.

One more thing to do.

She ducked down beside the bed, reached under it and hauled out a battered suitcase from beneath. She unlocked it with the tiny key which was wedged in one of the locks and flipped it open.

There were more clothes inside. Magazines, old birthday and Christmas cards she and Franklin had bought each other. But she dug deeper, sliding her fingers to the bottom, lifting the flap there.

There were two pistols in the hidden compartment. A nickel-plated Taurus PT92 9mm automatic and a Sterling .357 Magnum revolver.

Amy took them both, pushing them to the bottom of the overnight bag. She also pushed in two spare magazines for the Taurus and some extra rounds for the Sterling. That done, she closed and locked the suitcase and pushed it back under the bed, then she snatched up the overnight bag, took one more look around the flat and made for the front door.

When she reached it she paused before stepping out into the cold entryway. A short flight of stone steps led up to street level.

Amy locked the front door behind her then hurried up the stairs and out onto the street. She glanced warily to her right and left, not really sure what she was looking for. The wind whipped around her as she began walking. The road was virtually deserted. One or two cars crossed the junction about a hundred yards ahead of her, but otherwise there was very little movement. She felt suddenly exposed.

Her heart was thudding faster now. Franklin's words echoed inside her head.

Nowhere is safe.

She wanted to look behind her. Wanted to glance into the windows of shops and other buildings as she passed, but instead she kept on at a steady pace along the street.

From behind her she heard a car approaching.

Nowhere is safe.

She swallowed hard and kept walking. The car was slowing down.

Turn and look.

There were traffic lights ahead of her. The car engine rumbled. She saw it draw alongside her then pass her.

A taxi pulled up at the red light, the driver gazing out into the night. Amy hurried across to the black cab and was relieved when the passenger's side window slid down.

'Are you free?' she asked, her throat dry.

'I *was* knocking off, love, but as long as you're not going *too* far,' the driver smiled.

Amy pulled open the rear door and clambered in as the lights changed to green. She told the driver where she wanted to go and sat back, trying to control her breathing.

As the driver guided the cab along the dark streets, Amy rested one foot on the holdall and its lethal contents. She looked out of the side window but all that she saw was her own troubled reflection gazing back at her.

16

'He's going to die, isn't he?'

Cutler lowered his voice slightly as he looked across the lock-up towards the Ford.

On its back seat lay Jeff Adamson, his breathing low and ragged. Every now and then he would wake, murmur something unintelligible then slip back into unconsciousness again.

Franklin took a drag on his cigarette. 'I don't know,' he muttered.

'You *said* he was. You said if we didn't get him to a hospital he'd die.'

'I said a lot of things, Steve.'

The two men were seated on either side of a formica-topped table, close to a stainless steel sink and drainer on the far side of the building. Both had mugs of tea before them. Franklin had found two or three dusty tea bags in a box beneath the sink and made a brew. The table top was cracked and stained, the sink and drainer rusted and discoloured. The colour of dried blood, thought Franklin.

'I could have done with something stronger,' Cutler mused, looking down at his half-empty mug of black tea. He sipped at it and winced.

'I know what you mean.'

They sat in silence for what felt like an eternity, each lost in his own thoughts. Each mulling over the events of that night. The only accompaniment to their musings was Adamson's laboured breathing and the rain on the roof of the lock-up.

'The girls will be OK, won't they?' Cutler eventually asked.

'Course they will,' Franklin said, trying to inject a note of assurance into his tone. 'They can look after themselves.'

'Sue sounded scared when I rang her.'

'I'm not surprised.' Franklin swallowed some of his tea and took another drag on his cigarette. 'Anybody would be. They'll be all right now they've checked into that hotel. They'll be safe there until we get to them.'

'I wish I was as sure as you, Matt.'

Franklin said nothing and there was a moment of uneasy stillness between the two men.

'*I* was scared tonight,' Cutler admitted, his voice low. 'When it happened, when we found those bodies inside the van, when Two Dogs and George were killed. I wanted to run. I didn't give a fuck about anybody else. I just wanted to get away from there.'

'Didn't we all?'

'Yeah, but *you* went back for Jeff. *I* would have left him.' Cutler's voice cracked slightly.

'No you wouldn't. You *could* have driven off. You could have left me too but you *didn't.*'

Cutler cleared his throat and sniffed loudly.

'I don't want to die, Matt,' he said. 'Not like that.'

'You got a preference?'

Both men managed a smile.

'They both had families, didn't they?' Cutler continued. 'George and Two Dogs, I mean.'

Franklin nodded.

'Who's going to tell *them* they're dead?' Cutler wanted to know. 'The law?'

'Their families knew how they earned a living.'

'Is that supposed to make a difference? They're still fucking dead, aren't they? It shouldn't have happened.'

'But it *did*. And there's nothing we can do about it. I want to know who killed them too, Steve. I want to find the bastards who tried to kill *us*. I want to know why.'

Another heavy silence descended.

This time it was broken by Franklin. 'If they tried to kill us, they might go after Sue and Amy too,' he said, without looking up.

'You said they'd be all right.'

'They will,' snapped Franklin. 'But Amy . . .' He choked back the words.

'What's wrong? Is there something you're not telling me?'

'Amy's pregnant,' said Franklin softly.

There. I've said it. It's out in the open. No more secrets.

'Jesus Christ, why didn't you say?'

'What difference would it have made? I didn't know what the hell was going to happen tonight, did I?'

'You could have told me anyway, Matt. How long have we been friends?'

'Amy didn't want anyone to know. Not yet. She swore me to secrecy.' He forced a smile and took another drag on his cigarette. He gazed at the rising smoke as if hypnotised by it. 'Me, a dad. Can you imagine that?' His mood darkened rapidly. 'This should be one of the happiest times of my fucking life but I'm sitting here, one of my mates dying, two of them already dead, wondering if I'm going to be joining them. Wondering if I'm ever going to see Amy again and whether or not I'll ever see my kid.' He ground out the cigarette on the table top. The tip burned the cracked formica.

79

Cutler watched him in silence.

'What do they say? Life's a bitch and then you die,' snapped Franklin, reaching into his jacket. He pulled the .459 free of its holster, hefting it before him. 'Fuck that. We won't make it easy for them, Steve. *Whoever* they are.'

17

The roar of traffic from the Hammersmith Flyover barely seemed to diminish despite the lateness of the hour.

Amy Holden pulled back the curtain slightly and peered out into the darkness. There was nothing much moving out there apart from the seemingly constant flow of vehicles rumbling over and around them. She wondered if the other occupants of the Carlton Hotel had problems sleeping but then, she reasoned, they probably didn't have the same things on their mind that she and her companion did.

The hotel was small, consisting of just twenty rooms spread over three floors. There had been no trouble securing a double room when they'd arrived.

'Close the curtains, Amy,' Susan Harris said. 'Someone might be watching.'

Amy turned to look back into the room. Susan was barefoot, sitting on the double bed, legs pulled up to her chest. She rocked gently back and forth, the long blonde hair that framed her face unkempt. She looked tired and uneasy.

Frightened?

Amy knew how she felt.

Neither of the women had unpacked the overnight bags

they'd arrived with. Sue had locked the bedroom door as soon as they'd entered and had then sat staring intermittently at it for most of the duration of their stay. Amy, once she'd made the phone call to Franklin from a call box across the street, had made them some tea using the kettle and facilities in the room.

The two women hadn't spoken much. Sue, in particular, seemed preoccupied. She heard the floorboards creak outside the room and spun round to face the door.

'It's all right,' Amy assured her as the sound receded. 'Just someone going to their room.'

Sue reached for the pack of Silk Cut on the bedside table and lit one, ignoring the red NO SMOKING sign on the wardrobe door.

'What did you tell Matt when you rang him?' she asked.

'That we were all right,' Amy informed her. 'I gave him the name and address of the hotel. He said they'll meet us tomorrow.'

'Where?'

'He didn't say. I've got to ring him again in the morning.'

Sue exhaled deeply and lay back on the bed, her head resting against the headboard.

'First night off I've had in ages and this is how I end up,' she said, attempting a smile but not quite managing it.

'You enjoy your job, don't you?' Amy asked, turning away from the window.

'You don't have to make small talk with me, Amy,' Sue said, a slight edge to her voice. 'I know I'm scared but you don't have to humour me.'

Amy shot her a glance.

'I'm sorry,' Sue murmured, lowering her gaze. 'I didn't mean to snap.'

'Yeah, I know.'

'I just want to know what's going on. I want to see Steve again. Nothing like this has ever happened before, has it?'

Amy shook her head slowly then looked furtively out of the window once again.

She saw a dark blue Mondeo pull up outside the hotel. It sat there for a minute or two, the engine idling. She felt her heart speed up slightly.

Was anyone getting out?

The Mondeo remained stationary for a moment longer then pulled back out into the road and drove away. Amy relaxed slightly.

Come on. Get a grip. No one else knows you're here.

She moved away from the window and back to the bed where she sat down next to Sue.

'Do you want one?' Sue enquired, offering her the pack of Silk Cut.

'No thanks.'

'Oh God, sorry, Amy. I'll put this out. I forgot. You have to protect your voice, don't you?'

'No, Sue, it's all right,' Amy smiled. 'I smoke anyway. Besides, you should see the state of some of the places where I sing. It's like doing gigs in a coal mine.'

Sue nodded.

'You've got a really great voice, Amy,' she said. 'I hope something happens for you. You deserve it.'

'*Now* who's making small talk?'

Both women smiled.

The phone on the bedside table rang and they both froze. They stared at it as if it was some kind of venomous reptile, seemingly paralysed by its strident ringing.

'Don't answer it,' Sue said, her voice low, her gaze never leaving the ringing phone.

Amy hesitated a moment longer then finally reached for the receiver, her hand hovering over it.

'Amy, don't,' Sue persisted.

'It might be Matt or Steve.'

They'd ring on the mobile. You know they would.

She closed her hand over the receiver and lifted it to her ear. 'Hello,' she said, trying to keep her voice even.

There was a hiss of static.

'Hello,' Amy said again.

'I'm sorry,' the voice at the other end intoned. 'I have put the call through to the wrong room. I do apologise. I—'

The hotel operator never got the chance to finish. Amy slammed the phone back down, her heart racing.

Sue looked at her blankly.

'I've changed my mind,' Amy declared, swallowing hard. 'I *will* have that cigarette.'

Among Infidels

They were unremarkable-looking men. Both in their early thirties. Both dressed in jeans and trainers. The taller of them was wearing a battered denim jacket, the other was garbed in a dark-blue waterproof coat that reached to just below his waist. Two more strangers among a sea of nameless individuals.

They walked briskly across the concourse of Victoria train station, occasionally glancing at the other people milling around. Both of them carried holdalls. The taller one also had a rucksack on his back. He kept adjusting the shoulder straps as he walked. It was as much a nervous movement as an attempt to relieve the pressure of its contents. The second man performed a similar action with his sunglasses, constantly pushing them back up his curved nose. He could feel the sweat on his back and under his arms. It was beginning to bead on his upper lip too. He wiped it away with the back of one hand.

They saw two policemen as they drew closer to the entrance to the Underground. The men did their best not to look at the uniformed men, one of whom was giving directions to three Americans who were chattering and laughing loudly.

The two men swept past the policemen and made their way down the steps towards the Underground. The taller of the two almost collided with a man running up the stairs, sidestepping him as he struggled up the steps carrying a huge suitcase.

There were many people in the area around the ticket machines and both men hesitated momentarily. The shorter of the two fumbled in the back pocket of his jeans and pulled out a crumpled piece of paper. He unfolded it and held it before him, inspecting it with as much care and scrutiny as a pirate might study a treasure map.

The words upon the paper were scrawled in ink, some of which had run. However, both men could still read what was written there and, for a moment, they relaxed slightly, welcoming the sight of their native tongue. Neither of them spoke very good English. They could understand enough to get by but these instructions were crucial.

The taller man dug in his pockets for change. The exact amount was written on the piece of paper. Both of them crossed to a ticket machine and fed in the requisite amount of change. The machine spat out two tickets and they retrieved them, turning and narrowly avoiding a collision with a young woman and two small children. One of the children looked up curiously at the two men and said something to its mother that neither man understood, or *wanted* to understand.

They passed through the ticket barriers, consulted the piece of paper once again and took the escalator to platform level. More people here. They passed along the platform towards the yawning tunnel mouth at the far end and then waited.

A couple in their teens were kissing, leaning against a chocolate machine. The two men glanced at them with something akin to disgust.

There was a rumbling that signalled the approach of a

train and, moments later, it burst from the tunnel. As the doors slid open, the people on the platform pushed closer, leaving little room for those that the train disgorged to alight.

The two men waited until the platform was almost empty then they both stepped onto the train just seconds before the doors closed again. There was a loud hydraulic hiss and the train moved off, swallowed by the blackness of the tunnel.

The taller man tapped his companion's arm and motioned for the piece of paper. Once it was in his possession he studied it again, checking names and places against those on the map opposite him. Then, satisfied, he returned it to the other man who held it tightly in his hand as if it were some kind of icon.

There were several stops before they reached their destination and they would need to change trains. The instructions told them that much. But the men did not care. They stared straight ahead. They had no wish to gaze at the faces of those around them, no desire to look at the features of their fellow travellers.

There was no need to observe those they despised.

18

Franklin stared into the depths of his mug and looked at the dregs of cold tea. He waited a moment then raised the receptacle to his lips and prepared to down what was left of the fluid.

As he straightened up he felt something cold pressing against the nape of his neck. It took him a second to realise it was the barrel of a gun. As he sat paralysed, the mug still poised at his lips, he heard a metallic click as the hammer was thumbed back.

He wanted to say something, wanted to turn and face his opponent but every muscle of his body seemed to have gone into spasm.

The barrel was shoved more roughly against his flesh, the foresight actually grazing his skin.

Franklin slowly lowered his mug and spread his hands on the table top, fingers wide. His lips moved soundlessly and he spoke the same word over and over again. 'Amy.'

Somewhere inside his head he heard her laughter. Saw her face. Saw her holding his child.

Then the gun was fired.

Franklin sat up with a start, propelled from his nightmare

like a stone from a slingshot. He tried to swallow as he pivoted on his chair, realising that there was no one standing behind him. No gun pressed against his neck.

He was breathing quickly, his body trembling. The mug that had held his tea had been overturned and the dark fluid had spilled across the cracked surface of the table.

'Shit,' he gasped, looking around, blinking hard to force the last vestiges of the dream away. But, as they disappeared, so too did the sounds of Amy's laughter.

Amy.

What he wouldn't have given to be able to hold her. To take her in his arms right now. To have her with him. His breathing began to slow.

Somehow, he reasoned, he'd fallen asleep at the table the previous night. Weak, early morning sunlight was now groping its way into the lock-up through the grime-encrusted windows. Franklin massaged the back of his neck, aware of the murderous ache there and all across his shoulders. As his heart slowed its pace slightly he got to his feet, swaying uncertainly for a second. He looked at his watch. 7.39 a.m.

Outside, he could hear the sounds of traffic. A train passed through Harrow & Wealdstone station at high speed and it felt as if the lock-up was shaking. Franklin reached inside his jacket and touched the butt of the .459 as if for reassurance.

In the passenger seat of the Peugeot 405, Cutler also stirred, rubbed his eyes and swung himself out of the car.

'It's cold,' he said, shrugging his shoulders.

'How's the hand?' Franklin asked.

'It fucking hurts,' Cutler told him, regarding the bloodied bandage.

'Did you get any sleep?' Franklin queried.

'Three or four hours,' Cutler told him, yawning. 'What about you?'

89

Franklin nodded and ran a hand over his stubbled chin. 'About the same,' he said, taking a step towards the Cosworth.

'Jeff,' he called, moving nearer to the car.

The back door was closed. Adamson lay immobile across the back seat. Franklin chanced a look at Cutler then pulled open the rear door of the Cosworth. A rancid stench of blood and excrement met their nostrils.

Cutler recoiled, one hand to his face. Franklin leaned into the car, glancing down at Adamson's pale features. His eyes were slightly open, so too was his mouth. There was congealed blood and dried saliva on his lips. Franklin pressed two fingers to the older man's throat just below the jaw.

No pulse.

'He's dead,' Franklin mumbled, pulling himself out of the car. 'Let's get out of here.'

'What about Jeff?'

'The poor bastard's dead. There's nothing we can do for him now. Come on, Steve, we've got to go.'

Cutler looked into the rear of the Cosworth, taking one last glance at Adamson's inert form, at the blood on his clothes and also on the seat and floor of the car.

'Bring the SPAS,' Franklin said, jabbing a finger in the direction of the Ford.

Cutler snatched the shotgun from beside Adamson's body and hurried over to the Peugeot. He put it on the back seat with the Ithaca and covered them both with a blanket.

'We'll call the girls once we're on the way,' Franklin said. 'Tell them what time we're picking them up.' He was already behind the wheel of the 405, the ignition key in his hand. He started the engine, the sound deafening within the confines of the lock-up.

'Open the door, Steve,' he called, watching as Cutler hurried across to the metal entrance and fumbled with the lock. He pushed it upwards and daylight streamed in.

Franklin stepped on the accelerator and eased the Peugeot out towards the beckoning light, reaching across to push open the passenger door.

Behind them, another train rumbled past. Ahead, traffic was already building. Franklin glanced at his watch and guessed it would take them a couple of hours to get to Hammersmith. He heard the lock-up door slam shut. Heard Cutler walk back to the waiting car.

'Come on,' Franklin said wearily. 'Let's go.'

Cutler leaned forward to say something.

It was then that the bullet hit him.

19

It was as if someone had detonated an explosive charge inside Cutler's head. His eyes bulged momentarily in their sockets, his mouth agape as the top of his skull and most of his forehead erupted. Franklin was sprayed with pieces of bone, blood and brain matter.

'No,' he shrieked as Cutler's body fell forward onto the passenger seat, blood fountaining up from the remains of his cranium, bounced once then slid to the ground. It left a slick of crimson six inches wide on the seat.

Franklin had no idea where the shot had come from. He hadn't heard or seen anything.

Same as last night.

He stepped on the gas pedal and moved the Peugeot rapidly up through the gears, desperate to be away from this place, wondering if the next shot would take *him*.

The passenger door was flapping open but, as Franklin took a corner, it slammed shut. There was more blood on the inside. In the rear-view mirror he could see Cutler's body lying on the ground.

'Jesus,' Franklin hissed, guiding the car into traffic, anxious to put distance between himself and the latest scene of carnage.

What the fuck is going on?

He shot out into the road, narrowly avoiding an oncoming van. The driver hit his horn angrily but Franklin ignored it, sending the Peugeot past two more cars and towards a set of traffic lights ahead.

They were already on amber. He pressed down on the accelerator and sped through just as they glowed red. Another car blasted a warning but he ignored that too.

He swung the car left, overtook another vehicle then made a quick right. At last he checked his rear-view mirror. If anyone was following him, it appeared that he'd lost them.

Why do they need to follow you when they can pick you off from distance?

He looked wildly to his right and left. Was someone drawing a bead on him even now?

He wiped some of Cutler's blood from his face and then noticed, with rising nausea, that there were several gobbets of pinkish-grey matter splattered across the dashboard and the inside of the windscreen. He wiped them away with the back of one hand, his stomach somersaulting.

The inside of the car was like a charnel house. The passenger seat was covered with blood, the smell almost overpowering. Franklin's clothes were also flecked with it. He wiped a hand hurriedly over his jacket, bringing it away crimson as he gripped the wheel more tightly and drove on.

Slow down.

One part of his mind told him to slow his headlong pace while the other insisted that he *dare not*.

More traffic lights loomed up ahead. There were cars blocking both lanes at the approaches. He would *have* to slow down.

He drew up alongside a Corsa and chanced a look at the driver. It was a young woman, a little older than Amy.

Amy.

Franklin coughed, hawked and spat on the floor of the Peugeot. He could taste Cutler's blood in his mouth. Again his stomach lurched.

The lights were still on red.

Take it easy.

He inspected his reflection in the rear-view mirror, saw more blood. He wiped his face again with the back of his hand then dug into his pocket for a handkerchief. He then cleaned away the red smears as best he could, spitting on the handkerchief to aid the process.

Was there blood on the outside of the door? Was the young woman in the Corsa going to turn and look at it? Franklin glanced at her but she was staring blankly at the lights. They were changing. Glowing green. The cars in front began to move off.

The Astra at the front of the line stalled and Franklin hit his brake hard to prevent himself colliding with the vehicle.

'Come on, come on,' he said through clenched teeth.

The Astra's engine whined then died.

'Move the fucking thing,' snarled Franklin.

Again the Astra wouldn't start.

Franklin flicked on his indicator, waited for a gap in the traffic then moved out into the other lane. He drove on, his heart still beating madly.

Get off the road and check the damage.

He licked his dry lips and again tasted blood.

Franklin chanced another look in his rear-view mirror. There was a silver grey Montego less than twenty yards behind him.

Following?

He turned right.

So did the Montego.

Franklin reached into his jacket and touched the butt of the .459.

He guided the Peugeot across a junction.

The Montego turned right.

Franklin, perspiration now beading on his forehead, exhaled deeply.

Get further away from here then get off the road and get things sorted. Get the car and yourself cleaned up.

Franklin nodded to himself.

He gripped the steering wheel more tightly in an effort to stop his hands quivering so violently. And he drove on.

All Praise Be To Him

There were bodies lying all around the Armoured Personnel Carrier. Some were already dead, some in their death throes. Others were trying to crawl away from the blazing wreck. All of them wore the uniform of the Russian army. One of the men, his face a mask of blood, crawled with one arm ablaze from shoulder to elbow. The fact that part of his body was on fire seemed to matter little to him. All he wanted was to be free of the inferno behind him.

He crawled another two yards before a figure straddled him, placed the barrel of an AK47 assault rifle to the back of his head and fired once. Most of the man's skull was obliterated by the heavy-grain bullet and he flopped forward onto the ground, what remained of his head in the centre of a spreading pool of blood.

A hand gripped the dead man's collar and hauled him up slightly, thrusting his pulverised face towards the camera that was recording the events. There were shouts of triumph on the soundtrack too. Words spoken quickly and excitedly in the language of the men who gazed at the television screen.

There were six men in the small sitting room of the flat in Camden Town. All of them gazed raptly at the scenes flickering before them. They smiled as they heard the words and saw the pictures. One of them nodded, as if in agreement with what he was seeing. Another glanced from the screen to the video recorder that was squeaking slightly as it played. There were three more tapes lying next to the machine. They would watch those later. The men who had arrived a day earlier had brought one of the videos with them. The same men who had travelled across London from Victoria station and who now sat cross-legged on the bare floor, enraptured by what they watched.

The image on the television screen changed again and the six men found themselves looking at a solitary figure this time. A man like themselves. His head swathed in the folds of a white *imama*, his long grey beard cascading down the front of his jet black *jubba*. He spoke directly to the camera and his words were venomous. Delivered with fury. He spoke of the atrocities committed against all Muslims by the Russians in Afghanistan. He raged about the evil perpetrated by the Americans in Iraq. He cursed the Israelis. He damned the British and anyone else who supported the forces who opposed Islam. Only when some footage of the smoking ruins of the World Trade Center appeared did his tone soften and turn almost reflective. There was pride in his voice now.

As he continued, the picture on screen changed to one of a hospital in Iraq. Children, many with limbs missing, others horribly burned, cried into the prying lens of the camera. Mothers wailed and screamed as they kneeled beside beds where their offspring lay, bandaged and immobile, soaked in blood.

Two men were trying to pull huge lumps of concrete away from the remains of a house. Others were dragging bodies from inside the ruins. And the voice on the tape returned with renewed fury.

The six men who watched did so with anger etched on their faces.

The image changed again. A single truck was hurtling towards a roadblock. The camera this time was mounted inside the cab, it was pointing at the two women inside. Both had dynamite strapped to their bodies. They were calling loudly to Allah as they drove, the image blurring as the truck bumped over the uneven road. The two women screamed with a mixture of exaltation and anger as they sped towards their target. When the truck hit, the picture disappeared.

The six men watching the screen cheered.

Their cheers were for the two women. Patriots and martyrs as they would be. The women had given their lives to destroy the enemy. They had given their lives for Allah.

There could be no greater accomplishment. No finer tribute. All of them knew that *their* time would come soon. *They* would be blessed like the two women they had watched die. *They* would reach paradise and they would do it with the blood of thousands of infidels on their hands.

One of them whispered the name of the prophet. It was echoed by the others. Their time was close and they relished it.

All Praise be to Him.

20

At first Amy thought she was dreaming.

She heard the voice somewhere in her subconscious. A gentle knocking, then the voice. It was growing more insistent.

Then she realised that this was no dream. The tapping was on the bedroom door. The voice was coming from the other side of the wooden partition.

Amy sat up quickly and swung herself off the bed. She paused for a moment, glancing down at the black holdall just visible in the bottom of the slightly open wardrobe. She knelt swiftly, pulled the .357 from beneath some clothes and stuffed it into the waistband of her jeans, pulling her blouse over the butt.

Sue, now also stirring, watched silently.

The tapping on the door continued.

Amy could hear words being spoken. She drew nearer the door.

'Room service,' said the voice from the other side of the door.

Amy put her eye to the peephole and saw a man dressed in a white shirt and jacket and black trousers balancing a tray on one hand while he knocked with the other.

Sue looked warily at her but Amy unlocked the door and smiled cordially at the man.

'Room service,' he repeated. 'Your breakfast.'

'Sorry,' she said sleepily. 'Put it on the table please.'

The man set the tray down on the table close to the bed, nodding a greeting to Sue in the process.

Amy signed for the food and tipped the man a pound, closing the door behind him as he mumbled something about leaving the tray outside when they'd finished.

Sue exhaled deeply and rubbed her eyes. She stretched, the joints of her elbows popping.

Both women had slept fully clothed although neither had enjoyed more than a fitful slumber.

'I'm not hungry,' Sue said, massaging the back of her aching neck.

'Try and eat some toast,' Amy said, removing the paper napkin from around the underdone slices. She sipped at her orange juice and offered Sue a glass which she drank.

'I need to change these clothes,' Sue murmured wearily.

'I need a shower,' Amy added.

'When are you going to ring Matt?'

'When we've had this.'

'I hope they're all right.' Sue shook her head as Amy pushed a piece of buttered toast towards her.

Amy chewed her own toast slowly and glanced in the direction of the window, glad to see that it had stopped raining. She took the revolver from her waistband and laid it on the bed.

'Would you have used that?' Sue wanted to know.

'Matt said that nowhere was safe.'

'Would you have used it?' Sue repeated.

Amy swallowed hard. 'Look, Sue, I don't know what's going on,' she said. 'All I *do* know is that our lives could be in danger. Matt said that.'

'What if he's wrong?'

'Then he's wrong, but I'm not going to take that chance. Anyway, why would he say that if it wasn't true?'

Sue nodded slowly.

'The guns are for our protection,' Amy continued.

Sue looked at the polished frame of the Sterling glinting in the light of the room and shuddered involuntarily.

'When Steve first told me what he did for a living I didn't believe him,' she said, looking down at her carefully manicured nails.

'What did he tell you?'

'He said it was to do with the law. It was just that he spent his time out-running it.'

They both smiled.

'I said he was full of shit,' Sue continued.

'What about when you found out the truth?'

'I didn't care. I loved him so much by then I probably wouldn't have cared if he'd been a hit man.' She took another sip of orange juice. 'What about Matt? Did he tell *you* the truth about what he did?'

Amy nodded and smiled wistfully.

'He was more honest about his *dis*honesty than any other guy I'd ever been involved with,' she grinned. 'None of the others were like him. No one else ever *could* be.'

Tell her what a wonderful father he'll make.

Amy crossed her legs and continued to chew on her piece of toast. 'He'd laugh if he could hear me talking about him like this,' she added.

'So would Steve. He'd probably ask me to marry him again. Make an honest man out of him.'

'Why don't you?'

'A piece of paper isn't going to make any difference, Amy. I couldn't love him any more than I do now. Still, maybe one day . . .' Her voice trailed away into silence.

Both women sat without speaking for what seemed like an eternity, then Amy looked at her watch.

'I'd better make that phone call,' she said, getting to her feet. She pointed to the .357 lying on the bed. 'If you have to, Sue, use it.'

21

'Jesus Christ. Thirty-four?'

Detective Inspector Vincent Crane looked incredulously at his colleague.

'Thirty-four,' DS Kingston repeated, glancing down at the piece of paper he held as if for confirmation.

Crane exhaled deeply and sat back in the chair behind his desk, as if trying to sink into the leather and disappear.

'Did they all die the same way?' he wanted to know.

'We're still waiting for the pathologist's full report. We're not even sure about *cause* of death yet.'

'So the only thing that's consistent is the mutilation?'

Kingston nodded.

'Every single body, all thirty-four of them, has had the feet, hands and head removed,' he said.

'With what? What was used to remove them?'

'A cutting implement with a straight edge,' Kingston said, referring to his piece of paper once again. 'That's all we've got so far.'

Crane got to his feet.

'Somebody took the time and effort to cut the heads, hands and feet off thirty-four bodies then stuff them into a Securicor van and *that's* all we've got?' he said irritably. He crossed to the window of his office and looked out across London as if hoping to find an answer somewhere in the skyline of the capital. 'What about the others? The ones that were shot? Anything on them?'

'George Nicholson and Joe Maguire. They both had form. Maguire had done a five stretch. Nicholson had previous but nothing major.'

'What's the pathologist said about *them*?'

'Both were killed with the same type of weapon.'

'Well, that's something. What was it?'

'They think it was a rifle.'

Crane turned to face his colleague.

'They *think*? What the hell is going on here, Del? We've got thirty-four mutilated bodies and no one knows *how* they were killed *or* how they got into that van. Two guys are shot trying to hijack that same van and no one knows what they were shot *with*?'

'That's about it, guv.'

'Why the fuck would someone want to knock over a van full of dead bodies?'

'I'm guessing they didn't know that's what was in there.'

Crane managed a smile. 'I'm guessing you're right,' he grinned. 'That must have been a lovely surprise for them.' He stroked his chin. 'What's so mysterious about the murder weapon?'

'Like I said, they think it was a rifle. We found a couple of bullet fragments on the road. They're being analysed too. First reports confirm they were rifle slugs.'

'But no one knows what kind of rifle they came from?'

'The lab reckon either an HK PSG-1 or Sterling Model 81. But they can't be sure yet.'

'They're both sniper rifles,' Crane said, his eyes narrowing slightly. 'What about the bullets?'

'Well, as I said, they're still working on that, but word

is the rounds were titanium-coated. Traces of it were found in the bodies of both Maguire and Nicholson.'

'Titanium-coated bullets from sniper rifles. Which firms in London have got that kind of firepower to chuck around?'

Kingston shook his head.

'Any shell cases?' the DI wanted to know.

'Forensics organised a sweep five hundred yards in all directions from the van. Nothing.'

'Was the same weapon used to kill the guard and driver?'

'No. They were shot from close range with a standard 9mm.'

'By Maguire or Nicholson?'

'Forensics are checking it. We found a SIG P220 on Maguire. Two rounds had been discharged.'

Crane nodded. 'Doesn't it strike you as a bit . . . shoddy, Del?' the DI asked. 'I mean, this was a professional crew. The job must have been methodically planned and yet so many things went wrong. Where did they get their info in the first place? A tip-off? An inside job? Surveillance?'

Kingston raised his eyebrows and shrugged.

'All right,' Crane continued, 'in the meantime, let's concentrate on what we *do* know. Maguire and Nicholson. Small-time villains. Usually worked with the same firm, right?'

'As far as we know.'

'We've got four witnesses who say they saw three other men fleeing the scene of the shooting. One of them possibly injured. So check hospitals for anyone admitted with a gunshot wound.'

'That's already being done, guv. So far nothing.'

'Extend the search area if you have to. There must be five hospitals within a ten-mile radius of where the shooting took place.'

'Do you honestly think they'd risk that?'

'Depends how badly hurt the bloke was.'

'He's probably lying in a ditch somewhere now.'

'You could be right, Del. But let's be sure. And if he *is*, then let's find his body. I want a list of everybody Maguire and Nicholson have worked with during the past ten years. If we find their accomplices, we'll have a better chance of figuring out who might have wanted them dead. Then maybe some of this shit will start to add up.'

'*Nothing* about this lot adds up, guv,' the DS remarked. 'Maybe when the lab are finished—'

'If they *ever* are,' Crane said, cutting him short. 'Perhaps it's time we hurried them up a bit. Come on.'

He headed for the door of his office, Kingston trailing in his wake.

22

It had taken him longer than he'd expected to clean away the blood.

Franklin looked first at the bundle of sodden crimson rags gripped in his fist then back into the interior of the Peugeot.

A train thundered past on its way to Euston. Franklin watched as it sped through Wembley Central. He'd parked the 405 in the car park there, stopping first at the Sainsbury's nearby to purchase a plastic bucket, some bleach, kitchen roll and J-cloths.

No one had given the car a second glance, parked as it was in the furthest bay of the tarmacked area. The vast majority of the vehicles parked here, Franklin reasoned, belonged to commuters who had left hours ago to reach the hub of the capital. He had worked quickly and expertly without fear of disturbance.

Now he walked across to a large skip nearby and hurled the rags in with the other rubbish. Back at the car he used some clean kitchen roll to wipe his hands then he slumped in the driver's seat, perspiration beading on his forehead.

His head was spinning, his mind racing as it tried to make sense of what had happened earlier that morning.

He could still see the vision of Cutler falling into the car, his head blown apart.

How the fuck had they found them at the lock-up?

It had to be the same men who had killed Nicholson and Maguire *(and Adamson)* the previous night.

Who the hell else could it be?

Had they followed them? Staying at a careful distance. Tracking them to their hiding place?

Franklin rubbed his eyes.

If they'd known where you were last night they'd have come in blasting. They'd have taken all three of you out last night.

Whoever it was must have found the lock-up early this same morning. He tried to swallow but his throat was parched. His lips dry.

Franklin glanced into the rear-view mirror and studied his own reflection. The image that stared back at him was of a confused (frightened?), and desperate man.

You're on your own now, sunshine. They're all dead apart from you.

He shuddered involuntarily and reached for the ignition key. He had to reach Amy. That was his priority now. He must get to her. Help her.

Help her do what? You haven't been able to save any of your fucking mates. What are you going to do for her?

He started the engine.

The mobile rang.

He snatched it from his pocket, almost dropping it in his haste.

Amy.

'Hello,' he said, eagerly, clearing his throat.

'Matt, it's me.'

'Are you OK?' he asked.

'We're fine. Where are you? I've tried to call a couple of times before but I couldn't get through.'

'No. I switched the phone off while . . .'

'*While I scrubbed Steve's brains off the inside of the car.*' Is that what you wanted to say?

'Where's Sue? Is she with you?' Franklin asked hurriedly.

'She's all right. We're both fine. Just—'

'I didn't ask that, Amy,' he snapped. 'Is she with you now?'

'No,' Amy told him. 'Matt, please tell me what's going on.'

'Steve's dead.'

He heard a low moan at the other end of the phone.

'It happened this morning,' he continued. 'They were waiting for us when we came out of the lock-up. I couldn't do anything.'

There was silence at the other end of the line.

'Amy, listen to me,' he insisted. 'Don't tell Sue. Don't give her any idea that something's happened to him. *I'll* tell her when I get to you.'

'And what do I do if she asks me?'

'Lie to her,' he snapped. 'Say whatever you have to. Tell her you couldn't get through to me. Anything. It doesn't matter.'

'All right, Matt,' she said, her voice cracking. 'I'll take care of it.'

'She mustn't know, Amy,' he continued, lowering his voice again. 'Not yet.'

'I understand. What do you want me to do?' He heard her curse under her breath. 'I'm running out of money, Matt.'

'Stay where you are until I pick you up,' he said urgently. 'Which room are you in? I'll be there in two hours. I promise.'

She told him, then there was a moment's silence.

'Amy, I love you,' he said softly. 'Amy?'

There was no answer. The line had gone dead.

23

'I'll never get used to this smell.' Detective Sergeant Derek Kingston wrinkled his nose as he walked into the autopsy room. The smell of disinfectant was overpowering, mingled with an equally strong stench of bodily excretions and fluids. He glanced around the gloomily lit space, walking a pace or so behind his superior. On two walls there were metal freezer cabinets for storing bodies. To the right there was a sink. The tap was dripping, the sound echoing in the cold confines of the room.

DI Crane moved purposefully across the white tiled floor, his gaze moving swiftly between the four metal slabs that each bore the remains of a corpse. Above every one hung the scales used to weigh internal organs during an autopsy and, as he and Kingston moved closer to the furthermost slab, he saw the pathologist lift something dark and dripping from the cavity of the body he was hunched over.

It took Crane a moment to realise that it was a kidney.

The pathologist noted the weight of the organ and murmured something into the small microphone that was suspended over the dissection table. The tap dripped steadily in the background.

'What have you got, Howard?' Crane asked, moving closer to the slab and its grisly cargo.

Doctor Howard Richardson looked at the DI and raised his eyebrows.

'Not much, I'm afraid,' he said, in a tone that seemed entirely too cheerful for such mournful surroundings. Richardson was a tall, greying individual in his early fifties, with a pair of half-moon spectacles perched on the end of his aquiline nose. He reminded Crane of a vulture leering over a carcass.

'Tell me what you *have* got,' Crane insisted. 'What happened to them?'

Richardson's tone became somewhat more sombre as he waved a hand expansively over the body beneath him. 'You read my initial report?' the pathologist said.

Crane nodded.

'All the bodies were mutilated in exactly the same way,' Richardson continued. 'Heads, hands and feet were removed by a sharp object.'

'Any idea why?'

'You're the detective, Vince, not me. Why do you think?'

'To make identification more difficult,' Crane said. 'Without a head we can't check dental records. Without hands, we can't take fingerprints. And the feet . . . they're just a bonus.' He paused. 'Were all the injuries inflicted by the same person?'

'From what I've seen so far, I'd say that there were two, possibly three . . .' The pathologist paused as if searching for the words. 'How shall I put it? . . . "cutters?" The angle of the cuts isn't consistent. At least one of them was left-handed.'

Crane exhaled wearily. 'Three fucking maniacs,' he breathed.

'It looks that way,' Richardson confirmed. 'Although maniacs might be the wrong word. There doesn't appear

111

to have been any haste involved during the removal of the extremities. The cuts were made carefully. These bodies were mutilated by calm individuals working with precision. There aren't the usual signs of frenzy that you'd generally associate with this kind of thing. No hacking or tearing of the skin. Just careful, exact incisions.'

'What kind of man could do that?' Crane mused, looking at the stump of the neck on the corpse before him.

'A butcher?' Kingston offered.

'A surgeon,' added Richardson, smiling.

'So we raid every slaughterhouse, butcher's shop and hospital within a fifty-mile radius?' Crane asked. 'And hope we get lucky?'

'Any prints on the bodies, Howard?' Kingston wanted to know.

Richardson shook his head.

'Forensics said they found indentations on most of the bodies but they were all made by smooth gloves,' the pathologist continued. 'No fingerprints.'

'Calm *and* careful,' opined Kingston.

'Yeah, the worst combination,' Crane agreed. 'And all the victims were male?' he continued.

Richardson nodded.

'All white, all aged between twenty and thirty,' the pathologist told him. 'All of a similar height and build.' He pushed his glasses back up his nose.

'So, we could be looking for someone with a grudge against blokes. A man-hating butcher, a rent boy turned surgeon or Jack the fucking Ripper,' Crane offered.

The other two men in the room laughed.

Crane didn't seem to share the joke he'd made. A heavy silence descended, broken only by the steady dripping of the tap.

'How long had the bodies been in the truck?' asked Crane, finally.

'Twenty-four hours maximum,' Richardson answered. 'There's very little sign of even the earliest stages of decomposition. They were killed and mutilated in a very short space of time.'

'How the hell do you kill and cut up thirty-four blokes without anyone noticing?' Kingston asked.

'And then pack them into a Securicor van,' Richardson reminded him.

'What about *cause* of death?' the DI insisted.

'Nothing yet,' Richardson told him.

'Well find one, Howard, and find it quick. If the media get hold of this it'll be like a fucking feeding frenzy. If I have to go into a press conference I want *something* to tell them. Something to get them off our backs long enough to find out what the hell is going on here.'

24

Franklin was sweating. It wasn't warm but despite that, he could feel his T-shirt sticking to his back. When the traffic stopped at a set of lights he pulled off his leather jacket and dropped it onto the passenger seat. The .459, still in its shoulder holster, was already lying there beneath a damp cloth, hidden from prying eyes.

He watched the lights, waiting for them to change.

The red one looks like a bullet wound.

Franklin glanced first one way then the other. There was a white van to his left. A blue Nova to his right. He glanced at the drivers of both. A man in his early twenties in the van. A woman a little older in the Nova. Franklin checked the rear-view mirror and saw that there was a taxi directly behind him. He could see the driver's face quite clearly. Every now and then he turned and said something to his passenger.

Franklin switched on the radio, heard a couple of seconds of music then decided he could do without it.

A motorbike was moving up alongside vehicles on his right. The rider's visor was down.

Franklin slid his hand across to the passenger seat and allowed his fingers to touch the butt of the automatic.

The bike drew nearer.

Steady. Stay calm.

He swallowed hard, his gaze fixed on the bike and its black-clad rider. It was now less than ten yards from him. Franklin's heart raced. His eyes flickered from the bike to his rear-view mirror then back again.

The rider was less than five yards away now.

Franklin closed his hand around the butt of the Smith & Wesson.

There was a loud blast as the taxi behind him sounded its horn. Franklin jumped in his seat.

The bike was almost level with him.

Another blast on the taxi's horn.

The Nova and the van had both pulled away.

The bike swept up alongside then drove past and away.

He realised that the lights had turned green as the taxi driver blasted another warning.

Come on. Come on.

Franklin stepped on the accelerator and drove away, his heart slowing a little. The dispatch rider had already disappeared into a knot of traffic further up the road.

The Peugeot moved along evenly, as Franklin reached for his cigarettes and lit one. Christ alone knew he needed it. He sucked hard, feeling the smoke burn its way to his lungs. His progress from the car park at Wembley Central had been quicker than he'd expected. At least until he'd hit London's busiest areas. The roads were clogged like the arteries of a diseased heart. He drove with barely suppressed fury, desperate to reach his goal, conscious all the while that he may have been followed. That he could be under scrutiny at this very moment.

Could be in the cross-threads of a rifle sight?

He shuddered involuntarily and tried to force the latter thought to the back of his already confused mind.

Images and memories tumbled through his consciousness

and, as he drove, he tried to make sense of them. Tried to sort them into some semblance of order. It was useless. There were too many unanswered questions. Too many things that needed explanations and he was nowhere near to reaching any.

Who had killed his companions?

Who had performed the task with such ease and accomplishment?

Was he being followed?

Who had set them up the night before?

Who had been waiting for them?

Why?

Why? What? When? How?

Franklin shook his head, as if to dispel the endless stream of queries. He took another drag on his cigarette and drove on, wondering if he should call Amy from the mobile, tell her he was close now. That, within fifteen minutes, all being well, he should be with her.

What's the point?

He swung the car right, wondering what he was going to do when he reached her.

After you've told Sue that her boyfriend is dead you mean?

Franklin gripped the wheel tighter. He would somehow have to find the words to tell Sue what had happened to Cutler. But how? How could he look her in the face and tell her? And even if he did, what if she asked questions? What if she wanted to know if he suffered? What he said before he died?

Just tell her the truth.

Franklin exhaled almost painfully. He didn't know what the fucking truth was anymore. All he knew was that he had to reach Amy. After that . . .

The thought trailed off, lost among the other spinning, careening words and questions inside his mind.

He drove on.

116

25

'All right, let's run through this again.'

DI Crane raised his hand to attract the attention of those in the room and also to still the babble of chatter.

The Incident Room had been set up on the fifth floor of New Scotland Yard and it was crammed to bursting with both uniformed and plain clothes officers. Some sat alone, others huddled in groups but all were looking in the direction of Crane and the noticeboards and blackboards behind him.

The noticeboards were filled with photos of everything from the crashed Securicor van to every single one of the thirty-four mutilated bodies that had been found inside it. The grisly colour shots vied with pictures of the abandoned car vacated by Nicholson and Maguire. Next to those were half a dozen pictures of the dead men themselves, taken from every conceivable angle.

On the blackboards there were diagrams of where each car and every corpse had been found. There were also arrows, drawn in red, representing the direction from which the bullets that killed Nicholson and Maguire may have come. More pictures of the Audi that Adamson had been driving had been tacked to the rim of the board as had, in large letters, the names:

GEORGE NICHOLSON

JOE MAGUIRE

In addition, there was an Action Board at the back of the room, propped on an easel like an artist's canvas. It showed the location of every single one of the officers working on the case and which particular aspect of it they were connected with.

Crane kept his hand in the air until the babble died away, his eyes flicking across the myriad faces all fixed on him. He cleared his throat, glanced at DS Kingston as if for encouragement, then spoke again.

'I'd just like to say, before anyone else does, that I haven't got a fucking clue what's going on either,' Crane offered.

A ripple of laughter ran around the room.

'We've been over it again and again since last night but, so far, we've still got more questions than answers,' the DI continued. He took a sip from the glass of water on the corner of the desk which he stood before. 'Now it looks, taking all the information we've got so far into consideration, that what we've got here are two different crimes. Totally separate and unlinked. As far as we know, five guys, including these two,' he turned and pointed at the photos of Nicholson and Maguire, 'were in the process of robbing a Securicor van of its contents. What they actually found, as you all know by now, were thirty-four dead and mutilated corpses. The gang were then shot at. The two you see were killed, a third was wounded, but he escaped with the remaining two.' Crane began pacing slowly back and forth in front of the desk. 'So far we've got no information on the mutilated bodies other than that they were all white males.' He turned and glanced at Howard Richardson but the pathologist merely nodded.

'As for the men who pulled the job on the Securicor

118

van, we have positive ID on both of them. They both had form. I asked for any information on their known associates . . .' He looked at a uniformed officer in the front row.

'Both of them had worked with a man called Jeffrey Adamson, sir,' said the officer, consulting his notes.

'What about the other two men on the job?'

'More than likely Steven Cutler and Matthew Franklin,' the officer told him. 'Both had worked with Adamson before.'

'How come Maguire was the only one who'd done time?' Kingston wanted to know.

'All five of them had been held at various times but there was never enough evidence to make charges stick,' the uniformed officer explained. 'They all had top briefs any time they were in trouble.'

'Top briefs,' said Crane. 'The reason being that they were very good at what they did. These weren't petty thugs. They were career criminals and they were good at their work. Let's put it this way, I don't think we'd ever have caught one of them robbing an off-licence with "Born to lose" tattooed on his forehead.'

More laughter in the room.

'So, as far as we know, they planned the job thinking they were going to pick up money from the Securicor van,' Crane continued. 'As far as we can tell, the job was carried out *according* to that plan. Nothing went wrong until they opened it up.'

He held up one index finger. 'The first job was ostensibly a robbery,' he said. 'Pure and simple. The next question we need to ask ourselves is how those bodies got in that truck. Who put them there?'

'Shouldn't we be asking how they got in that state in the first place?' asked a plain clothes man near the back of the room.

There were murmurs of agreement.

'Yes,' Crane said, fixing his gaze on the man near the back. 'Any ideas?'

'Or where they were being taken?' someone else offered.

'Or coming from?' a uniformed policewoman added.

Crane nodded.

'Well, just to make things even more complicated,' said a plain clothes man wearily, 'we checked with both the Securicor depots that cover that area and *neither* of them had a job booked for that time *or* that location last night.'

'What are you telling me?' snapped Crane.

'That the van could have come from anywhere in the country.'

'Did you check the number plates with Swansea?'

'No record of them. No record of the van. It didn't belong to Securicor. Neither did the two guys aboard it. We're still waiting for ID on *them.*'

Crane glared at the plain clothes man as if he was personally to blame for the revelation. 'So someone stole a Securicor van and filled it full of dead bodies?' Crane said.

'No van was reported stolen. Securicor haven't had a vehicle nicked. It looks as if it was *disguised* as the real thing. That's why the specs inside were so basic.'

Crane shook his head. 'This is bullshit,' he snapped.

'It looks like a set-up, guv,' Kingston offered. 'Someone wanted to get to Adamson's firm.'

'It's pretty bloody elaborate, isn't it, Del? And that still doesn't explain the corpses,' Crane said. 'It also doesn't explain why the two guys riding the van were shot.'

'To stop them talking?' offered a plain clothes officer perched on the edge of a desk. 'Maybe they knew who the killers were.'

'But where was the van going?' another officer wanted to know.

Questions began to pour from all areas of the room until the melee of words grew in volume.

120

'All right, all right,' Crane said, raising his hands for silence. 'Quieten it down.' He drew in a deep breath.

'More questions and no answers,' murmured Kingston, looking at his superior.

'Our best bet at the moment is to find the other three guys who tried to pull the job,' Crane insisted. 'Maybe they can tell us exactly what happened last night. I also want other firms questioned. If it *was* a set-up, I want to know *why*. And I want to know where those fucking bodies came from. *And* where they were going.'

An undertone of mumblings began to fill the room once more as those present repeated aloud some of the things they'd just heard. Crane looked at Kingston who shrugged.

The door of the office opened and a uniformed man hurried in, watched by the assembled throng. He crossed to Crane, feeling the eyes of the watching officers boring into him.

'A mobile unit's just radioed in news of two of the men we're looking for in connection with what happened last night, sir,' said the uniformed man.

'Where are they?' Crane demanded.

'In a lock-up in Harrow & Wealdstone.'

Crane smiled.

'Let's go,' he said quickly, heading for the door.

'I wouldn't hurry, sir,' the officer called after him. 'They're both dead.'

Jihad

Their conversations were brief and sporadic. The six men who inhabited the flat in Camden Town barely knew each other's names.

It was the best way. None of them could see any point in forging close ties with their companions. They were united in their beliefs and in their unbreakable determination to succeed in their chosen mission. That was enough. Names, in matters such as this, were unimportant.

They ate together. They prayed together. They only ever left the flat in pairs. Three of them spoke passable English but it was barely needed. The inhabitants of the other flats were unconcerned by the comings and goings of these swarthy-skinned individuals.

An old woman three doors along had taken to peering out of her own front door every time she heard one of the men arrive or leave but, after a while, even that level of interest waned. And the men were able to move about freely among their enemies.

There was a large open area in front of the flats. It was concrete, many of the slabs cracked or broken. Weeds had thrust their way up through many of the fissures. Birds dug around for worms in the exposed earth beneath some of

122

the more badly damaged slabs. There had once been four wooden benches in this area too. All were now broken. One had been set on fire months earlier. Graffiti was sprayed on the remains of the others and also on the walls of the ground floor flats. It also covered the stairwells and lifts.

The six men who lived in the flat looked on the vandalism with contempt. To them it served to further illustrate the corrupt nature of their enemies. They despised these people who destroyed what had been given to them. Sometimes, one of the men would stand and watch while local children kicked a football about on the paved area. They shouted abuse at each other. They shouted it at him too if they caught sight of him. He recognised a few of the words.

On the wall of the living room, above the fireplace with its cracked tiles and broken gas fire, there was a map of London Blu-Tacked to the peeling paintwork. It was a large map. Fully three feet in width. It showed the centre of the capital.

Every day the men looked at it. Studied it. When they spoke about it, their tone was one of barely suppressed anger. What drew them to it time and time again were the red circles drawn in certain places on the map. Each was marked with a number. One to six.

Every day, one of them, the one who passed for their leader, would draw around those same circles once again using a red marker pen. He was the one who had been in the country the longest. The one who spoke the best English. He knew the city, but only because he had to. Like his four companions he had nothing but contempt and hatred for everyone who inhabited it. He, probably more than the rest, waited eagerly for the time that would be coming shortly. The time to strike back. To bring death and destruction to the city and those within it.

The man that the others looked on as a leader stood

before the map again and glanced at the six red circles, his eyes flicking to each one in turn. Then, after a moment or two, he took his marker pen and circled the locations once more. *Six red rings.*

One around the Houses of Parliament. Another encircling Oxford Circus. A third drawn around Covent Garden. The fourth at Euston station. A fifth around Piccadilly Circus. And the last one around Buckingham Palace.

He gazed indifferently at the circles. They looked as if they had been etched in blood.

His eyes focused on the one around the Houses of Parliament. That was *his*. He felt as if he was gazing at his destiny and he felt a swell of pride in his chest.

26

Franklin drove past the Carlton Hotel in Hammersmith, and glanced at the modest facade. He wondered if Amy was sitting at the window even now watching, waiting for him to arrive.

Franklin exhaled wearily. He knew that Sue would also be waiting. Expecting to see Cutler with him. The news Franklin carried was like a weight on his shoulders, pressing down on him.

What was he going to say?

He could always lie for the time being, tell her that Cutler was waiting somewhere for them. After all, he wanted to move as quickly as he could, get the two women out of the hotel. The last thing he needed was any hysterics from Sue.

You cold-hearted bastard. What the fuck do you expect her to do?

Franklin felt a stab of guilt.

How do you think Amy would react if Cutler was going to her with news of your death?

He administered a swift mental rebuke and slowed down slightly as he drove, glancing back towards the hotel. His concentration wavered slightly and the Peugeot swerved a little more than it should have.

A horn blasted behind him, shocking him back to reality. The driver of the car to the rear of him shot past, glancing angrily in Franklin's direction. He thought about raising two fingers in defiance but ended up lifting a hand almost in supplication.

He guided the car onwards through the stream of traffic until he found somewhere to turn around, then he steered the 405 back in the direction of the Carlton.

There were two or three parking bays outside and Franklin swung the car into one of these and sat behind the wheel, the engine still idling.

What are you going to do? Run in, drag them both out then floor it and drive out of London as fast as possible?

Franklin ran a hand through his hair.

Just what the fuck are you going to do? Where are you going to go?

He switched off the engine and pulled his jacket towards him, sliding the .459 from its holster. He pushed the shoulder holster beneath the passenger seat then stuck the automatic into the waistband of his jeans. He pulled his T-shirt out to cover the weapon. The SPAS and the Ithaca lay on the back seat, covered by a blanket.

For interminable moments he sat behind the wheel, listening to the vehicles roaring above him on the Hammersmith Flyover, then he reached for the ignition key and switched off the engine.

Time to go.

He glanced in both his rear-view and his wing mirrors, ensuring that there was no one near the car as he swung himself out from behind the wheel. Almost involuntarily, he looked up at the buildings around him, his heart thudding a little faster.

Are they watching you? If they are you'll never see them. Just like you didn't last night. Just like Cutler didn't see them before they blew his head off.

Franklin pulled his jacket on and walked with as much composure as he could muster towards the main doors of the hotel. He crossed to the deserted reception desk and stood there for a moment. Behind the desk was an open door. Franklin moved to the far end of the counter and tried to see into the room beyond but he could see nothing but the corner of a desk and some filing cabinets.

There was a small buzzer set into the counter with a sign proclaiming PRESS FOR SERVICE taped beneath it.

Franklin paused a moment longer then jabbed it a couple of times. No one came.

He could see room keys hanging up on metal hooks behind the counter.

Which room was Amy in?

He pressed the service buzzer again.

A swarthy man with jet black hair and a jacket a size too small for him emerged from the room behind the reception desk.

'Sorry to have kept you, sir,' he said, giving Franklin a professional smile. 'Can I help you?' He had a slight accent that Franklin thought was Mediterranean.

'I'm here to see Amy Holden,' Franklin told him.

'If you wait a moment, I will call up and tell her. Who shall I say is here?'

'No, I'll just go straight up, it's all right. She's expecting me anyway. She's in room nine, isn't she?'

Franklin was already heading for the stairs just ahead of him.

'Please wait,' said the man, emerging from behind the counter. 'What is your name, please?'

'I'm her husband,' Franklin said, not looking back.

'Her husband has already called for her this morning.'

Franklin turned to face the man. He suddenly felt as if all the blood had drained from his body.

127

'How long ago?' he said, his voice wavering.

'Ten, fifteen minutes.'

'Did she leave with him?' Franklin demanded.

'I didn't see.'

Franklin spun round. Taking the stairs two at a time, he hurtled up the narrow flight towards the first floor.

27

'Order. Order.'

The voice of the Speaker of the House of Commons cut through the vortex of sound. He rose in his seat, looking to both sides of the chamber in an effort to restore some semblance of peace.

MPs on both sides of the House were gesturing and shouting, some to those on their own side but mostly across the chamber to their opponents.

On the Speaker's left, members of the Opposition offered the most vociferous outbursts while, to his right, government ministers remained seated, for the most part. They seemed content to let the tide of abuse and protestation roll over them.

The Prime Minister looked across the chamber at his opposite number then, after a moment or two, he glanced at the Speaker again, as if willing him to quieten the unruly masses facing him.

Again the Speaker called for order and, gradually, the verbal tirade began to die down.

MPs reseated themselves on the green-leather upholstered benches.

The Prime Minister looked down at his notes, as much

to ensure that the noise had finally abated as to check his speech, then, gripping both sides of the lectern before him, he gazed slowly and deliberately around the lower chamber. Hundreds of pairs of eyes were fixed on him, waiting for his next words.

'As I have just stated,' he said, slowly and evenly, 'despite the protestations of the Opposition, these laws must come into effect immediately. The passage of immigrants into this country must be curtailed at this time.'

Mutterings again began to grow from the opposition benches but, this time, the Prime Minister merely raised his voice to counter them.

'This is not, as has been suggested, an attack on personal freedom,' he said, still gripping the lectern. 'Neither is it, as has also been suggested, evidence that this country is reneging on its duties as a refuge for those who seek to escape more oppressive regimes. It is, quite simply, a necessity. There is indisputable evidence that several gangs of suicide bombers, from a Middle Eastern country, are currently resident in Britain. To allow immigration to continue at the present rate will only make the passage into this country of more of these assassins both easier and, dare I say, inevitable.'

There were shouts of approval from around and behind him. More of furious indignation from opposite.

'I have spoken to New Scotland Yard, MI5, MI6, Special Branch *and* the Counter Terrorist Unit about this matter,' he continued, unfazed by the shouts. 'They are *all* satisfied that one or possibly more groups of suicide bombers are already in Britain and that those same groups are more than ready *and* willing to begin operating. The Chairman of the Metropolitan Police Authority himself has stated that an attack on London, carried out by a group of these Middle Eastern terrorists, is imminent. He said that evidence pointed to the fact that it was a case of *when* and not *if* such an attack would take place.'

Another chorus of supportive murmurs and confrontational complaints filled the chamber.

The Prime Minister paused for a moment then continued firmly. 'The danger to the public cannot and *should not* be underestimated,' he insisted. 'And this government will not stand idly by while its citizens are menaced.'

Another prolonged bout of verbiage swept around the House of Commons as the Prime Minister stepped away from the lectern and returned to his seat on the front bench. The man to his left leaned close and whispered something in his ear, seemingly oblivious to the racket around him.

The Opposition leader stood and took his stance across from the Prime Minister who was holding his notes tightly.

'Order, order, gentlemen,' shouted the Speaker.

'Even if these allegations are true,' the Opposition leader began, not waiting for the noise to abate. 'And if they *are* then may I state that the Opposition is fully behind the Prime Minister.' The babble began to die down. 'The measures being proposed appear somewhat draconian and also, I must say, a little late. The threat of terrorist attacks against this country has been looming for a number of years now. It would appear that the only new development is *how* they will be manifested.'

An uneasy peace had now settled over the chamber once again.

'If the intelligence reports that the Government has received are proved to be correct then I call upon the Prime Minister to make a full statement here and now as to how this threat is to be countered. We must be made aware of how the government plans to combat this situation.'

Several Opposition MPs echoed the sentiment with loud shouts of 'Hear, hear'. The Opposition leader turned and nodded smugly to his party members.

'Will the Prime Minister make a full Commons statement now?' the Opposition leader continued. 'As befits the apparent seriousness of the situation. How, if these suicide squads are proved to be in this country, are the government planning to combat them?'

There were more shouts and cheers as the Opposition leader sat back down and the Prime Minister returned to his lectern. He looked around him once again then cleared his throat.

'In reply to the Right Honourable gentleman,' he began. 'As is common knowledge, the nature of the attacks is expected to be of a type we have not experienced before, possibly using biological or chemical weapons. There could also be more overt action such as that we so sadly witnessed in New York on September the eleventh. The possibility of conventional bombs, hijackings and hostage-taking has also been considered.' Aware that he had the attention of the whole house, the Prime Minister continued, his words less hurried. 'What we *must not* do is create panic among the people. We have to be wary of acting on general information, of issuing warnings when they are not justified. Should we do this then we will effectively be doing the terrorists' work for them. Plans *are* in place to meet the threat posed against this country by these fanatics. To reveal the extent and nature of these plans would perhaps only succeed in playing into the hands of the very people who we seek to defeat. This country *will* protect itself by whatever means necessary against anyone who would presume to harm its people. If the *threat* is substantial, then the *response* must be even more potent. We will not shrink from making such a response.'

He stepped backwards and returned to his seat, the cacophony of noise growing to a crescendo all around the chamber.

As he sat, the man to his left once again whispered something quietly into his ear.

28

Franklin stumbled as he reached the top of the stairs. He tripped and slammed into the wall with enough force to knock the wind from him. Yet he remained on his feet. Breathing heavily, he looked to his right and left.

A sign on the wall proclaimed ROOM 1–5 THIS WAY. Beneath it, an arrow pointed to his left.

ROOMS 6–10 were indicated by another arrow that led him right. He pushed his way through the fire doors and ran along the short corridor, glancing at the room numbers in the process.

There was a sash window at the far end of the corridor. It was slightly open and a breeze ruffled the net curtain hanging there. It billowed as the wind stirred it.

Franklin passed room six. Then seven where a DO NOT DISTURB sign hung on the handle. He slowed his pace as he reached room number nine.

For interminable seconds he stood outside the door, trying to control his breathing. There was sweat on his face and neck.

Someone had been here ten or fifteen minutes earlier claiming to be Amy's husband. But who? And why?

Franklin sucked in a deep breath.

So many questions.

His heart was banging madly against his ribs, partly from the furious run up the stairs but also due to his barely controlled anxiety.

Amy.

He reached out and knocked four times on the door of room number nine.

There was no answer.

He knocked again. Harder and more urgently this time.

'Amy,' he called. 'It's me. It's Matt.'

Silence.

Further down the corridor a door opened and a man's head peered out. He ran appraising eyes over Franklin who met his gaze impassively. The man retreated back inside his room and shut the door.

'Amy,' Franklin called again, banging even harder.

Fuck this. Don't wait any longer.

He drove his foot against the door with terrific force and it groaned under the impact but didn't move. Again he struck, some of the panelling splintering in the process.

The same man who had peered out at him moments ago, eased his door open a fraction and watched as Franklin continued his assault, concentrating his blows on and around the lock.

It finally gave and the door flew inwards, slamming back against the wall and rocking on its hinges.

He almost tripped over the body.

Susan Harris was lying face down on the carpet, her head turned to one side. Her eyes were still open. Just above her right eyebrow there was a bullet hole the size of a man's thumbnail. The flesh at the edges of the wound was blackened and blood had run from the entry point down over her nose. It had spread in a wide crimson pool around her skull.

Franklin didn't bother to check for a pulse. There was no need.

'Amy,' he said, barely finding the breath, still staring down at Sue's body.

He glanced around the small bedroom and saw the breakfast tray. There were some discarded clothes on the bed. The wardrobe was open. He could see the black holdall inside it.

Franklin spun round frantically and noticed that the bathroom door was slightly open. There was more blood on the bottom of the door. Bright, vivid splashes of it.

He crossed to the bathroom almost reluctantly. Terrified of what he might find inside but knowing that he had to see.

His breath was coming in gasps.

He pushed the door but it would only open a few inches. There was something on the other side stopping it.

Through the gap he saw one booted foot. More blood was on the tiled floor. Lots of it.

Franklin pushed gently against the door and it moved enough to allow him to squeeze into the bathroom.

'No,' he whispered, tears welling in his eyes. 'Please.'

Amy was lying next to the bath, still fully clothed. There was one bullet hole in her left shoulder. Another in her right temple.

Franklin dropped to his knees beside her, tears now rolling down his cheeks. He reached out one hand and gently touched her face, as if to waken her. Her soft skin was still warm beneath his quivering fingertips.

'Oh, Christ,' he gasped, his body now trembling uncontrollably. He tried to speak her name but nothing came. When he tried to swallow it felt as if someone had stuffed rags down his throat. He wanted to sweep her up in his arms, to hold her tightly to him. But all he could do was stare down at her motionless form. Her lips were slightly parted, as if she were waiting for a kiss. Franklin traced the outline of those lips then he moved his hand to her stomach.

To where their baby would have grown inside her.

He wiped his nose with the back of his other hand and tried to straighten up. Part of his mind told him that he must get out of here, get away from this place of death.

The latest on a growing list.

The other part of him wanted to sink down beside her on the blood-spattered floor and simply lie there, gently stroking her face and belly.

Only by a monumental effort of will did he force himself upright. Eyes still fixed on her, he took a step back towards the door then paused. He couldn't leave her like this.

What else is there to do?

Franklin sniffed back more tears then crouched beside her once again. He kissed the tip of his index finger then pressed it gently to her lips. 'I'm sorry,' he whispered. 'Sorry.'

He stood up and moved back out into the bedroom. He grabbed the holdall from the wardrobe then headed for the corridor, stepping over Sue's body.

'Stop.'

The voice came from the end of the corridor.

The Mediterranean-looking man in the ill-fitting jacket was standing pointing at him.

'I will call the police,' he said, taking a step back, his forced bravado slipping somewhat.

Franklin slid his hand inside his jacket and pulled the .459 free, aiming the automatic at the man's head.

'Get on the fucking floor,' he roared. 'Now.'

The man dropped like a stone.

'If you move I'll kill you,' Franklin rasped as he passed him. 'You fucking stay there, right? You try to follow me you're dead.'

He pounded down the stairs, through the lobby and out

onto the street towards the Peugeot, the pistol still gripped in his hand.

He didn't care who saw him. Not any more.

He tossed the holdall onto the back seat, rammed the .459 back into its holster and slid behind the wheel where he started the engine. He reversed furiously, the tyres spinning on the tarmac. Franklin guided the 405 out into the traffic, narrowly avoiding an oncoming taxi. He wiped his eyes and drove on.

29

Gerald Collinson lifted a crystal tumbler and regarded its contents, listening to the sound of ice cubes clinking gently against the glass.

He was a tall man with grey hair and rimless glasses. Dressed in an elegant charcoal-grey suit that made him look perfectly at home within the confines of the room he now sat in. Comfortable in a high-backed leather chair, he glanced across at the other occupant of the room.

At forty-four, Edward Carter was three years younger than Collinson. He had been one of the youngest Prime Ministers ever to be elected when he had first come to power six years earlier. One of his first duties had been to appoint Collinson as his Home Secretary: a post he had held ever since.

The weight of power and responsibility had taken its toll on Carter's formerly youthful, almost boyish, looks. The lines around his eyes and across his forehead had deepened to harsh furrows and the grey in his hair that had, at the time of his election, only showed above his ears, was now more prominent. All the more noticeable because of the black lustre of the rest of his hair.

He stood by the window of his office, looking out over

the Thames, watching a sight-seeing boat making its way slowly up the middle of the river that wound through the capital like a dirty brown snake. Many of those on board the boat were taking pictures of the Houses of Parliament, Carter mused. This seat of government. This home of democracy. The bastion of free speech that was supposedly the envy of the civilised world. He smiled thinly and took a sip of his own drink, feeling the whisky burn its way down to his stomach.

'The speech went well,' Collinson said, sipping at his gin and tonic. 'I don't know why you're worried.'

'I realise diplomacy is our business, Gerald,' Carter said, still gazing out of the window, 'but you and I have known each other for twenty years. I think we can dispense with it between ourselves, can't we?'

'Meaning?'

Carter turned to face him. 'Within the walls of this office,' he said, waving one hand around expansively, 'we don't need rhetoric.'

'Your speech this afternoon was more than rhetoric. Don't devalue what you said.'

'Don't patronise me, Gerald. I know you have a gift for it but save it for those who don't know you as well as I do.'

'What *did* you want to say this afternoon?' Collinson asked. 'Because evidently it wasn't in the statement you made.'

Carter crossed to the drinks cabinet on the other side of the room and refilled his glass.

'I'm not comfortable with the situation,' the Prime Minister said slowly, as if to emphasise each word.

'That's hardly surprising. Suicide squads loose in London, the threat of terrorist activity and the use of biological weapons in the capital—'

'That isn't what I meant,' snapped Carter, cutting him short.

Collinson exhaled deeply and shrugged.

'Certain measures were taken,' he began. 'To combat the kind of scenario that we now find ourselves faced with. You were aware of those measures, Edward. You were fully supportive of them at the time. As you said in your statement earlier, the threat of force must be met with even greater force. Why baulk at using that kind of deterrent if the circumstances demand it?'

'At the moment they don't.'

'*At the moment.* Things may well change. In fact, I'll be flabbergasted if they don't. As you yourself said, it's a matter of *when* and not *if* these terrorists decide to strike.'

'I know what I said,' Carter muttered irritably. 'That doesn't detract from the fact that I'm still uncomfortable with the *nature* of the resistance we've chosen to be used against these fanatics.'

'Fanatics,' Collinson repeated. 'That is precisely what they are. They are more than enemies of this country. The men and women who will commit these atrocities, and make no mistake, they *will* act soon, are unlike any threat this nation has faced before. They themselves are different, they can only be countered by a different kind of force.'

Carter sipped his drink and returned to gazing out over the Thames, seemingly lost in his own thoughts.

'The people of this country would be in uproar if they thought that nothing was being done to protect them from the threat of these lunatics,' Collinson insisted. 'At least this government has taken steps to ensure that they will be protected. Even if you yourself aren't completely *comfortable* with the methods to be employed.' There was a note of scorn in his voice.

It was not lost on Carter who turned to face his colleague. 'I will do whatever has to be done to protect this country,' he said sternly.

'Then accept the decisions you made five years ago,'

Collinson said challengingly. 'It was you who supported these measures, Edward, you who insisted on their implementation. You made that decision as the head of this government and the leader of this country. You've done nothing wrong.'

'Thank you for that, Gerald,' chided Carter. 'I consider myself absolved.' He glared at the Home Secretary.

'You've been a politician for eighteen years, Edward. Don't start trying to acquire the one thing that no man in your position needs after all this time.'

'What's that?'

'A conscience.'

Carter held his companion's gaze for a moment then, once again, turned away, the glass held tightly in his hand.

30

Matt Franklin had cried before in his life, but never like this. Seated behind the wheel of the Peugeot, now parked in the multi-storey car park in Brewer Street, he felt his entire body racked by sobs that seemed to have no end. It was as if, here in this twilight world lit only by harsh fluorescent light, he had cried out all the emotion he had. It felt as if a hole had been punched through his soul. One that would never be filled.

He was thankful for the silence and relative privacy of the car park but it wouldn't have mattered. Such was the intensity of his pain he would have been helpless to control it no matter where he was. It was as if the very life itself had been sucked from him like poison drawn from a wound. But this was no cleansing and healing act. Torn from his life had been the one thing that made that existence worthwhile.

Even as he sat staring into space he could see the image of Amy's blood-spattered, bullet-pierced body swimming before his tear-filled eyes. The pain of loss was something he had heard about but the experience of it was something he could never have imagined. He was cold.

As cold as Amy's body.

The warmth had gone from him as surely as his will to continue. There was nothing left for him now. In the last twenty-four hours he had seen four of his closest friends die, and now the ultimate torment had been thrust upon him. He had lost the only person in the world he had loved.

No. Not lost. She'd been taken.

For the first time, somewhere deep within him, amidst the endless void of suffering, he felt another emotion. One that grew steadily the more he thought of the events of the past twenty-four hours.

He felt anger. Pure, naked, untamed anger.

Franklin welcomed the feeling because it seemed to somewhat neutralise the intolerable grief. He sucked in a deep breath and wiped the tears from his face, although he knew they wouldn't be the last. He slammed one fist down on the steering wheel with incredible ferocity. So hard that it hurt his hand. He struck it again. And again. Until one side of his hand was numb. But he felt no pain from the appendage.

Franklin caught a glimpse of himself in the rear-view mirror. His eyes were swollen and bloodshot, his face pale and streaked with tears. But there was something burning behind his eyes now. He realised it was the rage he felt growing inside himself that was blossoming. With each vision that flashed into his mind of his dead friends and murdered lover, the feeling grew stronger. And he welcomed it. Nurtured it. For while the rage mounted it kept the grief at bay. The fury he could cope with, but not the devastating sense of loss. That was too much.

Again he wiped his face with his hands. As he lowered his arms his elbow brushed against something in one of the breast pockets of his jacket. He unzipped the pocket and felt for the object. It was an audio cassette. There was one word written on the strip of paper at the top of it – Amy.

Franklin sniffed back more tears. He'd forgotten he even had the tape on him. He switched on the engine then pushed the tape into the cassette and turned up the volume slightly. The sound of a piano filled the car, followed by Amy's voice, gentle and controlled:

'. . . *I'm so tired of being here. Suppressed by all my childish fears . . .*'

Franklin looked down at the cassette.

'. . . *If you have to leave, I wish that you would just leave, 'cos your presence still lingers here, and it won't leave me alone . . .*'

He reached for the Off button then stopped himself, the words still filling the car.

'. . . *These wounds won't seem to heal, this pain is just too real . . .*'

He felt one single tear roll down his cheek.

'. . . *There's just too much that time cannot erase . . .*'

Franklin lowered his head.

'. . . *When you cried I'd wipe away all of your tears, when you screamed I'd fight away all of your fears . . .*'

He glanced across towards the passenger seat, as if expecting to see her sitting there beside him.

'. . . *I held your hand through all of these years . . .*'

Franklin switched it off, took the cassette out and slipped it back into his pocket, where he zipped it safely away. For what seemed like an eternity, he sat inside the 405, staring blankly ahead, Amy's voice still ringing in his ears. He wanted to touch her. To hold her again. To hear her whisper those words into his ear. But he knew that was not to be. Never again.

Franklin swung himself out of the Peugeot, dug in his jacket pocket and found his cigarettes. He lit one, ignoring the NO SMOKING sign on the far wall.

The dimly lit multi-storey smelled of petrol, warm metal and rubber. Franklin walked slowly back and forth in front of the car, drawing smoke deep into his lungs. After a few

144

drags he dropped the cigarette on the concrete floor and ground it out beneath his boot. He gently touched the cassette through the leather of his jacket then walked to the back door of the 405. He paused for a moment, then opened it.

31

Detective Inspector Vincent Crane looked down at the pale, waxen features of the man on the gurney then nodded almost imperceptibly.

One of the two paramedics at either end of the trolley reached around and zipped up the body-bag once more before pushing the body slowly towards a waiting ambulance.

'Jeff Adamson,' said Crane.

'We've got positive ID on him and on Cutler,' DS Kingston said, standing in the doorway of the lock-up.

Within a fifty-yard radius of the building, a police cordon had been set up. Crane saw officers ducking under it as they came and went about their business. He recognised men from a number of different departments all working the scene. They were using their own specialist knowledge to piece together what had gone on before they arrived.

'We were right about Maguire and Nicholson using the same firm,' Kingston offered.

'Any reports on the weapons that killed Cutler and Adamson yet?' Crane wanted to know.

'Rifles again.'

'What calibre?'

'7.62mm. Titanium-coated from either a PSG-1 or—'

'Or an AR-81,' Crane said, finishing his colleague's sentence. 'Same as the ones used to kill Nicholson and Maguire last night.'

Kingston nodded.

Crane walked into the lock-up and glanced around.

'Prints?' he said, appraising the building.

'Plenty,' Kingston told him. 'From all four dead men and from one Matthew Franklin – the fifth member of the team. He was a driver and explosives expert. By the look of it they've been using this place, on and off, for a while.'

'Where's Franklin now?'

'We're trying to find him, guv. It looks like he's the only one who got away in one piece.'

'He could be anywhere by now.'

'He left here in a Peugeot 405. Forensics found skid marks outside that match the tyres on that make of car. Unless he's changed vehicles we'll find him.'

Crane walked over to the table near the sink and looked at the tea-stained mugs that still stood on the cracked surface. Then he wandered across to the Ford. There were several forensics men around it gathering fingerprints, hair and fibre samples and anything else that might be of use. Crane looked briefly at the blood that had congealed thickly over most of the back seat.

'How come *they* can find them but we can't?' he mused.

Kingston looked puzzled.

'Whoever took out Adamson and the other three knew where to find them,' the DI continued. 'First, they were in position to hit them on the road last night. *Then*, they tracked them here. They almost finished the job. Once they get Franklin it's game over. I want him found. As much for his own protection as anything else.' He paused, turning to look out of the lock-up. Cutler's body was also being pushed towards an ambulance, housed securely in a

147

body-bag. It reminded Crane of some kind of macabre cocoon.

'So, we find Franklin,' said Kingston. 'What then?'

Crane could only shrug.

'I doubt if he had any idea what was in that Securicor van he helped to knock over,' said the DI. 'But he might have some idea about who'd want to wipe out his team. If we find Franklin, we're halfway to cracking this.' He ran a hand through his hair. 'Anything from pathology on the bodies in the van?' he asked.

'Nothing yet.'

'Well, tell Howard to get a fucking move on,' Crane snapped. 'I want those results before tonight. In the meantime, I reckon it's time we started talking to people.'

'Like who?'

'Rival firms. Anyone who might have wanted Adamson and his team dead. We'll start south of the river and work our way up.'

'I thought you said this was too sophisticated for a gangland hit, guv?'

'Humour me, will you, Del? I'm playing that well-loved game that we all play sometimes.'

Kingston looked puzzled.

'Clutching at straws,' Crane told him.

Two shotguns.

Two automatics and a revolver. Plenty of spare ammunition.

Franklin regarded the weapons evenly. The SPAS and the Ithaca lay across the back seat of the Peugeot. The Taurus and the .357 were still inside the holdall he'd taken from Amy's room. The .459 was in the shoulder holster he wore. Plenty of firepower should he need it.

He slammed the back door of the Peugeot and made his way slowly across to the door that led to the ground floor. A flight of cold stone steps took him to street level.

There was a control booth at the entrance to the multistorey. Franklin could see the operator inside, scanning his newspaper and sipping at a hot drink.

No other vehicles had entered the car park since Franklin himself had motored in. Or if they had, he reasoned, they hadn't stopped on the level where he was parked. He stood watching the attendant for a moment longer then ducked back into the stairwell and climbed the steps quickly and purposefully back to the level where his car was.

Below him there was the sound of an engine revving

but he paid it little heed. Instead, his gaze flicked from car to car as he headed back towards the Peugeot.

Vehicles of every shape and size were parked before him. A couple of Jags. A black Porsche. A Daimler. Even a Rolls Royce.

No. Too conspicuous.

Like a buyer in a car showroom, Franklin walked slowly along the lines of parked vehicles, appraising each with a professional eye. He paused for a moment beside a Mercedes 300SL.

Not practical.

He touched the round symbol on the front of the bonnet almost lovingly then passed further along the line of cars.

He stopped beside a black BMW.

Fast. Powerful. Anonymous.

Franklin walked around the vehicle then headed back towards the Peugeot, his footsteps echoing within the confines of the multi-storey.

From the boot of the 405, he took a small toolbox. He carried it nonchalantly back to the BMW, set it down beside the car and set to work.

It took him less than eight seconds to open the door and disable the alarm. He stood beside the car for a moment, glancing in the direction of the ramps that led in and out of the multi-storey. There was no sign of movement. Franklin opened the back door of the BMW then walked back to the Peugeot and transferred the shotguns and the holdall from the 405 to the other car.

He glanced once again towards the entry and exit ramps then, satisfied that he wasn't about to be disturbed, he pulled a small hammer from the toolbox. He struck the steering column with it, each contact reverberating around the inside of the car park. Franklin calmly pulled the driver's side door shut and continued battering at the column. There was a loud crack as the cowling finally shattered.

150

Wires dangled from the broken column like intestines from an eviscerated corpse. Moving with practised ease, Franklin took a Stanley knife from the toolbox and carefully stripped the plastic sheaths from the exposed wires to reveal bare metal. He twisted the ends of the battery and ignition feeds together and the dashboard lights flared.

So far, so good.

The third exposed wire was the most crucial. Franklin jabbed the starter-feed wire against the join of the other two and pumped the accelerator simultaneously. The engine roared to life. He eased up on the gas pedal, also taking care not to hold all three wires together for too long for fear of burning out the starter motor. Revving the engine once more, he allowed the starter-feed wire to drop away.

Job done.

He guided the BMW out of its parking space and down the ramp towards the striped barrier that barred the way from the multi-storey.

Franklin paid the attendant, collected his change and nodded good-naturedly, settling himself more comfortably behind the steering wheel. He'd dump the car in a couple of hours and take another. Remain anonymous. That was the key from now on.

He wondered if anyone was watching him. Had they found him already? They certainly hadn't had any trouble so far.

They didn't have any trouble finding Amy either, did they?

Maybe someone was perched high up on one of the buildings opposite right now. Were they drawing a bead on him at this second? Was a finger tightening around a trigger? Preparing to blast him into oblivion?

For the first time, the thought filled him not with dread but with anger.

Come and get me, you bastards. Show yourselves if you've got the fucking guts. Come and find me. Because I'm going to find you. Somewhere. Somehow. I'm going to find you.

He gripped the wheel more tightly and drove on.

In the Name of the Prophet

They prayed six times a day. Barefoot and with their fore-heads pressed to the floor, they offered up blessings to their God. In return they called upon Him to guide them in their work. When they felt as if their strength was failing, they asked him to imbue them with the power they knew they would need to complete their task.

Most of the time, it was sufficient for them to sit and watch the videos that showed the power of Islam. His power embodied in men and women like themselves. Men and women who sought only to destroy those who had wronged them. Those who had defiled their way of life and their beliefs. Those who had ravaged their countries and their culture, and murdered their people. Sometimes they shouted angrily at the screen when images of the Israeli Prime Minister or the American President appeared. When a speech by the British Prime Minister appeared on one of the tapes, two of the men spat in the direction of the television screen.

And, every day, they studied the map on the wall. They stared at the six red circles upon it and, as they did, each felt a shiver of anticipation. The time was near. *Their* time. A time to strike back. A time to show the West their dedication and their determination.

Their brothers in arms had done so before in other parts of the world. They had all rejoiced when the Twin Towers had fallen. Again and again they had watched that footage. Savoured every second of it. Envied their brothers who had carried out that act of war against their enemies. Likewise the explosions in Bali, Morocco and Israel. Every one a blow against those they hated and those who would oppose them. Those who sought to subjugate them, to corrupt the teachings of the Prophet. For it was in His name that they acted. It would be for Him that they would gladly give their lives.

They stared at the map of London with its six targets and they prayed. They were ready.

33

'Who found them?'

DI Crane moved slowly around room number nine of the Carlton Hotel in Hammersmith, his eyes scanning every inch of it.

He paused occasionally to look at a particular object. One of Susan Harris's boots lay close to the bed. He peered at it for a moment. It had already been dusted for prints. As had the wardrobe door that was still half open and had a plain white blouse hanging inside it. All of the surfaces and objects in the room carried the thin sheen of graphite that testified to the presence of the forensics department.

'One of the hotel employees, sir,' a uniformed officer told Crane. 'He made a call. We were the nearest unit. We found him outside the door when we got here. He was babbling away like a lunatic.'

'Has anybody managed to get any sense out of him yet?' Crane wanted to know.

'He gave a statement once he'd calmed down,' the uniformed man said. 'So has another guy who was in one of the rooms down the corridor. They both gave descriptions of the man they saw entering and leaving this room. The descriptions match. The bloke who came and went was definitely Matthew Franklin.'

Crane nodded.

'Thanks,' he said. 'I'll talk to them myself later.'

The uniformed man nodded, hesitated a moment then turned and walked out of the room.

'How did the killer get in?' Crane mused, looking at the door.

'They must have *let* him in,' DS Kingston offered.

'Then realised their mistake,' murmured Crane, taking a couple of steps towards the bathroom closely followed by his colleague.

'The murder weapon was a 9mm automatic,' Kingston said. 'Forensics found three shell cases in the room. No prints on any of them.'

'Same weapon that was used to execute the two Securicor guards last night?'

'Same MO – close range, through the head, execution style.'

'What about the wound in this one's shoulder?' Crane said, nodding towards Amy's body.

'She tried to run for it?' Kingston offered, shrugging his shoulders. 'Knew what was coming?'

Crane nodded.

'Christ knows where she thought she was going,' he said, quietly. 'Is the ID positive?'

'On both of them. Amy Holden, Franklin's bird. The poor cow in the bedroom is Susan Harris, Steven Cutler's other half.'

Crane drew in a deep breath.

'I don't get it, guv,' Kingston said.

'Join the club.'

'No, I mean, the hit on Franklin's team, that's sort of understandable. If it was another firm then fair enough. A

156

gang war or something. But why go after their girlfriends too? If this *is* a grudge thing then Franklin and his team must have pissed somebody off *really* badly.'

'Nicholson, Maguire and Adamson all had family, didn't they? It might be an idea to put a watch on them too. Just in case.'

Kingston nodded.

'I'll tell you the other thing that's starting to irritate me,' Crane said. 'We're always one step behind. We missed the lock-up and now this.' Again he nodded towards Amy's body.

The two men stood in silence for a moment until Kingston spoke, without taking his eyes from the bloodied body lying before him.

'Could it be Franklin, guv?'

'An inside job?'

'Well, he's the only one still alive, isn't he? Perhaps they let him in because they recognised him.'

'No. He wouldn't have shot his own girlfriend.'

'How can we be sure? If he turned—'

'No,' Crane interrupted.

'Just a thought.'

'I appreciate that, Del but I can't see it.'

Crane reached for his mobile as it rang.

'Yeah,' he said into the mouthpiece.

Kingston watched the expression on his face change to one of surprise.

'Jesus,' murmured the DI. 'Yeah, all right. We'll be there as soon as we can.'

'What is it, guv? Have they found Franklin?' the DS wanted to know.

'No. That was Richardson from pathology. He says he's found something that links the victims we found in that Securicor van.'

Crane was already heading for the door.

157

'What is it?' Kingston wanted to know.

'He doesn't know *what* he's found. He just said to get back as quickly as possible.'

34

When he heard the siren, Franklin resisted the temptation
to swing the black BMW into the first turning. Instead,
he glanced calmly to his right and left then checked the
rear-view mirror of the car. He saw the ambulance heading
through traffic, along Brompton Road, as fast as it was able.
Vehicles were trying to pull to one side to allow it better
access. It finally swept past, lights spinning madly and the
banshee wail of its sirens filling the air. Franklin saw it
disappear around a corner at the end of the thoroughfare
as he drove steadily on.

What if it had been a police car? he mused. Why should
he be concerned? As far as he was aware, the law were
looking for a dark blue Peugeot 405 – unless the BMW
had been reported stolen already. He wondered if it might
be time to change vehicles again. He'd been in this one
for over an hour now. Best to change as often as possible.
Or was it?

It wasn't the police who were occupying his mind at
the moment. It wasn't the law he wanted to find him. It
was the bastards who had wiped out his friends and lover.

Franklin checked his rear-view mirror once more.
Perhaps they were in the car that was behind him now.

He could see two men in the front of the Nova. Were they following him? Were they the ones he wanted? He drove on, almost disappointed when the Nova swung away to the left.

Franklin glanced over onto the back seat where the SPAS and the Ithaca still lay, covered by a blanket. They were within easy reach should the need arise. As were the Taurus and the Sterling .357, tucked into the top of the holdall. He still wore the .459 in its shoulder holster.

He stopped at a set of traffic lights, gazing blankly at the red light. Another hour and he should be where he wanted to be. He'd cross the river using Battersea Bridge, then make his way across towards Clapham.

If they came at him before then that was fine.

Whoever the fuck they were.

The lights changed and he drove on, a thought niggling at the back of his mind.

They won't come at you though, will they? They'll pick you off from a distance, just like they did with the others.

He shook his head, as if to dismiss the conversation going on inside his mind.

They got close to Amy, didn't they? Close enough for them to see into her eyes when they killed her.

He gripped the wheel more tightly.

Close enough for her to breathe her last breath into their faces.

He wondered what she'd thought in her last moments. Had she called his name? Wished that he'd been there to help her? Franklin swallowed hard. Had she felt any pain? He tried to drive the thoughts from his mind. Along that road lay madness. Part of him wanted to know, but the rest of his mind shrank from such knowledge.

A horn blared at him and he saw a bus cut in close behind him. A little *too* close.

Concentrate.

He shook his head then sucked in a deep breath and

160

held it for a moment. He was twenty minutes' drive from Battersea Bridge now. He was just another hour, perhaps less, from his final destination and the place where he hoped he might begin to find some answers.

35

As Crane and Kingston entered the room, Howard Richardson got to his feet and stepped out from behind his desk. The pathologist nodded cordially at the two policemen then motioned towards the chairs in front of the desk.

'You might want to sit down,' he said, the faintest trace of a smile playing at the corners of his mouth.

'Is it bad news?' Crane wanted to know.

'I'm not really sure,' Richardson admitted

The policemen sat. The pathologist perched on the edge of his desk, looking at each of them in turn.

'This had better be important, Howard,' Crane said. 'You pulled us away from a crime scene for—'

'I couldn't discuss it over the phone, it would have taken too long,' Richardson interrupted.

'So, what's the deal?' asked Crane. 'What have you got?'

'There's something in their blood,' Richardson said. 'All thirty-four of them.'

Crane looked puzzled.

'The bodies we took from the Securicor van,' the pathologist continued, his tone rising excitedly. 'I've received reports on each one now and the findings are the same in every case. There's something in their blood.'

'You mean you've found the cause of death? They were poisoned?' Crane offered.

'No. There are no traces of poison. No traces of anything toxic. Not even alcohol or nicotine.'

'So what the hell are you telling me, Howard?' the DI wanted to know. 'No alcohol or nicotine. So all the victims were good clean-living boys? How does *that* help us?'

'Just listen to me for a minute,' Richardson insisted, raising a hand for silence. 'Human blood is tissue, composed of three separate types of living cells set in unformed ground-substance. That ground-substance being liquid.'

'Howard, if you pulled us away from a crime scene for a lecture I'm not going to be very happy,' Crane said, holding the pathologist's gaze.

'Hear me out, please, Vince. This is important.'

'Go on,' Crane urged, waving a hand in the older man's direction.

'The blood is composed of plasma, red cells called erythrocytes and white cells called leukocytes. Right?'

The two policemen nodded.

'The bloodstream carries oxygen, glucose, water and waste products. Everything the body needs or *doesn't* need,' Richardson continued with barely concealed enthusiasm. 'Trace elements of anything from toxins to disease can be found on examination of the blood.'

Crane ran a hand through his hair. 'Just give me the punchline, Howard,' he said, wearily.

'All thirty-four bodies had a substance in their bloodstream.'

'What kind of substance?' Crane wanted to know.

'I haven't got a clue,' Richardson told him, smiling.

Crane looked first at his companion then back at the pathologist. 'So you got us here to tell us that you've got no idea what you've found?' he said irritably. 'Howard . . .'

163

Again Richardson raised his hand. 'That's the point,' he said. 'No one has seen anything like it before. None of my staff. Neither have any of the other members of the team who worked on the samples they were given. Whatever's in the bloodstream of those men is unique. It's new. A new strain.'

'Of what?'

'At first I thought it was a toxin, now I'm reasonably sure it's viral.'

'So they all had a disease?' Crane offered.

'No, not as such. A virus, as you know, *destroys* cells in the body. It attacks vital organs. There's no sign of that in any of these bodies. There is no damage to the hearts, livers, kidneys, intestines or any other internal organs.'

'Could the damage have been done to the brains?' Crane asked. 'Perhaps that's why the heads were cut off.'

'It's possible but it doesn't explain why the hands and feet were removed as well. I'm more inclined to think that our first thoughts on that were correct. The heads, hands and feet were removed to prevent identification of the victims, not to disguise the destructive effects of the virus they were all carrying.'

'Are you sure it's a virus?' Crane wanted to know.

'Well, that's the problem,' Richardson explained. 'Essentially, a virus isn't equipped with the chemical components needed for life. It can't provide its own energy. It has to *borrow* from a better endowed organism.'

'Meaning what?' Crane enquired. 'Try to keep this in plain English, will you, Howard?'

'Viruses are totally parasitic,' the pathologist continued. 'An isolated virus is just an inert speck of matter. It can't feed, grow or multiply. But when it becomes attached to a living cell, it diverts the cell's functions to its own needs and *then* it can multiply and grow. That's what makes this one different. As I said, there was no damage to any of the

164

internal organs in any of those thirty-four dead men. *This* virus isn't parasitic.'

'Then perhaps it isn't a fucking virus,' Crane said, a note of exasperation in his voice.

'Well, there is an absence of nucleic acid too,' Richardson told him. 'All viruses contain nucleic acid. Some of the smaller ones are nothing more than little parcels of nucleic acid. Nucleic acids control the synthesis of living matter. They are, not to sound overly dramatic, the very essence of life. The differences between species are determined by the structure of nucleic acids.'

Kingston shook his head.

'And yet the stuff you found inside the thirty-four dead men hasn't got any of this nucleic acid inside it?' the DS said quietly, wondering if he'd misunderstood something during the conversation.

'That's right. It's *behaving* like a virus but without showing any of the *pathology* of a virus.'

'You're losing me, Howard,' Crane confessed.

'In order to survive inside the body, some bacterial or viral infections, like tetanus, form spores. It's *their* way of protecting themselves against the body's immune system. The bacteria go into a kind of hibernation. They become dormant. In that state they're remarkably resistant to anti-biotics. Some bacterial spores can even survive in boiling water for up to thirty minutes. The virus, for want of a better word, inside those thirty-four men has already begun to form spores. It's going into a dormant stage.'

'What happens when the dormant stage is over?' Kingston asked.

'In this case, I don't know,' Richardson told him. 'Because I can't identify the virus.'

'Is it contagious?' Kingston asked.

'Again, I don't know until I can identify it.'

'Jesus, that's reassuring,' Crane muttered.

165

'You said you'd never seen anything like it before,' the DS persisted. 'If *you* can't identify it then who can?'

'Samples have already been sent to the Institute for the Study of Tropical Diseases here in London. I've also had specimens dispatched to the toxicology departments at Guy's Hospital and the Royal London Hospital,' Richardson continued.

'Did this virus, whatever it is, kill those thirty-four men?' Crane enquired.

'I don't know yet, Vince.'

'Even if it did, that doesn't explain why some mad bastard cut off their heads, hands and feet, does it?' offered Kingston.

'What I'm saying is, did someone infect them with it?' the DI mused. '*Deliberately* infect them? If they did, then this is a whole new ball game. Who the hell would want to kill thirty-four people using a virus? Who'd have the capability?'

'Could it be some kind of chemical?' Kingston said, looking at his superior.

'Like a chemical weapon?' Crane raised his eyebrows quizzically.

'The Prime Minister made a statement in the Commons about possible biological strikes against this country carried out by terrorists,' Kingston reminded them. 'It's not out of the question.'

'So now we're looking for terrorists, is that what we're saying?' Crane intoned.

'Surely we'd have heard,' Richardson said. 'If it was a chemical weapon there'd have been some news. Thirty-four people can't just disappear like that.' He snapped his fingers. 'Besides, if it was, who'd want to put the bodies in a Securicor van afterwards? Why do that?'

The DI allowed his head to loll against the back of the chair. 'A chemical weapon,' he murmured, his words directed at no one in particular.

166

A heavy silence descended, finally broken by Crane.

'Just assuming that this virus, or whatever the fuck it is, evolves in the same way as all the other ones you've ever seen,' the DI said slowly. 'How long before the dormant stage ends?'

'A month? A week? A day?' Richardson shrugged.

'And then?'

'I don't know, I've already told you, I can't say for sure—'

'Hypothetically,' snapped Crane, looking directly at the pathologist.

'The virus could spread.'

'How?' Crane insisted.

Richardson shrugged again.

'By ingestion, like typhus. By bodily secretions, like AIDS or . . .' he hesitated, as if reluctant to speak the other possibility.

'Or what?' Crane said, sitting forward in his seat.

'If it turns out to be airborne,' Richardson said flatly, 'it could be spread as easily as the common cold.'

36

Matt Franklin turned off the engine of the BMW and sat motionless behind the steering wheel for a moment. His gaze was fixed on the building opposite. It was a restaurant called the Wheat Sheaf. It was the kind of place that proliferated both in London and all over the country. An eatery and pub rolled into one. A plastic pub, usually serving plastic food, Franklin mused.

The car park was empty apart from a couple of battered second-hand cars, two builder's vans and, conspicuous by its newness and condition, a metallic-green Audi.

Franklin was parked on the far side of the tarmacked area. There was scaffolding over one part of the pub and several large skips full of building waste were outside the main entrance. Franklin eyed the place and saw two men moving about on the scaffolding. Two others were working lower down, one of them painting the window frames, the other planing what appeared to be a door that he had secured to a workbench. Wood shavings were falling around him like coiled confetti.

Franklin eased the .459 from its shoulder holster and pressed the magazine release catch. He checked that the weapon still held its regulation fifteen rounds then slammed the magazine back into the butt and worked the slide, chambering a round. He flicked on the safety catch. Then he clambered out of the BMW and shut the door. He set off across the car park, his face set in hard lines, his stride purposeful.

Now we'll see.

As he drew nearer the main door, the smell of wood shavings reached his nostrils. It seemed as if his senses had become more acute. The man planing the door looked at him then carried on with his work.

Franklin pushed on the brass handle of the main door and stepped inside. Straight ahead of him was the bar. To his left a collection of tables and chairs. To his right, under an archway of exposed bricks, the restaurant area of the Wheat Sheaf. There was a young woman in there. She was dressed in jeans and a white T-shirt, her brown hair tied back in a ponytail. Franklin watched her polishing tables for a moment then took a step towards her.

She turned to face him.

'We're closed,' she said. 'You might have noticed the workmen outside. Refurbishment.' She smiled.

'I want to see Jim Patterson, is he here?' Franklin told her, ignoring her words and her smile.

She wiped a hand across her forehead and ran appraising eyes over Franklin.

'He *does* still own this place, doesn't he?' he said, although it came out more as a statement than a question.

'He's upstairs in his office. I'll get him.'

'I know the way,' said Franklin, heading towards the rear of the building.

'I should tell him you're here,' she protested, stepping closer.

'I'm an old friend,' Franklin said, without breaking stride. 'He'll see me.'

She stopped where she was and watched as Franklin

reached the wooden door marked PRIVATE. He pushed it open and climbed the stairs beyond. They opened out onto a small landing. Three more doors confronted him. One marked STAFF, another displaying the legend TOILETS and the third bearing the word OFFICE. He moved towards that one, knocked once and walked in.

James Patterson was seated behind his desk. He was a rotund, balding man in his early fifties dressed in a pair of black trousers and a dark blue jacket. He was opening mail with a long silver letter opener.

'This is private,' he said, in a slightly high-pitched voice, his lips barely moving. He reminded Franklin of a ventriloquist.

'I know,' said the younger man. 'What I've got to say is private too.' He closed the office door behind him and sat down opposite Patterson who regarded him warily.

'Who *are* you?' Patterson wanted to know. 'You can't just come barging in here like this.' He reached for the phone with his free hand.

'Leave it,' snapped Franklin. 'I just want to talk.'

'What about?'

'Jeff Adamson.'

'Wait a minute,' said Patterson slowly. A slight smile fluttered on his thin lips. 'I know you, don't I? You work with Jeff. You're one of his firm. Franklin. Pat Franklin?'

'*Matt* Franklin.'

'Right. So, what brings *you* south of the river?'

'I want to talk about Jeff.'

'How is the old cunt?' Patterson grinned.

'He's dead. So are the rest of his team. I'm the only one left. Someone had them hit.'

Patterson looked on blankly.

'When?' he said, his voice barely more than a whisper.

'Last night.'

'How?'

170

'I was hoping *you* might be able to tell *me* that.'

Franklin pulled the .459 free of its holster and levelled it at Patterson. 'Well,' he said quietly. 'Tell me what you know.'

37

'What the fuck are you talking about?' Patterson's voice seemed to rise an octave as he saw the barrel of the automatic gaping at him.

'I want to know what *you* know about the hit,' Franklin said, his face impassive.

'I don't know nothing. I don't know what the fuck you're talking about. I never had anything against Jeff *or* any of his team.'

'Well, some fucker did.'

'Not me.'

'Then who? Who's got it in for us?'

'How the fuck am *I* supposed to know? Tell me what happened.' He laid the letter opener down close by him.

'There was a job with a Securicor van. It went tits-up. Somebody started shooting, killed Joe Maguire, George Nicholson and Jeff. The next day, the same people killed Steve Cutler. And a couple of other people too.'

The vision of Amy's bloodied corpse flashed into Franklin's mind. He swallowed hard and gripped the Smith & Wesson more tightly.

'I don't know anything about *any* of that,' Patterson said.

'Why the fuck would I want to wipe out someone else's firm?'

'More for you and your boys. One less competitor.'

'I've got no quarrel with Jeff. I've got no problem with *you*, except I don't like people pointing fucking guns at me.'

'Then talk to me.'

'What the fuck do you want to hear?' Patterson snapped, his initial fear giving way to anger. 'I've told you. I don't know anything about any Securicor job or about any fucking hit. I had no reason to want Jeff or his firm dead. Me and him never had any problems. We worked in different lines of business, you know that. Mine's always been diamonds, not cash. Jeff wasn't interested in stones.'

'If not you then who?'

'How do I know? I don't know who Jeff crossed, *or* who might have had it in for him.'

'Then think about it,' Franklin said, leaning forward in his chair, the automatic still trained on the older man.

'You've got a fucking nerve coming here and threatening me,' Patterson said, sweat forming on his bald dome.

'I need information. This was as good a place as any to start.'

'Well, you've wasted your time. I don't know nothing. Why don't you just fuck off before I get mad. Go on. Go now and I'll forget all about this.'

'Bollocks,' snarled Franklin. 'I want some fucking answers.'

'Then talk to someone else,' said Patterson through gritted teeth. 'The Turks run pubs and clubs on this side of the river. The Russians own most of the businesses in Soho. The Maltese have still got their fingers in plenty of pies. The chinks control Chinatown. The spades are everywhere. It's like the fucking United Nations here now. Firms from every country are into every racket you can think of.'

'None of them overlap with *our* businesses. You know that,' Franklin told him. 'The Russians and the Maltese run the porn business. The chinks and the spades are into drugs and smuggling. None of them are interested in the kind of work *we* do.'

'How do you *know* that?'

'I just know. They're all well organised but they haven't got the know-how. We were set up. Somebody was waiting for us. Somebody who didn't want *any* of us getting away. But they fucked up. *I* got away. And I'm going to find whoever did it.'

Franklin's face was contorted with fury and he leaned across the desk, the automatic pushed closer to Patterson's chest.

'Jeff knew what could happen,' the older man said flatly, looking from the barrel of the pistol to Franklin's face then back again. 'He knew the risks. We *all* do.'

'Who ordered the hit?'

Franklin thumbed back the hammer on the .459.

'I don't know who ordered the hit,' Patterson told him. 'And, to tell you the truth, I don't fucking care.'

'My girlfriend was murdered too,' Franklin said quietly.

'Shit happens,' smiled Patterson.

The movement was so rapid, even if he'd been aware of what was about to happen, Patterson would have been powerless to avoid it. Franklin snatched up the silver letter opener with his free hand and brought it down with incredible force and accuracy. The point tore through the back of Patterson's left hand, ripping through flesh, bone and tendon. It burst from his palm, pinning his hand to the desktop.

He shrieked in agony and looked down at the silver blade that had skewered him to the wood.

'Jesus,' he wailed, his eyes bulging as he stared at the weapon that had impaled his hand. Blood was pouring from the wound, spreading out around his hand to form a crimson puddle. White-hot agony shot the length of his arm.

Franklin stepped away from the desk.

'Where are your car keys?' he demanded.

Patterson was slumped forward over the desk, trying to work the silver blade free. Each movement caused fresh pain.

'Your car keys?' Franklin insisted.

'In my pocket, you mad cunt,' gasped Patterson, his head spinning as he looked at his ravaged hand.

Franklin moved swiftly round the desk and dug in the older man's jacket, pulling free a bunch of keys.

'You keep your fucking mouth shut about what happened here,' he said, backing away towards the door. 'Or else, once I've taken care of the bastards who nailed my mates and my girlfriend, I'll be coming back here for *you*. Got it?'

Patterson nodded, his face still contorted with pain.

He finally managed to wrench the silver letter opener free, letting out a huge groan as he did. He flopped back in his chair, close to unconsciousness.

Franklin hesitated a moment longer then holstered the .459, opened the door and stepped out, making his way back down the stairs. The young woman cleaning tables said something to him as he left but he ignorned her. He walked briskly to the green Audi and opened it. Then he slipped behind the steering wheel and started the engine. It purred into life and Franklin drove it across so it was next to the BMW.

Untroubled by the curious stares of the workmen, he moved his stuff from the BMW to the Audi, took one last look in the direction of the Wheat Sheaf and drove off.

There were other places he needed to go.

A Glorious Gift Awaits

The man in the denim jacket and jeans moved slowly among the crowd, careful not to touch any of them if he could help it. He did not want to feel their bodies against his. He wanted no contact with those he despised.

There were many of them in the road called the Mall. He heard many different accents. Some he understood, mostly the English and the American. The ones he hated the most.

Twice he stopped and checked the battered *London A-Z* he had been given. He'd stuffed it into the back pocket of his jeans when he'd left the flat in Camden Town an hour earlier. He and his five companions each carried one. They needed it to find their way to their targets. Just to be sure. They wanted no errors.

Every day they made the same journey. Each went to their designated destination, moving freely among their enemies. The man in the denim jacket looked contemptuously around him, finding it hard to conceal his loathing of those he walked among.

Men, women and children all elicited equal feelings of anger. The women were as vile as the men. Their only task was to breed more infidels. The children were no different. They would grow up to become a new generation of oppressors. He felt nothing for them. No sympathy.

He moved up the Mall, past two uniformed policemen who were talking, one of them saying something into a walkie-talkie. The man in the denim jacket passed them without fear. They had no idea who he was. Or why he was in their city.

At five other places in London, his companions, his brothers in arms, were also mingling with the oppressors. Reining back their anger and revulsion, knowing that, when the time came, they would destroy those they hated. And, as their own lives were lost, they would rise up to Paradise to claim the reward that awaited them.

He stopped near a fountain where dozens of people were seated, all of them gazing across at Buckingham Palace. Most were taking pictures. Smiling. Pointing at the building. Flags were flying on its roof, fluttering in the slight breeze.

The man in the denim jacket dug his hands into his pockets and walked on, across the road until he was at the very railings that surrounded the building.

Inside the courtyard he could see soldiers dressed in red tunics marching back and forth. He could hear laughter and excited chatter, most of which he couldn't understand. He stood watching the red-coated men for a while longer then stepped back from the railings and walked back through the crowd once again. There were thousands of people gathered around the gates, along the railings and over the road. More in the park beyond.

The man walked slowly now, looking for the best position. The ideal spot. A man bumped into him and apologised but he didn't answer, he merely looked contemptuously at the man. He hoped that man would be there when he returned. When he came back to this place, among the crowds.

But, when he next came here, by the time he had left, the ground would be stained with blood for a thousand yards in every direction.

38

'Wrong place, wrong time. Simple as that.'

DI Crane took a sip of his coffee, winced then remembered he hadn't added sugar. He used the cracked plastic spoon from the bowl on the counter to put some of the white granules in.

Kingston watched him as he stirred it. The Detective Sergeant was nibbling at the hot dog he'd purchased from the vendor's van. He picked a piece of fried onion from his teeth and dropped it onto the pavement. Kingston counted at least a dozen groups of tourists, herded around by guides, moving back and forth across the top of the Mall, mingling with the hundreds of other people who were milling about in front of the stunning edifice of Buckingham Palace. The man who owned the van had a Union Jack fluttering above it and the sound of the material could be heard every time there was a strong breeze.

He retrieved four cans of Coke from one of his fridges and placed them on the counter, taking the money gratefully from some Japanese tourists. Three of them posed happily in front of the van while the fourth prepared to take a photo, complete with the vendor beaming behind them.

Crane and Kingston moved away as the flash momentarily illuminated the scene.

'So you don't think there was any link between Adamson and his team and what was in that Securicor van?' the DS mumbled through a mouthful of bread and sausage.

Crane shook his head. 'Like I said, they were in the wrong place at the wrong time,' he continued.

'So how do you explain their murders and the two women as well? Why wipe out the firm *and* anyone associated with them?'

'So far, they've only got Cutler's and Franklin's girl-friends. The families of the other three dead men haven't been touched.'

'We've had round the clock guard on them, guv, that's probably why. Whoever blew away the other two women got to them before we had the chance to give them any protection.'

Crane took another sip of his coffee and headed across the pavement to the stationary car. He clambered into the passenger seat while Kingston slid behind the steering wheel, still chewing on his hot dog.

'What if the *bodies* are the thing that ties this case together?' Crane breathed.

'I'm not with you.'

'There are terrorists loose in this country equipped with biological weapons. Everyone from Special Branch to the Counter Terrorist Unit has confirmed that. Everyone's assuming that if there's an attack using chemical weapons it's going to be done down the Tube or at an airport or a shopping centre or something. That it's going to come in the form of gas or Christ knows what.'

'I'm still missing something.'

'Richardson said that all thirty-four of those bodies that we found in the Securicor van had traces of a virus or bacteria in their bloodstream. And that same virus is now

179

in a dormant stage. At the moment, he doesn't know what's going to happen when that dormant stage passes.'

'He said he wasn't sure.'

'Maybe *he* isn't because he's never seen a virus like it but I'd bet money that the terrorists who put it there know exactly what's going to happen.'

'Are you saying that someone pumped those thirty-four bodies full of a chemical knowing that the virus would multiply?'

'That's *exactly* what I'm saying. Every one of those corpses is like a biological time bomb waiting to go off. If they'd reached their original target then the virus would have spread without anyone having the slightest idea what was happening. No big gas attack, no bombs, no explosions, just thirty-four bodies, slowly decomposing, releasing the chemical weapon inside them. A virus that nobody's ever seen before. An infection that no one knows how to treat or stop.'

'But what was its target?'

'We'll probably never know, but Adamson and his firm ruined the plan when they hit that van.'

'You reckon it was the terrorists who killed them?'

'It's starting to look that way. The same terrorists who are still chasing Matt Franklin.'

39

The inside of the car smelled of sweat and gun oil. Matt Franklin wound down the driver's side window slightly, aware that the acrid odour of perspiration was his. As well as sweat, his hands were spattered with dirt and flecked with blood.

How much of it was Amy's blood?

His fingernails were filthy. He needed a shave. He wanted, more than anything, to feel the cleansing jets of a shower upon his body. He wanted to wash away the filth and the grime and the blood.

And the memories?

He sat at traffic lights, one arm dangling from the window, a cigarette clamped between his lips. On the passenger seat next to him lay the black holdall. Franklin reached inside gently and pulled out one of Amy's carefully folded T-shirts. He raised it to his face and inhaled deeply, drinking in her scent. He wished that she was here with him. Wished he could embrace her. Hold her tightly to him.

But that wouldn't be happening ever again, would it?

Franklin kissed the T-shirt then slipped it back into the holdall, pulling away as the lights turned green.

'I'm going to find them, babe,' he said, gazing ahead, guiding the Audi skilfully through the London traffic. 'And when I do, I'm going to fucking kill them. I'm going to make them sorry for what they did.'

He caught a glimpse of his own reflection in the rear-view mirror. Saw the emptiness in his gaze. It was as if someone had sucked the life from him. There was nothing left inside now except a searing anger and an overwhelming sense of despair. Of loss.

'I promise you,' he whispered.

As he turned he felt the cassette in his jacket pocket.

Amy's cassette.

For a second, Franklin thought about pushing it into the machine and turning the volume up to maximum so that her voice filled his head. He decided against it.

Thoughts tumbled through his head as he drove. Options. Desires. It was a fairly simple situation as far as he was concerned. Someone, somewhere, was trying to kill him. He had no idea why. He had no idea who it might be. But that wasn't what mattered. What mattered was that they had taken from him the one woman he had loved more than any other in his life. The woman who he would have lived out his days with. The one who would have borne his child. He gripped the wheel more tightly. When would they come for *him?*

The sooner the better.

He glanced around as he drove. At the traffic that passed him. Up at windows and roofs where someone might be concealed. He had no doubt that they would find him eventually. And for that he was grateful.

Come and get me.

If they got close enough then he would have a chance.

But they didn't get close, did they? They tried to blow your head off from Christ knows how far away.

He had to *let* them get close to him. He wanted to look

into *their* eyes as they died. Wanted to hear the last breath escape from *their* collapsing lungs. Wanted to savour the sound of the death rattle in *their* throats.

Franklin swung the car around a corner and pressed down gently on the brake as he saw a pedestrian crossing ahead of him. There were several people moving over the black and white striped portion of the road. One of them was a young woman holding a little girl by the hand. The girl was no more than five. Franklin watched the child trotting along beside her mother, dressed in a little blue dress and black shoes with white ankle socks. As she crossed before him, she smiled and waved at Franklin. He waved back.

Maybe your child would have grown up like that. But you'll never know, will you? Not now.

He clenched his teeth until his jaws ached. He could feel the tears building.

Then the little girl was gone. Swallowed by the crowd of pedestrians on the other side of the road. Vanished as if she had never been there and, for fleeting seconds, Franklin wondered if he had imagined her.

He drove on while despair so profound it almost suffocated him, gathered in his chest, like a cancer in his soul.

Another fifteen minutes and he would be back at the flat. Perhaps they'd be waiting for him there. He hoped so.

40

The church was about five minutes' walk from his flat. Franklin had passed it more times than he cared to remember and had never afforded it more than a passing glance. He wasn't even sure what made him stop the Audi close to the ornate front of the holy building. He switched off the engine and sat gazing at the edifice.

St Peter's was an Italian, Catholic church in Clerkenwell Road. Architecturally it was a hybrid – a mixture of new and traditional and with its marbled frontage, it seemed somewhat out of place among the red brick buildings that flanked it.

Franklin swung himself out of the car and stood looking up at the church for a moment, taking a last draw on his cigarette. He dropped it into the gutter, walked the three paces to the steps that led up to the main entrance of the church and climbed them. For a moment he thought about turning and looking up at the buildings around him, of checking the roof tops and windows for signs of a sniper but, instead, he merely put one hand on the church door and gently pushed. It opened noiselessly and Franklin stepped inside.

The solitude enveloped him like a cool blanket. So

different to the hustle and bustle of the busy street outside. As he closed the door behind him, it was as if he'd shut out not just the noise but also what stalked those streets searching for him.

Had they seen him enter the church? Would they follow him inside?

Franklin drew in a deep breath. It didn't matter if they did. Almost unconsciously, he slipped one hand inside his jacket and touched the butt of the .459.

His footsteps echoed as he walked from the main door to the rearmost row of dark wooden pews. The church smelled, not of incense as he'd imagined it would, but of polish. He saw a woman in her sixties close to the altar busily shining the chancel rail. She didn't hear him as he walked slowly down the central aisle, his gaze drawn to the huge wooden figure of Christ that dominated the wall above the altar.

Franklin stopped and stared into the blank eyes of the figure.

What are you looking for?

He sat down in the nearest pew, slumping backwards against the polished wood, his eyes still drawn to the carving. The woman turned from her task and saw him. She nodded, managed a smile then moved across to the altar itself where she began shining the already gleaming silver candlesticks that adorned the most sacred part of the building.

Franklin had never been a religious man. Like many, the only times he'd even been inside a church were for marriages or funerals.

There'll be a few of those coming up, won't there? Who's going to take care of Amy's?

The thought of her caused him to lower his head slightly, as if in reverence.

You've been to church for christenings too, haven't you? You

185

won't have to worry about organising one of those either, will you?
Not now that your kid's dead. Dead inside its mother.

Franklin ran both hands through his hair and sat forward, elbows resting on his knees.

'Why?' he whispered, his words drifting in the silence. He looked up at the figure of Christ once again, as if expecting an answer.

There was movement from behind him and Franklin spun round, his right hand reaching inside his jacket. The priest had walked silently down the central aisle until he now stood just a few feet from Franklin who surveyed him suspiciously for a moment then released his grip on the automatic inside his jacket.

The man was in his early forties and slightly greying at the temples. He was tall and lean. Powerfully built. Something that even the folds of his cassock could not disguise. He smiled benignly at Franklin who nodded a greeting.

'I am sorry if I disturbed you,' the priest said. 'I apologise if I interrupted your prayers or your thoughts.'

'I wasn't praying,' Franklin said flatly. 'What's the point?'

'It is our way of communicating with God.'

'I've got nothing to say to Him. But even if I had, I'm not sure He'd want to hear it.'

'God sees into your heart and your mind. He knows what you are thinking without you giving voice to it.' The priest smiled.

'He knows what I'm thinking, does He?' Franklin replied, his own features impassive. 'Does He know how I'm *feeling*? I doubt it.'

'If you speak to Him He will reply.'

'You believe that because you're a priest. It goes with the territory, doesn't it? It's a part of the job. Don't expect everyone else to believe it.'

'Don't you *want* to believe that He hears you?'

'What difference does it make?' Franklin rasped, fixing

186

the priest in a steely gaze. 'What's done is done. It's over. Finished. God can't change that. No one can.'

'May I sit, please?' the priest asked, putting his hand on the back of the pew behind Franklin.

'Help yourself,' said the younger man, hooking a thumb in the direction of the pew.

The priest seated himself and leaned forward slightly so that he was resting on the back of the pew that Franklin sat in.

'Why do you speak this way?' the cleric asked. 'Why is there so much anger in your words? Tell me, please. I may be able to help.'

'I thought God was going to help me,' Franklin chided. 'He knows everything, doesn't He?'

'He can only help you if you *want* His help.'

Franklin turned angrily to the priest.

'Then get Him to show me the men who killed the woman I loved,' Franklin hissed through clenched teeth.

'You have lost someone close to you. I am sorry. Many who have suffered a loss come here for comfort.'

'And do they get it?' Franklin snapped.

'They do if they believe.'

'Forget it. I'm not looking to join your club.'

The priest looked puzzled.

'People who've lost someone close come here to be comforted,' Franklin continued. 'Does God give them what they want? Does He give them back the person they've lost? I don't think so.'

'He knows what it is like to lose someone. He lost His own son. He watched His own son die. He allowed that to happen. It was an act of love such as none of us will ever be able to understand, but He did it because *He is* love.'

'He *allowed* His son to die. He had a choice. He could have stopped it. I *didn't* have a choice. I *couldn't* stop my girlfriend from being killed. I didn't *want* her to die.'

187

'No one who loses someone close to them wants that.'

Franklin sucked in a deep breath and closed his eyes for a moment.

'How can you still believe when you see what happens in this world every day?' he said quietly. 'Cancer. Child abuse. Death. Would a God that was good invent things like that? Would a caring God make people kill each other?'

'God does not *make* men kill. Men have that choice. God does not force them into evil.'

'Do you think it's evil to kill, Father?'

'Only God has the right to take life. He gives it and He takes it away when He feels the time is right.'

'Do you want to see *my* God?' Franklin said, his eyes blazing. He pushed his hand inside his jacket and pulled out the automatic.

'With this, *I* decide whether someone lives or dies.' He hefted the .459 before the priest who looked first at the gun, then at Franklin's contorted features.

'That is *your* choice,' said the priest quietly. 'Not God's.'

'Choice,' grunted Franklin, getting to his feet. 'Nobody has a choice any more.' He started off up the aisle, jamming the pistol back into its shoulder holster. The priest also stood but made no move to follow him. He merely watched the younger man striding angrily away from him.

As Franklin reached the door of the church he turned, a sardonic smile on his face.

'If there *is* a God, I'll tell you one thing He got right, Father,' he said, his voice echoing through the stillness of the church. 'All that stuff about an eye for an eye – he was spot on with *that*.'

Franklin pushed the door and walked out of the church.

The priest, the cleaning woman and the blank eyes of the carved wooden Christ watched him go.

41

Franklin sat outside his home for a long time before finally deciding to leave the relative safety of the car.

There were repairs being done to the building opposite. The front of the structure was criss-crossed by scaffolding. He could see men moving about on the wooden walkways. Every so often lumps of masonry would rumble down a long chute into a skip that was secured by the roadside. A pneumatic drill added to the cacophony. The sound was deafening but it was not noise that Franklin was concerned with.

Still in the driver's seat of the Audi, he squinted up at the scaffolding, watching each of the workers in turn as they went about their business.

Workers? Are the dusty overalls just a ruse? A disguise?

There were a dozen other places where a sniper could have hidden.

Franklin imagined the cross-threads being brought to bear on his head even as he sat there. His heart quickened its pace slightly.

Fuck them. You want *them here. You* want *them to come for you.*

He swung himself out of the Audi then locked it. The SPAS and the Ithaca were safely hidden on the back seat.

The holdall containing the Taurus and the Sterling .357 (and Amy's clothes) was on the passenger seat. He'd retrieve them after he'd checked out the flat. He fumbled in his pocket for the keys to his flat. *Their* flat. The knowledge that he hadn't set foot inside it since Amy's death suddenly seemed to hit him like a sledgehammer. He paused, not sure if he could actually take the steps.

Come on.

He opened the main door and moved quickly down the short flight of stone steps towards his own front door. The sound of the traffic and builders from the street above diminished considerably. Franklin was glad of the respite. He selected his key then ran appraising eyes over the door, checking to see if the lock had been tampered with. He ran one index finger along the door frame, feeling for any rough spots close to the lock that might indicate forced entry. The paint around it looked unscratched.

Franklin pushed his key slowly into the lock and prepared to turn it.

What if they took Amy's key after they killed her?

Franklin froze.

They could be sitting in there now, waiting for you.

He drew the .459 with his free hand and gripped it tightly, then he turned the key with infinite slowness.

The hinges squeaked slightly as he stepped into the narrow hallway. He could see that the living area was clear.

As Amy had left it.

The bedroom door and bathroom doors were shut. He pushed the bathroom door open with the barrel of the automatic.

Nothing.

Now, just the bedroom.

Franklin put his foot against it and pushed, simultaneously lowering the Smith & Wesson, prepared to pump the trigger if he had to.

190

The room was empty.

He lowered the pistol and glanced across at the bedside table on his side of the bed. There was a photo of Amy there. He'd taken it not long after they'd met, on one of their first dates. A picnic in Hyde Park. He thought about how beautiful she looked.

'Hey, you,' he said, quietly to the photo. 'I'm home.'

He picked up the picture and quickly took it from the frame, sliding it into one of his inside pockets, then he took off his jacket and laid it on the bed. He also took off his shoulder holster and dropped it beside the jacket. As he walked through to the bathroom he pulled off his T-shirt and tossed it aside.

Inside the bathroom he switched on the shower, poking his hands into the spray to test the temperature. He caught sight of his reflection as he turned. Franklin ran his fingers over the thick stubble on his cheeks and chin.

Time for a shave too?

He wandered back into the bedroom and pulled off his boots and socks then, standing in just his jeans, he rummaged through his drawers for a couple of clean T-shirts, some underwear and other necessary clothes. These he laid on the bed.

As the shower continued to sputter and the water warmed, he made his way to the kitchen and filled the kettle. He spooned coffee into a mug then reached for the fridge door. There were photos stuck to it. They were held in place with pieces of Blu-Tack or magnets. Pictures of himself and Amy together, Amy alone, smiling. In one of them she was blowing a kiss towards the camera.

Franklin opened the fridge door and took out the milk. He splashed some into his cup and replaced the carton, then he wandered back into the bathroom as he waited for the kettle to boil.

Franklin glanced down at his fingers and saw how thickly

191

the dirt and grime were encrusted beneath his fingernails. There were still some spots of blood on the back of his right hand too.

It was as he turned back towards the bedroom that he heard the sound of the main door opening. He heard muffled voices, then footsteps ascending the staircase.

Someone from one of the flats above returning, he reasoned. Franklin exhaled.

The kettle should have boiled by now, he mused.

Get a shower. Have a shave and get some coffee down you.

It was a start at least.

It was as he walked back towards the kitchen that he saw the handle of the front door move.

42

Franklin froze.

Eyes fixed on the door handle, he stood immobile, trying to control his breathing and the sudden thunderous pounding of his heart.

This is what you wanted, isn't it? You wanted them to come for you.

His gaze never leaving the handle, he backed into the bedroom and fumbled on the bed for the shoulder holster. He pulled the .459 free and gripped it in both hands, the barrel levelled at the door.

The handle moved again. There was no doubt. Someone was trying to get in.

'Come on then,' Franklin mouthed, his words virtually soundless.

The handle was still once more.

How many of them were out there? One. Two?

He had the advantage. They had to come in. Had to step right into his line of fire.

His mouth was dry where he had been breathing rapidly through it. His tongue stuck to the roof of his mouth, and when he tried to swallow he couldn't.

Come on.

He took a step nearer the door, straining his ears for sounds of movement on the other side but the stream of water from the shower was all he could hear.

They would hear that too. They would know he was inside the flat. They'd probably known from the time he left the Audi. They would have watched him enter the building. Bided their time.

Franklin heard a soft click as the door was unlocked and his anxiety was suddenly overwhelmed by fury.

Bastards. Had they taken Amy's key after they'd murdered her? Gone through her pockets? Fucking cunts. Come on. Come in now. Step in front of this gun barrel.

The door opened a fraction of an inch.

Franklin gripped the automatic more tightly and squinted through the crack between the hinges and the door frame. As far as he could tell there was just one man out there.

The door opened a little wider. It squeaked on its hinges.

Franklin sprang forward and drove all of his weight against it, slamming the door into the intruder.

He heard a grunt of pain and surprise as the man went tumbling back into the cold entryway outside the flat. Franklin tore open the door and made a grab for the dazed man. He caught him by the front of his jacket and hurled him furiously back into the flat where he slammed into the wall.

Franklin, the element of surprise still with him, drove one foot into the man's groin, watching with delight as he doubled up in agony and dropped to his knees. Another kick caught him in the side of the face and sent him sprawling, a red welt already rising just above his right cheekbone.

Franklin stepped towards him, the automatic aimed at his head.

'Fucking stay there,' he roared, as the man tried to rise.

194

The man raised a hand.

Franklin kicked him so hard in the groin that he felt his bare foot slam into the man's pelvic bone. He curled up into a foetal position, retching, so great was the pain, both hands clutching at his battered testicles.

'Are you alone?' Franklin rasped.

The man managed a strangled cry and rolled onto his back.

Franklin stood over him, seeing that his face had turned milk-white. His eyes were half-open and he still held his groin.

'Is anyone with you?' hissed Franklin, glancing towards the door.

The man managed to shake his head.

'If you're lying I'll kill you now,' Franklin hissed, pushing the pistol a little closer towards him.

'No one else,' the man managed to say, his eyes still screwed up in agony. He wiped his mouth with the back of one shaking hand.

'You're a fucking liar.'

Again the man shook his head.

'No,' he panted.

Franklin ran appraising eyes over him. He was in his mid-thirties and dressed in jeans, a Tommy Hilfiger jacket and a pair of dark blue trainers. He had thick brown hair that reached as far as his shoulders.

'ID,' the man said, trying to get his breath back, wishing that the fiery pain around his groin would diminish. 'Inside pocket.'

'*You* get it,' Franklin told him. 'Slowly. Use your left hand.'

He watched as the man fumbled inside his jacket and produced a slim leather wallet.

'Throw it over here,' Franklin instructed, kneeling quickly to retrieve it when the man did as he was told. He flipped

195

the wallet open and glanced at the contents, reading aloud, 'Detective Constable Michael Weaver.'

'Yeah,' gasped the man, trying to prop himself up on one elbow. 'I'm here to help you.'

43

'That's a fucking forgery,' snapped Franklin, tossing the ID back at the other man. 'You're no copper.'

He steadied the pistol, his finger tightening on the trigger.

'If you think I'm lying, then shoot,' breathed Weaver, one hand still clutching his scrotum. 'Either that or ring the number on that card. They'll confirm who I am.'

'Bollocks. This is all a fucking set-up.'

'Call the number.'

'How did you get in here?'

'I used a copy of your girlfriend's key.'

'The one that you took off her after you killed her, you cunt.'

Weaver shook his head. 'I didn't kill your girlfriend,' he said, swallowing hard. 'Or any of your firm.'

'How did you know I'd be here?'

'We've been watching this place since this morning. We thought you might come back. We've had mobile units all over London trying to find you.'

Franklin stared at the fallen man, his jaws clenched together so tightly they were starting to ache.

'Bullshit!' he hissed.

'It's true, but like I say, if you don't believe me then pull the trigger.'

There was a long silence, finally broken by Franklin. 'Even if this *is* true,' he said, 'and you're kosher, why would the police want to help *me*?'

'We want to know who tried to kill *you*. We need to find out who wiped out your firm and murdered Susan Harris and your girlfriend. Six people are dead. We need to know why.'

'How the fuck should I know?'

'You know the other firms operating in London. Why would they want you and your mates dead?'

'Ask *them*.'

'*You* beat us to it.'

'I want to know who's got it in for me.'

'Is that why you paid a call on James Patterson this morning?'

'What do you know about that?'

'You're driving his car, Franklin. You attacked him in one of his restaurants. He called us.'

'He grassed me up?'

'What did you expect him to do? You pinned his hand to a desk with a letter opener then stole his car. He's entitled to be a bit pissed off, isn't he?'

A faint smile touched Franklin's lips, but he still didn't lower the automatic. '*He's* entitled. What about me? Some bastard's hunting me. I'm not going sit around with my thumb up my arse waiting for them to blow my fucking head off.'

'I don't blame you.' Weaver hauled himself upright, one hand still rubbing his aching groin.

'Who told you to move?' Franklin asked him. 'Just because I haven't shot you yet doesn't mean I believe what you're saying *or* who you are.'

'Can I sit down?' asked Weaver, motioning towards the sofa.

198

'Help yourself but keep your hands where I can see them,' Franklin instructed, seating himself in the chair opposite.

Weaver winced.

'It's a good job I've already *got* kids,' he said, blowing out his cheeks and clasping his testicles. 'After that, I'm not sure I'll be fathering any more.'

'Join the club,' Franklin said bitterly.

'Yeah, I'm sorry. I saw the results of the autopsy. I know that your girlfriend was pregnant when she was murdered.'

Franklin lowered the automatic slightly until his hand was resting on his right knee. He kept the barrel pointed at Weaver's chest.

'If you *are* a copper,' he said quietly. '*If* you are, are you here to arrest me?'

'Well, for a start you *were* involved in an armed robbery two nights ago.'

'We didn't get much.'

'I know. I saw what was in the van.'

'We had nothing to do with what was in there.'

'Nobody thinks you did. My guv'nor just wants to talk to you. He thinks that whoever wiped out your firm and murdered your girlfriend is responsible for what we found inside that van. I'm supposed to take you into protective custody to make sure that you don't end up like the others.'

'What if I don't want to go?'

Weaver raised his hands.

'Then you risk going the same way as your mates and your girlfriend,' he said flatly.

'Do you think that matters to me any more?' Franklin said sardonically.

'I think you want to get whoever did it, and you might need our help for that.'

The two men locked stares.

'Protective custody?' Franklin murmured.

Weaver nodded.

'I'll get dressed,' said Franklin, getting to his feet and heading for the bedroom. 'Just one thing,' he added. 'I get to keep my guns. Because I'm telling you now, I'm going to get the bastards, *with* or *without* your fucking help.'

44

'You go first,' said Franklin, walking across towards the Audi. 'I'll follow you.'

Weaver hesitated a moment then nodded.

'Where were you watching me from?' Franklin wanted to know.

'That building opposite,' Weaver said, indicating the one festooned with scaffolding. 'The inside used to be a textile business. They're only doing work to the *outside*.' He smiled. 'Wait there while I get my car. I'm parked in the next street.'

Franklin watched as the policeman headed off across the busy street, then he unlocked the driver's side door of the Audi and prepared to slide behind the wheel.

If you go with him, they'll lock you up. They only want you to help them find the bastards who killed Amy.

Franklin drummed on the roof of the car with the fingers of one hand. Weaver had disappeared from view by now.

Once they get you back to New Scotland Yard, that's it. You can forget any chance of getting close to Amy's murderers.

He slipped a hand inside his jacket and pulled out the photo of her he'd taken from the flat.

Go. Get in and drive away.

Franklin slipped the photo back into his jacket, looking agitatedly around him.

You can be long gone before Weaver gets back. Go. Do it now.

The traffic lights ahead of him had just turned to green and a stream of vehicles was making its way down the street, led by a motorbike and a dark blue Mondeo.

Only when the bike was twenty yards away did Franklin notice that the rider was looking in his direction. Then he saw the gun.

In the split second before the barrel flamed, Franklin realised that it was a machine pistol of some kind.

There was a sound like a tremendously loud sewing machine as the bike rider opened fire. Bullets drilled across the pavement, ricocheting off the concrete in places, drilling into it in others. Several struck the car, blasting in one of the side windows.

Franklin pulled the .459 free of its holster as he dropped to the ground. The sound of empty shell cases hitting the road was audible even above the cacophony of gunfire and the roar of the traffic. He sprang up again, using the bonnet of the Audi as cover, steadied himself and pumped the trigger four times.

The first shot missed. The second struck a pannier on the bike. The third and fourth both hit the rider. One struck him in the shoulder, shattering his scapula, the other drilled into the small of his back. He tried to turn and fire another burst from the machine pistol but Franklin got off two more rounds, the pistol slamming back against the heel of his hand.

One of the 9mm bullets hit the motorcyclist's helmet. It blasted away the tinted visor, portions of it spiralling up into the air. The other shot hit him in the right shoulder.

The rider tried to retain control of the 500cc machine but it was hopeless. The bike veered across the street into the path of an oncoming taxi. The driver slammed on his brakes but couldn't avoid the bike.

The impact caused a shriek of buckling metal and Franklin saw the rider crash to the ground. He rolled over twice then lay still.

Franklin barely had time to register his victory. He straightened up slightly as the Mondeo swept past.

There was another devastating fusillade of gunfire from inside the vehicle and Franklin dropped to the pavement once again as bullets tore into the side of the Audi.

Sweat pouring down his face, he remained crouched behind the car, not daring to emerge.

The air stank of cordite. Spent cartridge cases littered the street like brass confetti. The sound of blaring horns, roaring engines, shouts and screams all melded into one hellish banshee shriek that seemed to reverberate inside his skull.

He hauled himself upright again and saw the Mondeo come to a halt. One of the men inside was scurrying from it, dragging the motionless motorcyclist into the back of the vehicle.

Franklin fired at the car. His first shot screamed off the boot. The second cut through empty air.

The Mondeo suddenly accelerated away, tyres screeching, leaving a cloud of acrid smoke hanging in the air.

Franklin tore open the driver's side door and clambered in, starting the engine. It roared into life and he spun the wheel, completing a U-turn. The Audi scraped an oncoming Volvo but Franklin kept a firm grip on the steering wheel and, as he straightened the vehicle, he pressed his foot down hard on the accelerator. Ahead of him, the Mondeo was trying to increase its speed. *Trying to get away?*

Hunched over the wheel, Franklin followed. There were traffic lights ahead, already blinking on amber. The Mondeo swept through.

Franklin saw the lights turn red but roared after the fleeing vehicle. The driver swung right into Farringdon

Street, scattering a number of pedestrians who were trying to cross. Most ducked back onto the pavement, one managed, by inches, to avoid the onrushing vehicle.

Franklin saw the man sprawl in the road and he twisted the wheel of the Audi wildly to avoid him.

The traffic on Farringdon Street was heavy but the driver of the Mondeo moved the vehicle with great skill, bringing it up alongside other, slower-moving traffic at speed, occasionally scraping the sides of vehicles if he had to.

But this was Franklin's province and he knew he had the measure of any driver. He pressed down harder on the accelerator, drawing nearer to the dark blue car, ready to ram it if he could get close enough.

Gripping the wheel with one hand he dragged the automatic from its holster and stuck it out of the open driver's side window. He squeezed off three shots.

The first exploded one of the Mondeo's rear lights. The second tore past it without making contact, but the third punched a hole in the rear windscreen.

Franklin gritted his teeth triumphantly as he saw the glass spiderweb. But the snarl of victory vanished as a gun barrel was thrust through the hole.

Franklin saw the long barrel and realised the man in the Mondeo was trying to draw a bead on him. There was a loud bang and the weapon spewed out its deadly load.

Franklin ducked involuntarily as the bullet blasted in a portion of his windscreen. Glass erupted backwards into the Audi and Franklin shielded his face with one hand, battling to keep control of the car. Several small pieces of glass cut his face and hand but he ignored them, more intent on keeping the Audi on an even course. The car had veered to one side, into the path of a bus. Franklin saw the driver slam on his brakes, saw his terrified face as he waited for the impact. It never came.

Franklin twisted the wheel, smacked into the side of a

van and shunted it towards the kerb, but he retained control of the Audi.

Cold air rushed into his face as he drove. It cooled the sweat on his skin and dried his mouth as he gasped for breath.

The Mondeo was still no more than thirty yards ahead of him as it sped towards the junction with Charterhouse Street doing fifty. The driver took a right: a sudden movement that sent more smoke rising from tyres battling to keep a grip on the tarmac.

There was a cyclist ahead, about to turn that same corner. The Mondeo hit him, knocking him onto the pavement where he collided with several pedestrians.

Franklin heard screams as he drove past, his gaze fixed on the Mondeo.

He was closing on it.

Twenty-five yards now.

Even if the Mondeo driver was aware of it, he was powerless to prevent it. The Audi was faster, more powerful.

Twenty yards.

Franklin steadied the .459 again and prepared to fire.

Fifteen yards.

Above the roar of the engine and the screaming of the wind, Franklin heard sirens. But it didn't matter. He was now less than ten yards from the fleeing Mondeo.

45

The two police cars both came from the direction of Hatton Garden, roof lights flashing and sirens wailing. Like Franklin and the car he was pursuing, they hurtled towards the vehicular bedlam that was Holborn Circus with terrifying speed.

The Mondeo swerved between cars, tyres screeching. It hit several other vehicles, grinding paint from their sides as it passed. The impacts were enough to slow it for precious seconds but not sufficient to stop it.

Franklin angrily jammed the automatic back into its shoulder holster, needing both hands on the wheel to guide himself through the moving labyrinth of vehicles into which he was travelling. The wind still rushed into his face but he squinted against it, his gaze never leaving the Mondeo.

One of the police cars smashed broadside into a bus, the impact bringing the two vehicles to a juddering halt. The police car's offside wing was buckled, the paint stripped from it. One tyre had burst, immobilising it.

Franklin glanced in his rear-view mirror and saw that the driver was slumped over the steering wheel. He gripped the wheel of the Audi more tightly and sent the car hurtling around a taxi, then a people carrier.

Ahead of him, the Mondeo was rushing down New Fetter Lane, the remaining police car still in pursuit.

Franklin knew that the men in it would be calling for assistance. In moments there would be more police cars. They would start sealing off roads up ahead. He had a choice to make and he had to make it quickly.

If the bastards in the Mondeo were the ones he wanted then he couldn't let them escape. He couldn't let the police stop them before *he* did.

There were two cars between him and his prey and the traffic on the opposite side of the road was coming too thickly to allow him to overtake.

Think.

He spun the wheel and drove up onto the pavement.

There was a bone-jarring thud as the Audi hit the kerb but Franklin held tightly to the steering wheel, aware that pedestrians were scattering in front of him. Many were shrieking in panic. A man dived into a shop doorway as the car roared past, missing him by inches.

Franklin screamed something unintelligible at those blocking his way as he drove, one eye on the Mondeo. He smashed into a waste bin and sent it spinning across the road where it struck another car like a missile, denting the door. Rubbish spewed in all directions, some of it flying up onto what was left of the Audi's windscreen.

A sheet of newspaper momentarily flattened itself over the splintered glass. Franklin, blinded for precious seconds, tore at the paper with one hand and pulled it free of his line of vision. As he did he saw what was before him.

Several metal tables and chairs had been set on the pavement in front of a cafe.

He could not avoid them. The people who had been seated there scattered like pheasants before beaters.

A second before he hit the first table, Franklin saw the pushchair.

There was no way round.

He saw the mother screaming. Saw her snatching desperately at the child in the pushchair, trying to lift him free.

The Audi hit the first table and sent it flying into the air. The second it shunted a full twenty yards further down the pavement. Several of the chairs went flying sideways, one of them smashing through the cafe window. Cups and mugs, bottles and glasses were all catapulted skyward to land seconds later, shattering on the flagstones.

Again Franklin roared some wild ululation that might have been voiced by a madman as he bore down on the mother and her child. He stamped on the brake, knowing it was a futile gesture.

The Audi hit the pushchair doing thirty.

The flimsy contraption was crushed beneath the wheels of the car, flattened by the impact and weight. A small teddy bear was flung across the pavement into the gutter.

Franklin twisted the wheel. In the wing mirror he saw the mother holding her child, sobbing hysterically, looking into the face of the small boy that she'd managed to pull to safety at the last second.

Now Franklin floored the right-hand pedal, still on the pavement but drawing level with the Mondeo. He yanked the wheel to his left and the Audi careered back onto the road and slammed into the other car with enough force to shunt it over into the path of oncoming traffic.

The driver of the Mondeo recovered quickly enough to avoid a head-on collision with an approaching Volkswagen.

Franklin drew the .459, still using the weight of the Audi to push the Mondeo further across the busy street.

Both vehicles, as if welded together, hit the opposite kerb and mounted it. They were heading towards the wide plate-glass window of a hairdressers.

Inside people ran towards the rear of the shop for safety, desperate to get away as they saw what was about to happen.

Franklin turned the wheel again, this time to his right. The Audi swerved back onto the road, screamed past a van and back into the other stream of traffic.

The Mondeo careered onwards.

It hit the window of the hairdressers and crashed through it. Massive shards of broken glass exploded inwards as the Mondeo skidded, spinning and finally slamming into the row of sinks on one wall. The porcelain shattered and water spouted from the broken conduits. More glass fell from the frame, raining down like crystal shrapnel, the strident clattering resounding all around.

There was steam rising from the bonnet of the Mondeo. Two of its tyres were punctured. One door was buckled and the paint had been all but stripped from its offside wing. As well as the back windscreen, two of the side windows were broken, one of them completely obliterated.

Franklin swung the Audi around in the road, blocking the flow of traffic, aware that the police car was somewhere nearby. He could still hear its sirens but his vision was obscured by the dust particles in his eyes. He wiped the back of his hand across his face and reached over onto the back seat where he grabbed the SPAS. Then he swung himself out of the Audi and ran towards the Mondeo.

He worked the slide on the shotgun, held it at hip level and fired one of the deadly rounds into the Mondeo. The shot tore easily through the metal. Still advancing, he fired again, and again, blasting holes in the stricken vehicle. Empty cartridge cases fell onto the road behind him as he walked.

Ten feet from the crashed Mondeo he stopped, the SPAS held in one hand, the .459 in the other, both trained on the other car.

If anyone was alive inside they weren't attempting to fire back.

Not yet.

Franklin's breath was coming in gasps.

'Drop the guns.'

He heard the shout from somewhere behind him.

'Franklin, drop the guns and lie on the ground.'

There was something vaguely familiar about the voice. He kept his eyes on the Mondeo. Somewhere in the distance he heard more sirens.

This is it. This is the end.

'Drop the guns or we'll shoot,' the voice insisted.

He could just see the men inside the Mondeo now. Three of them, including the wounded motorcyclist.

'Franklin,' that familiar voice roared more insistently. 'I'm not going to tell you again. I'm going to count to five.'

Where the fuck was that coming from?

'If you're still armed, we'll have no choice but to shoot. Do you understand?'

The other sirens were getting louder, they were coming from all around him. Still he kept his eyes on the Mondeo.

The driver turned and looked blankly at him.

Franklin raised the .459 and prepared to fire.

The Mondeo exploded.

46

The blast blew Franklin off his feet.

The Mondeo simply disappeared beneath a screaming ball of red, white and yellow flames. Portions of the riven chassis scythed out in all directions like red-hot shrapnel. What was left of the frontage of the shop also erupted into the street as the car was torn apart by the explosion.

Franklin hit the tarmac and lay there with his hands over his head as all manner of debris rained down into the street, propelled by the thunderous detonation. Lumps of the engine flew across the road, some of them striking the many vehicles that had come to a halt there. From fifteen feet away he felt the concussion blast and a searing wave of heat sweep over him as the Mondeo's petrol tank went up and a secondary explosion sent more flaming wreckage flying into the air.

Long rivers of blazing petrol spread across the thoroughfare like fiery tentacles, reaching for prey. The air was filled with millions of tiny cinders, floating on the hot blanket like a plague of minuscule insects.

As the flames diminished slightly, thick black smoke belched from the pulverised remains of the car and the stench of burning rubber began to reach his nostrils, mingled with a sweeter, more cloying smell that he assumed to be incinerated human flesh.

Franklin rolled over, one hand closing over the SPAS. He tried to struggle to his feet, suddenly becoming aware of a pain in his left leg. He looked down and saw blood running freely from a cut on his thigh. A sliver of hot metal the length of a sewing needle had cut through his flesh and muscle. His jeans were sliced open, exposing the wound. Franklin swayed uncertainly for a second, his head spinning. Voices and sounds were closing in on him, throbbing inside his skull. He put one hand to his head and brought it away stained with blood. Another piece of debris had caught him a glancing blow just above his hairline and opened a gash there.

Franklin tried to take a step towards the blazing remains of the Mondeo but his leg would hardly support him.

'Put the gun down.'

That voice was back again.

He turned this time, trying to locate its source.

'Franklin. Put it down.'

Crouching behind an abandoned car about twenty yards from him, he saw the face of DC Michael Weaver.

That's *why the voice sounded familiar.*

There were other policemen around Weaver, some in uniform, others in plain clothes. Members of the public were being ushered away though most didn't need to be told. The vast majority were running, desperate to be away from this horrifying scene.

Franklin suddenly felt as if he was the only one in the street, apart from the police who were surrounding him. Most of them had guns too.

'Put the shotgun down,' Weaver called.

What was that he had gripped in his fist? A Glock 9mm? Nice gun.

Franklin blinked sweat away from his eyes, wiped his face with a bloodied hand.

'They're dead,' Weaver informed him. 'You don't need that any more.' He jabbed a finger towards the SPAS. 'Let it drop and get on the ground. Don't do anything stupid, not now.'

Franklin looked down at his injured leg and winced. He sucked in a deep breath, a breath tinged with the smell of burned flesh, petrol and scorched rubber. He spat, trying to remove the taste of blood from his mouth.

Weaver stood up, the Glock still aimed at Franklin. He began walking slowly towards him, never lowering the pistol.

Franklin looked around and saw that the other armed policemen had remained behind whatever cover they'd first chosen. Many were holding rifles. Every single one of them was trained on *him*.

Weaver was less than ten feet away now, the 9mm still aimed at Franklin's chest.

He stepped over a tendril of burning petrol that had spread across the road. 'You got them,' he said quietly, inclining his head towards the blazing wreck of the Mondeo but never letting his gaze leave Franklin.

'No I didn't,' Franklin breathed, his head spinning even more violently. He blinked hard, wondering why his vision kept blurring.

'They're dead.' Weaver was close to him now. Just an arm's length away.

'Put down the shotgun,' the policeman said gently.

'*I* didn't kill them. *I* wanted to kill them. I wanted to see their faces when I pulled the trigger.'

'They're dead, that's all that matters.' Weaver held out his free hand for the SPAS. 'That's what you wanted.'

Franklin looked directly at the policeman, then glanced at the burning hulk of the Mondeo. Flames were still licking around the blasted chassis. They made everything look as if it was shimmering. Even when Franklin looked back at

213

Weaver, the image of the policeman swam as if he were gazing at him through a heat haze. It felt as if someone had filled his skull with helium.

'I wanted to watch them as they died,' Franklin mumbled.

He dropped to his knees, eyes rolling upwards in their sockets as he fell forward. He was aware, for brief seconds, of how hot the tarmac felt against his cheek, then Matt Franklin blacked out.

47

For a craft travelling at just under one hundred and sixty miles an hour, the EH-101 helicopter made surprisingly little noise. Driven effortlessly through the clear sky by its three CT7 turboshafts, it sped along majestically at an altitude of nine thousand feet.

Inside the spacious body of the helicopter, equipped to hold up to thirty people, the figures of Edward Carter and Gerald Collinson seemed dwarfed by the size of their transport. Other than themselves, the only passengers were two suited members of MI6, seated at the far end of the passenger area. One of them, like Carter, was gazing out of a window, looking down onto the landscape below.

'How long before we arrive?' the Prime Minister asked.

Collinson, who had been scanning a report he'd taken from a file, looked at his watch.

'About fifteen minutes,' he said, sitting back in his comfortable and plushly upholstered seat.

'And when we do?' Carter persisted, finally looking at his Home Secretary.

Collinson raised an eyebrow quizzically.

'What can I expect to find?' Carter wanted to know.

'Hopefully the answers to some of our present problems, Edward.'

Carter sucked in a deep breath and returned to gazing out of the window.

'Has there been *positive* identification of the terrorists?' he asked, still apparently more concerned with the landscape below.

'I have their names here if that's what you want,' Collinson told him. He held out a piece of paper but Carter merely shook his head, as if reluctant to touch the A4 sheet. 'We both knew this time would come. Everyone in the country knew it. It was only a matter of time before Middle Eastern terrorists struck Great Britain. You yourself have always been at great pains to stress that fact.'

'But, as yet, no action has been taken by those men,' Carter said, nodding towards the list of names held by his companion.

'The measures we intend to take are preventative, are they not? Why wait for an atrocity to be committed before acting? Why allow these men to strike against this country and then retaliate when they can be nullified before they are even *able* to act?'

'Nullified,' Carter mused, a thin smile on his lips. 'What a wonderful euphemism.'

'We both know the steps that must be taken to combat men like these.' Collinson tapped the sheet of paper bearing the names. 'We can't shrink from that course of action now.'

'I'm well aware of that, Gerald,' Carter said, disdainfully. 'I have no intention of *shrinking*, as you put it, from what must be done.'

'Then why the reluctance to go through with this final step?'

'Have I, at any time, indicated a reluctance to pursue our chosen course of action to *you* or anyone else?' There was an edge to Carter's voice that the Home Secretary was not slow to pick up on.

'Not openly.'

'Don't try to psychoanalyse me, Gerald. You know I'm committed to this project. If I wasn't, I'd have closed it down years ago.'

'I'm not asking you to defend yourself, Edward. I'm on your side.'

'It isn't a question of sides,' Carter rasped. 'It's a question of . . .' The sentence tailed off as he sought the word he needed.

'Of ethics? Of morality?' Collinson interjected. 'Do you think those two words are going to concern the suicide squads that we *know* are in London? Are ethics and morality words that the men on that list are even aware of?' He pointed to the sheet of paper. 'I doubt it.'

Both men were silent for a moment, the only sound either was aware of was the hum of the rotors.

'I agree with you,' Carter said, finally. 'I know the steps that must be taken and I have every intention of seeing my decision through but I'll tell you again, if anything goes wrong, anything at all, it won't be *my* job that's on the line. As far as you or anyone else are concerned my knowledge of this project goes only as far as I *say* it goes. Do you understand?'

'You mean you'll deny your part in it?'

'Why shouldn't I when I have colleagues who will protect me if necessary? That's what a Prime Minister does, isn't it? He delegates.'

'I believe the expression you're looking for, Edward, is passing the buck.'

Carter eyed his colleague silently for a moment.

One of the suited men approached. 'Excuse me,' he said. 'We'll be landing in five minutes.'

Carter nodded and snapped himself into his seat belt.

The EH-101 began to bank, gently at first, as it turned towards its destination.

217

48

'Fuck,' groaned Matt Franklin.

He opened his eyes slowly, blinking myopically, squinting as objects slowly swam into focus. The room he was in was about twelve feet square. The walls were bare, painted a colour that reminded him of sour milk.

He tried to swallow but his throat was parched. He coughed and looked around. Aware, as he did, of the pain in his left leg. Franklin slipped one hand tentatively under the sheet and ran his fingertips over the flesh of his thigh. Most of it was heavily bandaged. Again he coughed, trying to clear his throat.

'Want some water?'

The voice came from the other side of the room. Franklin turned slightly to find its source.

He didn't recognise the man seated near the door but he guessed, from his demeanour, what he was.

Detective Inspector Vincent Crane got to his feet and crossed to the bedside cabinet next to where Franklin lay. He poured water from the plastic jug into a beaker and handed it to Franklin who took it, nodded by way of thanks then drank.

'The doctor said you'd be waking up about now,' Crane

said, seating himself on a grey plastic chair beside the bed.

Franklin regarded the policeman evenly over the rim of the beaker. When he'd drained the contents he reached for the jug to refill the receptacle but the movement caused him a fresh jolt of pain from his leg.

Crane took the jug, refilled the beaker with water and handed it to Franklin.

'You've been unconscious since they brought you in,' the policeman told him. 'You'd lost a lot of blood and you were concussed. But the damage isn't bad. You got off lightly.'

'It doesn't fucking feel like it,' Franklin rasped. 'Who are *you*?'

'Detective Inspector Vincent Crane,' the DI told him. Crane reached into his jacket and pulled out his ID. He flipped it open for Franklin to see, watching as the younger man nodded.

'I thought you were law,' Franklin said, sinking back on his pillow.

'Spot us a mile off, can you, Matt?'

'Sometimes.'

'I suppose that's a bonus in your line of work.'

'I don't know what you're talking about.'

'Well, *this* time, I'm talking about a Securicor van full of dead bodies.'

Franklin gazed at the ceiling.

'I'm *also* talking about the murders of Jeff Adamson, Steven Cutler, George Nicholson, Joe Maguire, Susan Harris and Amy Holden,' the detective added.

Franklin's jaw clenched.

'*And* I'm talking about several attempts on *your* life,' Crane continued. 'With me now?'

'What do you want?'

'I want to keep you alive.'

'Why?'

'Because I don't like it when people keep getting shot. It makes more paperwork for me.'

Franklin looked at him.

'Who do you think killed your mates and your girl-friend, Matt?' Crane asked.

'The fuckers in that car that blew up.'

'You could be right. Do you know who they were?'

'No. Do *you*?'

Crane shook his head. 'Unfortunately, they're not going to be much good to us now,' he said.

'Fuck them. I'm glad they're dead. I'm just sorry I never got the chance to do it myself.'

'I can understand that.'

'Can you? Have you really got *any* idea what I'm feeling at the moment? I doubt it.'

Crane sat back on the chair and crossed one leg over the other. 'The three men in the car you were chasing were dead before it blew,' he announced. 'We found bullet holes in all three of their skulls. They all stuck guns in their mouths *before* the car went up.'

'Why would they kill themselves?'

'Because they thought they were about to be caught. They didn't want to be.'

Franklin exhaled deeply.

'Their bodies were burned beyond recognition,' Crane said. 'We can't even identify them from dental records.'

'Who do you think they were?'

'I'd be guessing. And some of what I *know*, irrespective of how little that may be, is confidential.'

'Bullshit. Those bastards killed Amy. At least tell me who they were.' He swallowed, then when he spoke again, his voice was low, barely more than a whisper. 'Please.'

'We think they could have been terrorists. There are several active cells that we know of in London.'

'Terrorists? You mean like the IRA?'

'No. *Not* like the IRA. These boys make the IRA look like beginners. They're from the Middle East.'

'What the fuck have Middle Eastern terrorists got to do with Amy or me or any of my mates? Why did they want *us* dead?'

'Like I said, I'm guessing but I think, when you and your firm hit that Securicor van, you stumbled onto something no one wanted touched.' He shrugged. 'Call it bad timing, shit luck, whatever. You were in the wrong place at the wrong time. Nothing more.'

'And what about Amy? Was *she* in the wrong place at the wrong time too?'

'They were being thorough. That's all. I'm sorry, Franklin. I don't know what else to say.'

'So now what? These . . . terrorists, are they all dead?'

'We don't know. But I doubt it. And if there *are* some of them on the loose, then chances are they're going to come looking for *you*. You're the only one left.'

'Good. Let them come,' Franklin said through clenched teeth.

'And what do you think *you're* going to do if they find you? Hit them over the head with your crutches? Besides, this is over for you now. If I wanted to I could have you locked up for ten years. I've got enough on you.'

'But you won't do that, will you?'

'Why not?'

'Because you want to catch these bastards.'

'And you're going to help me?'

'Yeah.'

'How?'

'Put me back on the streets. You said I was the one they wanted, the only one left. If they know I'm still alive they'll come for me.'

'You're not their only concern.'

221

'Who else are they after?'

'That's classified.'

'Bollocks. Who the fuck am I going to tell? What's *said* in this room *stays* in this room.'

'This isn't some *gang* war, Franklin. It's not two firms having a pop at each other with sawn-off shotguns over who runs which clip joint.'

'So what is it? You said they were terrorists. Who's their target?'

'Any poor bastard who gets in the way. They're suicide bombers. We also think they've got access to chemical weapons. This is a completely different ball game, Franklin. A lot of people could die. *Innocent* people.'

'Like Amy?'

Crane regarded the younger man silently for a moment.

'Put me back on the streets, Crane,' Franklin said calmly.

'You'd be dead in a day.'

'Try me.'

Crane shook his head.

'If I do, you're a sitting target,' he muttered.

'No I'm not. I'm bait.'

49

Crane looked at Franklin for a moment, the furrows on his brow deepening. 'Why would I want to do that?' he asked finally.

'I'm your best chance of catching them,' Franklin insisted. 'If you're right about them wanting me dead then they're going to come after me. Why not put a tail on me twenty-four hours a day? Wait until they come out of the woodwork again then . . . bingo!'

'You've seen how they operate, Franklin. They don't need to get *close* to you. Even if I agree to your idea it might not get me any nearer to the guys who are hunting you. They could take you out from seven hundred yards away. Then what? *They* walk and *I'm* left with another body to scrape off the pavement.'

'So what's *your* plan, Crane?'

'I haven't thought about it.'

'Perhaps you should.'

'Look, you're in no position to bargain, Franklin. Like I told you, with what I've already got on you, you could go down for ten years or more. This isn't the States. Don't try offering some kind of deal to keep you out of prison.'

'I'm offering you my help.'

'And I might not want it.'

'Then fuck you.'

'No. Fuck *you*,' Crane hissed, pointing at the younger man. 'You're the criminal here. Once the courts have finished with you, you'll be taking it up the arse in Pentonville for the foreseeable future.'

'And if you refuse my help then you'll have more than just *my* fucking body to scrape off the pavement. I could be your way in – your way to get to them.'

Crane stroked his chin thoughtfully.

'Why are you so eager to help me?' the DI wanted to know.

'Because I want them dead. You know that. They killed everyone close to me, Crane. They took away the only woman I've ever loved.' He swallowed hard. 'And they took my kid too. Amy was pregnant.'

'I know,' Crane said quietly. 'I'm sorry.'

'Are *you* married?'

'Yeah. For sixteen years.'

'Your old lady's got staying power then?'

Crane smiled.

'Any kids?' Franklin persisted.

'Two boys.'

'How would you feel if *they* were murdered? What would you do if someone put a bullet through your wife's head?'

'I'd feel the same as you do now.'

'Then do what I'm asking,' snapped Franklin. 'Put me back on the streets.'

'I'd be knowingly sending you out there to get killed. I might have crossed some lines over the years, Franklin, but I've never *tried* to get anyone killed before.'

'Since when did a copper let his conscience get in the way of solving a case?'

Crane got to his feet and began pacing slowly back and forth.

'How many of your own men are you prepared to lose to find these bastards?' Franklin wanted to know. 'Five. Six. More? If you use me you haven't got that problem. And *I've* got an advantage over any of your guys.'

'What's that?'

'I'm expendable. But even more important, I don't give a damn if I live or die any more.'

'A man with nothing to live for has no fear of death, eh?'

'What?'

'Something I read once.'

'It's true. Trust me. What's left for me now? Nothing. The only thing that stopped me from putting a gun in *my* mouth was the thought that eventually I'd be able to kill the bastards who murdered Amy.'

'It might not happen.'

'Maybe not, but I'll give it a fucking good try. And I swear to Christ I'll take at least *one* of them with me.'

Crane stopped pacing, placed both hands on the metal frame at the bottom of the hospital bed and looked at Franklin.

'So,' the younger man said. 'What's your answer?'

'If I agree,' Crane began. 'And it's a *big* if, Franklin, don't think you're going to walk at the end of it all. This isn't Hollywood. Even if you help us get them you're still looking at a ten stretch, minimum. And I don't care *how* good a brief you can afford.'

Franklin eyed the policeman indifferently.

'I don't want a deal,' he said quietly. 'I don't want to bargain.'

'As long as we understand each other.'

'There's just one thing I do want.'

'No negotiations, Franklin,' Crane said, cutting him short. 'We just agreed on that.'

'Hear me out.'

225

'Go on.'

Franklin sucked in a deep breath, held it for a moment then exhaled almost painfully.

'I want to see Amy,' he said softly.

50

'It's magnificent.'

Edward Carter held his glass in one hand. The Prime Minister sipped the contents approvingly and continued to walk slowly around the vast dining room.

As with most of the rooms inside Ravenscote Manor, the dining room was oak-panelled, high-ceilinged and reeked of wealth. The manor had been refurbished a number of times during its five hundred year history. Each successive owner adding to the opulence and splendour of a building first constructed as a country residence for the Stuart Kings of England just before the outbreak of the English Civil War.

It stood in over one hundred acres of densely wooded grounds, the entire perimeter protected by a twelve foot high stone wall. The manor was accessible by a single dirt road that wound tortuously through the woods before emerging onto a more recently laid, tarmacked stretch of driveway. The trees thinned out then finally receded until just oaks and poplars lined the final portion of driveway that led to the front of the manor.

Landscaped gardens and a wide expanse of perfectly manicured lawns formed a frontage to the main building. Stables and several other outbuildings were also visible upon closer inspection. Topiary animals kept silent watch over the entire scene. To the rear of the main building, surrounded on three sides by forest, there was a man-made lake.

Carter watched the sinking sun turn the surface of the water fiery red as he continued to gaze out of the mullioned windows.

Behind him, three other men sat at the expansive dining table. They too were sipping drinks and relaxing after the superbly cooked meal they'd just enjoyed.

Gerald Collinson looked around at some of the paintings that adorned the walls, impressed both by their quality and also by how much they must be worth.

The other two men seated at the table seemed less interested in the contents of the room than in the words and actions of Collinson and Carter. It had been the same for the duration of the meal they had shared. The conversation had been terse, occasionally punctuated by the kind of strained laughter that accompanies conversations between strangers. Now they sat, as if waiting for one of the politicians to break what was rapidly becoming an uncomfortable silence.

The first of the men was dressed in an immaculate charcoal-grey suit and dazzlingly laundered white shirt. His companion, two or three years younger, wore the uniform of a Colonel in the British army. Both men were in their early fifties.

'I think it's safe to say that niceties have been observed, gentlemen,' Collinson finally offered. 'I suggest we discuss the reasons for our presence here.'

'Those reasons are obvious, I would have thought,' Colonel Charles Napier concluded, his voice coloured by a gentle Scottish accent. 'Although it seems we spent the duration of dinner avoiding them.'

'Not avoiding them, Colonel,' Collinson corrected him,

smiling. 'I think we were all too preoccupied with the delights we were presented with to waste time on anything other than self-indulgence.' He raised his glass. 'My compliments to the chef.' The Home Secretary continued to smile but, looking at the other men in the room, saw that he was the only one who found any levity in the situation.

'Everything is ready,' said Doctor Alex Morgan, brushing a speck of dust from the sleeve of his grey jacket.

Carter took one last look at the blood-drenched sunset then joined the three other men at the table.

'The action we are about to undertake *must* remain top secret,' he began.

'I don't think anyone connected with this project ever thought otherwise, Prime Minister,' Napier said. 'In secrecy lies security. It's a maxim I've always lived by and it's served me well.'

'Can you guarantee the success of this project?' Carter wanted to know. He looked first at Napier then at Morgan.

'There's no need to expect anything *other* than success,' Morgan said.

'Guarantee it,' the Prime Minister insisted.

'Nothing in life is certain, Prime Minister,' Napier interjected. 'But this project is as near to perfection as is humanly possible. And, even if something *does* go wrong—'

'It can't,' Carter hissed. 'Not *this* time.'

'What happened before was . . . unavoidable,' Morgan said. 'Unfortunate but unforeseen. All the problems have been rectified.'

'The fact is,' Napier added. 'Project Sentinel was deemed necessary at the time and the work on it has proved successful.'

'That work was for a defined purpose,' Morgan added. 'For a specific time. That time has come.'

Colonel Napier got to his feet and looked at Morgan who nodded.

'I feel it may be more useful if you actually *see* the extent of what we've done here, Prime Minister,' the doctor said. 'Perhaps any reservations you may still have will be put to rest by seeing exactly what our work has produced.' Morgan also rose, pushing his chair back under the table. He and Napier looked expectantly at the Prime Minister.

Carter finished his drink and hesitated.

'Is this really necessary?' he wanted to know.

'It may be beneficial,' Morgan smiled.

'If you'll come this way, Prime Minister,' Napier said, ushering Carter towards the set of doors at the far end of the dining room.

'It might be an idea if you met the head of the project first,' Morgan said. 'He might be better equipped than myself or Colonel Napier to explain some of the finer points should you have any questions.'

Morgan turned to the Scot who nodded and wandered towards the double doors. He disappeared through them and Carter heard some mumbled words from beyond. A moment later, Napier returned, accompanied by another man.

Carter scrutinised the newcomer with a degree of suspicion.

He was tall and well dressed with a swarthy complexion, jet-black hair and thick eyebrows that met above his curving, aquiline nose. That, combined with his piercing gaze, gave him the appearance of a large bird of prey.

He stood before Carter, attempted a smile then bowed slightly. It was a curiously archaic gesture.

'Prime Minister,' Morgan said, ushering the newcomer forward with a flourish. 'I'd like you to meet the man responsible for the birth of Project Sentinel. Doctor Kalid Sharafi.'

51

Franklin had found that he could walk, even without his crutches, with more ease than he'd expected. Admittedly, his wound gave him some pain if he applied too much pressure to his left leg for too long but, despite the initial discomfort, he was glad to be mobile again.

The act of dressing had also provoked some pain and, for a time, he'd been unsure whether or not he'd be able to pull his jeans on over his strapped and bandaged thigh. He managed it though. Gritting his teeth when the pain grew in intensity, anxious not to reveal any suffering to Crane who was still with him.

Franklin had swallowed two painkillers before leaving the room.

They would do for now.

He'd seen a number of uniformed police officers as he and Crane had made their way along the corridor to the lift. Once they had reached the ground floor of the hospital he'd seen more. Doubtless, he mused, some of the other people moving around the building were also police, camouflaged by their plain clothes.

All this for me.

He had walked as briskly as he could to the car that was

parked outside the A&E, declining Crane's offer of a helping hand when he almost stumbled once.

The drive across London had been completed in relative silence, Franklin content to gaze out of the windows at passers-by. He was especially drawn to those who walked together as couples.

More than once he saw young women who reminded him of Amy. Her features superimposed on the visages of those he looked at, laughing, smiling, talking.

He didn't know whether to feel envy or hatred for those women and the men with them. For the people who were experiencing something he knew *he* would never feel again.

'Are you sure you want to do this?' Crane asked as he guided the car into a disabled space outside the Hammersmith Hospital. He switched off the engine and looked at Franklin.

The younger man nodded and pushed open the passenger's side door, using the car to support himself.

Moving at a moderate pace, they walked through the reception area of the hospital, Crane flashing his ID at one or two uniformed men. He spoke to one of the men posted close to a lift but Franklin didn't listen to what he said.

It wasn't important.

They rode the lift to the basement, each standing at either side of the wide car.

Franklin stared at the floor, closing his eyes momentarily.

'Are you all right?' Crane wanted to know.

'Yeah,' Franklin said, his voice barely more than a whisper. 'I need to see her.'

The lift bumped to a stop and the doors slid open. Both men stepped out into another long corridor. It felt colder to Franklin in the subterranean depths and he shuddered involuntarily as he walked slowly alongside Crane towards the end of the corridor and the white double-doors there.

232

'Why did they bring her here?' Franklin asked, his voice echoing slightly.

'It was the nearest hospital to where it happened,' Crane told him.

Franklin nodded.

'We couldn't trace any immediate family,' Crane said, almost apologetically.

'Her parents are both dead. Her sister lives abroad. She works in Spain. I can give you her phone number.'

'That'll be taken care of,' the DI assured him, noticing that the younger man's words were becoming faint. More distant.

Franklin paused at the entrance to the morgue, then looked at Crane.

The policeman led the way through the white double-doors into the cold environment beyond them.

There were three bare metal slabs in the centre of the room. A trolley bearing surgical instruments stood in one corner, most of the instruments covered by a white cloth. There was an empty gurney close by. To the right there was a door with a bevelled glass window in it. To the left, a large bank of what looked like stainless steel lockers. Franklin knew that was where the bodies were kept. A storehouse for sightless eyes. Crane crossed to one and prepared to slide it open. He glanced at the younger man as if for confirmation. Franklin nodded.

The drawer moved silently as the DI pulled it. The entire thing, including its cargo, slid out on well-oiled runners.

Franklin looked down.

'I'll give you a few minutes,' Crane said, quietly, his foot-steps echoing away as he left the room.

For interminable seconds, Franklin felt as if his body was frozen, as if the chill in the air had seeped into every one of his pores and prevented him from making even the slightest movement. It felt as though someone had injected

233

him with liquid nitrogen. The only warmth was on his cheeks and it took him a second to realise that tears had begun to course down his face the second he'd set eyes upon Amy's body.

He reached out slowly and touched her cheek. The flesh was cold but soft beneath his fingertips. Franklin allowed his shaking hand to move across to her closed eyes, brushing her long eyelashes. Then he turned his attention to her hair, feeling the silken strands, brushing it back with the palm of his hand.

He wanted to speak, wanted to say something to her but no words would come and that only caused his tears to flow more freely.

Say something.

His lips moved soundlessly.

Talk to her.

He withdrew his hand from her hair and gently kissed his fingertips then he pressed those two digits to her lips.

He wanted to tell her he loved her. That he would *always* love her, but he still couldn't find the words. His gaze moved from her head to her face and then further down her body, but he always returned to her face. Finally, he bent forward and kissed her lightly on the forehead, his own eyes closed now. When he straightened up his vision was clouded by the tears that had become an unstoppable flow. His body was shaking as he looked down at her.

One of his tears dripped onto her face and rolled over her cheek like a droplet of liquid crystal. Franklin wiped it away with incredible care, like a man desperate not to wake a sleeping child. But Amy would *never* wake.

He didn't even notice the morgue doors open.

Crane took a step inside, looked across at Franklin then stepped back out of the room, guilty at his intrusion. He did not return but instead stood silently outside in the corridor, waiting.

Beside Amy's body, Franklin took one final look at her then slowly slid the drawer closed.

One part of him wanted to join her in there. To be swallowed by that blackness. To leave behind the suffering. Another part of him wanted only to ensure that the men who had put her there would soon join her.

He wiped the tears from his face with one hand, took a deep breath and walked towards the doors of the morgue.

In the corridor outside, Crane glanced at him. Franklin held his gaze and nodded slightly. An acknowledgement passed, unspoken, between them.

Franklin set off along the corridor towards the lift.

He didn't look back.

52

Doctor Kalid Sharafi met the gaze of the Prime Minister and nodded a little stiffly.

The two men shook hands. Carter was surprised by the strength of the tall man's grip and made to withdraw his hand, but only when Sharafi deigned to release the pressure could he pull away.

'It is a pleasure to meet you, Prime Minister,' Sharafi said, his English close to perfect. There was a trace of an accent but, for the most part, he spoke confidently in his second language.

'Likewise, Doctor Sharafi,' Carter said, running appraising eyes over the newcomer. 'I've heard a great deal about your work. It's good to finally meet the man behind it.'

'I cannot take full responsibility for this project,' Sharafi said, glancing at Doctor Morgan. 'I have been aided by some of your finest minds.'

'And protected by our best security,' Collinson smiled.

'Perhaps if we sat down,' Morgan offered. 'There is rather a lot of information concerning Project Sentinel that you need to be given, Prime Minister. As a colleague of mine used to say, some information is best absorbed with the knees bent.'

A ripple of laughter ran around the room. Even Sharafi grinned as he seated himself in a high-backed leather chair near the fireplace.

The other men also took seats before the large and highly polished grate.

Napier poured each of them a drink then seated himself on a Chesterfield next to Morgan.

'Your English is excellent, Doctor Sharafi,' Carter observed.

'I have lived in your country for more than twelve years now,' Sharafi said. 'I would hope so.'

Collinson laughed politely.

'As you know, your predecessor in office was responsible for bringing me to this country,' Sharafi offered.

'Doctor Sharafi was removed from Iraq by a team of SAS operatives towards the end of the first Gulf War,' Napier explained.

'You worked for Saddam Hussein's regime,' Carter stated.

'Everyone in Iraq worked for Saddam Hussein. If you didn't, you died. It was a simple equation. I felt that my work was sufficiently important to continue with. Saddam's politics did not matter to me. I am a scientist, not a statesman. Most of my work was carried out on criminals,' Sharafi said. 'Or Kurds.'

'Or whoever Saddam Hussein *gave* to you? Did you ever question where the men you experimented on had come from?' Carter enquired.

'As I explained, Prime Minister, if I had refused to continue with my work for Saddam, *I* would have been the one killed. You do not know what it is like to live under such a regime.'

Carter shrugged.

'But your work was intended to be used against the allied forces in the Gulf, wasn't it?' he continued.

'As I just told you, I continued with my work because

237

I had no choice. Don't try to tell me that every scientist working in *your* country has never faced a moral dilemma of some kind, Prime Minister.'

Carter eyed the Iraqi evenly.

'We became aware of Doctor Sharafi's work through MI5,' Colonel Napier explained. 'It seemed to make more sense to have him on *our* side. That's why he was removed and brought to this country.'

'The same way the Americans took Nazi scientists from Germany at the end of the Second World War,' Morgan added, as if the analogy would change Carter's mood. 'They were the same men who eventually ensured America's success in the Space Race.'

'The important thing is how Doctor Sharafi can help us *now*,' Collinson said. 'Not what he may have done for a madman like Saddam.'

A silence momentarily descended on the room.

Carter sipped at his own drink then looked at Sharafi who was nursing a glass of water in his hand.

'Tell me how Project Sentinel works,' Carter said flatly.

In the Hands of Unbelievers

'This is barbaric,' hissed Edward Carter, his eyes fixed on the figure of the man in the corner of the room. 'Is this what we've come to?'

'This man is an enemy of the State, Prime Minister,' Napier offered, closing the door behind the group who were now gathered around the figure. 'How would you suggest we treat him?'

Carter looked at the other men in the room, as if for support. All of them merely gazed at the man who was sitting on the floor, his head resting on his knees. Polished metal chains attached to the manacles around his wrists and ankles anchored him to a wall.

The room into which they had moved was small. It contained a pillow, a blanket and a toilet. It was lit by powerful fluorescent lights, one of which flickered in the ceiling, buzzing like an angry bluebottle.

The man seated on the floor was dressed in a stained cotton shirt, black trousers and worn trainers. He didn't look up when the door of his cell was opened. He kept his gaze aimed at the floor, as if reluctant to look at his captors.

'Who is he?' Carter wanted to know.

'He is a key,' Sharafi explained. 'The key to the success of Project Sentinel.'

'What's his name?' Carter insisted.

'Jabir Al-Badri,' Napier informed the Prime Minister. 'He was captured by one of our undercover teams in London two days ago and brought here. He has known links with terrorist organisations in the Middle East. He was personally responsible for a bomb in a Tel-Aviv market two years ago that killed thirty-seven people. Intelligence also indicates that he helped to plant explosives in a hospital in Germany less than six months ago. There's every reason to believe he belongs to one of the groups of suicide bombers currently present in London.'

'One of the groups this government has promised to eradicate,' Collinson interjected, a slight smile on his face.

Carter looked at his Home Secretary for a second then continued gazing at Al-Badri who had now raised his head slightly. There were several small cuts and bruises on his face.

'You said he was a key,' Carter said. 'What did you mean?'

'He's been in contact with other members of his group,' Sharafi explained. 'Physical contact.'

'He carries their odours, their scents,' Doctor Morgan said. 'Those scents can be picked up by the subjects treated with the drug in the same way a bloodhound would pick up the scent of a rabbit. But *our* subjects can detect their prey a thousand times more accurately.'

'There's been little need for interrogation,' Napier interjected. 'Al-Badri was picked up just off the Euston Road. If any of his accomplices are within a mile of where we found him then we'll find *them*.'

'How?' Carter asked.

'I told you that the drug enhanced olfactory and visual capabilities when given in the correct dosages,' Sharafi said. 'The scents that have already been detected on this man's clothes will be picked up by our subjects when they are within range. They will be able to isolate those smells. Home in on them.'

'But this man must have brushed against hundreds of people while he was in London,' Carter protested. 'How can you isolate the scents of the men we need to find? How can you be sure which odours actually belong to the targets?'

'Particle analysis of his clothing,' Sharafi explained. 'There were a number of traces of leather or a similar material on his own garments. Muslims would not wear leather. That eliminated a large number of the scents. Food particles also helped to narrow the range considerably. The soles of his feet were the most useful.' Sharafi smiled.

'How?' Carter enquired.

'When Muslims pray, they pray barefooted. The only human scents found on the skin of Al-Badri's feet must belong to the men he has been close to.'

'It's just a matter of time before they are pinpointed,' Morgan added.

'And eliminated,' Napier smiled.

'And what happens to him?' Carter asked, nodding in the direction of the man on the floor.

'He will be kept here,' Morgan explained, 'until the operation is successfully completed. After that he'll be disposed of.'

'Just like that?' the Prime Minister murmured.

'This man is a murderer, Prime Minister,' Napier protested. 'If he hadn't been caught he would have been responsible for more deaths. The deaths of innocent civilians in *this* country. He has served a purpose. Don't trouble yourself over his fate. He doesn't care about his own life, let alone the lives of others.'

Al-Badri suddenly looked up and hissed something, looking at each of the men in turn as he spoke.

Sharafi smiled.

'What did he say?' Carter wanted to know.

'He said that you and everyone like you will burn in the fires of Hell,' the Iraqi explained. 'That your women are whores and your children will drown in lakes of blood.'

'He has a gift for melodrama,' grinned Collinson.

Carter turned away from the man and looked at Napier.

'What's the next step?' he wanted to know.

'We strike, Prime Minister,' said the Scot. 'And before this man's companions take their chance. We move quickly and with precision. We remove the threat.'

Carter nodded.

'You've seen what kind of man we're up against,' Morgan sneered, looking contemptuously at Al-Badri. 'He has no regard for the lives of any man, woman or child who doesn't share his own fanatical views. And more like him are waiting to strike at the very heart of this country.'

'They must be destroyed,' Napier added.

'Everything is ready, Prime Minister,' Morgan said, brushing the sleeve of his jacket. 'The time has come.'

53

Franklin sat motionless in the passenger seat of the car, staring blankly out of the windscreen.

DI Crane reached for the ignition key to start the engine then stopped and looked once more at the younger man, wanting to speak but almost reluctant to break the silence.

It was Franklin who finally spoke.

'So now what?' he muttered, still gazing ahead. 'What's your answer, Crane?'

'About what?' the policeman answered.

'You *know* what,' snapped Franklin, turning to look at the DI. 'My part in all this. I'm offering you my help. Are you going to take it?'

'You're offering to get yourself killed.'

'What does that matter to you? You said yourself you'll make sure I go down. Everything I had in my life is gone. Do you think the prospect of doing time scares me? According to you, I'll probably be safer inside anyway. It'll be harder for these bastards, whoever they are, to get to me there.'

'If they want you they'll get you, no matter *where* you are. You've seen what they're capable of.'

'Yeah, I've seen it. I've seen my friends killed. I found

the body of my girlfriend with a bullet in her head. Put there by these cunts who want to kill *me*.' His breathing was becoming more ragged. 'Let them try. *Let* them find me. How many fucking times do I have to say it?'

'And when they do, what am *I* supposed to do? Sit back while you try and kill *them?* Tell my men to hold off until you've had your revenge?' Crane shook his head. 'You've seen too many westerns, Franklin. It doesn't work like that. Not in *real* life.'

Again silence descended as the two men continued to glare at each other.

'How else are you going to find them?' Franklin said, finally. 'How many more people are going to die before you even get *close* to them?'

'We'll get them.'

'Yeah, right,' Franklin sneered. 'You've done a great job so far, haven't you? Amy's lying in there dead because you couldn't fucking find them quick enough.' He hooked a thumb over his shoulder in the direction of the hospital. 'How many people were killed or injured this morning during that chase?' He ran a hand through his hair. 'Without me, you haven't got a hope in hell of finding them and you *know* it. Why not just drop the bullshit and cut me loose?'

'You can hardly walk.'

'So what? I don't *want* to run from them, Crane. Not any more. Where am I going to run to? *Who* am I going to run to?'

The policeman drew in a deep breath, aware that Franklin's eyes were still burning into him.

'At least *tell* me that you know what I'm saying makes sense,' Franklin persisted. 'Do *that* much.'

'I *know* you're right.'

'Hallelujah!'

'I've known that from the beginning, but it's not that easy.'

'Why? You don't give a fuck whether I live or die. The only thing that matters to you is getting these terrorists. If you use me, you can do that.'

'Maybe.'

'From where I'm sitting, you haven't got much choice.'

'Don't dictate to me, Franklin. I've told you before, you're not in a position to bargain. You've got nothing to bargain with.'

'Yes I have. I've got my life. I'm willing to put that on the line.'

'To help *me*?'

'No. For my own sake. For Amy's sake.'

Crane reached for his cigarettes and lit one.

'My superiors would never agree to it,' he said finally.

'So don't tell them,' Franklin offered.

'And what the hell do I say to them? I had a known criminal in my custody and he escaped?'

'Tell them what you like. You're going to be the one picking up the medals when you nail these bastards. What does it matter if I'm dead or alive when it happens?'

'Part of my job is to protect the public. Even scumbags like you.'

'I'm not asking for your protection. I don't want it. I'm asking for a chance. *One* chance. To get the men who killed Amy. And if it helps you then fine. If they kill me then that's OK too. At least I'll have tried.'

'Very noble,' chided Crane, blowing out a stream of smoke. He pushed the lighter into the cigarette pack and set it down on the dashboard.

'It doesn't matter who *we* are,' Franklin said, pointing at the policeman then tapping his own chest. 'It's not important that you're a copper and I'm on the other side. I'm talking to you as one *man* to another. Give me that chance, Crane. I've never had anything in my life worth dying for but I've got plenty left worth *killing* for. What do you say?'

245

The policeman started the engine.

'I've got to talk to some people,' he said, guiding the vehicle out into traffic.

A slight smile played at the corners of Franklin's mouth.

'You got a fag to spare?' he asked.

'Help yourself,' Crane told him, nodding towards the pack.

Franklin lit one and drew hard on it.

'It's traditional,' he said evenly.

'What?'

'The condemned man always gets a last cigarette, doesn't he?'

Crane drove on.

54

'What's wrong with his eyes?'

Edward Carter spoke slowly, his voice barely more than a whisper.

He was looking down at the face of a man in his mid-twenties. It was an unremarkable face in many ways, distinguished only by the fact that there were no whites to the eyes. The entire area around each pupil was scarlet. Both orbs resembled swollen blood blisters. Each looked on the point of bursting.

The man before him was naked except for a pair of cotton shorts. His body was heavily muscled. The arms and legs in particular looked massive. Almost disproportionate to the rest of the body although the pectoral region and the shoulders were also highly developed. The man's chest was rising and falling slowly and rhythmically.

Carter, when he could finally tear his gaze away from the immobile man's eyes, noticed that there were several small punctures between the toes of the left foot. He was about to comment on them when Sharafi stepped in to answer his initial question.

'The blood vessels in the eyes sometimes expand when the drug is given in higher doses,' the doctor explained.

'Occasionally, the vessels rupture. That is what has happened in this case. There is no cause for concern. The condition is temporary and does not affect the vision of the subject.'

Carter glanced again at the man's eyes and shuddered involuntarily.

Along with Sharafi, Gerald Collinson, Colonel Napier and Doctor Morgan, he was standing in a room barely nine feet square. It was windowless. Accessible only by a single door behind them. Sharafi had punched in a six-digit code to open the door when they'd first reached it.

The room contained nothing but a bed and the man who lay upon it. The floor was bare, covered in dazzlingly white tiles. Spotlights built into the ceiling provided the only illumination and each was pointed at the bed. It was like an island of light in a pool of shadow.

'How is the drug administered?' the Prime Minister wanted to know, his gaze travelling over the unmoving man before him.

'By injection,' Sharafi explained. 'Here.' He pointed out a small red-rimmed puncture between two of the man's toes.

'What *is* the drug?'

'Well, to keep things simple, Prime Minister,' Morgan interjected. 'It's a derivative of a number of steroids. Predominantly Methenolone and Oxymesterone. There are other chemicals used too, obviously.'

'Obviously,' Carter muttered, his eyes still fixed on the man lying before him. 'How does it work on the subject?'

'It increases the power of the senses,' Sharafi said, his voice filling with pride. 'As well as giving physical strength it also heightens auditory, olfactory, visual and tactile abilities. The subject is able to hear, smell, see and touch far more acutely.'

'Can you be more specific?' Collinson asked.

'The subject can hear a cough a thousand yards away,'

Sharafi continued, warming to his subject. 'Can pick up a chosen scent among a hundred others. Vision becomes enhanced to such a degree that the subject is able to pick out a target as surely as if his sight were laser guided. The fingers can detect minute changes in the temperature of another's skin. If this man was to touch you now, he would be able to tell you your temperature to within one degree. To relay your exact heart rate and blood pressure.'

'My God,' murmured the Home Secretary.

'God has very little to do with this, Mr Collinson,' Sharafi smiled.

'And the side effects?' Carter enquired. 'We know there *are* some.'

'With every scientific advance there are drawbacks,' Sharafi said. 'Those surrounding this project have been minimised as much as possible.'

'What happens to the subject after they're injected?' Carter wanted to know.

'I've already told you,' Sharafi said sharply.

'Not *everything*,' Carter corrected him. For the first time since entering the room, the Prime Minister looked directly at the Iraqi. 'I want to know time scales. How long does it take to work?'

'After the initial injections, the subject reaches maximum capability within ten or fifteen minutes,' Sharafi said.

'What do you mean by maximum capability?'

'As I've said, the increase of all their sensory powers.'

'And then?'

'They are ready. Ready to perform the task for which they were created.'

'You make them sound like robots.'

'They are much more than that, Prime Minister,' Sharafi smiled. 'More powerful, more deadly.'

'How are they controlled?'

'All the subjects respond to commands. They function as you and I would in the same situation. They obey their superiors.'

'At all times,' Colonel Napier added.

'I hope to God you're right,' Carter breathed.

'Each of the subjects is also given a chemical inhibitor,' said Doctor Morgan. 'It's called Theodrylinol. It modifies the effects of the drug. I suppose the best way to describe it is a kind of super-powerful beta blocker. It has to be administered every twelve hours.'

'And what if it isn't?' Carter demanded.

'Then the subjects become less responsive,' Sharafi interjected. 'They revert.'

'To what?' the Prime Minister asked, a look of concern clouding his features.

'They can become violent and are sometimes unable to function according to their set parameters.'

'I think what Doctor Sharafi is trying to say—' Collinson began.

'I know what he's saying!' snarled Carter, cutting his companion short. 'You're turning men into monsters and then hoping you can control them with drugs. Only sometimes that doesn't work.'

'I am doing what I was instructed to do by your government,' Sharafi protested. 'They brought me here. They paid for my work because they wanted the end result. If I have created monsters then I have done so on *your* authority, Prime Minister.'

The Iraqi glared at Carter who found that his mouth was dry. He was having difficulty swallowing.

'I think we're getting off the point,' Collinson offered, looking at each man in turn.

'If the subjects *should* revert,' Sharafi said evenly, 'they cannot survive at full power for more than forty-eight hours without treatment.'

'What damage could they do in forty-eight hours?' Carter asked.

'Once that time has passed they *may* slip into a coma, some may die. The drug itself remains in their bloodstream,' the Iraqi said. 'But it takes on the appearance of a virus. That virus then forms spores, becomes dormant.'

'It is effectively harmless at that stage,' Morgan added, attempting to inject a note of calm into the proceedings. 'But it won't come to that, Prime Minister.'

'You'd better be right,' Carter rasped.

He looked down one final time at the man lying on the bed, his gaze drawn inexorably to the blazing red eyes.

55

Franklin looked at Crane as the policeman drove. He guided the car through London's night-time traffic, seemingly oblivious to the other vehicles on the roads.

Every now and then Franklin would reach tentatively for his injured left leg and gently massage the area around the wound.

You're not running anywhere *are you, sunshine?*

Crane had a cigarette jammed between his lips but he hadn't bothered to light it. He was merely chewing distractedly on the filter.

'So, what's your answer?' Franklin said finally. 'Do you take my help or not?'

Crane slowed down as the car approached a line of stationary vehicles waiting at some traffic lights. Still he didn't look at Franklin.

'Your help,' the DI murmured, tapping gently on the steering wheel.

'Like I said before, I'm your best chance of getting these bastards.'

'Bait, you said. Bring them out into the open. As simple as that.'

The lights changed and Crane drove on.

'How many people would *have* to know that you'd let me go?' Franklin demanded.

'Only half the fucking Met,' Crane replied acidly. 'Like I keep telling you, you're a criminal. You're wanted on a number of charges. Chances are if I let you loose you'd be picked up by a beat copper before those terrorists even got a chance to get near you.'

'Not if everyone knew what was going on.'

'And if everyone knew and it went wrong then I'm the one who gets it in the neck. *I'll* be the one writing parking tickets for the rest of my career. I've already got MI5 and Special Branch crawling all over this case. This is getting too big for me, Franklin. It's going to be taken away from me.'

'But if this plan works you'll be a hero.'

At last Crane glanced at his younger passenger.

'Franklin, there aren't any heroes,' he said flatly. 'Not any more.' He chuckled. 'Is that what *you* want to be?'

'A lot of people are already dead because of these fucking terrorists. It just so happens that some of them were good friends of mine. This has got nothing to do with heroics, Crane.'

'*If* it works, *if* they come after you. If we catch them. There won't be any deals. No negotiation.

A faint smile appeared at the corners of Franklin's lips.

'So, what are you saying?' he asked.

'I'm saying there are no deals,' Crane snapped.

'Fair enough. Maybe we'll *both* get what we want.'

Crane swung the car around a corner and, for the first time, Franklin glanced out of the side window at the buildings they were passing. The journey seemed to have taken an eternity.

'So what now?' he asked, recognising where they were. 'Are you taking me back to my flat?'

'It's the first place they came looking before,' Crane reminded him.

'And how am I supposed to defend myself when they *do* come?'

'Don't push it, Franklin. We'll sort that out when we get there.'

'How does this work then?'

'You go back to your flat. Get on with what passes for your life. Just like nothing's happened. We'll be watching you twenty-four seven. I'll get phone taps authorised. There'll be at least three armed plain clothes men within twenty feet of you every time you step out of your door but you'll never see them.'

'How long have I got?' Franklin wanted to know.

'As long as it takes.'

Franklin sat back in his seat.

He glanced up at the roofs and high windows they passed. Was he being watched now? Were they being followed? Part of him hoped so.

Crane finally stopped the car outside the block of flats and switched off the engine.

'Let's do this as quickly as possible,' he said, hauling himself out of the vehicle.

Franklin clambered out onto the pavement, feeling stiffness rather than pain from his leg now. He moved around to the boot of the car where Crane was standing. The DI looked around furtively, then opened it.

As Franklin watched, the policeman pulled away the blanket inside to reveal several familiar-looking weapons beneath.

The younger man reached for the .459 and jammed it into his belt. He took the SPAS as well, wrapping it in the blanket to hide it from view. As he prepared to pick up the Ithaca Crane shot out a hand to stop him.

'That's enough,' the DI said.

He was about to close the boot when Franklin noticed something else that caught his interest.

Jammed to one side, next to a toolbox, was the black holdall Amy had used. Her clothes were still inside.

'Can I take that?' he asked.

Crane hesitated a moment then nodded and handed it to him.

'Tomorrow, just go about your business,' the DI offered, his tone softening slightly. 'You could take care of the funeral arrangements for—'

'I *know* what I could do,' Franklin snapped, cutting him short. He sucked in a deep breath.

'There'll be men here within ten minutes,' Crane told him. 'They'll set up surveillance. Everything. Just watch yourself.'

'I know how to play this game, Crane.'

'That's what your mates thought. Look how *they* ended up.'

The two men regarded each other evenly for a moment. Then Crane spoke again. 'Now get inside,' he said. 'And just remember, I'm *not* letting you go. You're not being released. You're a means to an end, that's all.'

Franklin walked to the main door of the block and prepared to let himself in. He was about to turn the key when Crane called to him once again.

'Franklin,' the DI said. 'If it's any consolation, I'm sorry about what happened to your girlfriend.'

The younger man nodded.

'You know what?' he intoned. 'It *isn't* any consolation.'

He turned his back, opened the door and stepped inside.

56

'You should have told them everything.' Doctor Kalid Sharafi remained at the window for a moment longer watching the EH-101 as it rose effortlessly into the air, rotors spinning. The sound of the helicopter's engines seemed to shake the brickwork of Ravenscote Manor as it ascended higher into the night sky. Only when the machine's landing lights had been swallowed by the gloom did the Iraqi turn to face the two other men in the room.

There was still a look of irritation on his face and it was reflected in his tone. 'Did you hear what I said?' Sharafi demanded, looking at Alex Morgan who merely nodded.

'If I'd told them everything, this project would have been shut down,' Morgan said. 'We'd have been out of work and you'd have been returned to Iraq.'

'What exactly did you want us to tell them, doctor?' Colonel Napier mused. The Scot was sipping at a tumbler of whisky as he stood before the large open fireplace, one hand behind his back.

'They heard what they wanted to hear,' Morgan continued. 'They were pleased with the progress of Project Sentinel. It will go ahead. The Government will continue to fund our research. And after the first . . .' he paused as if trying to find the right word, '. . . the first incursion, they will be even more impressed with our work. *Your* work, Sharafi.'

'And the virus?' Sharafi said.

'They know what those treated with the chemical will do,' Morgan insisted. 'You explained it yourself very eloquently. You told them that the chemical will mutate into a virus unless Theodrylinol is administered. You also told them that the virus enters a dormant stage.'

'They were not told what happens when that dormant stage is over,' Sharafi protested.

'And how would we have explained that? How would we have made them understand? The Government *wanted* this project,' Morgan snapped. 'They've been willing to pay a high price to finance it for nearly thirteen years now. They've also been more than happy to pay all of those working on it a more than adequate salary – you included. If there are consequences to be faced then so be it. We've done all that was asked of us. We have supplied them with what they wanted. The responsibility is no longer ours. It now lies with the men who *use* what we have created.'

Sharafi thought for a moment then nodded in acquiescence.

'What happened before was unfortunate but unavoidable,' Morgan continued. 'There are always sacrifices to be made in the pursuit of perfection. The men that died did so to further our knowledge.' He looked at Napier. 'Wouldn't you agree, Colonel?'

'Thirty-four lives is a small price to pay,' the officer agreed.

'None of them had families,' Morgan said. 'None of them will be missed. When they joined the army they might have expected to give their lives for their country at some point and they did, just not in the way they might have imagined. And, as far as anyone else is concerned, they were all killed or were missing in action anyway. Lost in Kuwait, Bosnia, Northern Ireland.' He looked at Sharafi. 'Or Iraq.'

'And what of the men who found their bodies in that van?' Sharafi wanted to know.

'Only one of them is still alive,' Napier revealed. 'And he won't be for much longer. My men will find him and eliminate him just as they did the others.'

'So you see, Doctor Sharafi, everything is in hand,' Morgan smiled.

'Except the virus,' the Iraqi said.

'Even if it *does* progress beyond the dormant stage, it will only become active if it's exposed to air for a prolonged period of time,' sighed Morgan. 'And then, only in temperatures well below freezing.'

'The chances of that happening are incredibly small,' Napier added.

'I agree,' Morgan said, his tone taking on a harder edge. 'But we've all been aware of that from the beginning. It's a chance we'll have to take.'

57

Matt Franklin stood motionless outside the entrance of the Funeral Directors, oblivious to the people who passed him. Seemingly unaware of the traffic that glided by, it was as if he was enveloped in a vacuum, separated from the rest of the world by a transparent capsule. It had been like that since he'd left the flat, but now, faced with his destination and the stark reality of it all, he froze.

He'd found that he could walk a lot more easily than he'd expected on his injured leg. The slow stroll from the flat to his present location had taken him a little under twenty minutes.

The wound had been a little stiff on waking but that had gradually worn off. The painkillers that the hospital had given him were useful but not essential. The wound was an inconvenience rather than a hindrance.

He'd re-dressed it himself that morning before pulling on his jeans then he'd padded comfortably around the flat, eating a slice of toast and drinking coffee. The radio had been on but he'd hardly heard it.

As he'd bathed then shaved, his ears had been alert for any sounds of movement outside the door of the flat. When he'd been in the sitting room, he'd been careful to stay away from the windows. He was aware of what Crane had said about his would-be killers not needing to get close if they didn't want to. The thought didn't worry him unduly though. All that remained in his mind was a barely suppressed fury – a burning desire to confront one of the assassins.

To watch one of them die.

He'd been sitting on the bed sliding hollow-tip rounds into the magazine of the .459 when the phone rang. Franklin had answered it immediately and discovered that it was Crane at the other end.

The DI had wanted to check that he was still breathing. The night had been uneventful, Franklin had told him. He'd had trouble sleeping anyway so he'd been awake for most of it. If anyone had tried to get in they'd have walked straight into a face full of 9mm slugs or buckshot.

Crane had assured him that everything was in place. The surveillance and the plain clothes men.

Franklin had hurried the policeman off the line then returned to his task.

As he'd emerged from the flat, the automatic now tucked into its shoulder holster, he'd paused, wondering where the designated police officers were watching him from (*the building across the street perhaps, as they had before?*) and which of them were moving secretly among the pedestrians that flowed back and forth along Clerkenwell Road.

He had also wondered, for fleeting seconds, who *else* might be surveying his movements.

Now, as he stood before the main door of the Funeral Directors, nothing else seemed to matter. He took a step towards the door, his eyes fixed on the gold letters that spelled out the proprietor's name. Franklin swallowed hard, finding that his breathing was becoming more shallow. His mouth was dry. He wanted to turn and walk away but he knew he couldn't. He knew he *mustn't*.

Get a grip.

A vision of Amy flashed briefly into his mind.

He could feel his heart thudding against his ribs, the blood roaring in his ears.

Do it.

It took a monumental effort of will but he finally turned the handle and walked in. Franklin closed the door behind him and the sounds of the traffic seemed to disappear immediately. The silence within the building was over-whelming but somehow welcoming. Then, as he stood there, waiting for his heart to slow down a little, he realised that he was not standing in silence. There was music coming from somewhere. Not the kind of funereal tones he had expected but some kind of pastoral melody. Like muzak in a lift bound for Heaven.

He looked around him. To his right, there was a desk with a high-backed swivel chair behind it and two dark blue upholstered seats before it. To his left there was another and this one also had two wooden chairs in front of it. It also had several large leather bound books on top of it. Straight ahead was another door with a long, black velvet curtain hanging across it. The place smelled of fresh polish and new carpet.

From the central door a tall man dressed in a navy blue suit emerged. Despite his receding hairline, he was, Franklin guessed, in his late twenties. He smiled the kind of prac-tised smile he must have perfected over his years in the business and nodded his head slightly in greeting. It was a gesture that reminded Franklin almost of a bow.

'Good morning, sir,' the man said, still smiling. 'How can I be of help to you?'

Franklin coughed to clear his throat, still taken aback by the undertaker's appearance and demeanour.

What were you expecting? A black top hat and a crow sitting on his shoulder?

261

'I need to sort out . . . I mean, arrange, a funeral,' Franklin said, his voice cracking slightly.

There, you've said it.

'If you'd like to have a seat, sir,' the undertaker said, motioning to one of the blue upholstered seats. 'I'll just take some details from you.'

'I've never done anything like this before,' Franklin told him. 'I'm not sure what I've got to do.'

'That's what *we're* here for, sir.'

There was a warmth in the undertaker's tone that astonished Franklin. He knew the geezer must have done this hundreds of times before and yet he didn't sound as if he was running through a script.

Franklin looked at him and nodded gratefully, watching as he took a printed form from a drawer in the desk and smoothed it out before him.

'First things first,' the undertaker continued, taking a pen from his inside pocket. 'I'll need the name of the deceased.'

Franklin paused, his gaze dropping to the undertaker's hand, poised over the form.

'Amy,' he said finally. 'Amy Holden.'

58

Franklin had no idea how long he'd been sitting in the undertakers. It felt like hours. He glanced at his watch and realised that it had actually been less than twenty minutes.

The besuited man wrote some final details on the form and looked at him. 'That's everything taken care of,' he said quietly. The note of caring efficiency was still in his voice. 'We'll notify you when the time comes. You can visit Miss Holden in the Chapel of Rest if you'd like to.'

'Thanks,' Franklin breathed. 'I did that when my old man died. I can't remember much about it – I was only six.' He swallowed. 'My mum took me to see him. She said I should say goodbye to him.' He sighed. 'I didn't expect to be doing it with . . . with Amy.'

'You don't have to visit if you don't want to, Mr Franklin. It's just that many people find it a great comfort.'

'I'd like to fucking know how,' he said, holding a hand up by way of apology. 'Sorry.'

'I've heard worse,' the undertaker smiled.

'Yeah, I bet you have.'

'Seen worse too.'

'How do you mean?'

'Well, all of the people who come in here are distraught,

understandably. They've lost someone close to them so they're bound to be.'

'How do you put up with it, day in, day out? Seeing people so . . .' He couldn't find the words.

'Devastated?' offered the undertaker. 'I don't think you ever get used to it but you learn to switch off. I'm sorry if that sounds harsh.'

Franklin shook his head.

'You have to remember that you're there for the people who come to you for help,' the undertaker continued. 'People like you. I'm here to make sure that, when the time comes, you don't suffer any more pain than is necessary.'

'Just business, eh?'

'That's the way you *have* to approach it, Mr Franklin. It's the *only* way.'

'And you never find it hard?'

'The children are the worst. Trying to help parents pick out a coffin for their dead two-year-old isn't the *nicest* way to pass the time but it has to be done.'

Franklin nodded almost imperceptibly.

'We handle the burials for this council too,' the undertaker continued. 'You know, people who've been living alone, who've got no family. We take care of their burial.'

'Paupers' burials, you mean? Tramps. People like that?'

'Just people who are alone. Old people who might have lived alone for the last ten years of their lives. Some who've lived by themselves *all* of their lives. When you carry a coffin into a church where the only person present is the vicar, where there are no relatives or friends to say a last goodbye to the deceased, it makes you think.'

'Like the man said, when we die, we die alone.'

'Perhaps,' the undertaker shrugged.

The two men sat in silence for a moment then Franklin got to his feet. He extended his hand which the undertaker shook.

'Thanks,' Franklin said quietly. 'So, you'll let me know . . .' He allowed the sentence to trail off.

'I'll give you a call when things are in place,' the undertaker told him, walking with him to the door.

'There's just one thing,' Franklin said, reaching into his jacket pocket. 'I'd like this played at the funeral.' He held the audio cassette before him. 'It's Amy.' He cleared his throat. 'Some of her songs.'

'You'll have to speak to the vicar at the church but it shouldn't be a problem,' the undertaker assured him.

Franklin hesitated and opened his mouth as if to say something else, but no words would come. He merely nodded and opened the door.

For a moment he stood in the doorway then he slipped the cassette back into his pocket and stepped out onto the pavement among the other people passing back and forth.

There was a bar just down the road. Franklin set off towards it. He needed a drink.

Several pairs of eyes watched him cross the street.

59

'And the Commissioner agreed to it?'

Crane heard the words but, for a moment, he seemed more concerned with gazing out of his office window. The bright sunlight that bathed the capital reflected back off windows and other polished surfaces.

'What?' he said finally, his musings interrupted. He turned to face DS Kingston, his expression vague.

'Letting Franklin go,' Kingston continued. 'The Commissioner said it was all right?'

'I didn't let him go, Del,' Crane sighed. 'He's the cheese in a fucking mousetrap.'

'But the boss went for the idea?'

'He said he saw the reasoning behind it. I took that as a yes. He also reminded me that if Franklin did a runner *I'd* be hung out to dry. Like I didn't know that.' He lit a cigarette. 'Franklin's not going anywhere. I told the Commissioner that. He doesn't *want* to run.'

'*I* would if I was in his position.'

Crane shrugged.

'Maybe you would,' he murmured. 'Let's hope we never have to know what he's feeling. They killed his friends and his girlfriend. You can't blame him for wanting revenge.'

'I wonder why they haven't tried to kill Nicholson's wife? Or had a go at Maguire's family?'

'Just a matter of time, probably. They're still under twenty-four-hour guard, aren't they?'

Kingston nodded.

'Good,' Crane said. 'Let's hope it helps.'

'You don't sound too sure, guv.'

'You've seen how these bastards operate, Del. If they want someone bad enough, they'll get them, no matter how many men we've got watching. That goes for Franklin too.'

'Then why not just bring him in? Hold him in protective custody?'

'Because I'm not sure even *that'd* keep him alive if he is the next target. If he's on the streets it minimises the risk to our men as well. If Franklin gets his head blown off then we can at least say we tried.'

'How many innocent people are at risk if the information about suicide bombers is true?'

Crane shrugged.

'How many were killed or injured in that car chase Franklin was involved in?' he said. 'What happens to the suicide bombers is down to MI5, Special Branch, SO11 or the Counter Terrorist Unit now. It's their job to stop them. It's up to *them* to safeguard civilians. If we can help by using Franklin as bait then that's fine but our concern is *him* and this case.'

Crane sat down behind his desk and ran weary eyes over the paperwork there.

'How are Special Branch doing on the bodies that were found in the Securicor van?' he said finally.

'Still nothing.'

'What about the van itself? Anyone come up with where it was coming *from* or heading *for*?'

'No. Still working on it.'

267

Crane sifted through printed sheets, memos, reports and bulletins. He looked at each with the same vacant expression.

'Have ballistics tracked down the source of the bullets that killed Franklin's firm?' the DI asked.

Kingston shook his head.

'What about the men in the car that tried to kill Franklin? The ones that got burned?'

'Forensics said the bodies were too badly charred to get any positive ID. The car they were in hadn't been reported stolen. Neither had the motorbike that the first guy was riding.'

'*That* wasn't damaged. Were there any prints taken from it?'

'No. We checked the number plate. It was registered under a false name. There's no path back to who the rider might have been.'

'This is too well organised. I mean, it's *perfect*. There's got to be something we're missing. There's got to be.' He looked at the mass of paperwork before him once again. 'What about descriptions of the men in the car? There were plenty of people in the streets during that chase. *Somebody* must have been able to remember *something*.'

'A hundred and fifty-three witnesses have been interviewed. We got enough for a couple of identikits but not enough to really help.'

Crane sat back in his chair.

'Jesus Christ,' he gasped, exasperatedly. 'What *have* we got?'

'All departments are working on it round the clock but there's just nothing to go on. No leads. No fingerprints. Nothing.'

Crane nodded, wearily.

'All right,' he sighed. 'I know this isn't like anything we've ever dealt with before but I can't believe we've got *nothing*.'

'Nothing except Franklin.'

'This whole investigation hinges on him. We're relying on a criminal, a bloke who doesn't care whether he lives or dies to give us a leg up. And he's out on the streets like a rabbit in a shooting gallery.'

'*You* put him there, guv.'

Crane nodded. 'I know I did,' he said quietly. 'I just hope to Christ I did the right thing.'

The two men sat in silence for a moment then Crane leaned forward slightly.

'How's Richardson doing with that virus that was found in the bodies of the men we pulled out of the van?' he said.

'He's still working on it. He said he was waiting for reports from toxicology.'

Crane reached for the phone on his desk, hefting the receiver before him like a club.

'Let's find out if he's got them yet. Maybe *he'll* have something to help us.'

'Like what?'

'He said he'd never seen anything like it, didn't he? If it didn't just evolve on its own then it might have been manufactured artificially.'

'Manufactured? You make it sound like furniture.'

'If that virus was man-made then Richardson might be able to point us in the direction of who made it. Those terrorists got it from somewhere. Someone showed them how to use it. We've been looking for things, Del, but we might have been looking in the wrong places. Let's see what Richardson's got to say.'

He stabbed the required digits on the keypad and waited.

60

There were two men following him.

He'd spotted the first as he entered the bar. He was trailing along on the other side of the road about twenty yards behind Franklin. The second had come from the opposite direction and made his way in a moment later.

Franklin had clocked them both. One had bought a drink and gone to sit in a corner with a battered copy of the *Star*. The other was seated close to the dining area, next to three men in their mid-twenties all dressed in suits who were talking loudly and laughing raucously.

Out on an expense account lunch, Franklin thought, watching them for a moment as he sipped at his pint.

Noisy twats.

Franklin sat at the bar, with a clear view of the building's main entrance. He could see everyone who entered from his perch on the bar stool.

If the time came, he'd be ready.

It was noisy inside. Conversations were conducted at the loudest volume, amplified by the high ceiling and bare wood floor of the bar. It was frequented by businessmen mainly, like the three he'd been looking at.

He downed what was left in his glass and ordered another

drink from the barman. When it arrived he drank some then stared into the depths of the glass. As he did so, the sounds around him seemed to fade slightly. He was enveloped by his own thoughts. Of the undertakers. Of Amy. Of the impending funeral.

He looked up and glanced at the two men who'd been following him, studying each in turn.

They were both doing their best not to look at him, continuing with the charade.

Franklin slipped his hand inside his jacket and gently brushed the butt of the .459.

The man with the paper was in his late twenties. He wore tracksuit bottoms and a sweatshirt. The other one was slightly older, more heavily set. He was dressed in a pair of black jeans and a denim jacket. Franklin noticed that he kept looking at his watch.

Waiting for something?

Franklin sipped a little more of his drink then raised a hand to catch the barman's eye.

'Keep your eye on that, will you?' he said, nodding towards his drink. 'Toilets are through there, aren't they?' He indicated a dark wood door at the far side of the bar.

The barman nodded.

Franklin slid off the bar stool and made his way unhurriedly towards the toilets, aware that both the men tailing him had seen him move.

The one with the paper chanced the merest glance as Franklin passed.

At the bar, a man was struggling with three tall glasses, attempting to ferry them back to a table nearby where another man and a young woman sat. Just as Franklin reached him, the man dropped one of the glasses which promptly shattered on the floor.

All eyes turned towards the mishap. Franklin stepped

round the pool of spilled drink and continued on towards the toilet door.

The stockier man looked up, his attention drawn momentarily towards the accident. The other glanced over the top of his paper in time to see Franklin disappear through the door marked TOILETS. He waited a moment, glanced across at his companion then nodded.

The heavier set man got to his feet and moved swiftly across the bar towards the door through which Franklin had gone. He paused outside for a second then pushed it and walked through.

Franklin was standing at one of the urinals when the man entered the toilet.

He glanced around, saw that only he and Franklin were inside then he selected the urinal furthest away, close to the door.

For a quick getaway?

As Franklin stood there he was aware that the man to his left was at great pains to stare straight ahead at the tiled wall.

The sound coming from the bar was muffled and indistinct. When Franklin spoke, his voice echoed slightly within the room.

'You're one of Crane's boys, aren't you?' he said, without looking at the man.

Silence.

'I'm talking to you,' Franklin continued as he zipped up his jeans then turned away towards the washbasins behind him.

'Do I *know* you?' the man replied, his voice catching.

'Yeah,' Franklin smiled. 'You know who I am. You've been following me all morning.'

'I don't know what the fuck you're on about.'

'Yeah, you do. I've probably been in this business longer than *you* have. Do you think I've never seen tails working

272

before? Here's a tip for you. When I came in here, you shouldn't have come with me. You should have stayed outside and waited until I came out. Just like your mate out there with the newspaper. The best tails keep their distance. Remember that.'

'You must have got me confused with somebody else, mate. I don't know what you mean.'

'I'm not your mate and you know *exactly* what I mean.'

Franklin began drying his hands on the roller-towel.

'How long you been doing this?' he continued. 'Working undercover?'

The man didn't answer, he merely crossed to the sink and began washing his own hands.

'Did Crane tell you to stay close to me?' Franklin wanted to know.

The man shrugged.

'What are you carrying?' Franklin enquired. 'Nine mil? Something bigger? You're going to need it if things kick off.' Franklin smiled. 'Listen,' he said. 'I'm going to finish my drink and then I've got some business to sort out.'

The man glanced at him then began drying his hands, his expression darkening.

Franklin waited a moment then pushed open the door and walked out. He headed back into the bar and returned to his seat where he murmured something to the barman then settled himself.

In the corner, the man holding the battered copy of the *Star* shot him a furtive glance.

Franklin raised his glass in salute, nodded to the man then took a sip and turned away again.

61

'How many are being released?'

Edward Carter sat forward at his desk, his gaze flicking constantly between the man who sat in front of him and the door of his office. His tone was strained, his voice low and conspiratorial.

Opposite him, Gerald Collinson watched the Prime Minister dispassionately. He seemed unperturbed by the ever-deepening furrows that scarred Carter's forehead as he spoke, the phone held hard against his ear.

'How many?' Carter repeated.

The voice at the other end of the line answered his question.

'When?'

Carter drew in a deep breath.

'And Napier will be in command?' he insisted, digesting the answers as they were given to him. 'I want assurances that Colonel Napier will be handling the operation personally.'

From the other end of the line those assurances were duly given.

'Everything will be dealt with at this end as we agreed,' Carter told the voice. 'The media will be controlled.'

Collinson nodded in affirmation.

'I want my aides kept informed of the situation,' the Prime Minister continued. 'Do you understand?'

The person at the other end did.

Carter glanced at his watch.

At the other end of the line, the voice told him not to be concerned.

'Every hour,' he said sharply then he put the phone down.

'There's no going back now,' he breathed, looking past Collinson at the Lalique vase that stood on the mantelpiece above the ornate fireplace on the far side of the room. It was as if he wanted to look anywhere other than at his Home Secretary.

'What did Morgan say?' Collinson wanted to know.

'They're releasing twelve of them,' Carter said quietly. 'At six o'clock tonight. They should be on the ground, in London, by seven. Napier's taking charge personally. I insisted.'

Collinson nodded.

'How long does Morgan expect it to take?' he wanted to know.

'If what we were told, and shown, at Ravenscote Manor is correct, if they really *do* operate with such precision, then it should all be over by eight-thirty tonight.'

'And then?'

'Then it's *your* turn, Gerald. Make sure the media are fed the correct information. I want to be able to appear on the *Ten O'clock News* and inform the country that a crushing blow has been struck against terrorists. I want the people to be thankful that they can trust their government in matters of national security.'

'I wonder how the country would feel if they knew that one of the men responsible for their protection was responsible for taking the lives of their own troops?' Collinson mused.

'You mean Sharafi?' Carter said.

'Who else would I mean?'

'He's not the only one who's been involved in this.'

'He's the only one who was named as an enemy of this country during the first Gulf War.'

'His expertise has been invaluable,' Carter said. 'Or so everyone keeps telling me.'

'There's considerable public capital to be gained from this exercise, Edward,' the Home Secretary mused.

'I'm well aware of that. That's why I want everything finalised before nine o'clock tonight. I want every angle covered.'

'Including your own ignorance of everything that has gone on?' Collinson chided.

'I have had no knowledge of this project,' Carter smiled. 'I've told you that before.'

'You mean you have no knowledge of it, if it goes wrong,' Collinson said.

'Selective knowledge,' Carter corrected him. 'As far as the media are concerned, a unit of highly trained men will have wiped out the biggest single threat to this country's national security for twenty years. And that unit will have been funded by this Government. The men who perfected and trained that unit will have been *supported* by this Government. That in itself should be enough for another term in office. The public tend to look kindly on governments that allow them to sleep safely in their beds at night.'

Carter returned to staring beyond the Home Secretary. 'And what do you intend to say about these . . . highly trained men?'

'Obviously the situation is Top Secret so information will be released on a "need to know" basis.'

'Yes. God forbid anyone should ever find out the truth,' Carter chuckled.

'What *is* the truth, Edward?' snapped Collinson. 'What

276

do you *want* the public to know? You've always said yourself that certain measures have to be taken when dealing with the electorate. One of those measures is to not tell them too much. They don't care about details. In this situation, all they care about is their safety and the safety of their loved ones. This Government has given the people of this country, the people who elected it, security. How that security is maintained isn't important to the average voter, Edward. All that they're going to remember is that *you* were the Prime Minister who guaranteed that security they so badly need. *That's* what they'll remember when the next election comes around.'

Carter regarded his colleague evenly for a moment.

'By this time tomorrow, Edward,' Collinson continued, his smile returning. 'You'll be a hero – the man who saved his country from suicide bombers by his determination to act against them. It's a hell of a headline.'

'And if it goes wrong,' Carter reminded him, 'I knew nothing. Just remember that if you want to keep your job.'

62

As the train pulled into Farringdon station, Franklin didn't even bother to glance up and down the platform for his tails. He knew that the policemen were somewhere nearby, although the paucity of other travellers made it almost impossible for them to blend in unseen.

Franklin stepped onto the train and seated himself opposite a young woman reading a copy of *Cosmopolitan*.

He wondered if anyone other than the law were watching him. Tailing him. If they were, he fancied they were making a better job of it.

Whether or not the close proximity of the policemen was meant to make him feel secure he had no idea. Perhaps that had been Crane's plan, despite his assurances that Franklin would never know the tails were there. He was more inclined to think that the men entrusted with the job of watching him were simply not up to it.

The train pulled away and Franklin reached for a discarded newspaper on the seat beside him. He glanced at the sports pages then turned to the front and read the headlines. He kept the paper in front of his face, eyes scanning the words but not taking them in.

If someone takes a shot at you, newspaper's not going stop a bullet, is it?

He dropped the paper back onto the seat next to him and glanced across at the young woman. She was still immersed in her magazine. Franklin ran appraising eyes over her and she, as if aware of his probing gaze, looked up.

Could she be the one? Nobody had said it had to be a man who would come looking for him. She might well have been the one who'd put a bullet in Amy's skull.

Franklin continued to look at the young woman who did her best to avoid eye contact with him and seemed relieved when the train reached the next station and she was able to step off.

Others joined and Franklin regarded each one quickly.

It might be any one of them.

He reached inside his jacket and gently touched the butt of the automatic. If he had to pull it he would. This was close enough. The width or the length of an underground train carriage was fine by him. He'd still be able to see the bastard's face. That was all he asked.

The train was filling up. At the next stop even more people got on. One man was carrying a large shopping bag.

Big enough to hold a gun?

Franklin smiled to himself. A fucking shoebox was big enough to hold a weapon. Another thought struck him too. Just because Amy and the others had been killed by bullets didn't mean that was to be *his* fate too, did it? In skilled hands anything from a knife to a garrotte was effective. He thought about that Russian guy in the seventies (what the fuck was his name? Marklev? Marov?) who'd been stabbed with the tip of an umbrella. Poisoned. (Georgi Markov, that was it).

It was as easy as that.

279

Of course, if Crane was right, and those hunting him didn't give a fuck whether they lived or died then they might just decide to take him, themselves and any other poor sod who happened to be around, with them. Perhaps that shopping bag he was looking at was full of explosives.

Perhaps.

The train rumbled into Liverpool Street and Franklin swung himself to his feet, moving past the man carrying the large shopping bag. The doors slid open and Franklin moved swiftly among the crowd, following the signs that would take him towards the Central line.

It was crowded in the subterranean passageways but Franklin moved with relative ease, dodging between and around people moving more slowly than himself. If anyone was following him they'd have to keep up the same pace. And if they did *that*, they'd make themselves visible.

He took some stairs two at a time, glancing behind him before ducking through the archway to his left.

A man in his early thirties was at the top of the steps, his gaze fixed ahead. On Franklin. He hurried after him, bumping into two people in his haste.

The Central line platform was relatively quiet. Franklin walked towards the far end of it, glancing up at the electronic announcement board as he did. NEXT TRAIN APPROACHING flashed orange above him.

He heard the train roaring out of the tunnel as he looked back along the platform. No one was looking in his direction. He remained where he was, back pressed to the wall, watching as the train slowed down and the doors slid open. Still he waited, watching as passengers spilled off. A blur of faces moved before him and past him. The platform was relatively empty again apart from half a dozen people, also waiting.

Franklin looked down the platform then took a step towards the train. He stood still outside the open doors.

There was a hydraulic hiss. They'd be closing any second. The train would be moving off.

He stepped aboard.

Thirty yards away, so did the young man in his early thirties.

Copper or killer?

Franklin waited a second then stepped backwards onto the platform.

There was another loud hiss.

The young man, trying not to look in Franklin's direction, did the same as his quarry.

Got you.

The doors were about to close. Franklin moved forward and stuck his hands between them, somehow managing to slide into the carriage.

Further down the platform the young man tried the same manoeuvre but couldn't manage it. Couldn't squeeze himself through the dwindling gap.

Franklin smiled and sat down as the train pulled out of the station. He was sure there were others still tailing him; probably at least one was on the train even now. He'd be in touch with his colleagues by two-way radio. They'd know that he was on the Central line now. *How* long he'd be on it they *wouldn't* know, nor would they be aware of his next stop. Not yet.

And that was what Franklin wanted. He didn't need the police anywhere near him once he got to his final destination.

63

'What do you mean, you've lost him?' roared Detective Inspector Crane. He gripped the mobile so hard his knuckles turned white.

Inside the laboratory, DS Kingston and Doctor Howard Richardson looked at Crane and saw the fury on his face. Each time he spoke, his angry words tore through the relative silence like an axe through a plywood door.

'Where was he last spotted?' Crane continued, the veins at his temple throbbing furiously. 'There's supposed to be three men on him at all times, how the hell could you lose him?'

The DI listened to the voice on the other end of the phone for a moment, trying to regain his composure.

'All right, listen,' he said finally. 'If he's still on the train I want units waiting at every station as far as Leytonstone. Got it? Chances are, he's already got off or he's changed lines. Get cover to all the stations where he *could* change. I want surveillance set up on each of those stations. Find him. And do it before someone *else* does.' He stabbed the Call End button. 'Jesus Christ,' the policeman breathed, turning to face his two companions. 'Franklin's slipped the leash. He's lost his tails.'

'How?' Kingston wanted to know.

'Because he's quicker than *them*,' Crane snapped, tapping his temple. 'Because he's had to do it before. How the hell do *I* know?'

'But why, guv? He knows that he's in more danger *without* our guys covering him,' Kingston said.

'That's what he wants. He *wants* to be on his own. He thinks he's on some kind of fucking mission to kill the people who murdered his girlfriend and wiped out his firm.'

In the silence, the only sound was the plink of a dripping tap. Water hit the stainless steel sink and slid away.

'Sorry, Howard,' said Crane finally, glancing at the pathologist.

'That's all right,' Richardson told him. 'I can understand your concern.'

'Let's get back to what you were saying.'

Richardson motioned the DI back to the microscope that was set up before them on a stainless steel worktop. Beside it were several Petri dishes, some slides and a pipette.

'This microscope is a high power, or "sixth" objective,' Richardson explained. 'It has a final magnification of roughly two to four hundred times. The electron microscope that I also used and the ones used by the toxicology department I sent some samples out to for analysis can go as high as fifteen hundred times magnification.'

'Meaning?'

'More detail. More information.'

'So, do you know what this virus is or not?'

'Just have a look first and then I'll explain.'

Crane sighed.

'Bear with me,' Richardson told him, gesturing towards the implement. 'The blood sample on the left is a normal one,' the pathologist said, watching as Crane pressed his face to the twin eyepieces and peered at the slide beneath.

283

'The one on the right was taken from one of the men found in that Securicor van.'

'What am I looking at?' Crane wanted to know.

'You can see the virus in the sample on the right. It shows up as small dark blotches.'

'Yeah, I can see it.'

'Now look at *this* sample,' Richardson said, pushing another slide beneath the powerful lenses of the microscope. This one, however, had another slide tightly compressed upon it.

'It looks the same,' said Crane. 'I can still see the virus but that's about it.'

'Watch what happens when it's exposed to air,' Richardson said, and, using tweezers, he gripped the uppermost slide and raised it slightly.

'Jesus,' Crane murmured. 'It's moving.'

'It's growing, evolving,' smiled Richardson, dropping the slide back into position. 'Those spores were treated with liquid nitrogen prior to examination, to lower the temperature surrounding them.'

Through the eyepieces, Crane could see that the convulsive movements of the virus cells had ceased again.

'When it's exposed to air of a certain temperature, the cells multiply at a hugely increased rate. I said that they were in a dormant stage. Well, they are, but only until they come into contact with cold air. Once they do it activates them.'

'And then what?'

'The report from the toxicology unit I sent the samples to said that they had conducted their tests in a sealed environment and in various climactic conditions. They allowed the virus to multiply. Within an hour of first exposure to air colder than zero degrees Celsius it became transmittable. It was able to move from one subject to another.'

'How?'

'It's airborne. Like flu. The common cold. Once it gets

into the air it has the potential to spread like wildfire. Anyone who came into contact with it would be infected. It could be inhaled. It could even enter the body through a large cut or other break in the skin.'

'With what results?'

'We still don't know. The toxicology unit tried it on rats but there was very little metabolic change in the subjects. That would seem to indicate that it was never tested on animals. Which would make sense if it was created for use as a chemical weapon. It was only ever *tested* on humans because it was only ever intended for *use* on humans.'

Crane didn't speak but the colour drained slowly from his face.

'But, as I keep telling you, I can only guess what it would do to a *living* human being,' Richardson continued.

'So, guess. Tell me what you *think* would happen.'

Richardson shrugged. 'I'd say that the spores would form rapidly in the bloodstream of anyone infected. The same way they did in the circulatory systems of the men we found in the van. This would cause fatal blockages of veins and arteries. Aneurysms would form, blood clots too. The lungs would be starved of oxygen, so would the brain. The heart would stop pumping because it'd be clogged with spores. The blood supply would literally dry up.'

'And there'd be no way of treating it?'

'Without sufficient knowledge of a disease it's difficult finding a cure. We know so little about this virus that it could take years before anything like an antidote was perfected.'

'How long would it take for symptoms to show?'

'Well, again, it's impossible to say because I don't have enough data, but I did some calculations based on the speed of the metamorphosis from spore to active cells.'

Crane merely continued to gaze at Richardson who cleared his throat and continued, his mouth dry.

285

'Under the right climactic conditions, if a thimble full of blood containing that virus was released into the air, it could infect the whole of London in less than a week.'

64

As the train pulled out of Upton Park station, Franklin glanced at his watch. He walked to the wooden bench nearest him on the platform and sat down, waiting until the other six or seven passengers who had alighted at the same time had disappeared through the exit.

Franklin waited another two minutes before he finally got to his feet and made for the long flight of steps that led to street level. The pain in his left leg had subsided into a dull ache that felt more like a pulled muscle than the aftermath of an encounter with a lump of flying metal. He walked briskly, able to ignore the discomfort.

At the station exit Franklin paused and lit a cigarette before turning right into Green Street. He glanced around him, occasionally peering into the cars that drove past him.

Was someone following?

There was a profusion of market stalls set up on the roadside and across the pavement. Franklin moved between them, easing his way up and down the aisles until he emerged into a concrete courtyard flanked on three sides by shops and pubs. He stopped to let a young woman pushing a pram pass before him.

She smiled at him and moved on.

A baby.

Franklin could hear the baby gurgling happily. He tried to shut out the sound as he walked on through the throng of people. Passing a couple of large skips full of rotting vegetables he emerged into the relative peace of Queens Road.

Tower blocks thrust upwards into the overcast sky and it was towards the nearest of these concrete monoliths that he headed. As he walked he slipped a hand into his jacket pocket and found a single key. He glanced at the piece of metal then closed his fist around it.

There were three cars parked outside the first block, one with its tyres missing, the chassis rusted and crumbling. Opposite were some garages, paint peeling from their doors.

Franklin walked into the main entrance of the closest tower block and jabbed the Lift Call button on the left-hand side shaft. It arrived after a moment or two and he stepped in. Graffiti was sprayed on one wall. Bright blue paint formed sweeping letters and Franklin read the words:

CHELSEA CUNTS
FUCK MAN U

There was a dark stain on the floor in one corner and the small car reeked of something rotten, something decayed. He ignored it and sucked on his cigarette, blowing out a stream of smoke as if it were some kind of air freshener. He hit the button for the sixth floor and the lift began to rise.

Franklin finally reached the desired floor and stepped out. He noticed that the other lift was now moving upwards. He glanced at the numbers above the doors as they lit up and saw that the second lift had gone up to eight and stopped.

He waited a moment then walked along the narrow

corridor to flat number seven. He opened his fist, looked at the key lying on his palm then inserted it into the lock and stepped inside.

Behind him, the other lift began to descend.

It stopped at the sixth floor.

65

They'd all had a key to the flat. All of his firm. His team. His mates. His friends.

Dead friends.

Over the years, in his line of work, Franklin and his colleagues had learned, as had all men who plied their trade on the other side of the law, that it was essential to have as many safe-houses, lock-ups and bases of operation as possible. The more they could move around, the more addresses they had that remained undiscovered by the law, then the longer they were likely to stay working.

Franklin himself had found this particular place four years earlier. Like so many of the other flats in the block, it had been empty. Neglected by the council who purported to maintain it. Shunned by all but those most desperate to have a roof over their heads.

Now, he closed the door behind him and looked briefly around the flat.

The narrow hallway opened out into a small living area. Beyond that was a tiny kitchen. There was one bedroom and another door that hid a large and unlagged hot water tank. It was punctured and the water had been dripping from it for so long that the floorboards beneath it had rotted. That was one of the smells that clogged in Franklin's nostrils as he moved slowly around the flat.

There was no furniture in the living area. Two torn sleeping bags were laid out close to one wall. There were some yellowing magazines beside the cracked tiles of the fireplace, and where a gas fire had once been, a brass pipe protruded from the wall in the middle of the hearth. A portable television covered in a thick layer of dust was perched on an upturned cardboard box in another corner.

Franklin walked through to the kitchen. Here there was a small formica-topped table, two chairs and a miniature fridge. A mug tree, complete with three mugs, stood on one of the worktops. There was even a dusty box of teabags and a half-full jar of coffee close to it.

Cheap white hardboard cupboards and units had been fixed haphazardly to the walls. The cupboard doors were all closed. Black mould had crept halfway up two of the walls. The smell of damp was strong in here too.

Franklin pulled at the handles of the cupboard under the sink and opened the cracked doors. The mould was even thicker inside, not helped by the fact that water had dripped from a broken pipe leading from the plughole. There was a large metal toolbox in there, slightly rusted on one corner. Franklin knelt and pulled it out. He flipped open the lid and gazed at the contents: a couple of power drills, a circular saw, a blowtorch, hammers, chisels and several lengths of thick wire and insulating tape. The tools looked in remarkably good condition compared to the decaying state of the rest of the flat. There was even a thin sheen of oil on the blade of the circular saw.

Franklin stood up and opened two of the cupboards to his right. The first was empty. As the second door was opened a large spider scuttled for the safety of its web, spun across the back of the cupboard. There was a packet of rice and some tins of soup inside.

291

Franklin closed the cupboard and made his way back through the living area and into the single bedroom. What had been hung at the window hardly deserved to be called curtains but the single piece of dark blue velvet suspended there by nails had served a purpose.

The floor was bare of carpet and many of the boards were loose. They creaked protestingly as Franklin walked across to the large white wardrobe that stood in one corner of the room. He opened it and immediately began pulling at the wooden backing inside. It came away easily. The screws that had been put there to hold it in place spun free as he tugged.

What he wanted was in a black plastic bag taped to the back of the wood. Franklin smiled as he reached inside.

The 9mm Beretta 12S sub-machine gun was a little over twelve inches long and weighed slightly more than seven pounds. Franklin hefted it before him as he took it from the bag, the smell of gun oil strong in his nostrils. There were six spare clips in there too. All twenty round magazines. If necessary, the weapon could spew out five hundred and fifty rounds in one minute. Franklin hurriedly checked the firing mechanism of the weapon. It was working beautifully. He slammed in a magazine, chambered a round and slipped on the safety catch before dropping the 12S back into the bag.

That task done, he pulled the wardrobe door shut and prepared to leave.

He was at the threshold of the bedroom when he heard movement outside the front door.

66

Franklin felt his heart begin to hammer more rapidly against his ribs as he poked his nose around the door frame and glanced at the front door. He strained his ears to pick out the sounds beyond.

Was that the low whispering of voices?

He gripped the subgun, his finger resting on the trigger.

No. Let them come inside. Whoever the hell they are.

There was a moment of silence then he heard the movement again. Quiet. Furtive.

There was a scraping of metal on metal.

Franklin realised that whoever was outside the door was attempting to slip the lock.

They'd watched him come here. He knew it. Felt it. They'd probably been tailing him since he left the flat that morning.

Thoughts tumbled through his mind. Was it the police? No. He'd lost them on the Tube. No question. Besides, the police would have waited for him to come out. They wouldn't have needed to sneak around inside the building.

He held the Beretta more tightly and kept his eyes fixed on the door.

How do you play this?

He sucked in a deep breath. Once they got inside he would have to move fast to take them by surprise.

Franklin wondered how many there were, what they were carrying. Were these the bastards who had killed Amy?

Please God let it be them.

He was shaking slightly but convinced himself it was with suppressed fury and anticipation.

The lock gave. The door opened a fraction.

Come and get it, you fuckers.

Franklin stepped back inside the bedroom, pushing the door slightly shut. From outside he heard the front door hinges creak a little then there were footsteps in the narrow hallway.

How many of them were there?

The front door was closed.

Franklin tried to control his breathing. He was afraid that the intruder would hear him, as he was convinced that his heart's frantic beating was filling the flat with sound. Above the roaring of his blood in his ears he heard the footsteps moving towards the living area.

You're going to have to time this just right.

If there were two or more of them it could be difficult.

Just throw open the fucking door and start blasting.

He swallowed hard, trying to concentrate on the footsteps.

Whoever was now inside moved with stealth and predatory grace. The floorboards creaked slightly.

Franklin realised that the intruder was moving into the kitchen.

He's going to find you in a minute. This is the last room.

He sucked in a deep breath. His teeth were clenched together so hard he felt as if they would splinter.

Do it now. Shit or bust. No turning back.

The intruder was still in the kitchen, Franklin was sure of that.

If there was only one there was a chance he could get

to him through the living area. From behind. It might be his only chance. Franklin edged the door open slightly and listened.

Silence.

Had the intruder heard him?

He knows where you are. There's only the bedroom left.

There was movement outside the bedroom door.

Shoot him. For fuck's sake. Open up, right through the fucking door. Just shoot him.

Franklin stepped back, pressing himself against the wall.

The door swung open an inch or two.

With a wild yell of fury Franklin threw all his weight against the door. It slammed into the intruder and Franklin realised from the impact that it had caught the intruder a heavy blow. He heard a grunt and the sound of something hard hitting the floor.

Franklin tore open the door and saw the man ducking to pick up his dropped pistol. The silencer that was screwed into the barrel made the weapon look enormous.

Retaining the initiative, Franklin kicked out at his adversary and sent the man reeling backwards. He slammed into the wall opposite and Franklin was on him like a wolf on a sheep. He struck out with the subgun, catching the man across the bridge of the nose. Franklin heard the sound of shattering bone as the man's nose was broken. Blood spilled down his chest as he reeled backwards.

Again Franklin hit him. A hammer blow that caught him on the top of the head and opened another cut. As the man dropped to his knees, Franklin kicked him in the stomach and then the face.

He flopped backwards on the dusty floor and didn't move.

Franklin spun round, the blood-spattered gun gripped in his hand, his eyes alert for any other movement inside the flat.

Nothing.

The bastard was alone.

Franklin looked down at him and saw that his eyes were flickering slightly. He drove the heel of his foot into the man's face, the impact slamming his head back against the floor with a sickening crack. This time his head lolled limply to one side.

For a second, Franklin stood over the man like a hunter over his downed prey, then he turned and scooped up the gun the intruder had dropped. It was a Glock 9mm. Franklin looked at the polished metal of the weapon and its large silencer then he tossed the gun away. It landed in the kitchen beside the toolbox.

Franklin dropped to his knees next to the man and pressed the barrel of the sub-machine gun against the man's forehead, his finger poised on the trigger.

He stared into the man's face.

Are you the one who killed Amy?

Franklin held tight and prepared to fire. He steadied himself for the murderous salvo. He pressed the barrel hard against the man's flesh.

His breathing was coming in ragged gasps, as if he'd just run up a long flight of steps. Franklin tried to control it, tried to regain control of *himself.* This wasn't how he wanted it. Wasn't how he'd imagined it. He wanted the bastard to *see* his death coming. Just as Amy had. He wanted him to suffer as she had. Putting bullets in the skull of an unconscious man wouldn't achieve any of that.

Franklin pulled the gun away, noticing that the barrel had left an indentation on the man's forehead.

More questions began to tumble through his mind. How had he found the flat? How long had he been following him? Why hadn't he struck before? Were there others with him? Were they waiting outside even now? Why did they want him dead? Why had they killed Amy?

How could he even be sure this wasn't a copper?

His head was spinning.

Franklin stood up and dug the toe of his boot into the man's ribs, ensuring he was still unconscious. Working quickly, Franklin knelt again and slid one hand into the inside pocket of the man's jacket. He rummaged around unsuccessfully then tried the pockets of his jeans. He wasn't carrying a wallet. There was no loose change, no money of any sort on him. Franklin rolled him over onto his stomach and dug in the back pockets of his jeans. Nothing. No ID.

A copper would have had something like that on him. Who the fuck are you?

Franklin glanced in the direction of the kitchen. There was only one other way to get any answers.

67

The man was in his late thirties. Unremarkable in appearance, with cropped dark brown hair, green eyes and a thin face. He was dressed in a dark grey shirt, jeans, boots, tight leather gloves and a black jacket.

Franklin sat on one of the kitchen chairs gazing at the man. It had taken him a matter of minutes to tie the man to the other chair using the wire and masking tape he'd found in the toolbox. Satisfied that his captive was securely bound, Franklin continued to study him for a moment longer. There was still quite a lot of blood on the man's face and a stream of mucus had also now begun to dribble from one corner of his mouth. Occasionally, his head would loll onto his chest and he would make a low guttural sound deep in his throat. Once, his eyes opened slightly only to close again as quickly.

Franklin was sure that the man was alone. Or, at any rate, if he had companions outside, they had showed no signs of coming in after him.

Not yet.

Franklin got to his feet and slapped the man hard across first one cheek, then the other.

The older man burbled something unintelligible. Franklin slapped him again then shook him.

'Wake up,' he snapped.

The man blinked several times.

'Come on, you bastard,' hissed Franklin, striking him across the cheek again. Each impact seemed to be amplified inside the small kitchen.

The man coughed and looked evenly at Franklin. There seemed to be no fear in his eyes, not even in his general demeanour.

'Who are you?' Franklin asked. 'Who do you work for?'

The man didn't answer but he did keep his gaze fixed on Franklin. He made no attempt to struggle against his bonds.

'Why did you want to kill me?' Franklin persisted.

The man coughed, hawked, then spat a lump of bloodied sputum onto the floor close to Franklin's left foot.

'Where are your mates? Are they waiting outside for you? Or are you working on your own?'

Silence.

Franklin picked up the .459 and pointed it at the man.

'Do you *want* to die?' he said, quietly. 'Because if not, you'd better start answering my fucking questions.'

The man looked indifferently at the yawning barrel of the pistol.

'The police think you're terrorists,' Franklin told him. '*Are* you?'

No answer.

'How did you know we were going to hit that Securicor van that night? Were you there when it happened?'

Still no answer.

'A fucking hero, eh?' he said, sliding the automatic back into its shoulder holster. 'Fucking hardman.' Franklin slid a photo out from his inside pocket. He held it before the man, his face now set in hard lines. 'Do you recognise *her*?' he demanded. 'Her name was Amy. I want to know if you killed her. And if you didn't, I want you to tell me who did. And why.'

The man hawked and spat on the photo. His expression never changed.

'You cunt,' snarled Franklin, striking him hard across the face with the back of his hand.

He wiped the picture on the man's shirt, inspected it for a second then slipped it back into his pocket.

'You're going to fucking talk to me,' he said, quietly, his whole body feeling as if it was charged with electricity.

The man looked at him blankly.

'Not scared, eh? Couldn't give a shit about dying?' Franklin asked. 'Join the club.' He took a couple of steps across the room to the toolbox.

The man watched him, his features still untainted by any hint of emotion. He didn't even flinch when Franklin picked up the circular saw.

'I could take your fingers off one at a time with this,' Franklin told him. 'Or your hands. Or your feet. I could take the top of your fucking head off. Cut through it like a boiled egg.' He slammed the fearsome-looking tool down onto the table. 'Or I could use this,' he continued, picking up one of the drills. 'Drill through your kneecaps. Or your shins. Your ankles. Maybe even your balls.'

The man licked some blood away from one corner of his mouth.

Franklin banged down a pair of pliers on the table.

'I'll take out your fucking teeth one by one,' he rasped. 'Rip them out. And it'll get to the point where I don't care if you tell me the truth or not.' He looked at the man. 'You took away the only woman I've ever loved. But you don't care, do you? You don't care about her or about the friends of mine you and your mates killed. You were going to do the same to me, weren't you? Finish the job? Tidy up the loose ends. I can understand why you'd want to kill *me*. But why Amy?' He snarled the words through clenched teeth.

The bound man regarded him almost contemptuously.

'Fuck you,' Franklin breathed. He swallowed hard. Then, very deliberately, he picked up the blowtorch.

68

There was a low hiss as Franklin turned a valve to release the stream of gas. It poured from the cylinder for a second then he lit it with his Zippo, watching as it ignited. A dancing flower of yellow flame shimmered from the end of the nozzle.

Franklin gripped it firmly in one hand, regarding his captive through narrowed eyes. There was still no flicker of emotion on the other man's face, even as he looked into the flame. In fact, as Franklin glared more intently at him, he wasn't even sure that the man was looking at the fire. He was staring past it, right into Franklin's face.

'The yellow flame's not too bad,' Franklin said. He flattened his hand and passed it quickly through the heat. 'See.'

He turned the valve slightly and the jet of fire narrowed and turned light blue.

'That's a lot hotter,' he continued, aiming it at the formica top of the kitchen table.

The lance of fire cut easily through the plastic, blackening it and filling the room with an acrid stench as Franklin carved a line across the surface. Sooty black smoke rose into the air.

'These things can reach temperatures of nearly eight hundred degrees,' Franklin continued. 'They melt metal like it was wax. Now, unless you want to tell me who you are, I'm going to use this on you. Understand?'

The man looked down at the scorched table top then back at Franklin who had adjusted the valve once more. The flame that was now roaring from the nozzle was about two inches long, pointed and a dark bluish-purple in colour. With his free hand, Franklin reached foward and tore at the man's shirt. Buttons flew in all directions as he ripped it open, exposing his captive's broad chest.

'Last chance?' he muttered. 'Who are you?'

Nothing.

Franklin moved the blowtorch towards the man's bare chest with infinite slowness.

'You can change your mind at any time,' he said evenly. 'If you want to start talking then just do it.'

The man clenched his jaws together tightly.

'Talk to me,' Franklin urged, the tip of the blowtorch flame now only inches from the man's right nipple.

A single bead of sweat popped onto the man's forehead.

'Fuck you,' Franklin whispered. He pushed the blowtorch forward.

The searing flame incinerated the man's flesh with terrifying ease. Franklin drew it in a line from the man's right collarbone, downwards across his nipple and as far as his navel. The flesh rose in a hideous, red blistered weal. Any hair on the man's chest had dissolved. His nipple was scorched black by the incredible heat.

With his teeth still clamped together, the man strained in the chair, heaving against his bonds. There was a rasping screech deep in his throat that sounded like some badly wounded animal. It filled the room, drumming in Franklin's ears and reverberating around the kitchen. The smell of burned flesh filled his nostrils.

'How long have you been following me?' Franklin asked quietly. 'Who sent you?'

303

Before the last word had left his lips he pointed the blowtorch at the hollow of the man's throat and, again with infinite slowness, moved it down his body. He guided it between his pectoral muscles, across his sternum, his eyes moving back and forth between his captive's contorted expression and the channel of charred flesh that he was creating on the man's torso. He allowed the fire to blast into the man's navel for a second then pulled the blowtorch away for a second time. The air reeked of the sickly sweet stench of incinerated skin.

The man's head lolled forwards onto his chest but Franklin grabbed his chin and lifted it, looking into his eyes.

'Still feeling like a fucking hero?' he snarled. 'Come on. Whoever you are, whoever you're protecting, they're not worth *this*.' And he drew the blowtorch down the man's body again, this time guiding the flame over the left side of his torso.

Franklin wondered if he would be able to burn his way right through the man's ribs.

It was worth considering. It shouldn't be a problem. Straight through the bone to the lung. It might take that to get the bastard to speak.

The man's head flopped backwards and Franklin regarded his handiwork dispassionately.

The three marks were already weeping. The blisters that had risen on the flesh had burst and begun to spill their clear fluid. The whole of the man's torso was bright red, the burns even more vivid against the scarlet background of his overheated skin.

Franklin struck out with the back of his hand and caught the man across first one cheek then the other.

'Don't pass out on me yet, you bastard,' he snarled.

The man's pupils rolled upwards in their sockets but Franklin gripped his hair and shook his head violently.

304

The kitchen was hot and clammy, the stink of incinerated flesh almost overpowering. Franklin drew in a breath then spat.

'Tell me who killed Amy.'

The man's gaze moved momentarily to the blowtorch. His face and upper body were sheathed in sweat. His lips were moving slightly but Franklin didn't think he was attempting to speak.

Credit where credit's due. Most would have been blabbering as soon as the blowtorch was lit.

Franklin dug a hand into his pocket and pulled out his mobile. His gaze barely leaving his prisoner, he dialled a number and waited, listening to the ring tone.

'I'm going to make this call,' Franklin told the man. 'You think about what you're going to say. Because when I've finished, I'm going to start somewhere else on your body.'

At the other end of the line, the phone continued to ring.

69

'Where the hell are you?'

Franklin managed a slight smile and held the phone away from his ear slightly.

From the other end of the line, Detective Inspector Vincent Crane roared angrily at him, a mixture of fury and frustration in his voice.

'Can you hear me, Franklin?' Crane rasped. 'Where are you?'

'Later.'

'No, you bastard. You tell me *now!*'

'Or what? What are you going to do, Crane? Arrest me?'

'I want to know where you are and I want to know now. You're at risk out there without help.'

'Some fucking help *your* boys were. They might as well have been wearing neon signs on their heads saying "copper".'

'What are you playing at?' the policeman demanded. 'I put you back on the street to help with this operation. You were supposed to cooperate. I told you that there'd be men following you. *My* men. I'm not playing games, Franklin. Why did you dump the tails?'

'Crane, shut the fuck up and listen to me,' Franklin said quietly. 'I've got one of them.'

'Franklin,' Crane said. 'Just wait. We had a deal and—'

'Fuck you, Crane, you said *no* deals,' Franklin rasped, breaking in. 'I'm not doing this for *you*. I never was. I'm doing it for Amy. And right now I could be looking at one of the bastards who killed her.'

There was a moment's stunned silence at the other end of the line.

'Did you hear what I said?' Franklin repeated.

'What have you done?' the DI asked, his voice low.

'Your fucking job. The terrorists were following me, just like you said they would, except they were better at it than *your* boys. *They* found me. *One* of them did anyway. I've got him here with me now.'

'Who is he?'

'That's what I've been trying to find out.' Franklin looked at the three savage burn marks on the man's torso.

'What's he said?'

'Nothing. Not a word. Not yet.'

Franklin fumbled in his jacket for his cigarettes, slipped one into his mouth and lit it using the searing flame of the blowtorch.

'Franklin, listen to me,' Crane said, a conciliatory note in his voice. 'Tell me where you are. I'll send men to help you. You can't do this alone.'

'I've managed so far.'

'If *he* found you then so will the others.'

'That's what I'm hoping.'

There was another long silence at the end of the phone. It was finally broken by Crane.

'Don't kill him,' he said.

'Give me one good reason why I shouldn't,' Franklin answered, looking directly into his captive's eyes.

'I need him. If I'm going to find out who killed your girlfriend and your firm then I've got to talk to him.'

'Like I said, he's not saying anything and trust me, I've tried to persuade him.'

'If you kill him you'll go down for life.'

'I haven't got a fucking life any more. What do *I* care? What do *you* care for that matter?'

'Franklin, I'm *asking* you. Please don't kill him.'

Franklin looked evenly at his captive, the phone still pressed to his ear. He didn't speak, merely drew slowly on his cigarette then blew out a long stream of smoke. It hung in the air, mingling with the odour of burned flesh. His captive sat motionless apart from the odd quiver that ran through his body. His eyes were bloodshot.

'Franklin,' Crane repeated.

'Yeah, I heard you.'

'Please.'

'Half an hour, Crane. If you don't make it by then, this bastard's history. Got it?'

'Got it,' Crane sighed resignedly. 'Tell me where you are.'

'East London. Not far from Upton Park Tube station. There's a block of flats in Queens Road called Boylen Tower. I'm on the sixth floor, flat seven.'

'All right, I'm on my way.'

'Crane, you come alone. If anyone else walks in with you, I swear to God, I'll decorate the place with this fucker's brains.'

'Franklin . . .'

'Thirty minutes,' Franklin reminded him.

He hit the Call End button.

70

'Just you and me again,' Franklin said to the bound man as he slipped the mobile back into his jacket. He sucked on his cigarette, blew some smoke in his captive's direction then ground out the Marlboro on the table top. As a plume of smoke rose mournfully into the air, Franklin again reached for the blowtorch.

If the man strapped to the other chair felt any emotions they didn't register on his face or in his eyes; he merely looked fixedly at Franklin who took a step closer to him.

'The police'll be here soon,' said Franklin. 'But I don't suppose that matters to you, does it? I mean, what can *they* do to you? Nothing like *I've* done.' He nodded towards the man's badly burned chest. 'They'll question you, maybe leave you to sweat in a cell but that's nothing to you, is it? You see, they *can't* hurt you. They're not *allowed* to, not legally anyway.' He inhaled deeply, held his breath then exhaled again slowly. 'They could knock you around a bit then say you fell down some steps,' he smiled. 'It has been known. But that's it. And that's not going to make you talk, is it?'

Franklin was less than a foot away from his captive now, the blowtorch giving off a fierce heat that wrung droplets of sweat from Franklin's face too.

'The difference with me is that I can do what I want to you,' he continued. 'I *want* to hurt you. You and any like you who were involved in the murder of Amy and my friends. I couldn't give a fuck about your politics, your beliefs or anything else. This is personal. Now, tell me who you are and where I can find your mates.'

The man lowered his gaze slightly, moving his face infinitesimally as he felt the heat from the blowtorch coming closer.

'They should be proud of you for not grassing them up,' Franklin rasped. 'Maybe they'd think you were brave.'

He moved the searing flame towards the man's right cheek and allowed it to scorch the skin there. Beginning at the corner of the eye, where several eyelashes shrivelled under the incredible heat, Franklin played the flame down to the man's top lip.

The man strained in his chair, teeth clamped together against the indescribable pain, his eyes bulging madly in their sockets. Veins stood out like cords all over his face and neck, throbbing so violently it looked as though they would explode.

'Who are you?' Franklin snarled, holding the flame on the man's lip. It burned through the soft tissue with ease, briefly exposing the pink of his gum before it cremated that too.

Franklin whipped it away.

'No,' he murmured. 'If you're going to talk I need to be able to understand you, don't I?'

He walked behind the man and gripped the back of the chair, hauling it a foot or so away from the table. For a moment he regarded his captive in silence then, his expression still impassive, he lowered the blowtorch so that the flame was aimed at the man's genitals.

'You know what I'm going to do, don't you?' Franklin asked, pushing the searing flame nearer to the man's crotch. 'You know where I'm going to burn you?'

310

The man didn't respond, not even when Franklin shoved the flame against his testicles.

The fire burned easily through the material of his trousers and underwear and, seconds later, it was scorching the flesh of his scrotum. Skin and pubic hair were incinerated instantly. The stench was appalling.

Franklin saw one of the testes catch fire, the spherical object burned black by the fierce heat, charred until it resembled a scorched walnut. Blood, urine and clear fluid were immediately vaporised by the incredible heat.

The man's shrunken penis was also blackened as Franklin aimed the blowtorch at it, watching as portions of the foreskin actually ignited and peeled away before he cremated the glans, transforming it into a cracked and blackened lump of useless dead flesh.

The man had passed out again and Franklin stepped back.

This bastard was never going to talk. Never.

He stood silently, staring at the burned man before him.

What the fuck was wrong with him?

'Die then,' said Franklin softly.

The man's head suddenly snapped up as if pushed from beneath. He looked directly at Franklin who, surprised by the sudden movement, took a step backwards.

He put down the blowtorch and reached for the .459.

Was this mad bastard going to try and rush him? Even though he was strapped to a chair? Even though he'd taken enough to floor a fucking rhino?

The captive made no move to rise. Instead, his body began to shake madly, as if someone had pumped thousands of volts of electricity through him. He opened his mouth to emit the scream Franklin had been waiting for but the only sound that issued forth was a guttural retching.

Franklin trained the gun on him.

The man continued to tremble uncontrollably then he

stiffened, his bulging eyes fixed on Franklin. The veins all over his body were throbbing, becoming more prominent. Again, from his throat there was that vile retching and something that sounded like material being torn. A wet ripping noise then a mucoid rasp.

'Jesus,' Franklin murmured.

There was blood welling from both the man's ears and his nostrils. He began to shake his head back and forth with incredible speed, his mouth now fixed in an oval shape. Blood sprayed out from his nose and mouth, droplets landing on the table and the dusty floor.

His head continued to move from left to right impossibly fast, as if invisible hands were twisting it as rapidly as they could. Suddenly there was a loud crack that Franklin recognised as splintering bone. The man stopped shaking and his head slumped to one side, his mouth open, his tongue protruding.

Franklin waited a moment then, still keeping the .459 trained on the man's chest, he stepped forward and pressed two fingers of his free hand to the man's neck, just below his jaw.

There was no pulse.

Franklin pushed the man's head with the barrel of the gun. It lolled to the other side accompanied by the grating of bone on bone. His neck was broken.

'You bastard,' Franklin murmured, glaring at the dead man.

After a minute, Franklin holstered the pistol, then he lit a cigarette and sat down opposite the body.

Finish the cigarette then get out.

There seemed little point. Crane would be here soon.

71

The stench was almost palpable. As DI Crane opened the door of number seven Boylen Tower he recoiled slightly.

'Franklin,' he called. 'It's me.'

'Come through,' Franklin replied.

Glancing around at the dingy flat, Crane made his way through the living area, following the direction of the other man's voice. As he reached the kitchen, the policeman slowed his pace.

Franklin was still sitting at the table but it was towards the bound corpse that Crane looked.

'What the fuck did you do to him?' he breathed as he walked in.

'I didn't kill him,' Franklin said flatly, leaning back in his chair. He looked around, checking that Crane was alone. If he had back-up, Franklin guessed it was waiting for him outside.

Crane moved closer, wrinkling his nose at the acrid odour that filled the small kitchen. He walked around the body, his gaze taking in every injury and blemish.

'Tell me what happened,' he demanded, still staring at the corpse.

'He followed me here,' Franklin said. 'He would have

killed me.' Franklin pointed to the Glock that was still lying on the table. 'He was carrying *that*,' he said. 'It was a nine mil. that killed Amy, wasn't it? I saw the wound, remember?'

'Tell me everything,' Crane continued.

'There's not much to tell. He came into the flat. I took him by surprise. How much detail do you want?'

'I want to know if you burned him.'

'I needed him to talk. He wouldn't.'

'So you tortured him?'

'I was trying to make him talk.'

Crane shot Franklin a furious glance.

'So what did he tell you?' the policeman demanded.

'Nothing. Not even his name.'

Crane began going through the dead man's pockets as carefully as he could.

'He's not carrying any ID. I've already looked,' Franklin said.

'You killed the only lead I had,' Crane snapped.

'I told you, *I* didn't kill him,' Franklin rasped. 'He had a fit. Some sort of convulsion. It was nothing to do with me.'

Crane ran a hand through his hair.

'Nothing to do with the fact that you used a blowtorch on him?' he hissed.

'I told you. He wouldn't talk. What would *you* have done to him? Threatened him with twenty years inside? He'd have *really* shit himself then, wouldn't he?'

'You didn't have to . . .' muttered the policeman, unable to finish the sentence. He was staring at the hideous burn marks on the dead man's body, particularly the smoking hole where his genitals used to be.

'Listen, Crane, I told you that I was going to find out who killed Amy and I will. Just because *he* didn't tell me doesn't mean the next one won't.'

'The next one?'

314

'The next one they send after me.'

'You got lucky this time, Franklin. *You* surprised *him*. And what good did it do you? Did it help you find out what you wanted to know? Did it help *me* with my investigation? No. There isn't going to be a next time. I agreed to cut you loose to help me draw these bastards out, not so you could go around torturing them to death if you caught them. That's it. This is over for you.'

Franklin pulled the .459 free of its holster. He worked the slide and rested his hand on the edge of the table.

'What are you going to do, shoot me?' Crane said calmly.

'If I have to,' Franklin told him.

'I've got men outside the building. Snipers are watching the exits. If you walk out of here without me, they'll kill you.'

'On your orders?'

'That's right.'

'And that's supposed to bother me, is it?'

'No. I know you don't care whether you live or die but I know that you *do* care about finding the men who killed Amy.'

'Then put me back on the street.'

'No way. Not after this.' He inclined his head in the direction of the dead man.

'I told you, Crane. I didn't kill him. I wish I had, but I didn't.'

'So tell me what happened.'

Franklin shrugged.

'He had some kind of convulsion, I told you that,' he said. 'I think he was *trying* to kill himself. He broke his own neck.'

'There's only one way to prove that.'

'How?'

'A full autopsy. And until I get the results back I'm going to take you into protective custody.'

315

'No you're not.'

Crane slid his hand inside his jacket with lightning speed and Franklin saw the gleam of gun metal. He recognised the weapon immediately as a Sterling .357.

'I see that you came prepared,' he smiled.

'I've got hollow tips loaded into this.'

'You won't use it.'

'Try me. There are two ways out of here, Franklin – with me, or in a body-bag. It's your choice. After I get the autopsy results back we'll talk again. Trust me.'

'I don't trust anybody.'

'Then either put that gun away or pull the trigger now.'

The two men regarded each other silently for what seemed like an age, then Franklin looked at the automatic gripped in his hand. Slowly, he slipped the safety catch on then pushed the pistol back into its shoulder holster. He put his hands palms down on the table.

'That's sensible,' Crane said, holstering his own weapon.

'Have you really got snipers out there?' Franklin wanted to know.

'Walk outside without me. Find out.'

Franklin got to his feet.

'You asked me to come in here alone when you rang,' Crane reminded him. 'I gave you my word that I would. *Why* did you call me?'

'I don't know. Perhaps I'll end up wishing I hadn't.'

Together, they walked towards the door.

72

'Are you sure about this, Howard?' Crane asked, looking first at the pathologist then at the naked body of the unknown man lying immobile on the metal slab. His voice echoed inside the cold examination room.

'There's no doubting it,' Richardson said. 'The blood sample taken from this man contains the virus that was also in the circulatory systems of the thirty-four bodies found in that Securicor van.'

'You said the virus was activated by exposure to air,' Crane continued. 'If you start cutting this guy about, you'll release it.'

'The temperature in here is around ten degrees Celsius. As long as it stays above freezing the virus will remain dormant.'

Crane looked at the pathologist then at Detective Sergeant Kingston who merely shrugged.

All three of the men wore white plastic aprons. A trolley full of surgical instruments stood beside the stainless steel slab. They were covered by two sterile paper towels.

'Any word on ID yet?' Crane asked Kingston.

'We're still waiting for Hendon to get back to us about

his prints,' the DS said. 'Dental records are being checked too, guv.'

'Have we really got anything more to go on with this one,' Crane muttered. 'Any more than on the other thirty-four?'

'A *bit* extra,' Kingston observed, running appraising eyes over the dead man's features.

'What do you mean?' Crane asked.

'Well, at least this geezer's got his head, hands and feet,' Kingston mused.

Crane smiled.

'Do you really want to stay here while I do this?' Richardson asked, reaching for a scalpel. 'It could take some time.'

'You notify me as soon as you've finished,' Crane instructed. He and Kingston unfastened their aprons and laid them on the adjacent, unoccupied, metal slab. 'How long are you going to be?'

'It's difficult to say,' Richardson told him, adjusting the microphone that was suspended above the corpse. 'It depends what I find.'

Crane nodded and headed for the door, Kingston close behind him.

Richardson waited until he was alone then, taking a deep breath, he made the first incision.

The cell that Franklin occupied in East Ham police station was six foot by eight foot. It contained a single mattress laid on the stone floor, and a bucket. The walls were painted a dull slate grey. In places, names had been scratched into the brickwork. Dates. Crude drawings.

Franklin had surveyed each one with singular indifference. He glanced at his watch. It had been over an hour since he'd been placed inside the cell.

Now, stretched out on the mattress, head propped on

318

one arm, he smiled as he remembered the look on the duty sergeant's face as he'd laid the .459 on the counter. That intial look of bewilderment had been transformed into one of outright shock as the 12S sub-machine gun had been placed alongside it.

Contrary to usual procedure, and on Crane's instructions, he'd been allowed to keep his valuables, including his wallet. He now flipped that open and took out one of Amy's photos. Her image smiled back at him. Franklin traced the outline of her face with one index finger then kissed the photo and slipped it back into the wallet which he stowed in his jeans.

The other cells were currently empty but Franklin knew he wasn't alone in this part of the police station. At least two armed policemen had been placed outside his cell, again on Crane's orders.

Franklin wondered if the building was, even now, being watched. And by whom? Associates of the man he'd tortured?

Had they watched him and Crane walk from Boylen Tower to the unmarked car that had ferried him to the police station? Were they, at this very moment, waiting for him to be released? Waiting to strike?

Maybe they'll come in and get you.

Franklin stood up and began pacing the cell, pressing his forehead gently against the wall when he reached one end, and against the metal door when he came to the other. There was an observation slot in the door. It was firmly closed.

Would that or anything else stop them if they arrived?

There was movement outside the cell.

Were they here already?

Franklin looked round as he heard a key turn in the lock. A moment later, the heavy metal door swung open and a uniformed constable walked in carrying a tray with

319

a mug of tea and some toast on it. He set them down by the mattress.

'You must be pretty special,' said the constable, eyeing him up and down. 'Armed guards. Preferential treatment. The sarge said that some big nob from New Scotland Yard brought you in.'

Franklin stooped, picked up the mug of tea and sipped at it.

'So, what's so special about you?' the constable continued.

'Thanks for the tea,' Franklin said indifferently.

'Some kind of supergrass, are you?' the constable said. 'Dropped some of your mates in the shit and they've threatened to kill you. Is that it?'

'What does it matter to you?'

'I'm just curious.'

'Well, you know what curiosity does – it kills cats, sometimes coppers too.' Franklin sat down on the mattress. 'Careful the door doesn't hit you on your way out,' he said, without looking up.

The constable regarded him irritably for a moment then left the cell.

Franklin glanced at his watch again.

Howard Richardson checked the weight of the man's liver on the scales suspended above the slab. He muttered some observations into the microphone then continued with his work.

All of the internal organs, other than the brain which was dotted with pinprick haemorrhages, appeared normal in texture, weight and biological composition. However, Richardson paused as he inspected the slippery length of the large intestine in one tray. His expert eyes were alert for anything unusual.

'Evidence of prior surgery on the caecum,' he said. He pushed his spectacles back up his nose and gently scraped the blade of the dissecting knife over the length of entrail. 'There is some scar tissue indicating appendix removal. No evidence of other surgery.'

He put his hand over his mouth as he coughed, careful not to touch his lips with his bloodied rubber gloves. He shuddered involuntarily, aware of the necessary chill in the air. Behind him, a tap dripped. Richardson paused a moment then walked around the body, stopping at the feet.

There were small red puncture marks between the big toe and first toe of each foot.

Richardson mumbled this information into the microphone. 'It is possible that the virus was administered via these punctures,' he said. 'This could also be true of the bodies found in the Securicor van. Perhaps the feet were removed to hide that fact. Similar injections could also have been administered between the fingers. This could explain the removal of the hands and feet.'

He gazed at the body for a moment longer, then cleared his throat and returned to the microphone again.

'Examination of the body, both internally and externally, leads me to believe that death was caused by the rupturing of the second and third cervical vertebrae,' he said. 'Damage to these bones, combined with the many small haemorrhages in the brain, indicate that death was brought about by a convulsive reaction, possibly caused by an, as yet, unidentified chemical present in the bloodstream.'

Richardson looked down at the corpse once again. He shook his head slowly.

Crane finished stirring his coffee. He trailed the spoon through the foam on the surface then licked it off before sitting back wearily in his seat.

Opposite him, DS Kingston chewed on a sandwich, wiping his mouth with the back of his hand.

There was a newspaper laid out on the table between

321

the two men, folded over so that the headline showed: SUICIDE BOMBERS ARE REAL THREAT TO THIS COUNTRY!

'Do you reckon that geezer Franklin killed was one of them?' asked Kingston, tapping the paper with his index finger.

'He says he didn't kill him,' Crane answered.

'Just tortured him?'

'He definitely did *that* and he's not afraid to admit it.'

'What happens to Franklin now, guv?'

Crane shrugged.

'The fact that they came after him means he might still be useful to us,' the DI mused. 'But I don't know if I can risk putting him back on the streets. He's a loose cannon. And he doesn't give a fuck. *That's* what makes him dangerous.'

'And the terrorists? What about them?'

'Hopefully, we'll have more to go on when we get some information on the dead one. There's got to be a key to this somewhere. Maybe Richardson can find it.'

'Or the boys at Hendon. If they can match his prints.'

'If, if, if. We've got a body with no ID, a gun with no fingerprints and clothing with no labels.'

'But at least this time we have *got* a body, guv.'

Crane nodded, sipped his cappuccino and looked out across Parliament Square.

More than a dozen large concrete blocks, each at least twenty feet long and ten feet wide, had been laid across the tarmac area facing the Houses of Parliament. Crowds of tourists were gazing at the blocks with as much fascination as if they were at the parliamentary building itself. A cordon of armed policemen was stretched across the front of the edifice, trying to remain as inconspicuous as possible as they eyed the milling crowds.

'If they want to hit it, they'll hit it,' Crane said. 'They could drive past and fire a rocket at the bloody building. It would be gone before anyone knows what the hell's happening.'

'That's not what the Counter Terrorist Unit think, is it? Didn't they say they were expecting a suicide squad to drive a lorry-load of explosives at it?' He nodded in the direction of the huge building.

'They might be fanatics but they're not stupid,' said the DI. 'They'll have seen what's been done to protect the politicians. They're going to pick another target. Either that or they'll use a different method to get closer. Not a bloody lorry.' He sipped at his coffee and massaged the back of his neck with his free hand. 'It makes you wonder if it'd be such a great loss, doesn't it?' he smiled. 'If they blew up a load of politicians.'

Both men chuckled.

The shrill ringing of a mobile phone interrupted them.

'That's me,' said Kingston through a mouthful of sandwich. He fumbled in his pocket for the Nokia and held it to his ear. 'Kingston,' he said, then sat back as the voice at the other end spoke.

Crane finished his coffee then reached across and took a bite from one of his companion's sandwiches. He chewed slowly and looked back in the direction of the Houses of Parliament.

'Anything important?' he asked when Kingston finally switched off the phone.

Kingston merely nodded silently.

'What's wrong, Del?' Crane wanted to know, seeing the look on his colleague's face.

'Hendon identified the dead man from his prints,' the DS said. 'It was an eight-point match. His name's Robert Clifford. His prints were on file because he'd been arrested twenty-two years ago for driving while disqualified. Some of the team have been checking back, filling in details. He doesn't sound like a terrorist, guv.'

'What makes you so sure?'

'He joined the army sixteen years ago, did tours in Northern Ireland and Kosovo. Served in the Gulf War.'

'Any family?'

'A wife and son.'

'We need to talk to her, find out what he's been doing since he got back.'

'I don't think she'll be much help to us. According to our information, he was reported missing in Kuwait twelve years ago. They never found his body. He never *came* back. Mrs Clifford is officially a war widow.'

'What are you telling me?'

'I'm telling you what *I've* just been told, guv. Officially, the guy back there on the slab, Private Robert Clifford, has been dead for twelve years.'

73

Detective Inspector Vincent Crane raised his hands in an effort to still the chorus of conversation that was still sweeping around the Incident Room. Both plain clothes and uniformed officers babbled amongst themselves, seemingly oblivious to their superior.

'All right,' he called, shouting above the noise. 'Everybody, just keep it down.'

The excited chatter gradually faded away and Crane drew in a deep breath, glancing around the room at the stunned faces.

'I know it sounds crazy,' he said finally. 'But I'm just giving you the same facts that *I* received. I know it looks as if there's been a mistake somewhere, that what I've just told you is impossible, that someone must have mixed up the prints or something like that. Well, trust me, I'd like to believe that too but the fact is that everything adds up.'

'A dead man who used to be in the British army is now working as a hit man?' someone from the back of the room called.

Some nervous laughter accompanied the remark.

'A man who was *believed* to be dead,' Crane snapped.

'Which regiment was he in?' a uniformed officer enquired.

'The 95th. The Greenjackets,' the DI replied.

'Could *they* have made a mistake about Clifford?' the officer continued.

'What kind of mistake?' Crane wanted to know. 'Got his name wrong? No. And if it isn't *their* fault and no one here fucked up then that only leaves one explanation. As insane as it may sound.'

More bewildered murmurings greeted the remark.

Crane looked at Howard Richardson, seeking the pathologist's help. Richardson stood up, his imposing frame drawing the attention of the men and women in the room.

'The man I performed the autopsy on *is* Robert Clifford,' he said. 'Apart from the fingerprint match, I've checked his army medical records,' the pathologist explained. 'His appendix was removed by an army surgeon just prior to him leaving for the Gulf. 'The body I examined showed scar tissue in that area, indicating an operation of that nature had been carried out.'

'Thanks, Howard,' Crane said, as the pathologist sat down again. The DI turned back to face the others in the room. 'Let's think about this,' Crane offered, sucking in a deep breath. 'Clifford does his tours in Northern Ireland. He serves in the Gulf, right? He goes missing in Kuwait. He obviously didn't die out there. For some reason, he *wanted* people to think he was dead.'

'Including the army?' someone called.

'Possibly,' Crane mused. 'So, everyone thinks he's dead, including his family. He then makes his way back to this country somehow. Fake passport. Fake identity. I don't know. He must have had it planned. What we need to know is *why*.'

'Surely he'd have gone back to his wife,' a plain clothes officer near the front suggested.

'Not necessarily,' Crane offered. 'If he did fake his own disappearance and the army had then caught up with him then technically he'd have been classed as a deserter. He would have been looking at five to ten years in an army nick.'

'So, where's he *been* for twelve years, sir?' a woman PC wanted to know.

'It's not difficult to disappear if you really want to,' Crane said. 'If he had all this planned then he could have had fake ID waiting for him when he got back. A whole new life.'

'Someone would have had to have been working with him,' Kingston interjected.

'You're probably right,' Crane conceded. 'And if we can find *them* then that might open up this whole case. It could have been someone he was in the army with. Check on who he served with. Who was in his battalion? Check if any of them had any criminal connections.'

Some of the officers scribbled notes as Crane spoke.

'There's another possibility we should consider,' the DI went on. 'That Clifford was *brought* back to this country, that he was *told* to keep out of sight and to change his identity.'

'Who would have wanted him to do that?' someone queried.

'Good question,' Crane mused. 'Who'd have the *power* to do that? To make a man disappear for twelve years?' He slowly regarded each of the faces before him.

'So, for twelve years he lies low then, the first time he sticks his head out he's trying to kill some tuppenny-ha'penny criminal. Why?' Kingston looked at his superior as if expecting an answer. 'And if he was trying to kill Matt Franklin then who's to say he wasn't involved in the murders of Franklin's girlfriend and his firm as well?'

'It's entirely possible that he was,' Crane said.

'But I thought we'd agreed that terrorists were responsible

for those murders, sir,' another plain clothes man said. 'Middle Eastern terrorists. The suicide bombers that are loose in London.'

'That was the original theory,' Crane confirmed.

'But now it's not?' the plain clothes man asked.

'If it wasn't terrorists trying to kill Franklin, who *was* it?' Kingston wanted to know.

'Let's think back to where this all started,' Crane said, stretching his arms behind his back. 'Thirty-four bodies are found in a Securicor van that a gang of criminals think is carrying army money, right? Those criminals are wiped out, *we think* by terrorists. What if Clifford *was* one of the men who nailed Franklin's firm? Who would that make his most likely accomplices?'

'He could still be working with Middle Eastern terrorists, sir,' someone seated on a desk suggested. 'That geezer who let off that suicide bomb in Jerusalem not long ago, he was English. An English Muslim.'

'It's possible,' Crane agreed. 'But also remember that the bullets that killed Franklin's firm were titanium-coated. They were more than likely military issue.'

'But terrorists have access to all sorts of weapons and ammo, sir,' a uniformed sergeant protested.

'Have any shipments of arms or ammunition been stolen in this country during the last five years?' Crane asked. 'Specifically, sniper rifles and titanium-coated ammo, the kind used to take out Franklin's firm when they opened that Securicor van? If they had, we'd have known about it through Special Branch or one of the intelligence agencies. Now, if those weapons and that ammo weren't stolen then they were used with the full knowledge of someone in possession of that grade of armaments.'

'Are you saying that the British army are somehow involved in this?' Kingston wanted to know.

'I'm just thinking aloud,' Crane said cryptically.

'But that would also mean that the army were responsible for putting the bodies in the van in the first place,' Kingston offered. 'Bodies infected with a manufactured virus.'

'I said near the beginning of this investigation that we might be looking in the wrong places,' said Crane. 'It looks like I might have been right.'

'There's not enough proof to link all this to the army,' Kingston protested. 'It doesn't make sense.'

'It never has,' Crane muttered. 'What we *know* doesn't make sense. We haven't got all the facts. I'm willing to bet we never will have.'

'Are you saying there's some kind of conspiracy going on, sir?' a plain clothes officer asked.

'If there was, how high would it have to go to protect whoever's behind it?' Kingston asked.

'I don't even want to *think* about that,' Crane sighed. 'It'd have to be as high as governmental level to cover something of this size.'

'So, are we still looking for terrorists or not?' someone called.

'Without question,' Crane said. 'There are suicide bombers in this city, right now. All I'm saying is don't confine your investigations solely to *them*. And another thing, what's been said in this room today stays here. Got that? I don't want word of what we've discussed circulating. If I hear of anyone talking about conspiracies I'll be on them like a ton of hot horse shit.' He looked around at the men and women in the room for a moment longer. 'That's all. Let's get back to work.'

The room emptied quickly and in relative silence. As the door closed on the last officer, Crane turned and looked at the action board and the hundreds of photos that adorned one wall of the Incident Room.

'Were you serious about the army being involved?' Kingston wanted to know.

'We can't discount *any* possibility, Del,' Crane murmured. He reached for his cigarettes and lit one. 'Terrorists. A conspiracy. A virus that could infect the whole of London.'

'And nothing to link it.'

'Franklin. He's the link. He was one of the men who hit the van full of infected bodies. His firm and his girl-friend were murdered by whoever put those bodies in there and one of his own dead mates used to be in the army.'

'Jeff Adamson.'

'Right. He did three years in the same regiment as Robert Clifford. I think it's time to speak to Franklin again, I want to find out *exactly* how much he knew about his mate.'

'And then?'

Crane drew hard on his cigarette, his eyes still flicking over the collage of photos.

'There's one other person I need to speak to.'

74

Franklin heard footsteps outside the cell, then the sound of muffled voices. He got to his feet and, a moment later, the heavy door opened, swinging back on its hinges to reveal a familiar figure.

'Come to make sure I haven't escaped?' he said as DI Crane walked in.

The policeman pulled the door shut behind him.

'Take a seat,' Franklin said, motioning towards the mattress on the floor.

'I need your help, Franklin,' Crane told him.

'I thought that's what I was doing before you locked me up. Helping you. I'd be a fucking sight *more* help if I was on the street instead of banged up in here. Are you going to charge me? Because if you are, I want a brief here now.'

'I just want to talk.'

'So, am I under arrest or not?'

'You're in protective custody. I told you that. You're being kept here for your own safety.'

'Am I supposed to say thanks?'

'We've already had this conversation. Just listen to me, will you?'

'Go on,' Franklin murmured disinterestedly.

'It's about Jeff Adamson. How much did you know about him?'

'What do you mean?' Franklin demanded, his brow furrowing.

'What did you know about his background?'

'I *worked* with him. He was a friend.'

'How many jobs did you do together?'

'What the fuck has this got to do with anything?'

'Just answer me, Franklin.'

'I can't remember how many jobs.'

'You know that he was in the army for three years. Did he ever talk about it? About the people he served with? About the places he went?'

'Get to the point, Crane.'

'That guy you tortured. He was in the same regiment as your friend Adamson. They might even have known each other at some time.'

'So?'

'Why was Adamson thrown out of the army?'

'You're the detective, *you* tell *me.*'

'He was dishonourably discharged, wasn't he?'

'He didn't go into detail.'

'One of the first jobs you ever pulled together was the hijacking of an army weapons shipment. Who were the guns sold to?'

'How the hell do *I* know? Jeff took care of that side of things. He had the contacts. He knew where to go. As long as we got our money we didn't care where it came from.'

'So he could have sold them abroad for all you knew?'

'Like I said, as long as we got paid, we didn't care. One part of the shipment went to South Africa, that's all I know.'

'What about the Middle East?'

'I told you, I don't know. What's more, I don't *care.*'

'Did he have contacts abroad for shifting the gear?'

'We never talked about it.'

'Or you're just not saying?'

'Get me a brief, will you? If you're going to charge me I—'

'I'm not going to charge you,' Crane interrupted. 'Not yet.'

'So why the fuck are you here?'

The policeman walked to the cell door and opened it.

'You've got one more chance, Franklin,' the DI said, beckoning him towards the entrance. 'Forty-eight hours on the street to see if they have another crack at you. Whoever *they* are. After that, I'm throwing away the key.'

Franklin regarded the policeman suspiciously for a moment.

'This doesn't make sense,' he said quietly. 'Why am *I* so important to you? You've got me where you want me now. Why give me another chance? Jeff had family, so did George Nicholson. And Joe Maguire was married. Why not use *their* families as bait? You know *they* won't run.'

Crane exhaled wearily.

'They're dead,' he said flatly.

Franklin paused, the colour draining from his cheeks.

'When?' he wanted to know.

'Just over an hour ago,' Crane continued. 'Adamson's wife was shot. A sniper took her head off with a rifle. Nicholson's little girl had her throat cut as she was leaving school. The murderer killed the policewoman guarding her as well. Someone took out Maguire's wife while she was standing in her own kitchen, washing up.'

'Another sniper?'

Crane nodded.

'All the murders happened within ten minutes of each other,' the DI informed him. 'I was notified on my way here. They're tying up all the loose ends, Franklin. And you're the only one left. *That's* why you get one more crack at it.'

'I thought your men were guarding them all.'

'Like I said to you before, if these bastards want you, they'll *get* you.'

Franklin stepped out of the cell, his face fixed in hard lines.

'Keep the tails close to you,' Crane advised. 'If anything happens, they're there for your protection. You're going to need all the help you can get.'

'Your help didn't save the others, did it?' Franklin muttered dismissively. He turned and headed off up the short corridor.

'Forty-eight hours, Franklin,' Crane called after him. Then he allowed his voice to drop to little more than a whisper. 'If you last that long.'

75

Franklin paused before his front door. He stood silently for a moment, listening for anything like movement from inside. Then, carefully, he inserted the key in the lock and let himself in.

At the threshold he waited again then, satisfied that no one had gained entry while he'd been gone, he entered and locked the door behind him.

The flat felt cold. Lifeless.

How appropriate.

He moved through into the living area and filled the kettle then he switched on the television, not even noticing what was on.

Anything to break the unbearable silence.

He pulled off his jacket and threw it onto the sofa. The shoulder holster he kept on.

While the kettle was boiling he passed through into the bedroom, checking under the bed that the SPAS was untouched. He regarded the powerful shotgun through the clear plastic bag he'd wrapped it in, then pushed it back out of sight.

He sat on the edge of the bed for a moment, head bowed. Outside he could hear traffic passsing and, for a while, he sat there as if mesmerised by the noise. Then he wandered back into the other room, blew dust from a mug on the draining board and dropped in a tea bag. He opened the fridge, looking for milk. He gazed at the white fluid for a moment then banged the bottle back down on the draining board.

From the cupboard above the sink he took a bottle of Jack Daniel's. He hooked the tea bag out of the mug with his index finger and poured a large measure of the alcohol into it instead. He drank deeply, feeling it burn its way to his stomach.

As he glanced up he noticed that the call counter on the answerphone was showing a glowing red 2. He crossed to it and pressed the Play button.

The first message was from the local council. They needed to speak to the householder about some work that was to be done in the street outside. It could well involve an interruption of power to the premises.

Blah, blah, blah.

'Fuck off,' murmured Franklin, skipping to the second message.

It was the undertaker. Franklin swallowed hard as he heard the man's voice.

'Mr Franklin, this is just to let you know that Miss Holden's body will be in our Chapel of Rest as of nine o'clock tomorrow morning . . .' the message announced.

Franklin closed his eyes.

'. . . You're very welcome to visit whenever you feel like it . . .'

He rewound the message, then hit Play again.

'. . . *Miss Holden's body will be in our Chapel of Rest* . . .' And again.

'. . . *Miss Holden's body* . . .'

He pressed the Delete button. And then, for the first time in many days, he wept.

★ ★ ★

'Everything's ready,' Colonel Charles Napier said, checking his watch. 'I just thought I'd tell you. The Prime Minister wanted to be kept informed of events as they happened.'

The voice at the other end of the line concurred.

Napier waited a moment, still gazing serenely out of the Renault's windscreen.

'The targets have been pinpointed,' he breathed. 'The strike will commence in the next thirty minutes. I'll contact you when it's over.' He pressed the Call End button and slipped the mobile into his jacket.

Once again he checked his watch.

Franklin sat on the sofa, the empty bottle of Jack Daniel's on the floor beside him. He wondered why he wasn't drunk. Where was the oblivion he craved?

Amy's voice came from the stereo speakers, filling the room with sound. Filling his head. When the tape finished he rewound it and played it again.

As he sat there he looked down at the .459 lying on the coffee table, its outline glinting in the dull green light cast by the level indicators of the stereo. The rest of the flat was in darkness. A blackness as impenetrable as the hole inside his soul.

There was a gnawing pain at the base of his skull. Every time he inhaled deeply it felt as if someone was hammering away at the bone with a mallet. He closed his eyes and tried to sleep, tried to slip into unconsciousness but the solitude he wanted would not come.

He adjusted the volume on the stereo, Amy's voice growing louder as he pressed the key on the remote.

'. . . Has no one told you, she's not breathing? . . .'

Tears began to roll gently down his cheeks.

'. . . If I smile and don't believe, soon I know I'll wake from this dream . . .'

Franklin picked up the automatic and hefted it before

337

him. He flicked the safety catch off and turned the weapon so that it was facing him. He pressed it against his forehead, forcing the metal so hard against the flesh that it gouged into the skin there.

'. . . *I'm the lie living for you, so you can't hide, don't cry* . . .'

He closed his eyes tightly, his entire body shaking.

'Fuck it,' he snarled, dropping the weapon and slumping back, breathing harshly.

It would be so easy to pull the trigger. So fucking easy. He ran his hands through his hair and made a strangled sound deep in his throat. All around him, Amy's voice continued to fill the flat. When the tape finished he rewound it once more.

76

They didn't look like soldiers.

The six men that Colonel Charles Napier watched moving towards the front entrance of the block of flats in Camden Town were far more than that, far more than men even. A new breed? A new species? Napier didn't know what they were. He had no interest in any generic name that could be applied to them, nor in a term to describe them. They had once had names but he had never known what those names were. They weren't important.

All that mattered was what they were doing now, and what they were capable of doing. He was more than aware of *that*.

Six of them covered the front. Two more were covering the rear of the building. Another pair were already on the roof, preparing to make their way down. The final two men stood, one on either side of Napier, gazing through the gloom towards the flats. Watching.

If by some chance (and it was remote in the extreme) any of the targets should escape then *they* would deal with them.

'Move into position,' Napier said, his voice barely more than a whisper.

The men he could see moved with incredible speed, having heard his command.

Napier smiled.

No need for electronic communications when your troops could hear a pin drop at a thousand yards.

'Are they *all* moving?' he asked, glancing at the man on his left.

The man nodded slowly, his eyes fixed on the dark outline of the block.

'Stay here,' Napier instructed, hurrying across the concrete forecourt in front of the flats. He reached the hallway.

'Wait for my order,' he said quietly as he began to climb the stairs.

Anyone watching would have thought he was mad, talking to himself, his words floating away on thin air. But the Scot knew that the words had been heard and acted upon. He continued up the staircase, past locked doors and mostly empty flats. Some had lights burning in their windows, others had been boarded up. One, he noticed, had its front door missing. He slipped a hand inside his jacket and touched the SIG-Sauer P220 9mm automatic, prepared to draw it if necessary, although he doubted the need would arise.

He was the only one carrying a firearm. The other twelve men carried knives. Ten inches in length, razor sharp on one side and serrated on the other.

They were able to use every kind of offensive device, naturally. But knives seemed more suited to them when it came to close-quarters work. Sometimes they carried sidearms. Occasionally rifles or sub-machine guns. Weapons were issued to suit the operation. In this case, knives had been deemed the most appropriate.

As Napier reached the landing he paused, seeing six men moving like silent shadows along the walkway outside the flats. One or two of them looked around in his direction and fixed him in a gaze that penetrated the darkness with the ease of infrared.

The nostrils of another flared, recognising his scent. Instantly noting it as different from the smells that had drawn them to this place where they now waited.

All of them could smell the chemical that Napier carried. They knew its aroma well; even though the officer transported it around in twelve small glass phials they were still able to detect it. The acidic odour of Theodrylinol.

They could hear talking from inside the flat. Words being spoken in harsh, guttural tones.

Napier waited a moment, took a step back towards the landing, then whispered one word: 'Neutralise.'

Into Paradise

The door of the flat exploded inwards, pieces of splintered wood spraying into the narrow hallway.

The five men inside heard the deafening eruption and two of them hurried towards the sound. They froze momentarily, disorientated and confused by the sight before them. They were puzzled by the appearance of the figures hurrying through the remains of the door.

The intruders moved with incredible speed. They were so fast that it seemed their feet didn't touch the floor. The first of the men tried to shout a warning but a strong hand clamped around his neck like a vice. The hand squeezed with unbelievable strength. He felt fingers digging into his flesh, then tearing *through* the skin of his neck, gouging into the muscle and beyond, crushing the pharynx until they closed around the tube that was his oesophagus.

With one savage wrench, the hand tore his gullet out, ripping a huge length of the slippery tube free. It bulged like a bloated worm in the strong hand, blood spraying madly in all directions. The man dropped to his knees as the pressure was released, his eyes rolling upwards in their sockets.

The other intruders rushed past him, one of them seizing

his companion. There was a flash of steel as the knife was brandished. It cut with staggering speed, the blade carving across the man's face with such fury that it severed his nose. In one fluid, continuous movement, the weapon was wielded with breath-taking skill and precision. Another cut practically severed the man's head as it cut through his right carotid artery. The next cut, delivered with equal savagery, parted the head from the neck with ease.

On a geyser of blood, the head flew into the air then landed again on its stump, the eyes open. The body toppled backwards and lay twitching on the crimson floor, its muscles finally giving up their hold on life. The soft hiss of the collapsing sphincter muscle was clearly audible.

Already the hallway was like a slaughterhouse.

The intruders burst into the living room where two more of the men were. One of them dived for his jacket, pulling the pistol from inside it, trying to turn it on the infidels.

It was useless. There were too many of them and they moved too quickly.

A third man was grabbed by the wrist, his arm forced upwards, the bones in his arm shattering. The point of the shattered radial bone tore through the flesh of his forearm and, when he tried to shriek his pain, a fist caught him in the mouth. It stove in most of his front teeth, sending them backwards into his throat. Such was the power of the punch that the fist tore through bone and erupted from the back of his skull, pulverising the spinal cord.

The body was hurled to one side with the same disdain as a furious child might dispose of an unwanted doll. It slammed into the wall above the fireplace, cracking the plaster there before dropping to the ground.

The remaining man screamed oaths in his own language. He bellowed to Allah to give him strength and to allow him to strike back at these enemies.

343

A knife tore him open from sternum to crotch. His lower body simply opened up like a mouth, his intestines spilling onto the floor before him in a reeking pile. He looked down at the mass of offal and felt curiously little pain and, in spite of his eviscerated state, he made a clumsy dash for the kitchen where his last remaining companion waited with a Kalashnikov gripped tightly in his shaking hands.

He had wanted to die. They had all wanted to die. But in the name of the Prophet. In the struggle against those who would oppress and humiliate them and their homelands. They didn't want to die like this. Slaughtered like animals in a charnel house. Paradise awaited them but they had wanted to enter as martyrs, as warriors.

The man with the AK47 opened up, bullets spraying the kitchen, blasting holes in the walls. He kept his finger on the trigger, emptying the thirty-round magazine in less than five seconds. And as he fired he screamed his fury and his praises to the Prophet and it didn't bother him that several of the bullets he fired hit his companion.

The hammer slammed down on an empty chamber and he swung the butt at his attacker. The blow was deflected and the man saw the glint of a knife. It cut across his throat, then his belly and both of his thighs, deep enough to sever the femoral arteries and scrape bone. Blood erupted from the wounds. He hit the ground, crimson geysers spurting into the air.

The man on the floor reached out a hand towards the cupboard near him, aware of movement around him, of figures moving so quickly into and out of the room they appeared only as blurs to him. His vision was already fading and he knew that death was closing in but he had to try to fight back against these intruders. He had to ensure his entry into Paradise. If he was to share eternity with his brothers and with his God then he must resist.

He was aware of another man standing close to him. A

344

man who moved much more slowly than the others. An older man. He was looking down at him, watching him with little concern.

He heard words spoken in the tongue of his enemies but they meant nothing. He didn't care what they meant.

He pulled open the cupboard door and thrust his hand into a cardboard box, his fingers closing around something soft that smelled of marzipan. Something that had a detonator jammed into it.

The sounds around him suddenly became more frantic. He sensed fear in the words. He saw the arms of Allah opening to welcome him as the bullets began to drill into his body. The lump of plastic explosive he was holding went up. The world was on fire.

77

For a split second before the explosion, Colonel Charles Napier had a brief moment of unbearable clarity. As if everything inside the flat had been frozen, he found himself able to take in every detail as surely as if he'd been studying a painting.

He saw quite clearly the bodies of the terrorists lying around, gutted, decapitated and mutilated. The blood that covered the floor was like a heaving red carpet. The weapons strewn all around. The six men he commanded were drenched in the blood of their targets, looking unconcerned amidst the appalling slaughter. And he saw the bullet-riddled man at his feet detonate the plastic explosive.

Napier had known that there was explosive inside the flat. The odour had been detected by his men five or ten minutes earlier. How much there was he didn't know. All he *did* know, in that radiant second of realisation, was that he was going to die.

The knowledge brought a feeling of serenity he had never experienced before. It was as if a huge burden was suddenly lifted from his shoulders. A shadow that had been building for his fifty-two years on earth was suddenly pulled away like a blanket.

Napier felt as if he had time to consider exactly how much explosive might be hidden in the remainder of the flat. He thought it would be a lot. He thought that the combustive effect would be awesome. He was right.

The moment of serenity passed and, with it, Napier's presence on the planet.

Such was the ferocity of the blast the Scot was virtually vaporised by the explosion.

The initial detonation filled the kitchen with a shrieking ball of fire that quickly set off the rest of the Semtex hidden inside the room. In the blink of an eye that too erupted, roaring outwards into the rest of the flat, obliterating all it touched.

The thunderous salvo shook the entire block. Glass was blasted from window frames and pieces of debris, propelled by the screaming fireball, were sent hurtling into the air.

To those passing, the night was turned momentarily orange and white as the explosion tore a hole in the side of the block, ripping in all four directions to devastate everything around it. Flames belched from the holes in the building, licking like incendiary tongues over glass, concrete and stone.

A concussion blast strong enough to knock a man off his feet rolled outwards like an invisible tidal wave from the epicentre of the eruption.

On the courtyard outside the tower block, those of Napier's men who had managed to escape the blast moved quickly away from the scene of devastation. Due to their abnormal speed, three had escaped the blast inside the flat. The others had suffered the same fate as their commander.

They whispered words that were heard by their colleagues two or three streets away. Words that were heard over the roaring flames and the steadily growing cacophony of sounds now merging around the building. Screams, cries for help and the sounds of people dying echoed with

347

incredible clarity in their ears and inside their heads. They smelled blood, human waste, charred flesh and smoke. They felt the searing heat of the fire as surely as if they had been standing within the inferno.

Through the flame-tinted night they saw figures gathering around the remains of the block, pointing up at the fire and talking excitedly. Had they bothered to stop and listen, they would have been able to pick out every word.

But the myriad noises crowded in on them. The chorus of sound was painful to their ultra-sensitive ears. They needed to leave this place. To find somewhere secluded. A place where noise wouldn't be so painful. A refuge where the light wouldn't hurt their eyes.

They heard sirens. The emergency vehicles could still be over a mile away but the nine remaining men knew they must not be here when those vehicles arrived.

Their officer was dead and so was a man whom they had known once as a sergeant. In the chain of command, they looked to the one amongst them with the highest remaining rank and he responded. He knew what they had to do now. And he knew they would follow him without question. They were, after all, first and foremost, soldiers. Highly disciplined and highly trained. They had suffered casualties but they had accomplished their mission. However, they knew this was not the time for self-congratulation. It was a time to use their training in the pursuit of preservation.

The crowd gathering nearby was growing by the second. The emergency vehicles were drawing nearer. There would be police on the scene shortly.

The men moved away from the scene of death and destruction, the sounds still loud in their ears. They split up, moving either singly or in pairs. Careful not to attract attention, helped by their unremarkable clothes and the cover of the night. No one looked at them. No one

348

suspected them or what they might be, and that pleased them. They knew where to go and they moved purposefully towards that destination.

78

Franklin woke with a start and dropped the mug he'd been holding. The handle broke off as it hit the floor.

'Fuck,' he grunted, sitting up.

His head was pounding. He had trouble opening his eyes at first. For a second he wasn't sure where he was. The flat was in almost total darkness. The silence crowded in on him from all sides.

When he tried to stand he knocked over the empty bottle of Jack Daniel's that had been propped beside his leg.

'Fuck it,' he breathed again, slumping back down onto the sofa.

Why get up?

He tried to focus on his watch and the face finally swam into resolution.

'Shit,' he murmured.

He had no idea what time he'd fallen asleep. Or how long he'd lain where he was. He'd dreamed but he couldn't remember what about.

Amy probably.

He was angry with himself for not being able to recollect the threads of the visions that had passed through his unconscious mind. Afraid that there had been thoughts of Amy he might have wanted to savour that were now lost.

Franklin reached for the TV remote and switched the set on. He flicked channels, the sound still on mute. A couple of old films. A documentary. The news.

He sat forward slightly as he saw the smoking remnants of a tower block. The caption below read CAMDEN TOWN.

Franklin hit the mute button, raising the volume so he could hear what the newsreader was saying.

'. . . *earlier this evening. As many as twenty people are thought to have died in the blast which was originally believed to be a gas explosion. However, forensics teams are still working at the scene and a police statement issued earlier indicated that the blast may have been the work of terrorists, possibly one of the cells of suicide bombers known to be in the capital at present . . .'*

'Jesus,' whispered Franklin, rubbing his eyes and blinking myopically.

Still want them to come for you? Guns, that's one thing. But bombs . . .

He glanced at the .459 still lying on the coffee table. His mobile phone was next to it and it was *that* he reached for, jabbing in numbers. He pressed it to his ear and waited.

Edward Carter's study was lit by just the mellow glow of the anglepoise lamp on his writing desk. Ordinarily the ambience would have been welcoming. The room on the first floor of Number Ten Downing Street was Carter's private domain. It was a place where he could retreat, even within the relative seclusion of this house he had called home since being elected to the post of Prime Minister.

Carter found that the study was an oasis of calm within his hectic world. He enjoyed the welcoming solitude of

351

the room. Usually, he would go over business papers or answer personal letters but, more often than not, he would read. All his life he'd believed there was great therapeutic value in that pastime. The ability to escape in the pages of a book was a simple joy in his world, where simplicity was often just a word in the dictionary.

He'd read a little that evening, then relaxed in his sitting room with his family around him. The phone call that had interrupted him had sent him scurrying to his study.

The anglepoise lamp caused deep shadow in the corners of the study and Carter shifted uncomfortably in his seat, the phone pressed to his ear. He felt as if the darkness was steadily closing in around him. There was menace in those shadows.

'Are you sure Napier's dead?' he said, his face pale, his jaw set.

At the other end of the line, Doctor Alex Morgan assured him that there was no mistake.

'He was inside the building when it exploded,' Morgan reiterated.

'And there's no chance he could be alive?'

'None.'

'What about the . . .' Carter was struggling to find the words. 'The others. The ones under his command?'

'Three were killed. The rest left the scene.'

'Where are they now?'

'There's been no contact with them since the explosion. I think it's safe to assume they're still in London.'

'But where?'

'As I said, Prime Minister, there's no way of knowing that yet. Their original orders were to return to base should anything go wrong. Something like the death of their commander. As soon as they knew that Napier was dead, they'll have realised they had to make their way back here.'

'Can't you send more men after them?'

'At the moment this operation is still secure. No one other than those few directly involved even know those men exist. If we were to send more troops after them, we'd risk exposing everything.'

'So what do you propose to do?'

'The last dose of Theodrylinol was administered two hours before their attack. It won't begin to wear off for another five or six hours. They'll have secondary symptoms to begin with, but they won't revert fully until around noon tomorrow.'

'What kind of secondary symptoms?'

'They'll become sensitive to bright light. They'll experience occasional states of torpor and probably psychotic illusions.'

'You mean they'll become violent?'

'It's possible, but all they'll want to do now is get back here so that they can receive another shot of Theodrylinol. They'll do that as quickly and efficiently as they can. Without the Theodrylinol, they'll be like addicts going cold turkey. There *will* be a possibility of violence *then*.'

Carter exhaled wearily.

'My God,' he breathed. 'Can't you send someone after them? To administer more of—'

'Without fresh injections of the original drug, Sharafi's drug, some will die. *Some*, not all,' Morgan interrupted, in his most reassuring voice.

'And the virus that's in their bloodstreams?'

'It will remain dormant as long as it isn't exposed to air below freezing.'

'What about the men who were killed in the explosion earlier? Won't the virus spread from *their* blood?'

'The heat of the blast would have destroyed it. It can't survive in high temperatures.'

Carter sat in silence. He felt as if his head was stuffed with cotton wool.

353

'The terrorists were killed,' Morgan said. 'The operation was a success.'

'Don't call me again,' Carter said quietly. He gently replaced the phone.

79

Detective Inspector Vincent Crane took a drag on his cigarette and glanced at the feverish activity going on around him.

'What a fucking mess,' he breathed.

Beside him, at the wheel of the car, DS Kingston nodded slowly.

'What have we got, Del?' Crane asked, his eyes still fixed on the mass of uniformed and plain clothes men milling around. All of them, he assumed, were performing a duty of some kind.

'Forensics report that the explosion *was* caused by Semtex,' Kingston answered. 'An assortment of weapons were found inside what was left of the flat. Assault rifles. Pistols. Sub-machine guns. I think it's safe to assume that whoever hit them, hit the right people. And they made a bloody good job of it too.'

'Professionals?' the DI wondered.

'There's supposed to be more than one cell operating in this country, right? What if they got hit by another group of terrorists? A lot of these Middle Eastern groups are fragmented, aren't they? It might have been something personal between them, something religious.'

'No. If there is more than one lot of suicide bombers in London then their only concern is causing havoc among us. Westerners. The ones they see as the enemy.' His voice dropped to a whisper. 'So who *did* hit them?' he mused.

'So far only the bodies of the five terrorists have been identified. But all of the dead terrorists *were* names on our list. They were the cell we've been looking for.'

'*How long* have we been looking for them?' smiled Crane humourlessly. 'Months? Then tonight, someone else comes along and wipes them out just like that.' He snapped his fingers.

'Whoever hit them might have been tracking them for months too, guv,' Kingston offered.

'Yeah, you're probably right,' Crane shrugged. 'I suppose I ought to be dancing around the car because someone's done our job for us.' He took another drag on the cigarette, looking around at the plethora of emergency vehicles parked all around. Ambulances, fire engines and police cars, all with their blue lights turning silently, were blocking the road. A number were parked on the pavements. A fire engine had been brought to a halt on the concrete forecourt at the front of the block. Crane watched one of the uniformed men splashing his face with water that was dripping from a hosepipe.

Plain clothes officers moved among the mass of uniformed men too. All had specific duties and were going about their business with commendable efficiency. Crane focused on one man who stood back from the activity, speaking into a mobile phone. He didn't recognise the man.

'Do you know him, Del?' the DI asked, nodding in the direction of the stranger.

Kingston shook his head.

'Special Branch? The Counter Terrorist Unit?' Crane wondered. He fixed the man in an unwavering stare for a moment or two then looked across at his companion.

'Prints and dental records of the other bodies are being checked. But, so far, nothing,' Kingston told him.

'What a surprise.'

'There wasn't *that* much left to identify of two of them. The place went up like a firework factory. One of the bomb squad guys said there could have been over two hundred pounds of Semtex in there. The biggest miracle is that more people living in the block weren't killed or injured.'

'Any witnesses?'

'None. A few passers-by saw the explosion when it happened. But nothing that went on before. Nothing unusual. Most of the people in the block have been inter- viewed but no one saw anything. They didn't know that there'd been terrorists living near them for the last few months either.'

'They do *now*,' Crane stated, looking up at the smoul- dering wreckage of the flat. Smoke was still rising from the huge hole that had been blown in the side of the struc- ture.

His mobile phone rang and the DI pulled it from his pocket.

'Crane,' he said, still gazing up at the riven tower block. His expression darkened slightly. 'What do *you* want?'

Kingston looked across at him. Crane nodded a couple of times, as if the caller could see his reaction then he pressed the Call End button and looked disdainfully at the phone.

He said nothing.

80

The first two men could still hear sirens as they entered the ticket hall of Camden Town Tube station. But those sounds were growing increasingly distant now. Instead, from below them, they heard the roar of passing trains. They smelled the stink of oil and electricity. They picked up the dusty odour that permeated the tunnels, their nostrils flaring.

The smell didn't bother them. What they wanted was the darkness the subterranean catacombs offered, some relief from the light that was growing stronger by the minute to their oversensitive eyes.

And they were still following orders. Orders that had been issued to them by their commander. The man who had been killed along with three of their companions. He had told them to return to their base in the event of his death.

Ordered them, and they weren't about to disregard those orders now.

The first two of them glanced around at the people who moved back and forth in the hall.

There was a man in a blue shirt counting money behind the glass window of the ticket booth. A uniformed guard was standing close to the entrance of what resembled a glass sentry box. He was gazing aimlessly around, sometimes peering at the many advertising posters that decorated the walls of the ticket hall. One, a bikini-clad young woman on a sun-drenched beach, seemed to hold his attention for longer than most.

The first man murmured something under his breath and his companion nodded, easily able to pick out words that would have been inaudible to any other than those like himself. He turned and walked towards the ticket window. The first man headed for the turnstiles that marked the way to the escalators.

As he moved, the guard looked in his direction for a second.

The man vaulted the barrier with ease.

'Hey,' the guard called, taking hasty steps towards him. 'What are you doing?'

The blade of the knife flashed in the glare of the fluorescent lights. The guard barely had time to realise what was happening before the attack came.

They were two cuts of incredible power and accuracy. The first, across the guard's throat, opened a wound that looked like a fish's gill. It yawned wide and red. The second cut eviscerated him, carving him open from sternum to groin. His internal organs spilled onto the tiled floor as he fell forward in a huge pool of his own blood.

The man behind the ticket window shouted something but, seconds later, the sound was cut off as a fist smashed through the glass and seized him by the hair. He was dragged forwards, his neck pressing against the jagged shards that stuck up like crumbling teeth. His attacker shook him like a dog would shake a rabbit, grinding his neck back and forth over the glass, the pieces acting like a rasp. Blood erupted from the severed arteries and the attacker twisted the ticket seller's head violently to one side, breaking his neck with ease. The body flopped back inside the booth when it was released.

Now both men, their hands and clothes spattered with blood, glanced at each other and nodded. The lips of the first began to flutter soundlessly.

Seconds later, his seven companions moved quickly but unhurriedly into the ticket hall then across to the barrier. They all vaulted it effortlessly, one almost slipping in the guard's blood as he landed.

They headed for the escalators, still moving fast. Some of the people coming up from the platforms glanced across at them. The bodies in the ticket hall would be discovered soon but the nine men didn't care.

As they emerged onto one of the platforms they heard a scream but none of them reacted to it.

The platform was almost empty. There were just two young men and another man and woman walking arm in arm, heading for the exit.

One of the nine men wondered if they should be disposed of, his words audible only to his companions when he whispered them. Two more also voiced their concerns but the one who they had looked to for leadership whispered back that there was no need.

He looked into the yawning mouth of the tunnel. Into the welcoming darkness. Then, without another thought, he stepped off the platform edge and landed close to the nearest rail. The others followed.

They heard words behind them as they made their way along the Underground shaft.

Even in the almost pitch darkness they moved with ease, able to make out the position of the rails effortlessly.

The air was warm inside the tunnel. It smelled strongly of oil and machinery.

The nine men hurried on; vibrations in the ground that they had all detected were growing stronger. They heard the rumbling building, expanding until it filled their ears. They guessed that the approaching train was perhaps half a mile away. They moved on.

The nine men rested.

In the comforting gloom of the disused Underground tunnel they lay, wanting to escape the light. Needing respite from the brightness that had begun to sting their red eyes. They felt cocooned by the darkness. Safe within it.

None of them had even considered what they would do when the morning came. That wasn't important now. All that mattered were the shadows that welcomed them. And hid them.

81

Franklin wiped some crumbs from his mouth and returned to gazing out of the cafe window. He looked down disinterestedly at the folded newspaper on the seat beside him then took another sip of his coffee, wiping his mouth with the back of his hand.

There were other people inside the cafe. Some, like him, were seated alone. Others were in pairs. Talking. Killing time. Keeping warm. Sitting silently with their own thoughts.

Two of the staff, dressed in their slightly off-white uniforms, stood beside the counter chatting to the cashier in their native tongue. Franklin recognised it as Italian. There was a large poster of Juventus Blu-Tacked to the wall above the kitchen door. Sounds of activity filtered out from the hidden room, occasionally accompanied by shouts. He heard the sound of breaking crockery as a plate was dropped.

As he drained what was left in his cup he saw Crane cross the street and enter the cafe.

The policeman glanced around briefly then headed straight for the table where Franklin was sitting and dropped onto the seat facing the younger man.

'Nice place,' Crane said sardonically.

'You're late,' Franklin said.

'I've got other things on my mind,' Crane told him.

'Like the explosion?'

Crane looked at him, his face expressionless. When one of the waiters came over, the DI ordered a coffee.

'I'll have another one too, please,' Franklin added as the waiter nodded and retreated towards the kitchen.

'All right, Franklin, what do you want?' Crane said. 'Why did you want to meet me? And why here?'

'Because it's crowded. It's full of innocent bystanders.'

'What the hell are you talking about?'

'When I get up and walk out of here, you're not going to try and stop me. You're not going to risk any of *their* lives.' He hooked a thumb over his shoulder. 'You wouldn't want me to pull a gun on you in here.' He patted the .459 through his jacket. 'Just in case.'

'Why would you want to start shooting?'

'I told you. When I walk out of here, you might want to stop me.'

'What makes you think that?'

'Because I'm no use to you any more. You don't need me. The terrorists who wanted me dead were killed − I saw it on the news. I've served my purpose as far as *you're* concerned. You don't need any more bait. You've got no more reason to keep me on the streets and you told me before that you'd see to it I did time.' He lit a cigarette. 'I'm not going to prison, Crane.'

The waiter returned with the coffees, set them down and stepped away.

Crane dropped a couple of sugar lumps into his cup and waited for them to dissolve. 'How far do you think you'd get if you did a runner?' the policeman asked. 'You'd be picked up inside twenty-four hours. There's no reason for me to stop you walking out of here. If *I* don't arrest you there are hundreds of other officers who can.'

Franklin sipped at his coffee.

'The news said that there were five terrorists killed,' he said. 'Were they the ones who murdered Amy?'

'We don't know yet.'

'Who killed them?'

'We don't know *that* either.'

'What *do* you know?'

'That's none of your business.'

'I feel cheated. I never got the chance to pull the trigger on them.'

'You did a pretty good job on that geezer using a blow-torch.'

'I wish I could have done that to *all* of them.'

'It wouldn't bring her back, Franklin.'

'I don't give a fuck.'

'I know, you've told me before.'

'So, what happened in Camden?'

'That's classified.'

'According to you, I'll be locked up within twenty-four hours, so what harm's it going to do to tell me?'

The two men regarded each other across the table. Crane reached into his pocket for his cigarettes, cursing under his breath when he found that the pack was empty. Franklin pushed his own across the table towards the policeman who nodded gratefully and took one.

'Someone attacked them,' Crane shrugged. 'There were shots fired. The place went up. Bang. End of story.'

'What about the story I heard on the radio? It said that three people were murdered. Witnesses saw men escaping into the tunnels at Camden Town Tube station,' Franklin said. 'That's not far from where the explosion happened. Is there any link with what happened earlier? Could the guys who hit those terrorists have been the ones who did *that*?'

'Don't believe everything you hear, Franklin.'

'What the fuck is going on?'

'I told you. I don't know.'

'And even if you *did*, it's none of my business, right?'

'Spot on.'

Franklin took another sip of his coffee.

'I'm going to see Amy's body,' he said quietly. 'In the Chapel of Rest. I rang the undertaker earlier. He said it was OK.' Franklin managed a smile. 'I don't think they keep the usual office hours.'

'And then?' Crane wanted to know.

'I haven't thought about it.'

'Make a run for it? Where are you going to go?'

Franklin got to his feet.

'I know I'm not in a position to ask for favours,' he said. 'But I *need* to see her without having to look over my shoulder all the time.'

'You've been looking over your shoulder all your life, Franklin. It's an occupational hazard in your line of work, isn't it?'

'Just until I've seen her. After that, I'll take my chances.'

Crane nodded.

Franklin headed for the door.

'How far do you think you'll get before we catch you?' the policeman called without turning around.

He heard the door close. Franklin was already gone.

82

The undertaker looked up as he heard the door open. He smiled warmly at Franklin and got to his feet, extending his hand which Franklin shook.

'I'm not too late, am I?' Franklin asked, almost apologetically. 'When I rang, I thought . . . because it was late . . .'

'No, of course not, Mr Franklin,' the undertaker told him. 'Would you like to come through?'

He motioned towards a door at the rear of the reception area and waited for Franklin to follow but he remained where he was, looking reluctant to continue.

'Is Amy in there?' he asked quietly.

'Everything's ready, Mr Franklin.'

'Can I smoke?' Franklin said, trying to muster a smile. 'I think I need one.'

The undertaker nodded and motioned again to the door. This time, Franklin walked through when it was opened for him.

He found himself in a short corridor with white painted walls and three other doors leading off it – one to the right and one to the left. It was the one straight ahead that the undertaker led him towards. He gritted his teeth and stared blankly at the door ahead of him.

'If you'd prefer to go in alone, I'll be outside,' the under-taker said.

Franklin sucked in a deep breath.

'No,' he said, clearing his throat. 'That's OK. Thanks.'

The undertaker opened the door and stepped in.

Franklin followed, his fists clenched.

It was a small room. Painted white like the corridor. Lit only by dimmed roof lights that bathed the room in a comforting, almost welcoming, warm glow. There were three wooden chairs against one wall and a small vase of flowers on a high plinth in another corner. The coffin stood on two low trestles in the centre of the room.

Franklin gaped at it but found that he could not move nearer.

Seeing his reticence, the undertaker moved across to the box and looked down at Amy's body. He smiled warmly at her then at Franklin.

'She looks beautiful,' the undertaker said.

Franklin moved nearer and looked into the coffin.

She *did* look beautiful. Her hair had been washed and her make-up was immaculate. Mortician's wax had been used to fill the bullet hole in her temple. If he hadn't known where it was he wouldn't even have been aware of it. She was dressed in a dark grey crew neck sweater and a black skirt. Her hands were neatly clasped on her stomach.

'Who did this?' Franklin said softly, never taking his eyes from her face. 'Who dressed her? Did her make-up and everything?'

'My staff. I hope you approve, Mr Franklin.'

He nodded.

'I won't intrude,' the undertaker said cheerfully, and headed for the door.

'How long have I got?' He shrugged. 'How long can I stay with her?'

'As long as you like. If you need anything, just let me know.'

He closed the door behind him.

'Thanks,' Franklin whispered. Then he looked down at Amy again. He reached out and touched her hands. The skin was more pliable than he'd expected. He was half-surprised to find that it wasn't still warm.

If only it was.

'Hello, babe,' he said quietly, then he fetched a chair and sat down beside the coffin.

83

'*All* of them?' gasped Detective Inspector Vincent Crane. He gripped the mobile in one hand as he drove, squeezing the contraption so tightly it seemed he would crush it.

'Could someone have made a mistake, Del?' he continued, guiding the car through the traffic, the Nokia still pressed hard to his ear.

'It's been checked and double-checked,' DS Kingston told him from the other end of the line. 'Prints. Dental records. Everything.'

'You're telling me that the men whose bodies were found in that flat in Camden last night were all ex-army?'

'All missing in action, presumed killed. One in Kosovo four years ago, the other two in Kuwait back in the early nineties.'

'Just like Robert Clifford,' Crane said, narrowly avoiding a collision with a van just in front of him. 'Were they from the same regiment as Clifford?'

'No. One was a fusilier, the other two were from artillery regiments.'

'Have their regiments confirmed it?'

'According to the army, all three men went missing in action. They each received posthumous awards for gallantry. That's *all* they'd say.'

'Jesus.' He swung the car around a corner, just missing some pedestrians who were crossing the road. 'What about that virus? Any trace of that in their blood?'

'Richardson said all three were carrying it but the fire wiped it out.'

'*Four* other men died in that flat apart from the terrorists. What about the other guy?'

'The fourth man's still unidentified but forensics ran a test on some samples of his blood that were found in the flat. He was *not* infected.'

Crane drove in silence for a moment, attempting to concentrate on the traffic ahead.

'I've got to talk to Richardson,' he said urgently. 'Tell him I need to see the bodies and—'

'Guv, there's something else,' Kingston cut in. 'The Commissioner wants to see you.'

'What the hell for?'

'He didn't say. Word came down from on high, I'm just passing on the message.'

'No clues as to what he might want?'

'Nothing, guv.'

Crane nodded.

'Give me half an hour,' he said.

Franklin had no idea how long he'd been inside the room. It hadn't occurred to him to check his watch. Time, after all, seemed to have little meaning any more. He sat beside the coffin looking at Amy's face, occasionally reaching out to touch her cheek.

Only after a while did he realise that the room was not silent as he'd first thought, but that there was music playing softly somewhere. It was classical music adjusted to such a low volume that it was barely noticeable but just prominent enough to negate what would otherwise have been an unbearable stillness.

Franklin wondered if it was like this for others visiting loved ones. He knew that there were two other rooms in the Chapel of Rest where people could view (the undertaker's term) dead relatives. He wondered if there were visitors in those rooms even now. He tried to imagine who the others might be standing over. A dead parent? A dead spouse? A dead child?

A child.

Like the one that died when Amy died? The one that would have been yours?

These thoughts, along with many others, tumbled through his mind as he sat gazing at Amy.

He wondered why he wasn't crying. And, for a second, he felt a stab of something like guilt that he wasn't. Perhaps, he told himself, it was because she looked so peaceful. So untouched. So perfect. It was a marked contrast to the last time he'd seen her. He glanced at the point on her temple where the bullet had entered and, again, was amazed at how effectively the injury had been disguised.

Just like magic.

Franklin stood up and walked around the coffin, his head still stuffed full of thoughts, many of which he wished would leave him.

He stood at one end of the coffin looking down at the body of the woman he loved.

'I'm sorry,' he whispered.

Sorry for what? That you're alive and she's the one in the coffin? Sorry you couldn't protect her? Save her?

He swallowed and returned to his chair beside her. As he sat down and clasped her hand once more, a single tear welled at the corner of one eye and ran down his cheek.

84

There were four men in the room when Crane entered.

The first he recognised immediately. He was seated behind a large desk, dressed in a uniform, his greying hair short and immaculately groomed. His deep blue eyes were blazing, their glow undiminished by his fifty-three years. Police Commissioner David Oster nodded in Crane's direction and motioned him towards a chair that had been placed in front of the large desk that was the focal point within the room.

The two men seated at either end of it were both in plain clothes and Crane had no idea who they were. But the fourth man, reclining comfortably on the leather two-seater sofa against the right-hand wall, looked familiar to the DI. The man raised his head briefly and looked indifferently at the policeman before returning his attention to some files he was poring over. For a moment Crane wondered if his appraisal was wrong. He glanced at the man again and was certain of his identity. It only served to increase his sense of unease.

'Please, sit down,' Oster said and when he spoke there was a warmth in his voice not usually associated with men in positions of such power.

Crane did as he was instructed, glancing at the two men to his superior's left and right.

'I know you're wondering why you're here,' Oster began. 'So I won't waste your time, or *ours*, with irrelevant details. Suffice it to say that what passes between us in this room from this point on is to go no further. Is that understood?'

Crane shuffled in his seat and nodded.

'That isn't a request, by the way, it's an order,' Oster added. 'One which, if necessary, will be enforced with the sternest action possible. The gravity of the situation we're here to discuss makes that imperative.' Any warmth in the commissioner's tone had, by this time, disappeared to be replaced by a hard edge.

'May I ask which situation that would be, sir?' Crane enquired.

'I'm coming to that, Detective Inspector,' the commissioner told him. 'In the meantime, it's important that you know the positions held by my colleagues.' He gestured to the men on either side of him. 'Their names needn't concern you but their capacity should. The gentleman to my right represents the Counter Terrorist Unit.'

Crane nodded a greeting to the slightly overweight man with thinning hair.

'The one to my left is here on behalf of SO11,' Oster continued.

'Criminal Intelligence,' said Crane, a little warily. 'That's Top Secret.'

The man smiled.

'You sound troubled by that, Detective Inspector,' said the man. He was dressed in a dark blue suit. It was quite a contrast with his red hair, Crane mused.

'Should I be, sir?' the policeman wanted to know.

'The other gentleman present,' Oster went on, motioning towards the individual seated on the leather sofa, 'is here representing Her Majesty's Government.'

373

'Gerald Collinson,' Crane said flatly.

The Home Secretary nodded curtly, steepled his fingers and kept his gaze on the DI.

'As I said earlier, Crane, whatever's said within the confines of this office is not to be repeated outside it. There are matters of National Security at stake here. Information that must never become public knowledge.'

'I understand, sir.'

'Very well, then I'll get to the point. You and a team under your command have been investigating the attempted robbery of a Securicor van that resulted in the discovery of thirty-four bodies. Correct?'

'Yes, sir.'

'The men responsible for the robbery were killed, either at the time, or in the following few days, as were their families.'

Crane nodded.

'Your investigation led you to believe that the murders were carried out by a group of terrorists. One of a number of cells believed to be operating in London, comprised of Middle Eastern suicide bombers. Five of those men were killed in an explosion this evening, at a flat in Camden. All the deceased have since been positively identified as having links to various Islamic fundamentalist groups. That would be a fair summary of your investigation and findings so far, wouldn't it?'

The DI nodded and shifted position slightly.

'What you also discovered is that the thirty-four bodies that were found in that Securicor van had traces of a virus in their bloodstream,' Oster persisted. 'A virus so far unidentified, at least by name.'

'The pathology labs say that it could be highly infectious,' Crane interjected.

'I read the reports,' Oster cut in.

'Three of the men killed in that flat earlier this evening

374

had traces of the same virus in their blood, sir,' the DI continued. 'So did another man linked to this case.'

'Robert Clifford,' Oster stated.

'That's right. Clifford was reported missing, presumed killed, in Kuwait twelve years ago. I was wondering how he managed to turn up in an East End flat when he was supposedly dead. Three of the four men killed earlier tonight, the ones responsible for the deaths of the terrorists, had also been reported missing, believed dead. The army confirmed that. They were *all* ex-army.'

'And what does that lead you to believe, Detective Inspector?' the man from the Counter Terrorist Unit enquired.

'Well, sir, apart from confusing me, it makes me wonder what the hell the army have got to do with all this,' Crane declared.

'As far as you were aware, terrorists were responsible for the bodies in that Securicor van. Correct?' Oster regarded the younger man evenly.

'Yes, sir.'

'Evidence pointed to the fact that terrorists were responsible for the murders of the men who tried to rob that Securicor van,' the commissioner continued. 'As well as for the murders of their families. That *would* be a fair assumption, would it not?'

Crane nodded.

'Would it trouble you to discover that terrorists have never been remotely connected with the case that you've been working on?' asked the man from SO11.

'So who the hell have we been chasing, if you don't mind me asking, sir?'

'Are you a patriot, Detective?'

The words came from Collinson. Crane glanced in his direction, a slightly puzzled expression on his face.

'Do you care about this country?' the politician

continued. 'Its safety? The well-being of its citizens? Do you believe that certain measures should be taken to ensure its security is not breached? That there is a cost, both financial and moral, that comes with such measures?'

'You're losing me, sir,' Crane said irritably. 'What has my patriotism got to do with this case?' He looked at Oster and the other two men seated at the desk as if for clarification. They sat immobile before him.

'You accept that certain steps have to be taken to ensure that the enemies of this country are kept at bay?' Collinson continued. 'Just answer the question.'

'I suppose so,' snapped Crane. 'Yes. Is that what you want to hear?'

'This Government *took* those steps, some years ago,' Collinson said proudly. 'The unfortunate chain of events that have transpired during the last few weeks have uncovered what had previously been, of necessity, known to only a few.'

'Excuse me, sir,' Crane said, looking first at Collinson and then at the other three men. 'But I haven't got a clue what you're talking about. What has any of this got to do with my investigation? And, more to the point, why did you call me in here tonight?'

'Because you're being taken off the case,' Oster said, holding the DI in an unblinking stare. 'The investigation is being closed.'

85

'Why?' Crane gaped. He looked slowly at each of the four faces that opposed him, searching for some glimmer of an answer in their expressions. 'We're getting closer,' the DI said. 'We're putting the pieces together but it's going to take time and—'

'You said yourself that you had no idea what was going on,' Oster snapped, interrupting him.

'I'm finding it *more* difficult to understand what I'm being told in this room, sir,' Crane said, his voice rising in volume slightly. 'I'd also like to know why a major investigation is being terminated when it's nowhere near its conclusion. First I'm investigating the discovery of thirty-four dead bodies with the heads, hands and feet missing. Bodies, I might add, that are infected with a virus no one's ever seen before. Then, on top of that, I've got an attempted robbery and, within a few days, more murders to deal with too. I thought I was chasing terrorists . . .'

'Who do you think you *are* chasing?' asked the man from SO11.

'I was hoping someone in *here* might tell me that,' barked Crane. He looked around at the four men, his temper barely under control.

'This situation is more complicated and potentially more damaging than you could ever imagine, Detective Inspector,' Collinson offered.

Crane looked at his superior with narrowed eyes. 'Tell me what's going on,' he said quietly.

'The bodies in the Securicor van were ex-army too,' said the balding individual from the Counter Terrorist Unit. 'All of them. They were being removed for disposal.'

'Who killed them?' Crane wanted to know.

'Technically, no one. They'd all been listed as missing in action. Many of them as long as fifteen years ago. The heads, hands and feet were removed to prevent identification but I'm sure you'd worked that out,' he continued.

'Why were they being disposed of?' Crane asked.

'They were failed experiments,' Collinson interjected. 'The virus that was found in their bloodstreams was the residue of a drug that has been the subject of research and development for some time now. It had been used on those in the van but had not had the required results. There were other men escorting the van. The drug had been used on them but *with* the desired effect. They were ensuring that the vehicle reached its destination. That, as you know, didn't happen. When the van was attacked, its escort responded by shooting the men who ambushed it.'

'Those that weren't killed at the time were tracked down and eliminated at a later date,' Oster said. 'As were those connected with them. Their families.'

'The men escorting the van, the same ones who eliminated the criminals that attempted to rob it, were also responsible for the removal of five terrorists in Camden earlier this evening,' the representative of SO11 said, as if this portion of the story was his to tell. 'Unfortunately, three of *them* were also killed in the explosion, as was their commanding officer. Nine left the scene. There's been no contact with them since.'

378

'Where are they now?' Crane asked.

'They entered the Underground system,' Oster said. 'It's very possible they're using the tunnels to move around, to stay out of sight and to remain in the darkness.'

'The drug makes them sensitive to light,' the Counter Terrorist man added, almost as an afterthought.

Crane shook his head. There were so many questions whirling about inside his mind that he hadn't got a clue which to ask first.

'Jesus Christ,' he murmured. 'What *is* this?'

'It's a matter of National Security,' Collinson said. 'And that is what it must remain.'

'The Government knew what was going on,' Crane said, looking at the Home Secretary.

'Of course.'

'And the security forces? The army?'

'It was a very large undertaking,' Collinson smiled. 'But necessary.'

'But now it's gone tits-up,' Crane said quietly.

'There *have* been problems,' Collinson said. 'To put it in less *colourful* parlance.'

'We want you to find these missing men, Crane,' said Oster.

'How?'

'By searching the Underground system.'

'You told me I'm off the case, what's it got to do with me?'

'The case concerning the Securicor van and its contents *is* closed,' Oster snapped. 'The matter of these nine men is *not*.'

'It's insane,' Crane snapped. 'How the hell am I supposed to conduct an operation like that?'

'The nine men entered the tunnels just over two hours ago,' Oster told him. 'By one a.m. the entire London Underground system will have shut down. The only civilians moving around down there then will be cleaners and maintenance workers. No other members of the public.'

'You and your men will enter the system and search it,' the SO11 representative announced. 'Find the nine men and eliminate them.'

'I'm not trained for this kind of work, nor are my men. I'm a detective, not a member of the SAS. Why don't you use guys who've done this kind of thing before?'

'You'll be given command of several Armed Response Units,' Oster told him. 'A number of army details will also act as back-up and support.'

'We don't want to create a public panic,' Collinson added. 'If the population of London think that the Underground is filled with suicide bombers there'll be hysteria. You know how jumpy everyone got when there were rumours of a possible gas attack in the Tube system. Imagine the reaction if *this* got out. It has to be done quickly, efficiently and with the minimum of exposure.'

'There are plenty of derelict stations down there,' the representative of SO11 said. 'Many of them are still connected to the normal system by disused tunnels. You can move around quite safely using those where possible. We have schematics of the system that you can use. It'll give you and your men greater ease of movement down there.'

'Why not just let the army take care of it?' Crane snapped. 'They'd be sorting out one of their own fuck-ups then, wouldn't they?'

Oster glared at him.

'Can you imagine the public reaction to seeing armed troops in the Tube system?' Collinson reminded him. 'This operation is to be conducted with the minimum of exposure. That's why it's being conducted at night, when the system is not in use.'

'You'll have from the time the Underground shuts down

until the time it opens again tomorrow morning,' Oster told him. 'That should be more than sufficient.'

'And what will the Armed Response Units be told?' Crane demanded. 'What the hell do I tell my men?'

'That they're looking for terrorists,' Collinson interjected. 'The media have already been told that the police are searching for more possible suicide bombers. As far as the public are concerned, their safety is in your hands. You could come out of this a hero, Detective Inspector.' The Home Secretary smiled.

'Or a fucking corpse,' Crane grunted.

There was a long silence, finally broken by the DI. 'What kind of weapons are these men carrying?' he wanted to know.

'Knives,' Oster said.

'*Just* knives?'

'That's all they need,' the representative of SO11 declared. 'But they *will* utilise their other skills to protect themselves.'

'What other skills?' Crane demanded.

'Their five senses are a hundred times more developed than normal, due to the drug,' Collinson said.

'So what are you telling me? They'll *smell* us a mile away? Hear our footsteps half an hour before they even see us?'

'Not necessarily,' the red-haired man offered. 'If you're careful and you move sensibly you should be able to get close enough to do the job.'

'Can I have that in writing?' Crane rasped.

'Any more questions?' Oster said.

'About ten thousand, sir,' Crane protested. 'But I don't suppose asking them now would do much good, would it?' He looked at the men facing him.

There was another silence.

'How the hell do you think you can cover up something this big?' the DI demanded.

'Don't delude yourself, Detective,' the Home Secretary

smiled. 'Do you think this is the *first* time an undertaking on this scale has been attempted? Life is full of secrets, isn't it?'

He got to his feet and placed a sheet of paper on the desk. He pushed it towards the DI.

'The Official Secrets Act,' the Home Secretary said.

Crane looked at him then at Oster.

'Sign it,' the commissioner said. 'On the final page. There's no need for you to read it. You know what it says.' He turned the document towards Crane and jabbed an index finger at the relevent area.

Crane paused a moment then scribbled his signature.

'You may leave,' Oster said finally. 'And remember, what you heard here *remains* here.'

'What if we don't get them?' Crane asked.

'Then the matter will be passed to someone else,' the red-haired man said, matter-of-factly.

'Just like that?' Crane sneered. 'You don't *want* me to come out of there, do you? That's why you're only using the army as back-up. If *I* die down there then it doesn't *matter* whether this conversation ever happened or not, does it?'

He got to his feet, looked at his superior then at the other men in the room and thought about saying something else. He realised how futile it would be. What the hell was he going to say? He turned and walked towards the door.

'I hope you appreciate the trust we're showing in you, Detective Inspector,' Collinson called as he reached the door. 'Don't disappoint us.'

Crane paused, thought about replying but then decided against it. He stepped out of the room and shut the door behind him. It took all of his self-control not to slam it as hard as he could. His fists were clenched so tightly his nails were digging into his palms.

382

86

Time had lost its meaning for Matt Franklin. As he sat beside the coffin, head lowered, occasionally gazing at Amy, he realised that had been the case not just since he entered the undertakers that evening, but since this entire business began.

Ever since they'd opened the Securicor van on that rainy night. Since the first bullet had taken George Nicholson's head off, everything had fused into one long nightmare. Each day indistinguishable from the next. How long had it been?

Franklin closed his eyes for a moment.

Who fucking cared?

He tried to think back on what had transpired. The attempted robbery. The deaths of his friends. Of Amy. The attempts on his own life.

Now, as he looked at Amy, lying serene in her coffin he was beginning to wish that one of them had succeeded. There was nothing left for him now. Even the prospect of revenge had been taken from him. His only reason for living had been the knowledge that he might find Amy's killers. Now even *that* promise was lost. Franklin felt cheated. They were dead, but not by *his* hand.

He got to his feet and, yet again, walked slowly around the casket, his knees creaking protestingly. The music was still playing softly in the background, a soundtrack to his thoughts.

Franklin reached into his pocket and took out his cigarettes. He screwed one between his lips but made no attempt to light it. Pausing, he gently laid the palm of one hand on Amy's stomach.

What would it have been, he wondered? A boy or a girl?

No, don't. Down that road lay madness.

He took his hand away and, instead, gently stroked her cheek, his eyes fixed on her features. Features that, in a day or two, he would never see again. Once she was buried that was it. She was already gone from his life. In a couple of days she'd be further separated from him by six feet of earth. All he'd have left would be memories. Visions captured on film. Her voice on tapes. Her clothes. The sum total of twenty-eight years. Not much really.

Franklin chewed on the filter of the cigarette, shifting the Rothmans from one side of his mouth to the other until he finally pulled it free and dropped it into his pocket.

His stomach rumbled protestingly. He hadn't eaten since breakfast and he had no idea what the time was now. It was as if his refusal to look at his watch would somehow prevent the inexorable march of time.

He'd heard movement outside the room occasionally and wondered if the undertaker was going to come in and check on him. But no one had showed and for that he'd been grateful. The movement beyond the closed door could have been cleaners for all he knew.

He wondered if they might know how to wash away pain.

Very philosophical.

384

Franklin sat down and stretched, his joints popping. There were footsteps outside the door again. He heard a knock. It was hard and insistent. There were voices too.

A moment later the door opened.

'What the fuck are *you* doing here?' Franklin rasped.

He stood up, anger filling him.

'I thought you'd be here,' said the newcomer.

'Good for you. Now fuck off.'

'I tried to stop this intrusion, Mr Franklin,' the under-taker said apologetically.

'It's not your fault,' Franklin told him.

'We need to talk,' the newcomer said.

'You've got nothing to say that I want to hear. Get out.'

'At least listen to me.'

Franklin paused for a moment, glaring angrily at the newcomer.

'Not in here,' he said finally, glancing at Amy.

'The car's outside. We can talk there.'

Franklin hesitated a moment then nodded to the under-taker.

'It's OK,' he murmured.

Then he followed DI Vincent Crane out of the room.

'Why didn't you just whack the fucking cuffs on me in there?' Franklin hissed, indicating the undertakers.

In the passenger seat of the silver-grey Orion he lit a cigarette and drew hard on it.

'I didn't come here to arrest you, Franklin,' Crane told him.

'Why not? That's what you *want* to do, isn't it? That's what you're *going* to do?'

The two men regarded each other intently for a moment.

'You wanted a crack at the men who killed Amy, right?' Crane said finally.

'They're dead, remember?'

'No they're not.'

'Bullshit. They were killed in that explosion in Camden earlier tonight. All of them. You told me that.'

'I was wrong,' Crane said, his voice low.

'Why are you telling me this?'

'Because I thought you had a right to know.'

Franklin blew smoke in the policeman's direction. 'Since when did I have any rights as far as *you're* concerned? Why are you *really* telling me?' he said.

'I know where they are and I want your help taking them out. I thought you'd have jumped at it. It's a chance to pull the trigger on Amy's killers. That's what you wanted, wasn't it?'

'Who are they?'

'I don't know names, just *where* they are. So, what do you say?'

'Where are they?'

'In the Underground system.'

Franklin narrowed his eyes slightly. 'What the fuck are they doing down there?'

'It's a long story. What's your answer?'

'What if I say no?'

'Then I'll arrest you here and now. You won't even see Amy's funeral.'

Franklin smiled. 'Some fucking deal,' he chuckled.

'No deals, Franklin. I said that before.'

'How many of them?'

'Nine. And I'll tell you now, they're no mugs. Chances are you could end up buried beside your girlfriend before the end of the week.'

'Suits me,' Franklin said, a steely edge to his voice. 'But not before I've taken some of those fuckers with me.'

'So, are you in?'

'Yeah, and before you start trotting out any more shit about me getting a chance to kill the men who murdered

Amy, I *know* why you want my help. It's because I'm expend-able.'

'I'm beginning to know how you feel,' Crane murmured cryptically.

The detective swung himself out of the car and walked to the boot. Franklin joined him, watching as the policeman opened it.

'These belong to you,' Crane announced, gesturing towards the contents of the car's rear compartment.

Franklin looked in at the SPAS and the 9mm Beretta 12S sub-machine gun. He smiled.

'What's the catch?' he asked.

'There's a strong possibility you'll die,' Crane told him. 'Is that a big enough catch?'

'Tell me something I *don't* know.'

'Are you still carrying that .459?'

Franklin nodded.

'Good,' the DI muttered. 'You're going to need it. And anything else you can carry.'

87

The torch beams cut through the darkness of the tunnels, illuminating the cables that ran alongside the curved walls like entrails inside some vast concrete belly. Franklin shone his torch down at his feet every now and then, conscious, as were all the men, not to stray too near the central rail. The live one that carried fifty thousand volts. The one that would fry a man in the blink of an eye should he touch it.

The air was thick, almost palpable, tinged with the odour of oil, hot metal and rubber. Franklin took small, shallow breaths as if reluctant to fill his lungs with the cloying smell of the tunnels.

He walked just behind DS Kingston who cursed under his breath when a large mouse scuttled across his foot. At least he hoped it was a mouse.

The DS shone his torch in the direction of the movement and saw a long hairless tail disappear into a hole at the base of the tunnel wall opposite.

Crisp bags rattled in the soft breezes, some caught between the tracks. Franklin saw a Pepsi can roll past like some kind of metallic tumbleweed. A portion of newspaper was also stuck to the far rail. Yellowed and slightly burned at one corner, he could only guess how long it had been there.

Led by Crane, the men moved cautiously along the tunnel, away from the southbound platform at Warren Street, each of them pressed as tightly as possible to the wall of the tunnel.

'Why the fuck didn't they cut the power down here?' Franklin asked, shining his torch onto one of the live rails.

'Maintenance work,' Crane told him, moving cautiously onwards in the darkness. 'They test trains at night to make sure they're running properly. That kind of thing.'

'You mean there are still trains running down here?' asked one of the Armed Response Unit men.

'Only a handful,' Crane told him. 'The network's shut down for the night now.'

'What about the other units down here?' Franklin wanted to know. 'How do we communicate with them?'

'We don't,' Crane told him. 'Not *below* the surface. The army's insisted on radio silence. If we want to talk to the others someone has to go up top,' he gestured towards the tunnel roof. 'Do it by two-way.'

'Great,' Franklin muttered.

Thirty minutes earlier, fifteen teams of armed police, each of them equipped with Heckler & Koch MP5K submachine guns and protected by Kevlar body armour over their plain clothes, had entered the London Underground system at various points.

Fifteen teams of five men each (apart from Crane's team whose ranks had been swollen by the addition of Kingston and Franklin) were searching the Underground system from all points of the compass using both serviced and disused tunnels. Their search was to be exhaustive. The terrorists they'd been told they were hunting had to be found and wiped out. And before morning came.

It was unusually warm inside the subterranean shafts.

Franklin could feel sweat running down his back and his hands were clammy on the grips of the Beretta 12S. It was like breathing inside a cooling furnace and each breath made him want to spit out the impurities in the rancid air. The Kevlar was heavy. He felt as if he was moving in slow motion. He hoped that wouldn't be the case if he had to avoid an approaching train. He put his left hand against the tunnel wall as if trying to detect the vibrations that would warn of such an eventuality but all he felt was the accumulated dirt of decades. His fingers were black as he pulled them away. As he wiped some sweat from his forehead he left a dirty smear across his flesh. He wiped the remaining grime on his jeans as if it was contaminated.

Behind him, the other men moved with equal caution, each attempting to tread assuredly within the gloom. Franklin could hear one of them breathing heavily. The man at the rear of the line glanced behind him three or four times as they moved deeper into the tunnel. Power in all the stations had also been left on but the light from the tunnel mouth was growing fainter, the blackness swallowing them. Up ahead, the murkiness closed around them like some malevolent fist, squeezing out the light.

Franklin felt like a child, afraid of the dark. His own breathing was ragged and, all the time, the heat inside the tunnel seemed to be building. He wondered how much of that was fear.

Fear? Anticipation?

Now that he was closer to the men who had murdered Amy the desire to confront them was almost overwhelming. For the first time since this entire scenario had begun, he was confused. Driven by the need for revenge but apprehensive at what he might find. However, as he continued to trudge along inside the blackness of the tunnel he realised that his main concern was that it would be someone else who found these men first. He feared that another man would drill bullets into those he so desperately wanted to see dead.

At the front of the line, Crane kept his torch pointed ahead, the broad beam now his only source of light in the shadow. He had a map tucked into his belt, part of the schematic given to him by his superior. It showed the entire London Underground system, including disused stations, air vents, ventilation ducts and entrances in and out of the tunnel walls that were used by maintenance crews who worked on the subterranean network. Goodge Street, the next southbound station on the Northern line, was another quarter of a mile away. Crane estimated it would take them around ten minutes to reach it.

Once there, he and his companions could at least take a short break. Recover their strength. Crane was surprised at how draining the trek through the labyrinthine tunnels actually was. That, coupled with the constant vigilance and the ever-increasing tension, was enough to test the mental and physical stamina of any man. He wiped sweat from his forehead with the back of one hand and walked on.

'Why did the commissioner request *his* involvement, guv?' Kingston asked, pointing his torch at Franklin. The powerful light was secured to the sub-machine gun with masking tape.

'Watch where you're pointing that fucking thing, dickhead,' Franklin rasped.

'The commissioner didn't request him,' Crane snapped. '*I* did. Now shut up, both of you.'

Kingston slowly swept the beam away from Franklin and walked on.

Crane shone his torch along the wall, the beam illuminating the blackness. He steadied the light, his hands closing more tightly around the grips of the MP5K.

As they moved further along the tunnel, Franklin's heart began to thud a little harder.

88

'Nothing,' said Crane. 'Not a sign of them.' He ran a grubby hand through his hair and exhaled wearily.

Crane, Franklin, DS Kingston and the five officers of the Armed Response Unit were on the platform at Goodge Street. A number were seated, slumped against the advertising posters that decorated the walls.

'Nothing from any other unit either,' Kingston said, digging in his pocket for change. He wandered across to the chocolate machine nearby, fed in some coins and extracted a bar of Fruit & Nut. He had just returned from the surface and his face was oily with perspiration.

'Not one?' Crane muttered, exasperated.

'They all say the same,' Kingston told him. 'None of them have seen or heard anything since they came down here.' He broke off a square of chocolate and pushed it into his mouth.

'Perhaps there's no one to find,' Franklin said, reaching for his cigarettes. 'What if these bastards aren't even down here?'

'He's got a point,' one of the ARU men added. 'I mean, what kind of terrorists hide in a bloody Underground system anyway?'

Crane merely looked at the man.

Go on. Tell him who you're really looking for. Tell them all. Let them know what they're up against.

'What about the air vents in the tunnel?' Franklin asked. 'Someone could be using *those* to move about.'

'Do you want to go back and have another look?' one of the ARU officers called.

Some of his companions laughed.

'If it means finding out where these fuckers are hiding then yeah,' Franklin snapped. 'I'll go if *you* haven't got the balls.'

The policeman glared at Franklin and took a step towards him.

'Shut up, both of you,' said Crane wearily. 'No one's going back. We're moving on.'

'And how long do we wander around down here like idiots?' another of the men protested. 'We've already been down here for two hours.'

'Until we find the men we came *down* here to find,' Crane told him.

There was a loud metallic rattle as Franklin worked the slide on the .459. He regarded the pistol for a moment then slid it back into its shoulder holster. 'So what are we waiting for?' he asked, looking at Crane.

The DI pulled several pieces of folded paper from his jacket and opened them up, smoothing the top one out on the platform. Franklin moved closer and saw that it was a detailed map of the Underground system, with each station clearly marked. The other pages were similar but with dozens of other symbols on.

'What are they?' Franklin wanted to know.

'Ventilation shafts. Maintenance openings into tunnels. Air ducts,' Crane explained. 'The crews who work on the tracks use the openings. They lead from tunnel to tunnel as well as up to the surface in some places.'

'What are those?' Franklin asked. He was pointing at several dark lines leading off from tunnels. They were drawn in a different colour ink to the others. 'More vents?'

'They're disused tunnels,' Crane told him. 'Lift shafts or staircases that lead to abandoned stations.'

'There are dozens of them,' the younger man murmured. 'There must be at least twenty disused stations.'

'It's like a honeycomb down here,' the DI said, nodding. 'Some of the abandoned tunnels lead to unused platforms inside working stations. Others go into stations that were on lines that have been bypassed or discontinued. Like that one.' He jabbed a finger at Down Street. 'Not that far from Green Park.'

'Mark Lane. Bull & Bush. Northern Heights,' muttered Franklin, gazing raptly at one of the maps. 'And these are *all* disused stations?'

Crane nodded. 'Some of them have been shut since the thirties,' he said. 'Others have only been closed for five or six years.'

'Christ, there's one in Trafalgar Square,' the younger man exclaimed. 'St Mary's in Whitechapel. Holborn. Aldwych. Brompton Road.'

Crane said, 'We're about forty feet below ground level, some of these are eighty, ninety or a hundred feet below the surface.'

The other men had gathered round and were gazing at the schematics with equal interest.

'According to this there are deep level tunnels *here*, at Goodge Street,' one said.

'And at Camden Town, where the terrorists first entered the network,' Kingston added. He looked at Crane. 'Looks like they knew what they were doing *and* where they were going.'

'Maybe they had copies of your maps,' Franklin offered sardonically.

Crane looked at him then turned back to the drawings.

'We don't even know if they're still down here,' one of the other officers chided.

'Well, we keep looking until we find out one way or the other,' Crane told him. 'One of the units down here will find something.'

'Can we have that in writing?' a dissenting voice called.

'According to this, there's a disused tunnel halfway down there.' Crane gestured towards the tunnel ahead of them. 'It leads through to the Victoria line. Apparently they use some of the disused tunnels for maintenance work on trains. They park them in there until they're finished with them. Like sidings. But not that one by the look of it.'

'Are you sure?' one of the ARU officers wanted to know.

'I'm not sure about *anything* down here,' Crane snapped. 'All I *do* know is that these unused tunnels are filthy and unlit. So watch yourselves.'

'Good hiding places,' Franklin mused.

Some of the other men looked at him, concern on their faces.

Crane folded the maps and stuffed them back inside his jacket. 'Let's find out,' he said quietly. Followed by the others, he strode off down the platform towards the gaping mouth of the tunnel.

89

'Another twenty yards,' Crane said. 'The entrance is just ahead.'

'I hope that schematic's right,' Franklin muttered from just behind him.

As he walked he shone his torch constantly around the interior of the tunnel, aiming the beam first at the opposite wall, then sweeping it from ground to ceiling. Exactly what he was looking for he wasn't sure but the constantly moving light, together with the lights of the other men in the tunnel, gave him some small feeling of comfort in the blackness.

The tunnel curved to the right slightly, Franklin could feel the deviation as he ran his hand along the dirty wall. Crane stopped walking for a moment as he heard a distant rumbling.

A train moving through a far-off tunnel?

Franklin moved past him, sticking close to the tunnel wall. 'Crane.'

The sound of his name made the DI turn.

About ten yards ahead, Franklin was standing motionless, his torch pointing towards the wall of the tunnel.

The DI hurried to join him.

'The entrance to the disused tunnel,' Franklin proclaimed. He gestured towards a sliding metal gate set into the wall. It was slatted, the metal concertinaed like that which protected lift doors. It had been smashed in two. The thick metal was buckled in several places, the hinges practically ripped from the concrete. Pieces of the gate lay inside the yawning mouth of the tunnel.

'Looks like somebody got here before us,' Franklin murmured, aiming his torch into the gloom beyond. The blackness was so dense that the torch beam penetrated little more than three yards.

'Could it be one of the other teams, guv?' Kingston asked, joining his superior.

'No. We're the only ones covering this area,' Crane told him. He took a step forward, shining his light on the floor of the deserted tunnel.

As well as shattered pieces of the metal gate he saw foot-prints in the thick dust. They led off into the impenetrable umbra. 'Someone's been in there,' he said.

'But are they *still* in there?' Franklin wanted to know.

'You said that maintenance crews used these tunnels, guv,' Kingston offered. 'The footprints could belong to *them*.'

'Could do,' conceded Crane, his torch still aimed into the disused tunnel.

'Would a maintenance crew have broken that gate in half?' Franklin added.

'It's been forced from *this* side,' Crane confirmed. 'Somebody broke *into* the tunnel, not out of it.'

All the men stood silently for a moment looking into the gaping maw of the abandoned tunnel.

'Where does it lead?' one of the ARU officers wanted to know.

'Straight through to the Victoria line, heading towards Oxford Circus,' Crane said. 'It's about half a mile from here to the other end.'

Franklin shone his own torch around the mouth of the tunnel and then at the walls and floor. The dust was easily six inches thick. Black and sooty like the aftermath of a fire. When disturbed, it released small plumes into the air. A noxious odour that reminded him of rotting vegetation also mingled with the more cloying stench of neglect and damp.

'Are we going through?' one of the ARU men asked.

Crane nodded.

As if to reinforce his intentions, the tunnel in which they were standing was filled with a rumbling sound that began to grow in volume.

'Train,' Kingston noted.

'All right, come on,' Crane urged. 'But stay close and keep your eyes open. If there *is* someone inside then chances are it's who we're looking for.' He swallowed hard. 'But take it easy in there. Automatic fire in such an enclosed space . . .' He sucked in a breath. '. . . you don't need *me* to tell you the damage it can do. Make bloody sure of your target before you open up. If you have to.'

The roar of the approaching train was growing.

'Let's do this,' said Crane and he stepped through the remains of the metal gate into the enveloping gloom of the disused tunnel.

The other men followed.

90

It took Franklin a moment or two to realise that there were no train tracks on the disused tunnel floor. At first he'd thought they were merely hidden by the dense blanket of muck and dust that coated the ground but, as he stepped into the centre of the huge shaft, he found that his feet connected with nothing more than bare earth. The compacted detritus of decades beneath his feet made it feel as if he was walking on some vast, decaying carpet.

Each step sent more of the choking dust into the air, despite the fact that the men were moving relatively slowly. Most of them were coughing before they'd even got twenty yards into the seething darkness of the shaft. Franklin wasn't sure which was having the worst effect on his respiratory system – the dust or the foul stench that hung in the air.

The walls were black. The dust had accumulated there too. When touched, it came away in lumps.

He looked behind him and couldn't see the entrance to the tunnel. The world had been reduced to a few feet in all directions, visible only by the rays of light emitted by the powerful torches of the men who made their way through the pitch-black conduit. It was like moving through a vast cylindrical tomb.

At the head of the small group, Crane walked on slowly, his light constantly flicking from one side of the tunnel to the other then back ahead towards the funereal depths that awaited them.

Franklin had never known darkness so total. In places it seemed resistant even to the probing lights that the men carried. Motes of thick dust caught in the beams, twisted and turned as the men advanced.

Was the darkness of death like this?

A muffled symphony of sounds reached their ears as they walked. From above, the rumble of traffic. Behind them, the occasional passing train.

Franklin couldn't detect an incline to the tunnel floor but it felt as if they were constantly moving deeper into the earth, through a barrier of darkness that was growing more intense with each passing second. He was becoming convinced that, before they reached the end of the tunnel, they would be surrounded by blackness so total even their torches wouldn't be able to cut through it.

He had lost track of time again and was unsure exactly how long they'd been traipsing through the tunnel. It felt as if the blackness was penetrating his mind, his pores and his reason. His eyes stung. He was finding it difficult to breathe and it felt as if someone had filled his mouth with soot. More than once he spat, the sound echoing inside the shaft.

'Are there any air vents in here?' he said to Crane, his voice muffled by the dust and murky air.

The policeman shone his torch at the tunnel ceiling. All he could see were the circular steel bracings that ran around the inside of the shaft like curved ribs within a tubular chest cavity.

'There's supposed to be a lift shaft about halfway down the tunnel,' the policeman told him. 'But I reckon it will be sealed off. This tunnel's been closed for twenty-odd years.'

'How do the maintenance crews get down here then? Is there a flight of stairs from ground level or something?'

Crane could only shake his head. 'Probably,' he murmured.

He felt sweat running down the side of his face but didn't bother to wipe it away. The beam of his torch flickered slightly, turned briefly orange then flared more brightly again. 'Don't tell me the batteries are going,' he said, his voice catching.

Behind them, another train passed but it seemed a million miles away in the gloom. Even the sound had trouble getting through the choking atmosphere. One of the ARU officers looked back in the direction of the noise but saw nothing. The entrance to the disused tunnel was now invisible.

'I wonder how far it is to the next exit?' Kingston said, joining Franklin and Crane as they plodded on.

'I don't know how far we've come,' the DI said. 'It's hard to work it out in this.' He gestured around him at the darkness as if that were explanation enough. 'Like I said back there, this tunnel leads on for about half a mile.'

He looked back and saw the lights of the remaining members of the Armed Response Unit. They were, as he'd instructed, staying close. There was no more than five feet between each of them as they made their way along the tunnel.

Sweat glistened on the faces of the men and Crane knew they must be hot beneath the Kevlar, just as he was. He sucked in another breath, this time through his mouth, trying to minimise the stench that permeated the tunnel as best he could.

'Wait a minute,' said Franklin, slowing his pace, his torch beam trained on the filthy ground. 'There are no more footprints.'

Crane and Kingston both aimed their own torches at

401

the ground. Behind them, the members of the Armed Response Unit halted, two of them moving closer to the three men ahead of them.

'What's going on?' asked one.

'The footprints we've been following have stopped,' Franklin informed him.

'*Somebody* came in here,' said the ARU man. 'Somebody came through that gate back there.' He hooked a thumb over his shoulder in the direction of the tunnel mouth.

'They couldn't have got out again. They couldn't have got past us,' Kingston offered.

Crane shook his head slowly.

'Didn't you say there was a lift shaft or flight of stairs further down, guv?' Kingston wanted to know.

'The footsteps stop *here*,' Franklin reminded him, waving his torch at the ground. 'Look. There's nothing ahead.' He directed the powerful light before them.

The dense carpet of dust and grime was undisturbed.

'So where *are* they?' rasped Kingston, glaring at Franklin.

'There must be a ventilation shaft that's not marked on the schematic,' said Crane, shining his torch towards the ceiling of the tunnel.

'And if there is how the fuck did they reach it?' Franklin wanted to know. 'This tunnel must be twelve feet high.'

'What kind of terrorists *are* these, for Christ's sake?' one of the ARU officers demanded.

DI Crane ignored the question, contenting himself with sweeping the torch back and forth across the tunnel ceiling.

Tell them. Tell them they're not terrorists.

He swallowed hard.

You can't tell them the truth, can you? Because you're not even sure what the truth really is. You don't know what these men are that you're hunting. You're not even a hundred per cent sure they're men, are you?

'There are no vents up there,' snapped Franklin.

402

'So where are they?' one of the ARU officers replied angrily.

Crane could feel his heart pumping faster. 'Come on,' he said. 'There might be more prints further down the tunnel.'

'Fuck off, Crane,' Franklin hissed. 'They stopped *here*. What's the point of going on? We're not going to find anything. We might as well turn back and look somewhere else.'

'I agree,' said one of the ARU men.

'This isn't a union meeting,' Crane barked. 'I'm not asking for a vote. I'm giving an order. We're moving on.'

Franklin hesitated a moment, looking challengingly at the DI, his face etched with deep shadows in the torch-light.

'You're only here because I *allowed* you to be,' Crane said, leaning close to the younger man. 'Don't fuck me around, Franklin.'

'Or what? Are you going to arrest me? Here and now? Let everyone know who I am? *What* I am? The others might find it interesting.' He reached out one hand and touched the barrel of the MP5K. 'Perhaps it'd just be easier if you shot me.'

'Don't tempt me,' Crane hissed.

'So, what are we doing?' one of the ARU men called.

'Moving on,' said Crane, his gaze still fixed on Franklin. It was as he turned away that the scream filled the tunnel.

91

The sound reverberated inside the circular shaft, drumming off the walls, filling the men's ears. As one, they spun round in its direction, the high keening shriek still strong in the murky blackness.

'What the fuck is that?' one of the ARU men gasped, fear in his voice.

The sound had come from behind them.

They all turned their torches towards the spine-chilling noise, all the beams focusing on the area where the scream had originated.

The ARU officer at the back of the line was plodding slowly towards them, his feet barely leaving the ground, his eyes bulging wide. His companions could only look on as he opened his mouth, trying to form words.

Blood gushed over his lips and down his chest, splattering in the thick dust on the tunnel floor. He swayed uncertainly for a second but, just before he fell, they saw a gaping wound across his throat. So deep it had almost severed his head, the gash opened like the gills of a fish and more blood erupted into the air. His eyes rolled upwards in their sockets and he collapsed.

A figure was standing close behind the dead man. A figure holding a long, double-edged knife.

One of the remaining ARU men quickly slipped the safety catch of his subgun off and squeezed the trigger. In the confines of the tunnel, the sound was incredible.

For brief seconds, the entire shaft was lit by the blinding white of the muzzle flash and Franklin found himself wincing at the strength of the glare.

He thought his eardrums had burst, so intense was the roar of gunfire and, a second later, it became even more unbearable as another of the men opened up.

Firing in short bursts, the men raked the area where the figure with the knife had been standing. The others in the tunnel shone their torches in that direction.

Nothing.

There was another scream.

Another of the ARU men was clutching at a wound in his arm that had opened the limb to the bone from elbow to shoulder. He dropped his gun, the torch bulb shattering as it hit the ground. He clutched at the riven arm, blood gushing through his fingers. He squeezed hard, trying to hold the two edges of the wound together, but it was useless.

Franklin tried to train his light on the rapidly moving figure. He saw it move with incredible speed from one side of the tunnel to the other, moving among the men. The bloodied blade of the knife it carried flashed in the light. He fired two bursts at it.

Again, the sound of gunfire deafened him. Bullets sang off the walls of the tunnel, some blasting chunks of the rotten walls away. Brick dust filled the already choking air. The scream of ricochets added to the madness.

The wounded ARU man was hurrying along as best he could, teeth gritted against the pain, and now all of the men in the tunnel found that they were running deeper into the shaft, desperate to be away from their attacker. And, as they ran, they fired behind them, not caring what they hit as long as *some* bullets struck the intruder.

Franklin saw another figure moving along the right-hand wall. Then another.

Crane, his breath coming in gasps, steadied his own sub-machine gun in one hand and fired a burst that almost emptied the magazine. Empty shell cases spewed into the air and landed noiselessly in the thick dust on the tunnel floor.

'Jesus,' gasped Kingston, looking up.

In the momentary blinding brilliance of another muzzle flash, he looked up towards the ceiling of the shaft. Two figures were moving along the tunnel roof. Crawling like animals, hand over hand on all fours but travelling with unbelievable speed and assurance. They moved so expertly and easily that it seemed as if the tunnel had been inverted and they were simply scrabbling along the floor, such was the pace with which they scuttled.

Kingston fired upwards.

One of the figures fell, blood spouting from five or six wounds. His body crashed to the ground with a thud. The other one kept coming. Making his way inexorably along the tunnel roof, keeping pace with the fleeing men below.

Franklin fired into the blackness again. He saw another figure and realised that there were at least four of them now inside the tunnel.

Two of the ARU men were almost shoulder to shoulder, firing short bursts, attempting to run backwards while facing a foe they only caught sight of in sporadic flashes of searing light.

Another figure went down, blood pumping from a wound in its stomach but it was up again and running on, still moving with the same unbelievable speed.

Franklin felt something heavy slam into him with such power he was knocked off his feet. He went flying, sprawling in the filth on the tunnel floor. Coughing, he tried to pull himself upright, his hand still gripping his gun. He knew that without it, whatever slim chance he had was gone completely.

There was another tremendous impact against his chest and he realised that he'd been stabbed in the stomach.

The knife was torn upwards towards his sternum but the tip only rasped against the Kevlar.

From point-blank range he fired again and saw, in the cold white light from the muzzle, that his shots had found their target. He saw his attacker stagger backwards. Saw him drop his knife as he slammed into the far wall of the tunnel, propelled by the energy of the 9mm rounds.

And then, from beside him another burst of fire drilled across the wall at head height, ripping most of the left side of his attacker's skull away. The figure's head was slammed back against the tunnel wall, lumps of pulverised bone and slicks of brain matter coating the filthy stonework. The body remained upright for a second longer then slid to the ground, leaving a trail of blood smeared on the wall behind it.

Crane struggled to find another magazine as the hammer slammed down on an empty chamber. It had been he who had finished what Franklin had started. He dug in one pocket, found more ammunition and slammed it into the MP5K, eyes scanning the blackness for more movement.

The men still ran headlong down the tunnel, adrenalin surging through their veins. Fear quickening their steps.

Kingston looked upwards again but, this time, saw nothing. He wondered if the figure on the ceiling had managed to get ahead of them so he fired a brief burst in the direction in which they were running.

He could see nothing. Nothing but the blackness that swallowed them all and hid both the positions and the number of their attackers.

Shouts, groans, gasps and the occasional ear-splitting eruption of gunfire filled the tunnel as the men ran on, dashing headlong from an enemy they could not see. They ploughed through the dust carpet, sending up great choking clouds of the reeking matter that was ankle-deep. Every now and then the light of a torch would cut through the gloom. Sometimes it would pick out a figure still pursuing them. Occasionally, one almost alongside them, preparing to strike.

Ahead, Crane heard a low rumbling sound that he recognised. 'We must be getting near the end of the tunnel,' he gasped, his throat and mouth dry, clogged with the filthy dust.

There was another shout from further back. One of the ARU officers opened fire again.

Franklin tried to pick out movement in the momentary flash of light.

'Two left,' he said, barely able to force the words from his bursting lungs.

Two that you can see.

Holding the 12S in one hand he fired, bullets screaming off the walls and ceiling of the tunnel.

The injured ARU officer was running along close by, his arm dangling uselessly at his side. It looked as though the limb had been dipped in red paint from fingertips to shoulder. In the brief flashes of light, Franklin could see bone gleaming whitely within the crimson mess.

The man suddenly pitched forward, weak from blood loss and exhaustion. One of his companions stopped close by him and fired another burst into the darkness, while the other man attempted to drag him to his feet. Like a drowning man treading water, his feet rose and fell uselessly for a moment as he was hauled upright.

Kingston joined them, his eyes still drawn towards the ceiling of the tunnel. The vision of that swiftly crawling figure burned into his brain.

More gunfire. More deafening noise. Franklin felt

something warm and wet seeping from his left ear and realised that his eardrum must have ruptured.

That realisation was cut short as he collided with something so solid that it knocked the wind from him. He fell to the ground again, rolled over in the clinging muck then dragged himself up onto his knees. He looked around frantically in the blackness to find where the attack was coming from.

In front? Behind? From above?

Torch light blinded him and he heard heavy footsteps coming closer. He prepared to pull the trigger but then heard a voice he knew.

'Franklin,' Crane called breathlessly, hurtling towards him so fast it seemed they must collide. 'How far to go?'

'We're there,' the younger man told him, coughing. 'But it's a dead end.'

92

'No,' roared Crane. The sound that exploded from him was a combination of anger and desperation.

And fear?

Franklin was leaning against the brick wall that formed the end of the unused tunnel, the 12S in one hand and the .459 in the other.

'There's nowhere to run,' he gasped.

Crane slammed one fist madly against the wall, as if hoping that the brickwork would crumble. 'Bastard,' he roared, spinning quickly to see that the remaining men under his command were drawing nearer, their juddering torch beams looking like strobes in the inky blackness.

The two ARU men were dragging their injured companion while Kingston covered them, firing back into the tunnel in the general direction of their pursuers.

Finally, exhausted and drenched with sweat and blood, he backed up towards the wall with the others, the subgun hot in his hands.

'Come on, you bastards,' he hissed, squinting into the gloom.

Franklin and Crane, weapons also pointing into the umbra, stood close to the DS. Neither could see anything moving. Crane picked up a torch that had come away from a gun barrel and shone it ahead of him. He swept the beam back and forth, up and down each wall and finally the ceiling.

'If they're still there, I can't see them,' he breathed.

'They're too far back for the torch to pick out,' Franklin said.

'But not out of range of the guns,' snarled Kingston, raising his sub-machine gun.

Franklin pushed the barrel down. 'Save your ammo,' he advised.

'Fuck you,' barked the DS. 'I'm not just going to stand here waiting to be cut to pieces.'

'He's right, Del,' Crane interjected. 'Wait.'

'You're siding with this bastard now?' Kingston said breathlessly.

'It's not a matter of sides,' snapped Crane. 'He's right. Save your ammunition. We're going to need it.'

One of the ARU officers shone his torch on the wound that had incapacitated his companion. 'Fuck,' he wailed. 'It almost took his arm off.' He dug in his pocket for a handkerchief and attempted to tie a rough tourniquet around the other man's arm, near the shoulder. It barely halted the flow of blood and the injured man was close to unconsciousness.

'Who are they?' said the third man evenly.

Crane could just make out his features in the torchlight. There were slicks of blood on his cheeks and forehead.

'What kind of terrorists fight like that?' the man persisted.

'They were crawling along the *roof* of the tunnel, I saw them,' Kingston said, his eyes bulging, his breathing ragged.

'So did I,' said the other ARU man, his gaze never leaving Crane. 'I'll ask you again. Who are they?'

'What the hell does it matter who they are?' Franklin cut in. 'What *we* should be thinking about is how to get

411

past them because it's the only way out of here.' He banged the brick wall behind him as if to emphasise what he'd just said.

'It's impossible,' said the man kneeling beside his stricken companion.

'We dropped two, maybe three of them, back there,' Franklin reminded him. 'We can do it again.'

'We don't know how many there are,' one of the ARU officers insisted. 'The whole fucking tunnel could be full of them.'

'Only nine came down here in the first place,' Crane said. 'Even if *all* of them are here in this tunnel, Franklin's right. There's only six or seven left now.'

'Only six or seven,' the ARU man murmured sardonically.

'Six or seven of *them* and six of us,' Crane emphasised.

'It's going to take two of us just to carry *him*,' Kingston said, indicating the injured man lying close by.

'Leave him here,' Franklin offered.

'And let him die? No chance,' snapped one of the ARU men.

'If we take him there's a chance we could *all* die,' Franklin hissed.

'I'm not leaving him,' the ARU officer insisted.

'Then you die here *with* him,' Franklin said through clenched teeth. 'But there's no way *I'm* waiting until those fuckers decide to come in and pick us off when *they* feel like it.'

There was an uneasy silence, then Franklin continued. 'How many torches have we got left?'

'Three,' said one of the ARU officers. 'The others were damaged. Some of the weapons were lost too.'

Franklin banged one hard then looked at the fading orange glow coming from the filament. There were three large cracks across the thick plastic face of the torch. 'This one's almost had it,' he said wearily. 'Another twenty minutes and we won't be able to see a hand in front of us. We've *got* to get out, while we've still got a chance.'

'Is there no way through that wall?' Kingston wanted to know, gesturing towards the brick blockade behind them.

'If we had sledgehammers and dynamite maybe,' Franklin intoned. 'Otherwise, forget it. It's probably two or three feet thick.'

'Where are the army?' Kingston wanted to know. 'I thought they were supposed to be providing back-up.'

'Only *above* ground,' Crane told him. 'Anyway, with radio silence maintained, they've got no way of finding us.'

'What you're saying is, we're on our own,' Franklin muttered.

'Nine terrorists came down here, you said,' one of the ARU officers offered tersely. 'Nine. Are you sure that was all?'

'Who cares?' Franklin rasped. 'All that matters is that they're trying to kill us. Well, fuck that. I'm not going to stand here and wait for them to make the first move.'

'And what are you going to do, hero?' an ARU man snorted.

'I'm getting out of here and I'm going to kill those bastards in the process,' Franklin told him. 'If you want to stay here with your mate while he bleeds to death that's *your* business. Now, if anyone wants to come with me that's fine. Otherwise, I'll take my chances.'

He looked around at the other men.

'It doesn't seem as if we have a choice,' Crane said finally. 'We've got to go back the way we came in.'

'Right through whatever's waiting back in the tunnel?' breathed one of the ARU officers.

'Spot on,' Franklin hissed. 'Right *through* them.' He brandished the 12S defiantly before him.

413

93

The first body they found was lying about a hundred yards away.

Crane, moving slightly ahead of the other men, fixed it in the beam of his torch and halted immediately. Franklin stepped up to join him, his own weapon aimed at the immobile figure sprawled on the tunnel floor, head turned away from the advancing group.

'We'd better check it,' the policeman said quietly. He looked back at Kingston. 'Cover us, Del.'

The DS nodded, standing motionless, sweat running down his face. The heat inside the tunnel seemed to have increased during the last thirty minutes, not helped by the furious combat and the mad dash to the dead end the men had been forced to endure.

Behind Kingston, one of the ARU men swept his torch constantly back and forth and up and down, attempting to illuminate the tenebrous gloom. His companion was supporting the third ARU officer who had slipped into unconsciousness and whose gaping arm wound was still weeping out blood slowly and steadily.

'If Kingston opens up, I hope to Christ he hits what he's aiming at,' Franklin murmured as they drew nearer to the body.

Crane didn't answer. His attention was riveted on the body which was now only feet ahead of them, twisted like a rag doll. He kept his gun aimed at the motionless figure and prodded it gently with the toe of his boot.

Franklin ran the beam of torchlight up and down the body and saw that it had been hit in several places by bullets. One had torn through the left thigh. Another had punctured the small of the back. Two more had drilled holes in the chest. There were two large exit wounds near one shoulder.

Crane kicked the body harder and it flopped over to face him.

Franklin looked at the eyes. They were both blood-red, the pupils invisible. Dust was sticking to the waxy flesh of the corpse as well as to the clothes.

Was this the man who'd shot Amy?

He watched as Crane pressed the first two fingers of his left hand to a point close to the figure's jaw. Not surprisingly, he found no pulse.

'At least they can be killed,' the DI whispered.

'What did you say?' Franklin wanted to know. 'What do you mean "they can be killed"?'

'Forget it,' Crane protested, straightening up.

'No. Maybe it *is* about time we all knew what we're up against.'

'I thought you only wanted revenge, Franklin.'

'Yeah, I do but I want to know what *you* know about these bastards.'

'What difference would it make?'

'You tell *me*.'

'If we get out of here alive, I will.'

'Maybe I don't want to wait that long.'

'So, what are you going to do, shoot me if I don't tell you?'

In the torchlight, the two men glared at each other for

415

a moment then Crane turned away and continued up the tunnel. Franklin hesitated a second then joined him again, the other men keeping fairly close behind them. Each of them regarded the body with a mixture of anger and curiosity as they passed. The dust was still thick on the ground but, in many places, it had been disturbed by running feet. In the torchlight, empty shell cases occasionally glinted. Franklin saw splashes of blood here and there on the filthy walls.

There was another body slumped against the side of the shaft.

Crane didn't even bother to check for a pulse. Half the head was missing, blasted away by bullets.

'Two,' said Franklin, under his breath.

'Maybe the others *have* gone,' Crane murmured.

'Or they're just waiting for us somewhere else.' Franklin swept his light up and around the tunnel. 'Shit,' he said, seeing the eviscerated body of another ARU man.

Franklin licked his lips and tasted salty sweat. The walk back up the tunnel seemed to be taking far longer than their frenzied flight down to the dead end had done.

'The geezer back there with the slashed arm's dead unless we get him out of here,' Franklin said, his gaze constantly moving back and forth.

'If we can get him to the next station, I'll call for help. Get him some treatment.'

'How far is it?'

'Once we get out of here? Half a mile? I'm not sure.'

'He'll never make it,' Franklin intoned, inclining his head towards the men following.

'Shut your mouth,' one of the ARU officers called back, his voice quavering. 'I'm going to make sure he gets out. He's got a wife and kids.'

'He's lucky,' Franklin replied without looking round.

'There's another one,' said Crane suddenly, the beam of

416

his torch wavering in the darkness. He took a step closer to the third body. This one was lying on its back, shot through with at least half a dozen bullets. The red eyes were still open, pieces of dust sticking to them.

'*Six* left,' Franklin muttered.

Another hundred yards and they came to a more familiar sight.

It was the body of the ARU man killed during the earlier attack. His upper body was sticky with congealed blood from his gashed throat. Franklin crossed to him and picked up the MP5K that he'd dropped.

'What the hell are you doing?' one of the other officers called.

'Like I said back there,' Franklin told him. 'We're going to need all the ammunition we can lay our hands on. Besides, *he* doesn't need it any more.'

They traipsed on. Exhausted by the heat. Blinded by the darkness. Choked by the ever present, putrid dust that filled the air like toxic waste. It looked as if millions of minute cinders were swirling in the beams of the torches.

Franklin's ruptured eardrum was throbbing but at least it had stopped bleeding. Sound was partially muffled, as if he was listening through a sack. His hands were so sweaty they could barely cling onto the grips of the sub-machine gun. Holding the weapon in first one hand then the other, he wiped his palms on his filthy and bloodied jeans.

Up ahead, there was a distant rumbling that all of them recognised as a passing train.

'We can't be more than a few hundred yards from the main tunnel by now,' Crane said hopefully. 'When we get there, we'll make our way down to Tottenham Court Road.'

'How come trains are still running?' Kingston asked.

'I told you,' the DI answered. 'Maintenance.'

Franklin suddenly raised the Beretta 12S, pressing the

barrel of the sub-machine gun hard against Crane's cheek. 'Drop the gun,' he said quietly.

'What the hell are you playing at, Franklin?' the policeman said through clenched teeth.

'Do as I say,' the younger man repeated. 'The rest of you too,' he called more loudly. 'Lower your weapons. If anyone tries anything, I'll blow his fucking head off.'

94

'Franklin, you don't know what you're doing,' Crane said, the sub-machine gun shoved against his face. The light from the torch strapped to the barrel was shining directly into his eye, making him wince.

'I know *exactly* what I'm doing,' the younger man said. He looked back at the other men in the tunnel.

Kingston had taken a step forward.

'If I was you, I'd stay where you are,' Franklin advised. 'Unless you want your boss's brains all over the inside of this tunnel.'

The Detective Sergeant remained where he was, his own gun still levelled at Franklin.

'Go on then,' the younger man chided. 'Open up. There's quite a kick on those things, isn't there? Even if you manage to hit *me* and not him, even if you kill me outright with the first shot, then chances are my finger's going to tighten up on this trigger. Bang. He'll still die.'

'Is *this* your way of saying thanks?' Crane asked under his breath.

'Don't try to appeal to my better nature, Crane. I'm not sure I've *got* one any more.' He looked back at Kingston. 'Put the fucking gun *down*,' he said, pronouncing each word carefully, as if the DS had just learned English.

'Do as he says,' Crane added.

Kingston hesitated a moment longer then complied.

'You,' Franklin continued, looking at Crane. 'Take the magazine out and put it in your pocket. Slowly.' He watched as the DI pressed the magazine release button, catching the slim metal container in one hand. He shoved it into his jacket.

'Satisfied?' Crane asked, glaring at the younger man.

'The rest of you do the same,' Franklin told them. 'Clips out but keep them close in case we need them.'

The waiting men reluctantly did as they were told.

'Keep the Glock,' Franklin said, tapping the policeman's side with the end of the sub-machine gun. 'But don't try and pull it.'

'Now what?' the DI demanded.

'We walk to the end of this tunnel, just like you said.'

Crane's eyes narrowed slightly as he looked at Franklin who stepped back towards the tunnel wall, pulling the policeman with him.

'The rest of you, get in front,' Franklin called, watching as the other men filed past and continued along the tunnel. 'And if anyone tries anything, I'll cut Crane in half first and then the rest of you. Got it?'

He waited until the others were five or six yards ahead then prodded the DI in the small of the back with the barrel of the sub-machine gun. The two of them began walking.

'By the way, don't even *think* about trying to talk me out of this, Crane,' the younger man began. 'Forget the *"you don't really want to do this"* bullshit. It won't work on me. According to you, I'll be lucky to get out of here alive anyway and, from what I've seen, you're right. But even if I do make it, I know that I'm looking at doing time. *You*

420

told me that. So if I'm going down, it makes no difference to me if it's for armed robbery or murder.'

'I don't doubt you'll pull that trigger if you want to, Franklin. That's what that speech was all about, wasn't it?'

'I'll only pull it if I *have* to. Don't make me. I'm not interested in killing *you* or any of the others.' He nodded in the direction of the other men ahead of them. 'You know who I want. The same guys I've wanted since Amy was murdered. Three are already dead. That leaves me six.'

'And if we *do* find them? And you manage to kill them? What then? I don't understand why you're doing this, Franklin.'

'I'll feel a little bit better when it's over.'

'But you won't have Amy back.'

'What do *you* care? You want these bastards dead too, don't you? Once they are, everybody's happy.'

They both felt a blast of warm air from up ahead.

'We must be close to the end of the tunnel,' Franklin murmured. He raised his voice when he spoke again. 'All of you. Get over against the left-hand wall. Slowly.'

'I hope you know what you're doing,' Crane whispered.

'Walk,' Franklin told him, prodding him again with the Beretta.

There were pieces of twisted metal lying on the ground all around them. Franklin could see the remains of the shattered gate hanging off its hinges at the entrance to the abandoned tunnel. Beyond was the working shaft that led south towards Tottenham Court Road. He heard the rumbling of an approaching train and pushed Crane towards the opening.

'What are you doing?' the DI protested. 'There's a bloody train coming.'

'I know,' Franklin said, standing close to him. 'Step out onto the track.'

'You're not going to shoot me, you're going to electrocute me instead?'

421

The train was drawing nearer. Several large fragments of debris, dislodged by the growing vibrations, detached themselves from the filthy roof and floated to earth.

Franklin looked at the small group of men to his left. 'No one move or I'll kill him,' he said sharply.

Crane hesitated.

'Onto the track,' Franklin urged, shining his own torch at the gleaming rails to be sure of his footing in the gloom.

Crane stepped over the first rail and down into the shallow concrete trench over which the live rail ran. A second later, Franklin joined him.

'Use your torch when the train comes,' Franklin told the policeman. 'The driver'll see us. He'll stop.'

'And what if he doesn't?'

'Then I'll shoot him.'

The ground beneath their feet was shaking now, the rails humming as the oncoming train drew nearer. Its headlights shone brightly on the curved wall of the tunnel.

'What the hell are you playing at?' Crane asked, looking down nervously at the live rail that he was only inches away from. 'You're going to kill us both.' His voice was little more than a whisper.

Seconds later, the train burst into view, bearing down on them like a creature unleashed from a nightmare. It thundered forwards like an enormous bullet exploding from the barrel of an impossibly large weapon.

Both men waved their torches back and forth, pointing them in the direction of the startled driver.

They heard the sound of screaming metal as the brakes were applied and the wheels locked. The train skidded on towards them, its headlights dazzling in the blackness of the tunnel.

'It's not going to stop in time,' murmured Crane.

The smell of oil and diesel filled their nostrils. The shriek of brakes drummed in their already pulverised ears.

422

Franklin winced as the headlights blinded him.

The train was slowing down. Sliding to a halt. It juddered to a stop only feet away from them. Franklin hauled himself out of the concrete trench and walked carefully towards the train's cab.

'Open up,' he shouted to the driver, pointing the sub-machine gun at the terrified man. He hesitated, partially paralysed with fear. 'Open the door or I'll blow the fucking windscreen in.'

The man complied.

'Get the others,' Franklin called to Crane who had also carefully hauled himself up onto the trackside. 'Get them on the train. I want *you* in the cab with me. There's been a change of plan. We're going for a ride.'

95

The cab was cramped and unbearably warm. Designed for occupation solely by the driver, it was hardly big enough to fit Franklin and Crane in as well. They stood to one side of the sweating driver who looked around occasionally, his eyes wide with fear.

'Do as you're told and you'll be fine,' Franklin told him.

'What do you want me to do?' the driver asked nervously.

'Drive. But keep your speed down to ten or twelve miles an hour.'

Crane looked quizzically at Franklin.

'I can't,' the driver said, his voice quavering. 'There are other trains down here, you know.'

'Ten or twelve miles an hour,' Franklin repeated. 'If you build up too much speed, and try hitting the brake suddenly or press one of those switches,' he nodded towards the array of yellow, red and green buttons dotted around the cab, 'without telling me what you're doing, I swear to Christ I'll kill you. Take us to the next station.'

'Hijacking?' Crane asked, glaring at the younger man.

'We tried finding these bastards on foot and they nearly killed us all,' Franklin said, looking at the policeman. 'I reckon we've got a better chance like this. They might have been able to outrun *us*, but it'll be harder for them to outrun a train.'

'So what do you intend to do? Run them down?'

'If they're still in these tunnels, then yeah. You got a better idea?'

'They could be anywhere, Franklin, you know that. In one of the disused tunnels. Hiding in—'

The younger man cut him short. 'Maybe they are, but we'll find them quicker like this,' he interrupted.

The train trundled along, juddering every now and then as if the slow speed was more difficult to maintain.

'I should contact Nine Control,' said the driver, without looking over his shoulder. 'They're going to know something's wrong soon.'

'What's Nine Control?' Franklin snapped.

'It's like the nerve centre for all the trains on the network. The controllers can keep in contact with drivers, give instructions. They let us know if there have been any delays or accidents. That sort of thing. They call us on that.' He gestured to what looked like a microphone set into the front section of the cab, just below the right-hand side of the windscreen.

'Can *they* hear *you*?'

The driver nodded.

'All I have to do is just press that button and . . .'

Franklin pushed the barrel of the 12S hard against the man's neck.

Crane looked on impassively, the knot of muscles throbbing at the side of his jaw. He was gazing ahead, out of the train window as if what was going on around him wasn't important. As if his mind was elsewhere. He felt anger building deep within him.

This has gone far enough.

'You better be fucking sure you're pressing the *right* button,' Franklin snapped.

'I swear to God,' the driver babbled.

'Don't contact them yet,' Franklin said quietly.

'No. Do it. Do it now,' Crane said, leaning forward slightly. 'Tell them that your train is under the control of the police. Tell them you're acting on police instructions.'

Franklin looked in bewilderment at the DI.

'Tell them to clear the tracks for the full length of the Northern line in both directions,' Crane continued. 'Better still, let *me* speak to them.'

96

'What are you doing?' Franklin demanded, a look of astonishment still on his face.

'I'm finishing this once and for all,' Crane told him, his features set in hard lines. 'I'm just sorry it took me this long to figure out we're both on the same side. There *is* an enemy down here, Franklin. You've seen that. But there are others too.'

'More of them? Where?'

'Contact Nine Control,' the policeman said, tapping the driver on the shoulder.

'Crane,' Franklin said impatiently. 'What about radio silence? You said the army wanted radio silence at all times.'

'Fuck the army,' snapped Crane.

The driver hit a switch just in front of him. 'The channel's open,' he said, looking around quickly at the DI.

'I want to speak to whoever's in charge,' Crane said loudly. There was a moment's silence then a voice filled the cab.

'Who *is* this?' the voice demanded.

'My name's Detective Inspector Vincent Crane. I'm in the cab of a train heading south on the Northern line towards Tottenham Court Road.'

'No one's authorised to be in the cab except the driver—' the voice began.

'Fuck authorisation,' Crane shouted. 'Did you hear what I said? Now I'm telling you, there is an emergency situation here. If you've got other trains moving down here then stop them. Do you understand? Repeat, there is an emergency situation.'

'We're aware of it,' the controller told him flatly.

It was Crane's turn to look puzzled. He glanced briefly at Franklin who could only shrug. 'How many fucking emergencies have they *got* down here?' the younger man questioned.

'What information do you have?' Crane asked, leaning closer to the microphone.

'A train was taken less than five minutes ago,' the controller's voice told him. 'We haven't even had time to alert the other drivers yet.'

'What do you mean *taken*?' Crane demanded.

'A number of men boarded a train at Russell Square,' the voice of the controller said, his words filling the cab. 'They killed the driver. At least one of them is in the cab now.'

'How many men?'

'No one's sure. Five or six. We don't know. One of the cleaners managed to get off, that's how we know what happened, but—'

'Are there still people on the train?'

'Yes. Three or four cleaners.'

'Where is it now?'

'Moving south on the Piccadilly line.'

'Same direction as us,' Franklin interjected.

Crane nodded.

'It's them, isn't it?' the younger man continued.

'Where's the nearest station, from here, where the Northern line and Piccadilly line cross?' the DI asked the driver.

'If both trains are heading south, it'd be Leicester Square,' the driver said. 'But they couldn't get that far.'

'Why not?' Franklin asked.

'The train'll be stopped by ATP.'

'What's that?' Crane demanded.

'Automatic Train Protection. All trains stop automatically at red lights. Even if someone was driving, as soon as the train tried to go through a red light the ATP would stop it.'

'If that happens and they get off we'll lose them again,' Franklin said.

Crane nodded. 'Have you tried to stop the train?' the DI asked Nine Control.

'It hasn't come to a red light yet,' the controller's voice informed him.

'Don't stop it. Let it through.'

'What about the people on board?' asked the controller.

'Switch all the signals on the Piccadilly and Northern lines to green. And get every other train out of the way. I want the track cleared. Do you understand?'

'We'll try.'

'Don't *try*. Do it. I don't want that train stopped.' He tapped the driver on the shoulder. 'Speed up.'

'But he told me . . .' the driver protested.

'*I'm* telling you. Speed up.' Again he leaned close to the microphone. 'Can you track the progress of that train? I need to know where it is now.'

There was a moment's silence then the controller's voice filled the cab again.

'Approaching Holborn. There's a red light that'll trip it.'

'I said turn all the fucking lights green!' Crane roared.

There was a painfully protracted silence broken by the voice. 'It's through,' the controller announced with relief. 'All the signals have been changed.'

'What are you doing?' Franklin wanted to know as their own train accelerated.

429

'You're right. If they get off that train, we'll never find them again. And the only thing that's going to *stop* them getting off is if it keeps moving. If we can get to Leicester Square before them, we've got a chance of stopping them once and for all.'

Franklin nodded. 'You'll need this,' he said quietly.

He handed the MP5K to the policeman who nodded almost imperceptibly and took it from him. He slammed in the magazine and chambered a round.

97

The train roared through Tottenham Court Road station, its speed now touching sixty. For fleeting moments, the lights of the station illuminated the interior of the cab then darkness swallowed the speeding train once more. It tore into the gaping tunnel mouth and sped on. Franklin pressed himself against the rear wall of the cab, trying to keep his balance as the train took a slight curve at increased speed.

Crane, meanwhile, leaned forward towards the microphone once again. He was forced to raise his voice to make himself heard over the churning wheels. 'Where's the other train now?' he shouted.

'Heading for Covent Garden,' the voice told him.

Crane wiped sweat from his forehead and straightened up again.

'We're not going to make it,' Franklin murmured. He pushed his face close to the driver. 'How far?'

'Another couple of minutes at this speed,' the terrified man said breathlessly.

'Come on, come on,' muttered Crane.

The entire cab was suddenly lit by a vivid white flash.

'What was that?' Franklin demanded.

'A short,' the driver told him, raising his voice. 'It happens all the time. It's nothing.'

The train continued on at breakneck speed.

'Keep going,' Crane urged him.

The policeman inspected his sub-machine gun, glancing at the safety catch. He flicked it to Off and continued to gaze out into the blackness of the tunnel that was pierced only by the twin headlights of the train.

'Is there any way a train could stay on the move without someone in the cab?' he asked, his brow furrowing slightly.

'No. No way,' the driver told him. 'There has to be pressure on the drive control at all times.'

'What if it was weighted down with something?' Crane persisted.

'Do you think they might have got off somehow?' Franklin wanted to know.

'I was just wondering,' muttered the DI.

'They'd have had to jump from a moving train,' Franklin observed. 'One doing over sixty miles an hour.'

'We've seen what they're capable of. I wouldn't put *anything* past them.'

Up ahead, the lights of Leicester Square station began to glow.

'What do you want me to do now?' the driver asked.

'Stop the train in the station,' Crane told him. He leaned closer to the microphone. 'How long until the other train reaches Leicester Square?'

There was a brief silence then the controller's voice filled the cab again, the words reverberating in the cramped area. 'Less than a minute.'

The train had barely come to a halt when Crane threw open the cab door and rushed out onto the platform.

Franklin followed him, seeing doors slide open along the full length of the now stationary train.

Bewildered passengers spilled out onto the platform. Several protesting loudly. 'Get out of here,' Crane shouted. 'Move!'

DS Kingston hurried across to his superior. 'What's happening?' he wanted to know.

'Southbound Piccadilly line,' the DI gasped. 'Now.' He looked at the wounded ARU man. 'One of you stay with him,' he told the man's colleagues.

The other man joined Crane, Franklin and Kingston as they hurtled through the nearest archway in their haste to reach the other platform.

Franklin reached the top of the stairs first. Crane followed, feet pounding the concrete.

The sound of the men's heavy panting filled the Underground tunnel as they ran on, their only desire to reach the Piccadilly line platform in time.

Franklin heard a familiar low rumble and realised that the train was close. He vaulted a hand rail then ran on, leaping the last three steps to land with a thud on the concrete. He skidded, fell to his knees but hauled himself upright and ran onto the platform just as the sound of the approaching train grew to thunderous proportions.

'Shoot the driver,' Crane bellowed from behind him. 'Fire at the cab.'

The train was emerging from the tunnel. Franklin raised the 12S and pulled it tight into his shoulder. He opened up.

The sound of the sub-machine gun reverberated thunderously inside the cavernous shaft. The noise melded with the roar of the train to create one, monstrously deafening symphony that might have been piped directly up from Hell.

Empty shell cases flew into the air as Franklin fired again. The first two blasts punched in the windscreen of the train, pieces of glass flying back into the face of the driver.

Franklin was aware of a figure beside him and, seconds

later, Crane began pumping rounds at the cab with the Glock, which he'd drawn from inside his jacket.

His third shot hit the driver in the chest and slammed him back against his seat. Franklin also fired two long bursts of automatic fire at the front of the train, bullets drilling into the figure who was driving, each 9mm round causing the body to jerk and convulse epileptically as it struck flesh and bone.

The cab of the train was nearly level with them now.

Franklin saw another figure inside it. Saw him pulling at the bullet-shredded form of the one who'd been driving. He fired again but the hammer slammed down on an empty chamber. Cursing, he reached for a fresh magazine and slammed it into place.

The train began to slow down as pressure on the drive control was eased.

'We've got to get on,' shouted Crane, stepping towards it.

If there were people on the train then they were not in view. Franklin couldn't see anyone inside the carriages.

The train had slowed to a crawl.

'Come on,' Crane urged. He tightened his finger on the trigger of the MP5K and blasted in a window.

Kingston followed his example.

Now, Franklin heard screams from inside the train and realised that the terrified cleaners were lying on the floor.

The cab was past them, the front of the train trundling slowly into the mouth of the tunnel. Another two carriages followed it.

It was their one and only chance.

Running alongside the train, he emptied the remaining rounds of the 12S at a window, using the butt to knock out more glass, then he grabbed at the frame and began trying to haul himself inside. The toes of his boots scraped on the platform as he struggled to clamber aboard.

A little further behind him, Crane was doing the same. Kingston too.

The last remaining member of the ARU raked the door of the train and clung on as the metal juggernaut began to pick up speed.

Franklin rolled through the shattered window and landed heavily on the floor of the carriage. He looked through into the next carriage and saw that both Crane and Kingston were also safely on board.

The ARU officer was still hanging onto the door, trying to struggle through the small gap.

The train was now moving more quickly, building up speed and Franklin realised that the other figure who'd been in the cab must have taken the dead man's place. As Franklin struggled to his feet, trying to stay upright as the train rocked and shuddered, he glanced back once more to see that the ARU man was now trying more frantically to gain entry to the carriage. Pieces of glass that were left at the edges of the frame cut his flesh and shredded his clothes as he struggled.

'Get inside,' Franklin bellowed helplessly. He looked ahead and saw the tunnel mouth gaping. Felt the train increasing its speed.

The ARU officer had his head and part of his upper body inside the carriage now, but his legs were still flailing about madly as he too realised that he had mere seconds to slide into the carriage.

He was still struggling when the carriage sped into the tunnel.

98

Wedged in the narrow gap of the smashed door window, the ARU man was only too aware of the fate that awaited him. He made one last desperate effort to get inside, his face now a mask of fear.

His body was bent backwards at the waist as his hips and legs hit the tunnel mouth. His spine snapped with a hideously loud crack that seemed to fill the carriage.

The top portion, from the navel upwards, flopped into the carriage spraying blood madly in all directions. Lengths of intestine landed with a loud, liquid splat on the floor while other internal organs also spilled from the riven body.

The legs and lower half of the corpse merely fell away into the darkness of the tunnel, spraying more blood all over the tracks. One length of pulsing duodenum, caught on a piece of glass in the frame, flapped like a length of slippery, bloated bunting from the now speeding train.

Crane advanced quickly and tore open the door into the next carriage. The hot air rushed through the broken windows into his face. DS Kingston was kneeling on the floor sucking in lungfuls of air and shaking his head slowly. Crane gripped his shoulder hard then helped him to his feet.

They blundered through into the next carriage where Franklin was standing.

'We got one in the cab,' he said breathlessly. 'The other four must be in the carriages near the front of the train. They'd have had a go at us by now if they were behind us.'

'How many carriages away from the cab are we?' Crane asked.

'Can't be more than two or three,' Franklin suggested. 'But I can't be sure.' He slammed a fresh magazine into the sub-machine gun.

'How many people are in there with them?' Kingston breathed.

'The train controller said three or four – if they haven't killed them already,' said Crane. 'We've got to get to the cab.'

'There's no way into it from the front carriage,' Kingston offered.

'We'll have to *find* a way,' the DI said defiantly.

'Once we've got past the others?' Franklin said wearily. Crane nodded.

'Why doesn't someone stop the train?' Kingston asked. 'They could shut it down. Cut the power.'

'Because your boss told them *not* to,' Franklin stated sardonically. 'That's why.'

Crane shot him an irritable glance.

'*We're* the only ones who can stop this train now,' Franklin continued.

The three men paused at the door that linked the carriage they were in with the next one.

'No sign of any of them,' said Crane, scanning the interior of the carriage. 'It looks safe to go through.'

Franklin reached for the handle of the door and opened it. The three of them stepped through into the adjoining carriage, weapons levelled, ducked low, until they reached the next door.

Kingston almost overbalanced as the train took a bend at incredible speed.

'Four of them,' Franklin said, pointing in the direction of two dark-clad figures in the centre of the following carriage. There were two more at the far end. If any of them had spotted their opponents then they certainly gave no indication of it.

'Four of *them* and three passengers,' Crane sighed, looking at the trio of figures lying prone on the floor.

'We can't open fire on them,' Kingston protested. 'We could hit anyone. We could kill one of the passengers.'

'Then how the hell are we supposed to take *those* bastards out?' Franklin snapped. 'The passengers are dead anyway. There's no way they're coming out of this in one piece. Let's just go in blasting.'

'No,' Crane said, looking fixedly at Franklin.

'They don't look as if they've seen us,' Kingston murmured, his eyes flicking from one man to another.

'They know we're here,' Crane said, a note of conviction in his voice.

'So, what do we do?' Franklin enquired. 'Sit around here waiting for them to die of old age?'

Crane, chewing his bottom lip, was watching the figures intently. He slipped one hand inside his jacket and pulled the Glock 9mm free. 'We might have a chance of picking them off,' he breathed, gently pulling back the slide.

Glass suddenly exploded into the carriage, spraying all three men with shards of shattered crystal. Franklin hissed as a sliver cut his face.

One of the figures in the centre of the carriage had run at the three watching men, shoulder-charging the central door linking the carriages. It had been his collision with the glass that had smashed the windows.

Franklin tore the .459 free of its holster and swung it towards the figure, his finger pumping the trigger.

From close range, the 9mm shells, travelling at over one thousand feet a second, slammed into the figure. The first hit him in the chest, tore through one lung and erupted from his back. The second obliterated his left elbow. The third drilled into his jaw just below his left ear. The bullet exploded from the top of his head, carrying with it a geyser of pulverised bone and brain matter.

The figure swayed for a second, his blood-red eyes rolling upwards in their sockets.

Crane put two more shots into him from the Glock, watching as he fell forwards with a loud thud, a pool of blood spreading out around him.

'The other three have gone through to the next carriage,' Kingston said, stepping around the body.

'Yeah, and they've taken the fucking passengers with them,' Franklin observed.

'Come on,' Crane urged and the three men passed on into the next conveyance, through the twisted remnants of the battered doors.

'Four left, including the one in the cab,' Franklin said, looking back at the body of the man he'd shot.

Were you the one who killed Amy?

The train rocked again as it roared through Green Park station.

'We must be close to the cab,' Franklin said.

They continued to advance.

There was a sound from above them, but the churning wheels and the air rushing into the carriage masked it. The three men moved on, oblivious to the noise.

A scraping they didn't hear.

'Another station,' said Franklin, as the train burst out into light once more and swept through Hyde Park Corner.

He looked out at the empty platform and, as he did, he

saw something dark on the outside of the train. 'Jesus Christ,' he gasped.

It was then that the window imploded.

99

For a split second before the eruption of glass, Franklin realised what was happening.

One of the figures from the forward carriages was clinging onto the platform side of the train, hanging there like some massive insect.

Franklin wondered if he'd somehow managed to crawl all the way from the other carriage like that. Then suddenly it didn't matter any more.

The window was driven in and the figure was among them.

Crane got off a burst of fire from his sub-machine gun but it went astray and blew out another window instead.

Franklin saw the flash of steel in the figure's hand. Realised that the knife was being wielded with incredible speed.

The blade caught Kingston as he raised his arm to protect himself. It sheared effortlessly through bone and cartilage and the policeman's right hand went spinning into the air, blood spraying from the stump.

Before the other two could react, the figure had struck again, this time driving the blade forwards towards Kingston's chest. The point buried itself just below the sternum and was ripped downwards as far as the groin.

Fortunately for the DS, the Kevlar he was wearing was strong enough to prevent him being gutted as had been the intention. However, no amount of body armour would have prevented what happened next.

The figure struck out again with lightning speed and awesome power. A backhand stroke shaved off a large portion of the top of the policeman's head, scalping him. Blood ran down his face from the hideous gash and he was still reeling when the knife was brought down again, this time into the top of his skull. It penetrated his brain, was torn free, then plunged into his throat, shattering his larynx.

He dropped like a stone and Franklin tried to bring his weapons to bear on the attacker. He got off two rounds from the .459. The first missed. The second pulverised the man's left hip.

Crane aimed the MP5K but the short burst was again wide of its mark.

The knife flashed at him and the point tore open his right cheek.

Franklin managed to grab the wrist of the figure and he held on like a ferret to a rat. With his free hand he slammed the 12S into his opponent's face, shattering his nose and momentarily stunning him.

He brought one knee up with stunning power into the figure's testicles. It seemed to have little effect. He felt a hand grip his throat. A hand whose fingers dug into his flesh, burrowing deeper as they sought his windpipe.

White stars spun before his eyes, searing pain enveloped his throat. He could taste blood in his mouth.

There was a thunderous roar as Crane fired the Glock.

Franklin felt the pressure on his throat ease suddenly and, as he struggled to focus on his attacker, he saw the bullet hole in his opponent's temple. An exit wound large enough to stick a fist in had been blasted in the other side of the figure's skull. A sticky flux of blood and brain was splattered all over the inside of the carriage.

The figure swayed then dropped to its knees, finally sprawling beside Franklin who was coughing and massaging his neck.

Warm, rancid air rushed in through the broken windows. Franklin hauled himself up onto his knees and looked first at the figure on the floor, then at Kingston.

The policeman was already dead.

Sitting upright on the floor, his head lolled backwards, blood still spurting from the monstrous wound in his throat.

Franklin tried to speak but it was too painful. Every time he attempted to say something it felt as if a hot corkscrew was being twisted inside his throat.

He hawked, spat blood onto the floor and rolled over onto his side, sucking down painful breaths.

'Franklin,' gasped Crane, kneeling beside him. 'Are you all right?'

The younger man raised a hand and tried to nod. All he finally managed to do was cough again.

Both he and Crane were covered in blood, some of it their own. Franklin felt his head spinning and thought he was going to pass out. He loosened the Kevlar slightly and, again, tentatively touched the gouged skin of his throat.

This time when he tried to speak he managed to utter a sound like a wounded seal.

'Come on,' Crane said, shaking him gently. 'Just take it slowly.'

Franklin tried to swallow once more but couldn't. He coughed painfully and spat more blood-flecked sputum, this time onto the body of the figure who'd tried to kill him.

Another moment and he nodded, drew in a deep breath and was relieved to find he could swallow. It was painful but he managed it again.

Crane crouched beside him, his sub-machine gun pointed towards the forward carriage. Another attack could come at any second. And, he thought with a shudder, from any direction.

The train thundered on.

100

They passed through Knightsbridge station at incredible speed.

Crane looked back at Franklin who was massaging his throat gently.

'Two of them left,' Franklin croaked, still rubbing his throat. 'We take *them* out then it's just the one driving.'

Crane nodded, his gaze flitting from one figure to the other. They were both standing close to the rear wall of the cab, facing impassively towards the policeman and his younger companion.

'If we go in blasting we'll kill the passengers too,' the DI murmured.

'What choice have we got?' Franklin wanted to know. He coughed and winced painfully. 'Besides, they're not going to stand there waiting forever. If *they* come at *us* we'll have to open fire.'

'I wonder why they haven't killed the passengers?' the policeman mused. 'All three of them are still alive in there.'

Franklin slammed a fresh magazine into the butt of the .459 and chambered a round.

'Not for much longer,' he hissed.

'Franklin, we can't,' said the DI.

'How are we supposed to stop this fucking train? The line is clear, remember? *You* cleared it. There's no *need* for them to stop. What's at the end of the Piccadilly line? Heathrow, right? And the line goes round in a loop there. They can turn this fucking thing straight round and come back the same way.'

Crane continued to gaze into the forward carriage. The last carriage.

'Three passengers, Crane,' Franklin said. 'Three lives. If that's what this is going to cost then what choice have we got? What choice have *you* got? How many have they killed already?'

'I can't.'

'*You* can't.'

Franklin hauled himself up onto his knees, the 12S gripped in one hand, the .459 in the other.

'No,' the policeman snapped, grabbing at Franklin's arm.

'The passengers are lying down,' Franklin insisted. 'We've *got* to do it.'

Crane shook his head slowly.

'I said I was going to kill them and I am,' Franklin snarled, pulling free.

Crane swung the MP5K around, the barrel pointing at Franklin's chest. 'I won't let you do it,' he said through gritted teeth. 'I can't take the risk.'

'Then pull the fucking trigger now. Because that's the only way you're going to stop me.' He inclined his head towards the body of Detective Sergeant Kingston. 'You saw what that one did to your mate. You've seen what they're capable of. You've *known* all this from the beginning, haven't you?'

Crane swallowed hard, the sub-machine gun still pointing at Franklin's chest.

'If *you* can't pull the trigger, I understand,' Franklin muttered. 'I'm not asking you to. I'm *telling* you that *I* will.

And the only way you're going to stop me is by killing me. My life or theirs, Crane. Your choice.'

The two men glared at each other for interminable moments.

Crane's head was spinning. He looked up quickly and noticed that the nearest cleaner was a young woman, no more than twenty. She was curled up on the floor in a foetal position, crying softly. Beyond her, sitting in the aisle between the seats was a woman in her mid-forties, her head bowed as if in prayer, her face drenched with sweat. Beyond her, another woman. Black. Also seated on the floor. She was rocking gently back and forth, her eyes tightly shut.

The youngest of the three women was closest to the two figures with their backs to the cab. Crane noticed she had lost a shoe.

Three people. Three souls.

Three sacrifices?

'Wait,' Crane said quietly.

'We haven't got time for any more of this shit,' Franklin insisted.

'Just shut up,' hissed the policeman, swinging the gun back at him. 'Don't say a word.'

101

As Franklin watched impatiently, the DI dug a hand into his pocket and pulled out a biro.

'What the fuck are you doing?' Franklin wanted to know.

The policeman raised his hand angrily to silence the younger man while he continued to rummage in his pockets, finally pulling free what looked like a credit card receipt from one of his back pockets.

He put down the subgun, rested the piece of paper on his thigh and scrawled;

they can hear us

He showed the paper to Franklin.

'They what . . .'

Again Crane raised his hand to silence his companion.

He scribbled once more on the back of the receipt, the pen gouging through the flimsy material at one point.

do not speak

Franklin nodded, still looking suspiciously at the DI as the older man found room to scribble something else.

He showed the words to Franklin who smiled thinly and nodded. Again the policeman held a hand to his mouth to ensure Franklin said nothing.

Crane held up three fingers.

Franklin nodded.

Both men were still crouched next to the door that led through into the last carriage.

Crane's three fingers were shaking. He folded one down to his palm and held it with his thumb. A second later, he lowered the second.

Franklin kept his eye on the last remaining digit, his own heart now thudding so hard against his ribs he felt it must explode.

The train took another curve at tremendous speed and the two men shot out hands to steady themselves, trying to control their breathing. A single droplet of sweat ran down the side of Franklin's face and dripped to the floor. His eyes were still on Crane's finger as his hands squeezed the grips of the sub-machine gun so hard it seemed they would crack.

The DI nodded, closed his index finger to his palm and brandished the resultant fist.

Franklin understood.

Both men stood simultaneously, fingers tightening on the triggers of their weapons.

The 9mm slugs shattered glass and tore into the next carriage.

The deafening retort of the weapons mingled with the shouts and screams of terror from the three passengers. Bullets tore across the back wall of the cab. Both of the figures standing there were hit.

One went down immediately, hit in both eyes and the forehead by the heavy-grain shells that blasted away the back of his skull and plastered it on the metal partition like dripping paint.

The other, struck in the shoulder and chest, grabbed at the young woman close to him and hauled her to her feet.

Franklin and Crane couldn't stop firing in time.

Bullets tore into her, turning the blouse she wore crimson. And, as they continued to fire, they saw the other figure stumble backwards.

Franklin dropped the empty 12S and began pumping the trigger of the .459. The first two shots hit their target. The third screamed off the rear of the cab. The next blasted a path through the figure's sternum, cracking two ribs and puncturing a lung in the process. Franklin advanced into the last carriage, firing one-handed. More shots went astray but another drilled into the figure's heart. Long before the slide shot backwards to signal an empty magazine, Franklin was standing over the prone body, his face fixed in a grimace of fury and triumph.

Crane joined him, ushering the other two terrified women back along the carriage then stooping over the young woman lying between the two immobile figures. He didn't need to check her pulse to know that she was dead.

Franklin pressed the magazine eject button then slammed a fresh one into the automatic. Only then did he look down at the dead woman.

Not much younger than Amy.

He let out a weary breath and kicked at each of the two motionless figures in turn.

Crane pulled off his jacket and laid it over the dead woman's face.

He and Franklin looked coldly at each other but neither spoke.

What were they going to say?

The train roared on, its speed, it seemed, increasing.

'Pull the fucking emergency cord,' Franklin hissed.

'Pulling it tells the driver there's something wrong,' Crane told him. 'It can't *make* him stop.'

Franklin caught a brief glimpse of a green signal as the train tore through Gloucester Road station. 'Green all the way,' he coughed, the stink of cordite strong in his nostrils. 'How do we stop this fucking train?'

102

'There's no way into the cab from here,' breathed Crane. 'What now?'

'Get the controller to switch the lights back to red,' Franklin offered. 'Stop it automatically.'

'We'd have to get into the cab to do that. It's impossible.'

'They must know it's a runaway by now. Why don't they just cut the power?'

'Because, as you keep reminding me, *I* told them not to.'

As the train hurtled through Barons Court station, daylight suddenly flooded into the carriage. The first blazing rays of a brilliant dawn.

From ahead of them, there was an ear-splitting caterwaul of pure agony.

'What the fuck was that?' Franklin hissed, spinning round towards the cab wall.

'Jesus Christ, it's the daylight,' Crane told him. 'They're sensitive to light. The one who's driving must be in agony with the sun in his eyes.'

'The rest of the route's overground,' Franklin said, a faint smile on his face.

'The bastard's going to suffer but he's not going to stop the train.'

'No way of contacting anyone?' Franklin mused.

'Only from inside the cab,' the policeman reminded him.

'Hey,' Franklin said suddenly. 'You said they could hear everything.' He hooked a thumb in the direction of the cab.

'They can,' Crane said. 'But what's he going to do? If he comes back in here to get us, he stops the train.'

Franklin nodded then steadied himself again as the train sped into Hammersmith. He shot out a hand to prevent himself falling, his bloodied fingers closing over something cool. Something metal.

He looked down at the fire extinguisher.

'Jesus Christ, that's it,' he exclaimed. His gaze was fixed on the side of the red cylinder. 'Crane, listen to me. Go back down the train and bring the fire extinguishers from all the carriages.'

'Why?'

'We can use them. If we do it right we can get them to blow up.'

'But they're full of water.'

'Not *full*. The propellant is pressurised CO_2. It's highly volatile. Enough of it should do the job.'

Crane looked at him silently for a moment.

'If it works,' he said. 'What about the rest of the carriages?'

'The only one that'll blow will be *this* one. With no cab, the rest of the train'll stop automatically.'

'It could derail. Hit the wreckage of the front carriage—'

'That's a chance we've got to take,' Franklin snapped.

'How do we set it off?' the policeman wanted to know.

'With bullets. All of the extinguishers are under pressure. Puncture them in the right place and they'll blow. Chances are there'll be sparks off the round when it hits the canister anyway. Once the CO_2 ignites that'll be it. Bang. When *one* goes they'll *all* go.'

'I'll get the other fire extinguishers,' Crane breathed. He was about to walk away when he turned back to the younger man. 'How do you know this is going to work?'

'Trust me.'

'That's asking a lot, Franklin.'

The younger man managed a smile. 'Go,' he said, watching as the DI scurried off down the aisle towards the connecting door that led into the next carriage.

Franklin sat down on the floor, his eyes fixed on the red cylinder before him. He lit a cigarette and sucked hard on it, the entire carriage vibrating around him as the train tore onwards.

Moments passed, he finished his smoke and ground it out on the floor of the carriage. From behind him he heard a loud clang and turned to see that Crane had returned with three of the other extinguishers. One of which he'd dropped.

'Careful with those,' Franklin snapped, taking the first of them from the sweating policeman. 'We don't want them exploding while we're still inside the carriage.'

He laid it carefully at the base of the cab partition then did the same with the others.

'I'll get the rest,' Crane called, turning and running back down the aisle.

Franklin looked around him.

Something to ensure the cylinders remained tight to the partition.

He grabbed the outstretched arm of the nearest dead figure and hauled the bullet-ridden corpse across the floor, jamming the extinguishers behind the bulk of the dead weight.

'At least you'll be useful for something, you bastard,' he murmured, looking down at the blood-drenched body.

Crane returned again, then stood back, recovering his breath as Franklin jammed the last of the cylinders into position.

'Help me,' he said, taking hold of the other figure's feet.

Crane grabbed the arms, ignoring the fragments of bone that fell from the obliterated head of the figure.

'Put it on top of the other one,' Franklin gasped. 'When the blast comes, their bodies'll absorb some of it, send it against the cab.'

'Now what?' the DI wanted to know, his breath ragged.

'We get the fuck out of here,' Franklin said.

Both men hurried towards the rear of the carriage. They paused beside the door that would lead through into the next conveyance, glancing at the row of red fire extinguishers lined up against the rear wall of the cab.

Crane slipped through the door first then stood back as Franklin followed him.

The train took a slight curve and they both glanced ahead. There was another few hundred yards before they reached the next station.

'If we're going to do it we've got to do it now,' Crane said, looking at his watch. 'The whole network will be up and running by now. If there are any people on the platforms when this blows . . .' He allowed the sentence to trail off.

Franklin understood and raised the 12S so that he was squinting down the sight. 'Ready?' he asked, as a particularly bright beam of sunlight flooded the carriage.

Crane pulled the MP5K tight to his shoulder. 'Ready,' the policeman told him.

They opened fire simultaneously.

103

The carriage was filled with the staccato rattle of machine-gun fire as both men squeezed the triggers. No short controlled bursts this time, just concentrated fire towards the front of the first carriage.

Bullets ploughed into the corpses that had been laid before the fire extinguishers, the 9mm rounds blasting lumps from the bodies. Others dug holes in the floor or screamed off metal. A few punched out portions of the windows and some raked the rear of the cab. Spent shell cases flew into the air, the smoking remains landing with a loud metallic clink on the floor of the carriage in which the two men crouched.

Who fired the round that punctured the first of the canisters, they never knew. It didn't matter anyway.

All that *did* matter was that one of the heavy-grain slugs finally hit an extinguisher, tearing through the metal.

The pressurised carbon dioxide inside erupted immediately. Fire shot in all directions, the incredible temperature immediately setting off the other extinguishers. A chain reaction of fury happened in the blinking of an eye.

As the first blast ripped through the carriage, both Franklin and Crane threw themselves down, hugging the floor of their own carriage as glass cascaded over them. The windows were blown outwards by the force of the blast and it grew in intensity until there was a deafening eruption as all the canisters went up almost simultaneously. It was as if a portion of Hell itself had been unleashed inside the leading carriage.

A plume of fire fully twenty feet high exploded skywards, ripping effortlessly through the roof, sending fragments of the pulverised transport spinning towards the heavens.

More searing flames shot to the left and right, blasting huge holes in the sides of the carriage. The main force of the detonation took out the cab. The entire structure, a ball of fire, was hurled thirty yards up the track, spinning over repeatedly like a massive catherine wheel. As it rolled, pieces of red-hot metal flew out all around it and it trailed a choking tail of thick black smoke behind it. More smoke belched from what remained of the front carriage, rising into the sky to form a noxious man-made cloud that hovered over the destruction like a shroud.

Franklin held tightly to the floor, feeling the wave of scorching heat sweep over him. It sucked the oxygen from the atmosphere and made it hard to breathe for a second. Then they were engulfed by choking smoke. Cinders danced like gnats in the boiling air.

The entire train lurched violently to one side and, for terrifying seconds, it seemed as if it was going to derail.

The leading carriage had been split almost in two and, as Franklin finally raised himself up slightly to inspect the incredible wreckage, he saw that the entire structure was ablaze.

And it was still moving.

Carried on by the momentum of its high-speed journey, the train rolled along, over pieces of burning debris.

The first carriage was fast approaching the remains of the cab.

Franklin felt a hand on his arm and realised that Crane was already on his feet and trying to pull *him* upright too.

The younger man understood and both of them began running back down the train, trying to put distance between themselves and the imminent collision.

The train was slowing down slightly but, Franklin feared, not enough.

They crashed through the first set of doors and into the next carriage, sprinted down the aisle and burst through the next set.

As they reached the third carriage the entire train slammed into the blazing remains of the cab. The leading carriage merely folded like a piece of foil, buckling and splitting from front to back. What glass remained in the windows was shattered. Fire licked hungrily at the seats, melting the plastic where it touched it.

Franklin was thrown off his feet by the impact of the collision, then hurled against a door. He grunted in pain as his head snapped sideways and connected hard with the glass and metal. He felt something warm running down his cheek and realised that a cut had opened on his temple.

Crane was attempting to drag himself upright, holding one shoulder, a look of suffering on his blood-flecked face. It felt as if his left collarbone had broken.

The train continued to roll onwards, but now both men could feel that it was definitely slowing down.

From further down the train they could hear the screams of the remaining two passengers.

Franklin looked towards the front of the train and saw only fire and smoke. Thick, reeking clouds of it that blotted out the morning sky.

He walked slowly towards the front of the carriage, leaving Crane still crouched on the floor clutching his injured shoulder.

The air smelled of hot metal, burning oil, melted plastic

and incinerated flesh. It clogged Franklin's nostrils with each breath he took but he seemed unconcerned.

As the train finally juddered to a halt he stood gazing at the wreckage before him, his red-rimmed eyes focused on the twisted mass of metal and fire that had once been the cab.

No one could have got out of that *alive.*

The knowledge should have brought a smile to his face but it didn't. He merely stood, transfixed by the devastation he had helped to create.

'Burn, you bastard,' he whispered breathlessly. A gust of air swept across the tracks, causing the smoke to dance in its wake. Franklin smelled fresh air.

In the distance, he could hear sirens.

104

Franklin tugged at the straps of the Kevlar, pulled the bullet-proof vest free and dropped it on the floor of the carriage. He walked slowly back to where Crane was still crouching, holding his injured shoulder.

The strident wail of sirens was now louder.

'They'll be here in a minute,' Franklin said. 'Ambulances. Police.'

Crane looked up at him and nodded.

Franklin glanced down at the MP5K still gripped in the policeman's hand.

'If I try and walk, you'll shoot me, won't you?' the younger man said quietly.

'Gun's empty,' Crane informed him.

He lifted the sub-machine gun, pointed it at Franklin's chest and squeezed the trigger. The hammer slammed down on an empty chamber. The policeman dropped the weapon.

'The Glock's not,' Franklin said.

'I can't reach it anyway,' Crane told him. 'I think my shoulder's broken.' He winced.

'So what do we do?'

'If you're going to walk, you'd better do it now.'

'You said you'd find me if I tried to run.'

'You said you didn't *want* to run.'

'That was before.'

'Before you got your revenge?'

'You were right, it won't bring Amy back.'

'So, are you going to run or not?'

'Will you come after me?'

'What do *you* think? It's my job.'

'Is that the only thing that matters? The job?'

Crane nodded.

Franklin smiled. 'You told me back there we were both on the same side,' he mused.

'We *were*.'

'But not any more?'

Crane didn't answer.

Franklin dug in his pockets for his cigarettes. He lit one, took a couple of drags then leaned forward and screwed it between Crane's lips.

'You look like you need it more than me,' the younger man exclaimed.

It was Crane's turn to smile. 'Get out of here, Franklin,' he said. 'Go now, while you still can.'

'What did you mean about there being others?' the younger man wanted to know. 'You said that if we got out of this alive you'd tell me.'

'I said a lot of things.'

'Who *were* they? The men we killed? The ones who murdered Amy?'

'It's a long story and *you* haven't got time to listen.'

'I want to know.'

'I gave you the chance to kill them. What more do you want from me?'

'The truth.'

Crane chuckled. It was a hollow, humourless sound. He winced and clutched at his injured shoulder. 'I forgot what that was a long time ago, Franklin,' he intoned. 'I'm

461

not even sure it matters any more. Get out. Go on. Go now.'

The younger man hesitated a moment then walked to the end of the carriage and pushed open the door.

Three or four feet below him were the tracks. He noticed a piece of material lying on the gravel to one side of the left-hand rail. It was smouldering.

Had it come from one of the dead men? The one who'd killed Amy?

Franklin jumped down, landed heavily then he steadied himself and set off across the debris-strewn tracks.

Ahead of him, the remains of the first carriage still burned. Behind, the first of the emergency services were already swarming around the rest of the train.

He looked up at the sky. There wasn't a cloud to be seen, just the man-made smog of smoke and fumes still belching from the remnants of the train.

Franklin hurried away.

105

The waves of applause from the Government benches were deafening. Accompanied, as they were, by shouts of encouragement and approval, they reverberated around the lower chamber. Edward Carter smiled and gratefully accepted the adulation.

Even those on the Opposition benches were clapping enthusiastically.

He finally turned away from the lectern, roars and applause ringing in his ears. He seated himself next to Gerald Collinson. The Home Secretary smiled at his colleague and tapped him on the arm.

'An excellent speech, Edward,' Collinson murmured close to his ear. 'A problem solved, one might say.'

Carter nodded slightly in thanks but, for now, all that concerned him was the unceasing applause that still rang around the House of Commons.

Doctor Kalid Sharafi paused for a moment and sat back from his desk. Then he got to his feet and crossed to the window of his office.

The midday sunshine spilled across the perfectly manicured lawn, and with the window slightly open, Sharafi could smell the delightful scent of freshly cut grass. Somewhere close by he could hear birds singing in the branches of the trees close to his office. It was a beautiful day.

Allah be Praised.

The Iraqi remained at the window for a moment longer, looking out over the beautiful tableau before him, watching a sparrow dip its beak into the fresh water of a birdbath before fluttering off into the clear azure sky.

Sharafi returned to his desk and continued writing. His notes would be typed up for him later by a secretary then stored on a hard drive. The set that he wrote in his native language he would keep locked away in the bottom drawer of his desk as he had always done.

He was the only one with a key.

He continued to write in his elegant style, copying the names of chemicals from a computer printout that lay on his desk. Beneath that was another list. Of men's names.

Men who had once been members of the British army. All missing in action, believed dead.

He would come to that list soon enough.

Outside his window, the birds continued to sing and, again, he thanked Allah for such a beautiful day.

106

Matt Franklin looked at the headstone. He wiped a single tear from his cheek.

AMY DANIELLE HOLDEN
THE BRIGHTEST FLAME BURNS QUICKEST

The dates of her birth and death were engraved beneath, almost obscured by the flowers that covered the grave. As Franklin stood there, the scent of the flowers mingled with the smell of freshly turned earth.

A slight breeze had sprung up. The cellophane wrapping around the flowers crackled as the cool gusts grew stronger. Franklin stood a moment longer, his gaze on the fluttering petals of some red roses.

'I remembered that the funeral was today.'

The voice startled him and he spun round. 'What are *you* doing here?' Franklin wanted to know.

Detective Inspector Vincent Crane took a step forward. His left arm was in a sling and he winced occasionally when he moved.

'I went to your flat. When I couldn't find you there I thought it made sense to come here.'

'How did you know where Amy was going to be buried?'

'I'm a detective, remember?' He stepped alongside Franklin and looked at the grave. 'I went to the undertakers. Asked him what time the funeral was and where.'

Franklin nodded. 'There were a lot of people here,' he said quietly, his own gaze fixed on the headstone. 'A lot of people liked her.'

'And now they've gone.'

'I wanted some time alone with her.'

'I understand.'

Franklin glanced at the policeman. 'How's the shoulder?' he enquired.

'Painful.'

'Good.'

Crane smiled. 'Thanks for the concern,' he murmured.

The breeze blew strongly again and the cellophane rattled.

'You know why I'm here, Franklin,' Crane said and it came out as a statement, not a question.

The younger man nodded.

'I've got to take you in,' Crane continued.

'Why?'

'Because it's my job.'

'And that's all that matters, right?'

Crane nodded.

'You've got a wife and kids, haven't you?' Franklin stated.

'Is that important?'

'Is that why you do the job? For them?'

'I've never really thought about it but, yeah, you're probably right. Apart from the job, they're all I've got.'

'You're lucky. At least you've got *something*.'

Crane stepped back. 'If it's any consolation,' he said, 'I'm sorry.'

'You said that once before. It wasn't any consolation *then* and it isn't *now*.'

466

'The car's waiting, when you're ready. I'm parked outside the main entrance.'

'Are you on your own?'

'Yeah. I didn't think you'd do a runner.'

'And what if you were wrong?'

'If you were planning that you'd have been gone by now. Besides, you can't run forever, Franklin. I'd find you eventually. Or, if not me, somebody else.'

'How long will I do?'

'I told you. Ten years. Maybe more.'

'Just one thing. Tell me *now* what you meant – about there being others. About the *real* enemy.'

'You see them every day in the newspapers and on TV. Politicians. Heads of State. Prime Ministers. Presidents. I spend my whole life chasing guys like you when *they're* the ones I should be locking up. *They* killed Amy. Not some terrorists.'

'Bollocks,' hissed Franklin.

'This isn't the time or place for a lecture. Believe what you like. Believe that *you* killed the men who murdered Amy if it makes you feel better.'

Franklin glanced at the policeman. 'Can I have a minute with her?' he asked.

Crane nodded. 'I'll be in the car,' he said quietly, turning and making his way from the graveside.

'Don't you want to cuff me?'

'I trust you,' Crane called over his shoulder.

'That's asking a lot,' Franklin murmured, a slight smile on his face.

He kissed the tips of the forefinger and middle finger of his left hand then touched the digits gently to the cold marble of the headstone. 'I love you,' he whispered, tears welling in his eyes.

The wind blew again. A single red petal came free from one of the bouquets and fluttered away.

Franklin watched it drifting heavenward on the breeze. He waited a moment longer then turned from the grave and set off towards the main entrance.

He didn't look back.

'All governments are liars and murderers . . .'
Bill Hicks (1961–1994)

'Churches, laws – everybody seems to think that man is a noble savage. But he's only an animal, a meat eating, talking animal. Recognise it.'

Sam Peckinpah